W9-AZO-946

How far
would
you go?

The siren howled, drowning out their words. "A call just came in," Dondi explained, eyes fixed on the road. "Domestic disturbance, officers on the scene. There's been an injury."

Paul's head was spinning, free floating anxiety waiting to ignite. "Yeah? And?"

Dondi's features were pale in the dim dash lights. He wracked the wheel and sliced across the intersection, blatting the horn at anything that even looked as if it might get in the way.

"What's going on, Dondi?" Paul barked. "Why are you flipping over a damned domestic?"

"It's the address," Dondi said, still white-knuckling the wheel and downshifting. The big rig roared, gear teeth gnashing beneath their feet. "It's Marley Street, Paul. The address is 514 Marley Street."

"What are you saying?" Fear spread, mental kindling crackling. Paul was sweating now. "Dondi, did somebody break into my house?"

"We got a description . . . Caucasian female, multiple blunt trauma to the head . . . " Dondi paused, throat constricting, his face a mask of dread determination.

The logical part of Paul's brain tried to make a connection but failed. "Who is it, Dondi?"

Dondi said nothing.

And just like that, it all clicked nightmarishly into place.

"Bare-knuckle popular fiction—a book that burns like a five alarm fire."

Peter Atkins

TO BURY THE DEAD

CRAIG SPECTOR

HarperTorch
An Imprint of HarperCollinsPublishers

This is a work of fiction. Names, characters, places, and incidents are products of the author's imagination or are used fictitiously and are not to be construed as real. Any resemblance to actual events, locales, organizations, or persons, living or dead, is entirely coincidental.

HARPERTORCH
An Imprint of HarperCollins*Publishers*
10 East 53rd Street
New York, New York 10022-5299

Copyright © 2000 by Craig Spector
ISBN: 0-380-79305-9

First HarperTorch paperback printing: December 2000

HarperCollins®, HarperTorch™, and ❦ ™ are trademarks of Harper-Collins Publishers Inc.

Printed in the United States of America

Visit HarperTorch on the World Wide Web at www.harpercollins.com

10 9 8 7 6 5 4 3 2 1

To Keith Gordon Spector
"Rusty"
1956–1999
brother, father, husband, friend

"No man may keep you in the dark
any longer, walk now in the light."

—Anonymous, left at murder site

Acknowledgments

The author would like to extend deepest thanks and appreciation to the following people: to my literary agent, Anthony Gardner, for sage counsel; to my editor, Jennifer Sawyer Fisher, for navigating the changes; to Richard Christian Matheson, Peter Atkins, and Peter Straub, for heartfelt friendship and extraordinary insight; to Dr. Leib Lehmann, Lance Bogart, Matthew Jorgensen, Buddy and Holly Martinez, Kimbra Eberly, and Karl and Diane Heitmeyer, for being there; to Roy Smith, Michael Shoemaker, Dan McGuire, and Pat Lobrutto, dot-comrades and co-conspirators; to Ed Yashinsky and Paula Guran, for tenacious energy and expertise; to Bob, Jan, Dick, and George, stealthy angels all; to Mike, for the grisly forensics; to Rob and Nan Wickman, just cuz; to Christa Faust, Poppy Z. Brite, Peter and Gail Clough, Peter and Tania Hopps, Jim Hagopian, Robert Pineda, Richard and Tara Sutphen, Jason McKean, Preston Sturges, Leslie and Adam, Ervin and Elizabeth, Donna Ebbs, Scott Lew, and only sister, Kim, for the moments along the way; to Janet Burrows, in memorium; to Lubov and Alexander Vasilenko, for love and courage and the divine Ms. V.; to Deb, Ash and Jake Spector, with hope; and to Lou Aronica, for discovering me twice in a lifetime.

Singular thanks and love to my wife, Vera, for her patience and devotion, and for putting up with me.

In all chaos, there is a cosmos;
In all disorder, a secret order.

—Carl Jung

Nothing is intrinsically good or evil,
but its manner of usage may make it so.

—Saint Thomas Aquinas

so·ci·o·path·ic (*sousi:oupæthik*)
adj. 1. of, relating to,
or characterized by,
asocial or anti-social behavior.
2. a psychopathic personality.

—*Webster's Dictionary*

PART ONE

Running Hot

1

Dondi wiped blood from his arms as Paul Kelly smoked, impassive. "Bleeders," Dondi muttered. "Christ, I fuckin' hate 'em."

Paul blew a smoke ring and said nothing, leaning on the back bumper of the rig as Dondi stripped off thin rubber surgical gloves and changed into a fresh shirt, his third of the night. The air was cold and clear, stars faintly visible through the backwash of urban illumination. They were parked butt-in to the ambulance bay of St. Anthony's Medical Center, the harsh glare of sodium vapor lamps casting sickly green shadows around them.

Tom and Joli were still inside, dragging ass under the guise of paperwork as they scoped the graveyard shift's new booty count—word was there was a new nurse on tour, a tight little Dominican named Liza, who could give rigor mortis a whole new meaning. If Paul had been in a better mood, he would have been inclined to joke that the only sheets his two crewmates would ever share with her was the one she'd pull over their heads, should they ever even try.

Paul said nothing. The gloves went into the medical

waste bin recessed into the rig's inner wall. The discarded shirt was blotched and spattered, powder blue stained Rorschach red courtesy of a multiple stab wound off the industrial crack-ho section of Elizabeth Street in Glendon.

"You know," Dondi continued, "I don't mind the hours, the stress, the bullshit, every damned thing. But this—" He pulled a fresh shirt out of his gear bag, his last. It was powder blue, well-worn, with an embroidered patch emblazoned on the left sleeve and chest: GLENDON FIRE/RESCUE, in little red and gold letters. Dondi stashed the wadded ball of cloth in a baggie behind the driver's seat and donned the clean shirt, then slipped on his dark blue nylon bomber, still bitching. "Man, Connie's gonna shit," he said. "Fuckin' bleeders. They're the worst."

"What about floaters?" Paul spoke at last, blowing another blue ring of smoke and chilled air. His tone was soft, droll. "Last night you said floaters were the worst."

"Them, too," Dondi groused. "I swear to God, between the bleeders and the floaters, I don't know what to tell ya. Least he didn't puke on me." Dondi checked his arms for stray spillage; Paul glanced up offhandedly.

"You missed a spot," he said.

"Where?" Dondi craned his neck, peering into the reflective surface of the wall. It was clean. "Very funny." Dondi scrutinized his reflection, then pulled another premoistened antiseptic towelette from one of the recessed metal supply drawers and wiped himself down anyway. "Shit," he grimaced, "fucker probably gave me the AIDS."

Paul shrugged as Dondi grunted and buttoned up. His grousing was as familiar as the claustrophobic confines of the wagon, a nightly ritual; mental kevlar, staving off emotional shrapnel. And gallows humor aside, Paul knew that it was a fair enough concern—fully one-third of their street calls these days were HIV-positive, if not full-blown cases. Addicts, mostly—people who'd started out using a needle or a pipe, and ended merely used up, pinballing from lockup to detox to rehab and back again, their humanity evaporating into a greasy residue. But working fire/rescue was like that;

you seldom saw the best people, or the ones you did at their best.

In Glendon these days, doubly so—the blue-collar out-lands west of the industrial wastebelt rimming the Big Apple were gradually sinking under a steadily rising tide of junkies, homeless, and third-generation working-class trash.

Paul thought back to this evening's latest casualty: a lonely little thirty-seven-year-old Russian immigrant named Eddie, who cruised the barren stretch of parking lots that ringed the Jersey Transit station in the bottom-feeder section of downtown. Eddie made his rounds in a blue Suzuki Side-kick, offering rides and blow jobs to hapless commuters who failed to snag one of the smatterings of after-hours gypsy cabs that lurked at the base of the platform. He had even picked Paul up one sub-zero December night years ago, as Paul trudged home with an armload of Christmas presents for Julie and Kyra, over streets iced thick from storms until it lay like urethane. He'd mistaken Eddie for a gypsy cab, found out too late that Eddie had other destinations in mind. Eddie mumbled to his hopefuls with a thick, Slavic tongue and kicked-puppy eyes: "Eye-am lookeeng for sumvun." Paul had wished him luck and gotten off at the next corner. He'd seen him literally dozens of times since, a puttering sexual scavenger, slump-shouldered and leering, but harm-less enough.

Thirty minutes ago they had found Eddie slumped in the driver's seat, leaning against the horn, his little Japanese shitbox bleating out a cry for help into the late October air, his blood black and steaming on the dash and glass. Eddie had three stab wounds worth mentioning, including one per-ilously close to the carotid artery, which accounted for the shirt-destroying spray, and a half-dozen superficial lacera-tions of the face and hands. Defense wounds. Apparently, Eddie was still looking for love in all the wrong places.

Sadly, it was nothing new. There were a lot of psychos out there, and according to the cops Eddie's was a squirrely little loon who thought he was Jesus; the pocket savior swore up and down that he was back from the dead, and he was pissed. Apparently, he hadn't much cared for Eddie's offer to eat of his flesh, either, and had expressed his righteous rage at his latest luckless supplicant with a steak knife. They'd probably sell the story rights, Paul thought, make it into a cheesy Z-grade slasher film. Paul could see the poster now—*INRI: Portrait of a Serial Killer*. Morons.

Glendon PD might have the big J doing communion with Velveeta sandwiches and Thorazine-laced Kool-Aid up at Haverford by morning, but for the moment all Rescue could do was to bring Eddie in viable and hope for the best. Anything more was left to the wheels of justice and the tender mercies of the greater New Jersey health care system. If God had anything to say on the matter, He kept it to Himself.

Oh, well. Eddie would live. Until next time, anyway.

Which was more than Paul could say for their prior run: a six-year-old Hispanic girl, three inches to the left of DOA before they ever wheeled her through the ER's big double doors. Father AWOL, mother strung out on whatever latest chemical enslavement aid was currently making the rounds on Hurley Street, near the piers, where the distant sprawl of Manhattan shimmered across the fetid Hudson.

Apparently she'd been a bad girl, spilled some bathwater one too many times today, or some other capital crime. And Momma's latest live-in hump had decided that the best way to assert his parental proxy was by making her squat in a scalding tub and keeping her down by whacking her with a clothes hanger. Her baby brother got to watch, absorbing important life lessons on obedience at the ripe old age of two.

By the time Rescue rolled in, a heartbeat after the cops, boyfriend was cuffed and cursing. Momma stumbled home in the middle of the melee, and they busted her, too. But the girl was unconscious and adrift, a bruised and blistered rag doll. Multiple contusions and second-degree burns covered three-quarters of her slight, spare body. As Social Services arrived, her sibling just stared with eyes dark and dead, the nightmare forever burned into his impressionable brain. Outside, TV crews shuffled and craned for a better angle, hovering over the promise of slow-news-night filler.

She seized up and arrested on the way in; Paul did everything he could, intubating her and hitting her up with as many cc of epinephrine as he dared as Tom and Joli played backup and Dondi hit the siren and howled down the cramped boulevards, running red lights, racing death. But by the time they turned her over to the ER orderlies who wheeled her into trauma, she'd already gone cyanotic, and the last Paul saw of her was a little blue-faced angel, arm flopping loose and limp from the edge of the cold metal cart, waving bye-bye. She didn't make it.

Score: Russian perverts, one. Children, zero.

And it was only eleven-thirty.

Paul entered through the rear, hunching to miss the five-foot clearance of the wagon's stainless steel interior, tossing the butt just before the doors slammed shut. The cigarette sparked and winked out on the macadam behind him, lost in the darkness. He wasn't supposed to smoke on board, but at the moment he just didn't give a damn.

So far, things were shaping up to be just another night in Jersey. They weren't even supposed to deal with half the shit that had flown into their fans tonight—they weren't equipped for much beyond basic triage and stabilization. Big stuff was traditionally reserved for the ambos, the ambulance crews, but tonight had just been too goddamned busy.

To compound the festivities, it was unseasonably cold: bitter, biting, and heartless. The kind of weather that froze vagrants in their sleep—limbs curled and brittle, faces frosted with snot-cicles. Popular wisdom held that cold snaps were low on assaults but high on domestics, DUIs, and the homeless; anything below the freezing point tended to not excite the criminal element, but the resulting move into bars and bedrooms only brought the headaches home. And the homeless . . . well, the homeless were eternal.

Since coming on this morning they'd already responded to some two dozen calls, including six false alarms, two drunk driving crack-ups—the latter with the driver pinned behind the steering column of his compacted LTD, a Jaws-of-Life endorsee if ever there was one—a trash fire in an abandoned building, a John Doe floater fished out near the docks, and a heart attack.

The floater was a suicide, a jumper, maybe three days dead. There was no note, and by the time they fished him out there were no extremities or facial features, either. Rats. They bagged him and let the county coroner's office do the rest. With luck, they'd ID him from dental records. If not, well . . . one more faceless stiff wasn't going to make or break anybody.

The heart attack was a three-hundred-pound retiree who blew a hose during an after-dinner argument with the wife. Rescue found him laid out on the kitchen tile, deep in the grip of a V-fib—multiple points in the heart beating like a coronary conga line dancing out of synch and into oblivion. Paul and Dondi had moved with practiced economy, wasting no time as Tom and Joli brought the back board and straps. They shocked him twice and bagged him, performed CPR and hit him up with Lidocaine to stave off any premature ventricular contractions that might pitch him back into V-fib before he got his rhythm up. By the time they rolled into St. Anthony's he was breathing regularly, good beat on the monitor, even bitching about his IVs. Score one more, for cranky old fat guys.

His wife was an irascible immigrant dumpling with a bad perm and ten-dollar housedress. She was blubbering but grateful as they left; apparently she hated her hubby enough to wish him dead but loved him too much to actually want him so. She blessed them profusely, which was both unexpected and appreciated. It was rare to be thanked, and it felt good.

But Paul was still creeped about the kid.

Dondi picked up on it as Paul squeezed into the shotgun seat and hunkered down, one foot propped on the dash, eyes gazing out at the harsh-lit bay. They were a team-within-the-team, as different from Tom and Joli, or even each other, as two men could be. Dondi's swarthy mass, smartass smile, and wiry nest of oil black hair was as much a genetic one-eighty from Paul's lean frame and fair, fiery Irish good looks as his wisecracking demeanor was from Paul's dry, brooding moodiness. Tommy DeAngelo and Joli Pelligrisi were younger, twenty-six and twenty-eight respectively, and both seemingly sprung from the same beefy, Italian-stallion gene pool: all cropped hair and barely contained testosterone. When not on runs, they pumped iron in the station house basement until their seams burst.

But time and experience had fused them all into a symbiotic unit—seasoned professionals whose cumulative skills, knowledge, courage and expertise would easily have commanded twice the salary and three times the social standing were they working in any field where the collars were white and not sweat-stained blue. They were pals, and bros, and family, and they were tight.

Firefighters were like that. They were an odd breed: mythological anachronisms, archetypal unsung working-class heroes. They routinely went where no one in their right mind would go to do a job no one in their right mind would want to do, risking life and limb to protect a public that ignored as much as it relied upon them. Joe and Jane Civilian would vote down referendums for better equipment if it hiked their property taxes a dime, park in front of hydrants to buy milk or bitch when they pulled over to let a rig or an ambulance go screaming past, all because it inconvenienced them in some way, stole a dollar or a moment from their busy, busy lives. They complained when sirens woke them up at night or a two-alarm tangle made them go around the block, unless of course it was their block, their house, their life or loved ones facing the flames. They saw firemen as ciphers when they saw them at all, faceless functionaries in clunky gear and funny hats. They just didn't get it.

But for men like Paul and his crew it was different; exactly the opposite, in fact. Wearing the shield was more than just a steady job with a pension at the end, more than simply a means of escaping the grueling monotony of factory work or the stultifying hive-mind of the corporate yuppie warrens. To be a firefighter was to live a life that was never boring. It was a chance to make a difference in an indifferent world. Being a firefighter mattered.

Paul and Dondi had grown up together, taken their department entrance exams together, graduated from the academy together, and saved each other's butts more times than either could count if they ever tried, which neither ever did. They loved and sometimes hated each other as only the closest of friends could. But for all Dondi's annoying personal habits, which were legion, he possessed one sterling trait that Paul valued above all others: he knew when to shut up.

This he now did, as they sat in the silent confines of the big red rolling meat wagon that was Rescue One. Outside, the managed panic of St. Anthony's raged on, distant, oblivious. A muted voice squawked urgently over the intercom; heads and blue scrubs bobbed on the far side of the gritty safety glass, and were gone. Paul let out a long sigh as the knot unbound inside him.

"I dunno," Paul said at last. "I just hate it when it happens to the kids."

Dondi nodded—so that's what the silent treatment was about. "At least we got the other one out," he offered. It sank as fast as he said it. Dondi shrugged. "Anyway, Social Services got 'im, and with any luck mom and her hump'll do some serious time."

"Great, three more wards of the state," Paul replied. He gave a short husky huff that Dondi knew was Paul's characteristic weight-of-the-world warm-up. "I mean, doesn't it ever get to you that we follow these people practically from cradle to grave, mopping up after them? Jesus. It's like this big dysfunctional machine, churning out assholes like snack chips. They ruin their lives, they ruin everyone else's lives, and we get to clean up the mess."

Paul stopped. Dondi watched, concerned; it was the longest speech Paul had made all day. Something else was eating at him, simmering just beneath the surface. What it was, Dondi couldn't say, and he knew better than to ask. He shrugged again.

"Hey, we did what we could, you know? You can't save everybody. Last time I checked, you didn't have a big red P on your chest." He looked at Paul, deadly serious. "But if it'll make you feel better," he added, "I'll pee on your chest."

Paul smiled at that one, and Dondi winked. Just then Tom and Joli pushed through the ambo bay doors, snickering and zipping up against the cold. From their posturing it was clear that they'd failed miserably in the pickup department and didn't mind a bit. They climbed aboard, took their customary positions in the rig's rear jump seats. Joli leered at Paul and Dondi.

"She wants me," he said.

"Oh, yeah," Tom scoffed, then explained, "she invited him to self-administer an enema, bag first."

"Hey, at least she talked to me." Joli punched Tom on the bicep; the two started mock-sparring across the aisles. Dondi rolled his eyes.

"Girls, girls," Dondi admonished. "Recess over. Duty calls."

The two calmed down marginally. Business as usual was restored for the moment. Dondi keyed the ignition. The big Mack diesel rumbled to life. Dondi leaned toward Paul, who still looked miserable. "Buck up, binky," he said. "The night is young."

Just then a harsh crackle blasted on the radio, as another call came in.

And it got a little older.

2

The siren wailed, high and keening. In the cab, a nasty little nasal voice came over the headsets, cutting through the engine noise, pinging in their ears.

"Heh-heh . . . heh-heh-heh . . ."

Paul and Dondi rolled their eyes as the second voice chimed in.

"Huh-huh-huh . . . Fire!"

Behind the partition separating the cab from the rest of the truck, Tom and Joli were on their Beavis and Butt-head jag again. The two animated idiots had become a timelessly annoying running joke for them since they'd first glimpsed them on MTV, and they egged each other on mercilessly.

"Fire!"

"FIRE! Heh-heh-heh!"

"Knock it off," Dondi barked into his headset mic.

"FIRE! FIRE!"

"Fire is cool! Huh-huh . . ."

"WOULD YOU TWO MORONS PLEASE SHUT UP?"

Silence. Then, *"Heh-heh . . . huh-huh-huh . . ."*

"Jesus," Paul groaned, smiling despite himself. It was too

stupid. He looked at Dondi. "At least they haven't picked up on South Park yet."

From the backseat, a pause. Then a screeching falsetto, *"Omigod, they killed Kenny!"*

"Heh-heh-heh."

Paul and Dondi both groaned. Then Paul glanced out the shotgun side window, and funtime was over. "Heads up," he said. "We're here."

The joking stopped instantly. They cleared the corner, saw thick black smoke billowing from the windows of a three-story brick structure on the corner of Helm and Chelsea streets. It was an older residential building in a lower-middle-income neighborhood, prey to bad wiring, bad landlords, and falling real estate prices. Engine Company 13 and Ladder Company 33 were already on-site: men in black canvas turnouts scrambling amidst gleaming machines as red light flashed off the reflectorized strips on sleeves and backs and legs. Rescue One inched forward through the morass; they glimpsed tongues of flame flitting in the roiling blackness above.

"Fuck me," Paul muttered. The others nodded. This was a bad one.

Rescue One weaved its way through the chaotic sprawl, past five-inch feed lines snaking from the hydrants to the pumper, getting in as close as possible. They could see the building's inhabitants scrambling out of doorways, clutching crying children and shivering pets, clothing and toys, TVs, boom boxes, family portraits, whatever came to mind. Heavy coats were hastily thrown over pajamas and slippered feet, refugee chic. The team parked and jumped out, sussing the situation as they grabbed their gear.

Georgie, the fire chief, was already shouting orders, directing operations, improvising a game plan. Fighting a fire was coordinated chaos, synchronizing teams against an elemental adversary that was as voracious as it was unpredictable. Easy to die if you screwed up, easier still to kill someone else. Ladder 33 was busy smashing glass from hallway window frames, ventilating the upper floors as the Engine Company divided into teams and hauled the attack lines into position. The walkie-talkies on their belts buzzed a hornet's nest of cross talk.

Georgie paced and stewed like a Rolaids poster boy. Every chief was different, and each ran the show according to the dictates of his style and personality. In Georgie's case this was not happy news—Georgie was a hard-core workaholic with flaming ulcers and a prostate like a thermite grenade, and he liked to share the wealth, lodging as great a pain in everyone else's butt as the fire that ever throbbed in his own. He was a thick and grizzled fifty, with a full head of gray hair under his helmet and surprising power in his rotund form. When pissed he spoke in booming tones almost devoid of consonants, like one great vowel movement, and he seemed truly happy only when he was bitching at someone.

Right at the moment, that someone was Tom and Joli, who had pissed Georgie off simply because someone had to. "Whaddafuckah yas doin?" Georgie bellowed, gesturing to the huddled inhabitants. "Gedd ovahdeyah!"

Tom and Joli grabbed a medbox and hustled toward the rattled evacuees as Paul and Dondi yanked oxygen bottles and donned their bulky SCBA gear. Paul called out to a short, stocky man at the pumper's control panel. "Hey, Maytag, what's up?"

"Dunno yet," Maytag replied. His real name was Bobby Maitland, but everyone called him Maytag because he was built like one. His dark skin glistened from perspiration and spray. "Started in the basement," Maytag added. "Looks like Mr. Toast has struck again."

He said the last part casually, not taking his eyes off the pressure gauges. Paul nodded. Mr. Toast was the tag they'd given a mysterious firebug who'd popped up three years ago around Halloween. No doubt inspired by the coverage of Detroit's annual inferno, some twisto had tuned in and found his true calling, creating his own personal Devil's-Night-on-the-Hudson. His burns always started in the basement; after a while, any blaze of suspicious origin invariably invoked his name. He was a bogeyman and an unofficial mascot.

Maytag threw the pumper's switches and the hoses

charged and grew fat with thousands of gallons of pressurized water. Just then Georgie caught sight of them.

"O'Connell 'n' Kelly!" he said. "Whaddaya waitin foah?"

"Say no more, Chiefie," Dondi said. "We're already there."

Georgie growled and turned, directing his attention to more pressing matters. Despite his rancor, his curtness was a sign of respect; he knew they would do their job, and thus felt no need to elaborate. They were Rescue, and their job was exactly that: search and rescue. They were free agents on the scene.

Paul grabbed his helmet, pausing to glance at the stained Polaroid tucked into the webbing: Julie and Kyra, mugging for the camera. Kyra was eight at the time, and his wife and daughter were smiling and serene, light-years from this madhouse scene. A reminder. Paul grabbed his mini-Haliburton tool, an eighteen-inch titanium bar with a head that flattened into a short blade on one side and a thick spike on the other. Among other things it was an all-purpose entry tool and could force locks or pop hinges on virtually any door. That and a flashlight were all he carried on a search; Paul walked point, and he liked to travel light.

He sucked in a breath and pressed the SCBA mask to his face, cinching the straps until it hugged his skull. For the second it took to thumb the feed valve on he was encased in a claustrophobic vacuum. Then the oxygen hissed in, and he could breathe again.

Paul donned his helmet and looked to Dondi, who was now likewise thoroughly encased in boots and turnouts, thick gloves, hood, helmet, and airtank. He had the other medbox in hand. The black rubber mask hugged his face like an alter ego, colors refracting off its scratched Plexiglas visor. His voice came over the headset, a muffled squawk.

"Ready when you are, pal."

Paul gave Dondi a clumsy thumbs-up.

And in they went.

* * *

Darkness. Total, complete. Heart pounding, adrenaline pumping senses into overdrive. Breath huge, aqualung gasps. Regulator hiss.

Move.

The hall lights were off, but it wouldn't have mattered; if it had been broad daylight, it would have made no difference. Fire loved the darkness, and hated any luminance not its own. Gray smoke drifted on currents, swirls and eddies sucking through the door and up the stairs. It quickly choked off visibility as they checked the first floor, then climbed upwards and came in low, searching door to door, room to room.

Hot. Sweat, clammy under heavy gear. Sight useless through poison clouds. Follow sound: garbled cross talk, the sound of flames feeding. Move by Braille, hugging the walls. Stay close. Ignore instinct. Keep going.

The second floor was clear: nobody living, and even better yet, nobody dead. But the third-floor hallway was worse, a thick sea of swilling smoke swallowing their flashlight beams, tracing oily patterns in the air an inch in front of their faceplates, which was as far as either of them could see. They pushed forward into the swirling void, working together but utterly alone, listening for cries and feeling for heat. Paul thought of the old fireman's saw about finding a fire dick-first, felt his own shrivel like a hibernating turtle even as his thoughts attenuated down to the next moment, the next move, the next step.

Find a door. Check the knob. Locked. Pop it. Pause. Kelly's first law: fire is cunning. Fire eats available oxygen, then goes out. Tricky. Heat rises. Gases expand. Pressure builds. Thirteen, fourteen, fifteen hundred Fahrenheit. Waiting. Charge in too fast, and boom! Reoxigenation, ignition, explosion, fireball: backdraft. Or incinerate down like a molten sky, burn from ceiling to floor in two seconds flat: flashover.

Either way: death.

Remember. Fire is more than force of nature, more than physics of combustion and cubic room volume of air and science of oxidation. Fire is alive. It breathes. It feeds. It grows

and breeds. Fire has personality, jealousy, ambition, hunger.
Fire loves and hates and needs. Fire is alive.

And, like all things greedy with life, it wants more.

Paul stopped. There was something heaped before him on the floor. Paul leaned closer, saw. A body. Curled fetal, turned in on itself. Paul couldn't see the face, but he could tell by the arc of the hips that it was a woman.

"Got one!" he called out.

Up ahead in the hallway, it was hot now, very hot. The fire was lurking there, somewhere in the roiling clouds. Paul rolled the woman over. She was Hispanic, maybe twenty. Black mucus striped her lips, her chin. He brushed her hair back, saw her eyes were rolled back in her head. She was already gone.

But she had left something behind.

"Holy shit," he gasped. Dondi scrambled forward, hunkered down on hands and knees, caught a glimpse of Paul's discovery—a toddler, maybe eighteen months, still and clad in its bargain flannel Barney pj's and wrapped in a wet blanket. Paul couldn't tell its sex, but the grim tableau was all too clear. The woman, presumably the mother, had tried to get out and had been overcome by smoke just as she'd cleared the dead bolts. In her last moments she had thrown herself over her child, instinctively protective. For all the good it had done.

"Leave 'em," Dondi said. "We'll get 'em on the way back—"

But Paul was already scooping up the child's limp form, inching back through the portal. As he turned Dondi got a glimpse of his eyes behind the visor. There was no arguing with that look.

Behind them, the first fire team was already down the hall, engaging the blaze. Engorged hose splayed across the floor, water hissing against a dull red roar.

"Great," Dondi muttered as he hefted the body of the mother. "I get all the fun."

* * *

They made their way back, dodging hose and sploshing through the impromptu waterfall cascading down the steps. Inside, the fire teams were busy knocking down the flames. Outside was a circus: the blaze had been stepped up to three-alarm status, with another Engine Company and additional ambulance crews called in to handle the overspill. An Action 9 minivan had already set up shop on the perimeter; their local man in the field, Link Lenkershem, was busily sniffing the scene for camera-ready carnage and practicing his warm-up pitch, a casual ghoul in Dockers and an L.L. Bean parka.

"Tragedy strikes as dozens flee into the frigid night," he intoned for the cameras, "as a mysterious blaze claims yet another Glendon property . . ."

Joli came up as Paul reached the back door of the nearest ambulance, grabbed a thermo blanket, and deposited his tiny bundle on the gurney bed. The paramedics were off tending to the disheveled survivors on the front lawn. Paul stripped off his mask and unslung the airtank, coughed, and spat on the pavement. Joli glanced from the fire to Lenkershem, then saw what Paul was doing.

"Shit, man," Joli exclaimed. "You okay?"

Paul nodded and gestured back to Dondi, who was sucking wind as he labored under the mother's dead weight. Joli ran over and pitched in, lifting her as gently as possible off the older man's shoulder and onto the frigid grass. Dondi collapsed beside her, peeling off his helmet and mask and gloves. Joli started to check for a pulse, but Dondi shook his head.

"Don't bother," he said, red-faced, exhausted. He looked to Paul.

But Paul was not done yet. He checked for a pulse, then peeled open the child's jumper and placed his ear to its chest.

Just then Tom came up, sweating, overwhelmed. "Hey, I could use some bodies over here . . ." he began, then stopped. Paul was working feverishly now, tipping the child's head back, placing his mouth over its slack lips, blowing air into deflated lungs. He pressed on the tiny chest, counting one thousand one, one thousand two, one thousand three. Nothing. He repeated the process. Time crawled. One thousand one, one thousand two, one thousand three . . .

Dondi came over just as the camera crew caught sight of the dead woman on the lawn and the tense drama playing out at the back of the ambulance. Five-hundred-watt battery-powered halogens swept across them as Lenkershem's crew zeroed in, video vultures scoping fresh kill.

"Let it go, man," Dondi said. "You done what you could." But Paul continued to labor over the tiny body, his features intent, grimly focused. "Paul," Dondi said, reaching out. "Paul, man, it's over . . ."

But Paul just shook him off, grabbing his oxygen tank and disconnecting the face mask. Dondi shrugged and pitched in, opening the valve on the tank as Paul placed the hose directly over the child's mouth and nose. The tank hissed, feeding pure oxygen. The babe's half-lidded eyes were fixed and dilated, pupils milky. Paul pulled the hose away, listened to its chest, massaged it again.

As he worked, a small crowd began to form: refugees and rubberneckers, all drawn to a fleeting glimpse of a fate worse than their own. The paramedics returned, pushing through the throng. Lenkershem's eyes were fixed and dilated, as well, but for another reason entirely. He signaled to his camerawoman; she nodded and zoomed in.

Suddenly the little chest heaved.

A collective gasp sounded; Paul laughed, a nervous release, then redoubled his efforts. "C'mon, honey, c'mon," Paul murmured, part pep talk, part prayer. "You can do it, I know you can. Breathe . . . breathe . . ."

And then, as if in answer, the child hitched and gulped. Its eyes fluttered and squeezed shut, and in the next moment the air was filled with a raw-throated banshee wail. It squirmed in his grasp, full of fear, full of pain and rage and indignation.

But it was alive.

The crowd watched, amazed. Paul was laughing out loud now, blinking back tears. He scooped the child up in the blanket, hugged it to his chest as the paramedics moved in

and Dondi and Joli shouted and high-fived each other, giddy
with adrenaline and victory. Someone started to clap. A torrent of applause followed, a rippling wave of jubilation and
relief. Lenkershem smiled, sentiment-surfing the moment,
but the glint in his eyes said he would have been just as
happy either way.

The child bawled like nobody's business. It was royally
pissed. Paul handed the toddler over to a waiting ambo crew,
and a trip to St. Anthony's.

"Way to go, champ," Dondi said, clapping him on the
back as they stumbled onto the lawn and collapsed, dog-
tired. "Way to fucking go."

Paul nodded thanks, too spent to speak. As the ambulance
pulled away Paul fumbled inside his turnout coat for a cigarette, his mind a merciful blank. Dondi beat him to the
punch, offering a Montclair 100.

"Jesus, how can you smoke these things," Paul grimaced
as Dondi lit him up. "If I'm gonna kill myself, at least give
me a Marlboro."

"You're welcome."

Paul leaned back and exhaled smoke and frosted breath,
realized he had completely forgotten about the cold. Somewhere in the deeper recesses he knew that there was a world
of hurt awaiting the life he'd just reclaimed: hospitals, insti-
tutions, buried memories, nightmares, a lifetime of damage.
But at the moment, he was simply happy that there was any
life at all. That had to count for something.

Behind them, the second Engine Company had fired up
the remote water cannon, Super Squirt, and aimed it at the
roofline. As the chromed nozzle roared, a white arc of pressurized fog curtained down, sweeping gracefully back and
forth. Lights refracted off the mist, an aurora borealis shim-
mer. Ice glistened everywhere, magical and surreal at a distance, punishing up close. The fire was abating, knocked
down at last.

Dondi shivered. "C'mon. I'm freezing."

They stood, joints creaking, reeking of smoke and sweat,
and made their way back to the rig. It was twelve-thirty and,
technically speaking, a new day. But there was still cleanup

and salvage to do, victims to transport, gear to repack, a dozen other tasks in the aftermath. And miles to go before they slept.

Georgie glanced over as they passed, and he nodded, then went back to bitching at his men. Coming from him, it was tantamount to a ticker-tape parade, a combination of good job, congratulations, and don't let it go to your heads.

Paul laughed through chattering teeth.

"What?" Dondi asked. "What's so funny?"

"I was just thinking," Paul replied. "Was it a boy or a girl?"

"Beats me, pal. I forgot to ask it."

Paul smiled. Another day, another one hundred and sixteen dollars and seventy-one cents, before taxes. Tomorrow, they'd sleep in.

And then they'd get up, and do it again.

3

The needle was short and sharp, the hand that wielded it soft, casually precise. It was a habit borne of years of experience, and as Paul watched, Julie jabbed the hypo into the tender flesh of her hip without even breaking her train of thought.

"So there's this new program the district wants us to implement," she said, leaning on the rim of the sink and twisting for a better view. "It's all about alcohol and drug abuse. Simpson wants us to have our classes come up with a series of posters that illustrate the perils of drug abuse, says he wants to use them in a regional show. Very hard-core, makes D.A.R.E. look like the Grateful Dead—you know, smoke pot once and you burn in hell. Can you believe it?"

"Hmmph," Paul mumbled tiredly.

"That's what I said," Julie continued. "I mean, I told him this isn't art, this is propaganda. We've been told to work the theme that if they ever even so much as think about smoking a joint or drinking and driving, they'll die. They're in third grade, for God's sake." She rolled her eyes and finished the injection, swabbed the site with an alcohol-soaked cotton ball, and let the nightshirt slip back over her hips.

"So then one of my kids, she's with her dad and he stops to get a Big Gulp at the 7-Eleven, and when he gets back into the car with it she starts crying, and she says to him, 'But, Daddy, you're drinking!' I mean, the poor kid thought he was gonna crash and burn from having a Pepsi."

Paul grunted. Julie laughed; ironic, angry. "Things are really getting nuts," she said. "I've already got one kid who's scared to do the creative visualization exercises because his parents are born-again Christians and they told him that imaginary worlds are unbiblical."

She clipped the tip off the needle and tossed the disposable syringe into a little hardwood trash container reserved for that purpose. Her daily insulin injections were as much a part of the rhythm of life as going to work or bitching about the system, or watching her blood sugar levels, or getting up too damned early on a Sunday.

"Plus," she continued, "now they're talking about mandatory urine tests for teachers and students. I couldn't believe I was hearing this. So I said to Simpson, leaving aside for the moment issues of the First Amendment and the Bill of Rights, just how do they propose to pay for all this? And guess what Simpson said. Guess whose, quote, nonessential, unquote, budget they want to cut?" Julie paused dramatically.

But Paul just grunted again. Julie looked at him and frowned. "Glad to see you share my rage," she said, only mildly sarcastic.

"Sorry," he replied. "I'm beat."

"Poor baby." She softened, let it slide. It was less righteous rant than end-of-the-week wrap-up, anyway, and she could see he looked thrashed. "Tough night?"

"Yeah, kinda." Paul sat on the fuzzy covered toilet seat, trying to jump-start his consciousness. He was bleary-eyed and rumpled, clad only in black boxers and a wrinkled Ren and Stimpy T-shirt that read *I'll keeeel you, you stinking blob of protoplasm!* His hair was plastered flat on one side of his head, unfortunately emphasizing his receding hairline. He felt about three hundred years old.

Julie, by way of glaring contrast, was maddeningly fresh and chipper for 10:00 A.M. on a Sunday. She was two years younger than Paul but looked ten, and was the kind of cheerful spirit who aged so gracefully that it appeared she barely did so at all. She was also a morning person by nature and could roll out of a dead sleep at the crack of dawn, do her yoga on the braided bedroom rug, then be showered and dressed and ready for action before Paul could even remember where his eyelids were, much less how to use them. It both annoyed and endeared him by turns, and he loved her for it, though Paul would be the first to admit that the fact that they only slept together three nights a week helped immensely.

"Heads up," Julie said and leaned past Paul, going on tiptoe to place the insulin kit on the top shelf of the cabinet: another habit, though Kyra was certainly old enough by now not to worry about it. As she moved Paul could smell his wife's warm body scent tinged with the faintest trace of perfume, a soft and musky woman-smell, delicate and familiar. The nightshirt was an anniversary present from Victoria's Secret; it hung loose around her shoulders and unbuttoned to mid-sternum, and as she brushed against him he caught a glimpse of small breasts beneath patterned flannel, nipples dark against her pale skin. He nuzzled his face between them and wrapped his arms around her waist. He started to growl. Julie giggled girlishly, then realized he was doing it less out of lust than pure exhaustion, and it wasn't a growl but a snore.

She squirmed in his grasp. "God, babe, if you're that dead, go back to bed," she said. "Sleep in for once."

"Can't," he mumbled, face still buried. "Gotta meet Dondi at the house at noon." By "the house" he meant the little row house on Marley Street, the latest in an unending parade of Paul's side projects. Paul said something else that featured the words "Sheetrock" and "fixtures," but it was otherwise unintelligible. Julie mussed his hair.

"You work too hard," she replied, then leaned forward and

kissed the thinning spot at the crown of his head. Her own hair was a loose cascade of dark curls, unbound in weekend day-off celebration, and it spilled over her shoulders like an ebony waterfall. Her nose crinkled. "Ugh," she said. "Shower immediately. You smell like a charcoal briquette."

Paul nodded tiredly. He'd already had one at shift's end at the station house, but the stench of burnt property and cindered lives lingered on, in his pores, in his bones, probably in his DNA. Julie pushed away and Paul stood, stripping down and turning on the water.

As he stepped into the stall Paul saw Julie slip her nightshirt off and stare fretfully over her shoulder into the full-length cheval mirror that stood in the corner. Like the rest of the house, the bathroom was done up in a kind of Ikea *cum* Town-and-Country casual, with a dash of Frank Lloyd Wright: an eclectic mix of rustic and modern, oak, honey maple, burnished cherry, and black lacquer, all in a funky, comfortable hodgepodge. Pennsylvania Dutch stenciling and quaint Shaker reproduction sat side by side with clean, stark Scandinavian, with the odd touch of Greenwich Village bohemia, Santa Fe terra-cotta, and Navajo thrown in for ballast. It was pure Julie and it suited her to a tee, and like everything else in their home, she somehow made it all work.

They had been married for seventeen years and together for damned near twenty, but in Paul's eyes she was still the same amazingly lithe Italian girl from the South Shore who'd come to New York to study at Parson's. She met Paul at a loft party in Hoboken, once upon a time. They spent the evening talking about everything from Monty Python to the Shroud of Turin, were living together within a month, married within a year. It was an instant and mutual lust that had blossomed into friendship, ultimately ripening into a deep, abiding love. She was his other half, his better half, and the embodiment of all he considered good in the world.

After Kyra's arrival Julia's figure had morphed from willowy girlishness into a wonderfully feminine lushness, though she still wore a size six and labored ceaselessly to keep it so. The long, thin C-section scar that arced across her belly was, by any estimation, her sole imperfection, and though it bothered her endlessly, Paul loved it simply because it was hers. But he could tell by both her body language and the way her brow was knitted that it was coming, the inevitable follow-up to the genial week's-end bitchfest: the dreaded question, a marital pop quiz, as immutable as the tides.

Paul ducked under the shower massage's pelting spray, but it was no use: the water pressure wasn't loud enough, and the stall was a dead end. Julie's voice came over the curtain, mock-casual, a practiced anxiety.

"Babe," she called out, "does my butt look big?"

Paul pretended not to hear. Pointless. "Hon-ee?" Again, singsong.

"Of course not," he called out. "Don't be ridiculous."

"Seriously," she continued. "I think my ass is getting really huge. Do you think?"

Paul was wide awake now. This was marital no-man's-land; there was literally no right answer, and booby traps galore. If he said no again, she'd say he was lying and torture him relentlessly until he gave in, at which point he was doomed. If he said sure, but that just means there's more of you to love, he was dead meat. Pretending he had soap in his ears was out of the question, as was the real reply, the one he could never say because it wasn't part of the game and cut too close to the bone, besides. The real reply went something like, *What are you talking about, I'm the one with the wrinkles and the creeping hair loss, I'm aging in dog years while you just get better with every passing birthday, you're more beautiful now than when I first married you, and after all this time I still can't believe I ever got you in the first place . . .*

Instead, Paul dodged, invoking their daughter as a kind of psychological human shield. "Babe, where's Kyra?"

As if by some secret signal, a thudding rap groove suddenly sounded from her bedroom on the other side of the wall. Paul winced. It was a girl-thing, a subconscious conspiracy. They were ganging up on him.

"Answer me." Tone shift. Uh-oh. Though his feet were

firmly on Italian tile, they might as well have been skating on thinnest ice.

"Julie, trust me," Paul said in the most egregiously earnest tone he could muster. "You are not fat, you do not look fat, you are light-years from fat. You are the archetypal anti-flab. Other women hate you for this. I know. I took a poll."

"But my butt looks big."

"Your butt is perfect," he corrected. "Your ass is a work of art."

"Yeah?" she called back skeptically. "Which artist?"

"Michelangelo," Paul offered.

"Michelangelo liked men," Julie countered. "All his women were dumpy and had fat thighs."

"Maxfield Parrish, then," he said, going off the other end of the map entirely. No good. "Frank Frazetta?" Nope. Paul cast wildly, assiduously avoiding Dada and cubists. "Um, Vargas?"

"Please," she scoffed. "My tits are too small. Vargas women have breasts like zeppelins."

"Botticelli's *Birth of Venus*?" he offered. No sale, and no points for his grasp of art history. Julie poked her head through the curtain. "If you say Rubens," she said, "you're a dead man."

"Eeek." Paul threw his hands up in a passable imitation of Munch's *The Scream*, hoping the irony would not be lost. Julie did not look amused. Paul sighed.

"Ya got me, babe," he confessed. "I give."

Julie's lower lip pursed, pouting. "So you're saying I'm fat."

"On the contrary," Paul countered, turning and wincing into the water. "I'm just saying there are some things that no artist, living or dead, could ever hope to capture. They're just too perfect."

Behind him, a hint of draft as the shower curtain widened. Warm hands slid around his waist, followed by the warmer press of flesh on flesh. Paul turned and placed his big hands squarely on the subject of their debate, and pulled her under the steaming spray. Barefoot, Julie was a tiny thing, the top of her head just brushing his chin. She tilted her face up toward his.

Fatigue went out the proverbial window as little head replaced big head in the driver's seat, and Paul found himself growing instantly energized. The little fireman was awake now, too. Julie's hand reached down to greet it, as she nuzzled his neck.

"Good answer," she murmured.

4

"**N**o shit?" Dondi said, grabbing the heavy board and hefting his end. "You actually said that?"

"Yup." Paul nodded.

"Damn," Dondi added, "remind me to call you when I need to brush up on my bullshit."

The two men were heaving-ho into the last of a pile of Sheetrock stacked in the center of what was once and would one day again be, God willing, a living room. The house at 514 Marley Street was what real estate agents euphemistically referred to as a "cozy fixer-upper with terrific investment potential!!"—which was a polite way of saying it was dingy, gutted, and would cost more to fix than it did to buy it. A run-down, two-story Edwardian row house sandwiched into a block of similarly borderline buildings, it harkened back to an earlier elegance, with high ceilings, wide casement windows, and hardwood floors, though the decades and socioeconomic changes had clearly taken their toll. Outside, the weather had pulled a schizophrenic and flu-inducing one-eighty, turning balmy and warm. It was a gorgeous day.

Inside, Paul and Dondi were grimy and tired in jeans and thermals, half-toasted off the dwindling supply of Old Bohemian stashed in an Igloo chest in the ravaged kitchen. It was five-thirty and they'd been at it all afternoon, though as the day wore on they spent more time drinking and kvetching than actually working.

"I dunno," Paul sighed, "it's like this game we play, except sometimes she's serious. The bitch of it is, I never know in advance where the joke part ends and the serious part begins."

"Of course you don't," Dondi responded. "That would be too easy. That's how they get us—you're standing there with your mouth hanging open and your foot sticking in it, and they're like, what, you didn't get the memo?"

Paul laughed. They laid the sheet down in the equally hammered dining room, then walked back and grabbed another one off the pile. "Yup," he replied, "and God forbid I ever give the same answer twice. She remembers all of them."

"Got that right," Dondi said. "Connie's memory has a half-life like plutonium." He shook his head. "She can remember every dumb thing I ever said, going back to before we even met. There should be some kind of moratorium on stupid comments—a general amnesty, statute of limitations, something like a Miranda warning on the marriage certificate: anything you say can and will be used against you, til death do you part." Dondi paused mock philosophically. "Why do they do that, anyway?"

"Because they can," Paul laughed. "It's like this weird power they have, for total emotional recall. With Julie, it's gotten so it's half seduction, half loyalty oath." He paused and swigged his beer, genuinely stumped. "Ever since she hit thirty, she worries that she's over the hill or something."

"Yeah, right," Dondi said, wistful. "Connie should still look so good. I think it runs in the family; one night I said something about how if her mom's butt got much bigger someone was gonna have to ride around behind her with one of those wide load signs, and you know I'll be hearing about *that* one until the galaxy collapses."

He paused, looked around reflexively, as if expecting to get hit. "You think they know we talk about 'em like this?"

"Are you kidding?" Paul replied. "They make us look like punters. I heard Julie on the phone, talking with a college friend once: they talk length, girth, and which way it bends."

"Ouch," Dondi winced. He grabbed two fresh brews from the Igloo and tossed one to Paul. "Still, consider yourself lucky," he said. "Connie won't give it up while the kids are in the same time zone." He paused. "So where was you-know-who while all this connubial bliss was going on?"

"Where else?" Paul replied. "In her room, with the stereo blasting. We could have pounded the plaster off the walls and she wouldn't have noticed." He switched gears then, mildly annoyed. "What is it about sixteen-year-olds, that they suddenly want to play everything so loud their brains liquefy?"

"Oh, gee, grandpa, I don't know," Dondi chided. "Remember Blue Oyster Cult at the Meadowlands? I seem to recall you couldn't hear for a fucking week."

"Yeah, but that was different," Paul bitched. "At least they could play."

"Tell me about it," Dondi said. "All this Dawg-E-Dawg, E-Z-E, Chuck-E-Cheez crap. Like, what, suddenly every middle-class white kid in America became a homey from Compton?"

Paul nodded. "It's like the bad pants thing—now all the kids wear these big, baggy, hanging-off-the-crack-of-their-butts-style pants, so now we're having *that* fight. And she's already pissed because last week she wanted to do her hair in dreads, and I told her I don't feature our kid looking like Buckwheat from an *Our Gang* episode. She's been pouting around the house ever since."

"Man, you're gettin' cranky in your old age, you know that?" Dondi warned.

"I know," Paul groaned, nailed. "It's like a nightmare. I'm turning into my fucking stepdad."

"One of life's nasty little ironies," Dondi said. "Like the first time you catch yourself saying 'Because I said so!' "

Paul laughed then, and Dondi smiled. "Hey," he said, "you remember that night we pinched your stepdad's Chevy and blew down to Asbury Park with Gina Lorenzo and whatsername . . ." Dondi squinted, searching his mental archives. "Bobbi," he came back, then luridly amended, "Roberta Janeskew."

"Oh, God," Paul echoed, then laughed guiltily. The name alone was enough to induce a time-tripping grin. Gina was Dondi's high school squeeze and cute enough, but Bobbi Janeskew was the adolescent wet dream incarnate of every good Catholic boy at St. Thomas High, and most of the bad ones. She was an erogenous timebomb in plaid skirt and knee socks, and more than one venal sin had been committed in her name during Paul's junior year. He had set out in conquest of her like Don Quixote on a testosterone bender, only to discover to his unending delight that Bobbi Janeskew lubed for streetwise bad-boy types.

It was a doomed revelation, as Paul quickly found out. Because Bobbi Janeskew's succulence came with a heavy price tag. Ma and Pa Janeskew were second-generation old school from Warsaw, and they held some very particular ideas about their little girl's virtue. And Paul Mister-idle-hands-are-the-devil's-playground Kelly soon found himself designated persona non grata at the Janeskew household, banished in near-record time.

Old man Janeskew, in particular, hated him with a passion normally reserved for Nuremberg war criminals. He was a Polish pit bull—jowly, thick-necked, and bug-eyed—and he watchdogged his daughter's virginity as if it were a piece of the one true cross.

Roberta, of course, had rebelled at every opportunity, surreptitiously cutting loose from her good-girl persona whenever she thought she could get away with it, which was never. It looked like true love was destined to die in utero.

Until that one fateful night . . .

Bobbi had miraculously conned her parents into letting her sleep over at Gina's under the guise of working on a school project together, and with assurances of parental guidance and an eleven o'clock lockdown. The Lorenzos were totally cooperative in this.

But the girls had other plans.

Paul had performed his bit of familial larceny like a pro, sneaking downstairs shoeless after his mom and stepdad had turned in for the night, lifting Ken's keys from the eyehook in the kitchen on his way out. He and Dondi had motored over and coasted up with the lights off and the engine dead, a rolling ninja funmobile. Bobbi and Gina slid out her bedroom window, and together they slipped into the night.

They cruised all the way down to the Jersey shore, shotgunning cheap Mexican and sucking down brews, tripping out on Supertramp, Pink Floyd's *Dark Side of the Moon* and Robin Trower's *Bridge of Sighs*, getting utterly, thoroughly wasted. And then, while Dondi and Gina amused themselves elsewhere, Bobbi had ended up fulfilling the fantasies of a lifetime by doing the bone-dance with Paul under the boardwalk: all full lips and ripe curves and precocious carnal abandon, her nubile teenage flesh shining otherworldy and electric in the shadowed moonlight.

They dropped the girls off by the dawn's early light, undetected, and rode away like masters of the known universe. Paul had let Dondi off a block from his house, then secreted the Malibu back in the driveway and snuck back inside: shoes off, smug, satisfied. It was the perfect crime, with one small exception.

Ken. Waiting for him. In the kitchen.

The moment Paul stepped through the door . . .

"God, I remember," Dondi groaned. "Bastard kicked the living shit out of you . . ."

"Yeah, but it was worth it," Paul laughed, then shrugged. "Screw him. He always said I was a dirtbag, anyway."

"You were," Dondi snickered, "but then, so was I." He raised his bottle in toast to lost youth. "Kinda scary, ain't it? We were exactly the kinds of kids we hope our kids never meet."

"Tell me about it," Paul replied. "Every time some little roving hormone shows up for Kyra and I see that look in his eyes, part of me just wants to pin his head to the floor. It's like, yeah, sure, you can take my daughter out . . . just check your dick at the door, and I'll give it back to you when you bring her home." He paused. "How'd we ever end up on the other side of this equation, anyway?"

"Karmic payback, I guess," Dondi laughed, and gazed around the interior. "Anyway, I wish you better luck with women than you have with real estate. This place is a piece of shit."

"What?" Paul shot back, offended. "It's an investment."

"It's a goddamn firetrap, is what it is." Dondi gestured to the walls, which were laid bare down to the joists, exposing ragged clots of plaster and skeletal wood, frayed wiring and copper pipe. "Wiring's fucked, plumbing sucks, the boiler . . . I don't even want to talk about the boiler." He swigged his beer. "Why the whole damn place hasn't been condemned is beyond me."

"Your problem is, you got no vision," Paul replied. "I'm telling you, another five, ten years, max, this place is gonna be a boomtown. Better than Hoboken in the eighties."

"Uh-huh. Sure."

"Seriously. I paid five grand for this place," he said. "I figure, pump another twenty into it to bring it up to code, rent it out for a few years, it'll practically pay for itself."

"Yeah? How you gonna do all that on twenty-five large?"

"Ruthlessly use my friends," Paul grinned, wiggling his eyebrows. "It'll give you something to do with your hands."

"Fuck you, I've got something to do with my hands. You're the one getting laid in the shower."

Paul ignored him. "Anyway, Kyra's gonna settle down one of these days, after she finishes school and college. I mean, eventually she's gonna get married, want to start a family of her own. This is kinda like an early wedding present."

"Gettin' a little ahead of yourself, ain'tcha, hoss?" Dondi commented. "She just got her driver's license."

"Yeah," Paul said. "But I never really knew my old man, and Ken didn't give me a damn thing growing up. When I turned eighteen he just opened the door and said, 'There's the world.' And then he booted me out into it." Paul drained his beer and crumpled the can. "I just want to give her what I never had."

"Nothing wrong with that." Dondi drained his as well, then let out a luxurious burp. "Better tack another five onto the budget, though. For beer." They laughed and tossed the crumpled cans into the trash, and then Dondi stood and clapped his friend on the shoulder.

"Well, this is all fine and dandy," he said. "But before you go strolling down the aisle and picking fabric swatches and all, lemme show you what's wrong with this piece-of-shit boiler you got." Dondi ambled toward the back corner of the kitchen and the door that led to the basement, gesturing for Paul to follow.

"Among its many other charms," he continued, "there's some severe fuckage in the gas mains. You don't get it fixed, and you're liable to blow this place sky-high. And then I'll have to come ID your crispy ass, and that'll just ruin my whole day."

They were just about to descend when Paul stopped and peered at the back door immediately adjacent to the basement steps, in what the real estate agent had laughingly referred to as "the mud room."

"Hey, Dondi, check this out," he said.

One of the panes of glass nearest the doorknob had been neatly broken, stray shards littering the floor directly beneath. Dondi smirked.

"Like I said, great neighborhood," he chided.

"Goddammit," Paul muttered. "Why would anyone want to break into a gutted house? S'not like there's anything to steal."

"You kidding?" Dondi replied. "They were probably looking to rip out the plumbing or the wiring for the copper. Junkies, man. They'll steal anything."

They opted to check the rest of the house to make sure it was secure. It was barren, but intact, and there were no signs of looting.

But as they reached the end of the second-floor hall Paul pushed open the master bedroom door and sent something hard and brittle skittering across the hardwood planks. The door swung wide, and Paul and Dondi peered in.

"Looks like someone's been hanging in Daddy Bear's crib," Dondi said.

And he was right. A squat had been set up in the big bedroom; in one corner a dropcloth and an old sleeping bag lay piled like a nest, empty beer bottles and cigarette butts strewn around it. Even the fireplace bricks were blackened with ash and bits of burnt plywood scrap.

"Don't see any works or vials," Dondi said, the tip of his boot nosing through the clutter. "If they're junkies, they're awful careful about it."

But Paul was not amused. It was clear this was more than an annoyance to him; it was tantamount to a violation. Dondi nudged him. "Something else to put on your shopping list," he said. "New locks."

Paul frowned.

5

The sun was just setting as Paul drove his black '86 Ford F350 pickup down the street, heading for home. John Mellencamp's "Case 795 (The Family)" from the *Human Wheels* album played on the Sony CD player, the volume pumped up to bleed. Paul liked Mellencamp, even back in the "Jack & Diane" days, before he lost the goofy "Johnny Cougar" moniker his label had saddled him with early in his career. He liked his nicotine-saturated voice, straightforward guitar-driven tunes and the working-class pathos of his lyrics, which were like little stories sliced from the heart of life. But mostly he liked him because Mellencamp was a frank anachronism and didn't care who knew it.

Paul sang along shamelessly about how everything's all right with the family, everything's safe here at home, all the while drumming the steering wheel to the driving beat. He couldn't sing to save his life, but who cared? The truck was a big, testosterone-spewing gas pig with dualies on the back, a fiberglass shell covering the bed, a winch on the front bumper and a hundred and sixty thousand miles on the engine, but it was paid for, and all his.

The song wailed on, Paul's tuneless voice drowned out by two hundred and forty watts of RMS power. A big, tuned-port subwoofer in the back of the king cab vibrated his ass like a magic fingers at the Kozy Kove Motor Lodge. All in all, life was good. Paul wheeled into the driveway, fat tires crunching on crushed gravel laid by his own hand.

The neighborhood was a quiet, middle-income enclave, mercifully removed from the neat but unbelievably tacky abodes that characterized the bulk of Glendon, where fake wood-grained aluminum siding ruled, offset by postage-stamp lawns now festooned with pumpkins, ghouls, and all manner of macabre ornamentation for Halloween.

Coming home at the cusp of dusk was one of life's little pleasures that Paul never tired of, the windows of his house aglow and golden against the deepening blue background, radiating warmth and welcome. Indeed, the Kelly house was a rambling and romantic old manse on a lot dotted with oak and elm and poplar, far from the seedy human backwash that was Paul's standard stock-in-trade. The house bristled with peaks and gables and gingerbread trim, all painstakingly restored by Paul and Julie, down to the wraparound porch and leaded glass windows that made rainbow prisms of the morning sun.

He wheeled around back and pulled into his slot, noting that Julie's midnight blue Honda Prelude was tucked in the garage. Paul keyed off the engine as Mellencamp disappeared in a puff of sonic smoke. He wistfully wished for a two-car garage, parking space ranking second only to closet space in marital power-brokering. His clothes had long ago been squeezed from closet to armoire; when Julie got the Prelude, his truck had similarly been banished. God help him when Kyra got wheels, which, given the fact that she'd just scored her license, should be imminent. He'd probably end up parking on the roof.

Paul grabbed his ripstop nylon ditty bag and climbed out, heading up the patio leading to the back door. The patio itself was inlaid brick from a demolished factory downtown—trucked in by the ton after a deal Paul made to install smoke detectors in the contractor's home—and was covered with fallen leaves that rustled and crunched underfoot as he made his way toward the kitchen door. A lot of work went into making the Kelly house a home, a lot of time, a lot of love. The property taxes were murderous. But it was worth it.

As Paul approached he noticed that the gutters and rainspouts were clogged with leaves again—Kyra hadn't done her weekly chores, which, among other things, included raking duty in the fall. He grumbled momentarily, then his stomach rumbled as he caught the first aroma of food. Thoughts of parental reprimand instantly vaporized; he was starved. And dogged as his schedule tended to be—no matter what he was doing, or where he was doing it—Paul always made it a point to be home in time for Sunday dinner whenever he was off.

It had ever been thus, was in fact one of the few traditions that held sway in the face of the hectic juggling act that comprised the Kelly family's daily lives. Fast food and microwave might rule six days a week, but Sunday was still a sit-down deal, and he always looked forward to it.

Paul entered. The kitchen was warm and spacious, with broad exposed hardwood floors and unexpectedly urban forties-style brushed steel cabinets refinished in gloss black lacquer. The window over the sink was filled with plants and crystals; a Felix-the-cat clock hung on the opposite wall, sly plastic cartoon eyes sweeping back and forth in perfect syncopation with its curved, swishing tail, a sardonic little grin on its molded face, as though it were perpetually privy to some particularly juicy secret.

The counter next to the fridge was the familial dump zone, stuffed with mail and papers, car keys, magazines, and bills. A police scanner sat atop the fridge, the volume tuned low, neat little rows of LEDs sweeping the audio horizon for danger. Taped to the freezer door was a list of relevant call monitor frequencies, and numbers for every engine or ladder company in Glendon, as well as Paul's beeper code. A clunky butcher block table dominated the far end of the room, next to the bay window that looked out on the back-yard.

"Hey, babe," he said, kicking his boots off and hanging the bag on a hook by the door. As he did, a gangly black Doberman came loping in, grinning a big doggie grin. The dog jammed his nose into Paul's crotch without further ado. "Spock," Paul said, "give it a rest, already." Spock's stumpy tail waggled cheerfully; Paul scratched the dog's clipped and pointy ears, then turned and opened the door. "Go, go."

The dog bounded out into the yard. Paul shook his head and entered the kitchen.

"Good timing." Julie looked up and smiled. "Wash up. You're just in time to make the salad."

"Yes, ma'am," Paul replied and exited. He came back a moment later, scrubbed and ready, pulling on a clean sweat-shirt. Julie had already pulled the ingredients from the fridge and laid them on the counter; Paul grabbed a beer, then pulled a chef's knife from the butcher block and set about slicing and dicing. As he worked, Julie glanced at him.

"Saw you on TV."

"What? Oh, yeah," he said, remembering Lenkershem. "Scumbag."

She kissed him on the forehead. "I don't know whether I'm pissed you didn't tell me, or glad you spared me the gory details."

"Thanks," he said, hand brushing the small of her back. "Did they say, was it a boy or a girl?"

"A girl, I think," she replied. "They said she's in stable condition."

Paul nodded, changed the subject. "I see someone didn't do their chores today," he said ominously. "There's more leaves in the gutters than in the damn trees." Julie said noth-ing. Paul looked around. "Speaking of which, aren't we missing someone?"

Julie paused. "Um, she's staying over at Jennifer's tonight."

Paul stopped chopping. "Say what?"

"Well," Julie explained, "they had to work on the float for the Halloween pageant, and I said it was okay . . ."

"Tonight?" Paul blurted, annoyed. "It's Sunday . . . it's a *school* night . . ."

"Yeah, well, this is the night they're doing it." Julie donned a pair of mismatched oven mitts—one a lobster, the other a great white shark—and pulled a steaming tray of lasagna from the oven. "Don't worry, she took a change of clothes, and Loren promised me they'd get to bed at a decent hour. They'll be fine."

"Yeah, well this is also the only night this week that we get a chance to be together, you know?"

"So instead we'll have a romantic dinner for the two of us." Julie smiled, ever the effortless mediator, smoothing troubled waters. She slipped past him, heading for the table, and as she did she cocked her hip into his, playfully butting him.

But Paul didn't want to let it go. He glanced at the fridge, where a color yearbook proof of Kyra hung suspended from a little Keith Haring magnet. She was a beautiful girl, fine-boned and delicate, with Julie's features and Paul's eyes, her face framed by thick, curly hair; her smile was simultaneously wholesome and sly. Her eyes were winsome and bright, radiating both intelligence and soul in abundance. A good kid.

Paul resumed chopping, the blade slicing at a head of lettuce. "I mean, what is it with her these days?" he bitched. "She used to help out around here. We used to do all kinds of stuff together. Now it's like trying to get an audience with the queen."

Julie paused in gathering the plates and silverware, grabbed ahold of Paul's hand. "Hmmm," she murmured, inspecting his knuckles.

"What?" Paul asked.

"Interesting," she said, deadpan. "I just thought they'd be whiter, from holding on so tight."

She let go of his hand, continued on. Paul watched. "Very funny," he said.

"Relax," she told him. "It's not a plot."

"What is it, then?"

"It's called being sixteen," Julie interjected, setting two places at the table. "And it'll pass."

"Yeah, and become seventeen," Paul muttered. "Then eighteen, and nineteen . . ."

"Life is a bitch," Julie replied, then came up behind him with a glass of wine and patted him on the butt. "I think that's done now," she said drolly, gesturing to the pile of butchered veggies. "Unless maybe you're torturing them for information."

Paul put down the knife. "Sorry," he said, then began scooping the greens into a big wooden bowl.

"What's with you?" Julie said, eyeing him. "This isn't about missing dinner . . ."

"I don't know." Paul paused, then muttered, "Halloween, I guess." He sighed. "I don't know . . ."

Julie nodded. She did. And suddenly it was perfectly clear.

Another Kelly family tradition, almost as big a deal as Sunday dinner sit-downs. Halloween had always been one of Paul's favorite holidays, outstripping Thanksgiving and Easter cold, even giving Christmas a run for its money. And his appreciation had evolved over time, from a simple handing out of trick-or-treat goodies with a bedsheet over his head and a flashlight under his chin to a full-scale production of gothically Spielbergian proportions.

Every year, Paul's basement workshop would become a beehive of sinister, clandestine activity. Noxious fumes and the whine of power tools would seep through the floorboards until the wee hours. And by All Hallows' Eve, the Kelly home would be transformed into a macabre wonderland: blood-colored lights in the windows, Styrofoam tombstones on the lawn and leering gargoyles on the roof, rustling skeletons hanging from the trees or clawing themselves free from their ersatz graves.

But the pièce de résistance was the big front porch: its normal shady comfort magically mutated into a grand, spook-house-style maze. Trick-or-treaters would ascend suburban front steps only to find themselves plunged into a makeshift Dantean underworld. Ghastly sound effects would emanate from hidden loudspeakers; rubber bats and spiders would bob before shrieking faces, suspended on elastic tethers. A life-sized corpse would tumble from its upright coffin in the creped-out living room window, plastic head thudding against the cobwebbed glass, LEDs glowing in its empty eye sockets. And at the end of the line, there would be Kyra: presiding over a full-size bubbling dry-ice cauldron and handing out the treats, as Paul played a doting Igor, the hunchbacked assistant, or a towering Frankenstein's monster, or a slavering Lawrence Talbot, complete with dog collar and make-believe lycanthropic fleas. Or a pale and blood-lusting vampire. Or one of the shambling undead, hungering for child-sized human flesh.

As time went on and the all-too-real dangers of freelance trick-or-treating had driven most parents into voting on curfews or hauling their kids to shopping malls for watered-down fun, other members of the Fire Department got in on the action, supplying construction skills or dressing up themselves, to aid and abet the thrills. After year five, the Fire Department more or less officially recognized it for the great community relations tool that it was and voted Paul a small budget.

But at the heart of it, always, was Paul and Kyra's annual father-daughter conspiracy. At one time or another, they had worked their way through virtually the entire Universal Studios monster repertoire—with the possible exception of the Creature from the Black Lagoon—and quite a few others in the lexicon of modern horrors. This year, he had planned on dressing up as Pinhead from the *Hellraiser* films, adding a little Cenobite action to liven things up.

Kelly's Hell-House had practically become a local legend. They occasionally got local TV coverage, and it was de rigueur for some reporter or another to do a piece to list in the Things to Do section of the *Glendon Herald*. They had alternately delighted and/or scared the living shit out of every kid in Glendon for most of the last decade, and had earned the unique honor of being one of the few households in Glendon that never woke up on November 1st to find its car windows soaped, or its landscaping wearing a mile or two of sagging Charmin garland.

As for Kyra, she had been in on the act since she was old enough to say boo: going from curly-haired toddler-goblin to the Head Witch herself, grande teen-diva of the undead, a vibrant, integral part of a time-honored ritual.

And now, suddenly, it was stupid.

"Those were her exact words," Paul lamented. " 'It's stupid.' " He sighed. "This really sucks."

"I know." Julie shook her head sympathetically. She knew how much Paul enjoyed it all, and the thought that their daughter was not only no longer interested in the familial festivities but was off doing something similar with strangers was doubly damning.

"Let's face it, hon," she offered, somewhat philosophically, "she's growing up. Every kid eventually reaches a point where they'd rather be with their peers than their parents."

"I hate it when that happens," Paul mumbled, knowing full well that she was right. Still . . . "How'd we suddenly get demoted to geek patrol?"

She just looked at him. She didn't even have to say it.

"I know, I know," Paul said resignedly. He'd studied psych in school and knew enough handy headshrinking buzzwords like *individuation* and *establishing boundaries*. "But we're still gonna have some *rules* around here," he added, waxing paternal. "From now on, no skipping out on Sunday night dinners."

"Yessir," Julie said, smiling.

"And no work-ee, no mon-ey," Paul added.

"Okay, Dad," she replied, underscoring the D word with just a hint of sarcasm.

"I like this," he said, puffing his chest out magisterially.

"Don't push your luck," she warned. Julie grabbed the lasagna, gestured to the salad and dressing. "C'mon," she said. "Let's eat. If you're really good, I'll give you something special for dessert."

"Like what?" he asked.

Julie just smiled and headed for the dining room.

Paul grinned. He grabbed the salad bowl and made to follow her, when the phone suddenly rang. Paul reached for it; Julie's voice called out from the other room. "Let the machine get it!"

Too late—besides, it might be Kyra. Paul picked up.

"Hello, Kellys'," he said. From the other end, nothing. Paul spoke again, louder. "Hello?"

Silence. He could hear the presence of the caller on the other end, the dim wash of background street noise.

"Good-bye!" Paul called out, then hung up. "Asshole," he muttered.

Julie's head popped around the corner. "Who was it?"

Paul shrugged. "No one," he said.

6

The room was dark, moon high and full through dormer windows, bathing the interior an ethereal, lunar blue. The house was still and silent. A low squeak sounded from the big brass bed.

Paul moaned as Julie moved on top of him, angling her hips into a long-practiced and wonderfully familiar position. Her bare skin was hot, laced with the cool sheen of exertion; hers and his. Her hair hung sweat-flecked in a thick dark spill of loosely coiled curls, momentarily obscuring her features. She reached up and brushed it back, biting her lower lip provocatively. Her eyes were heavy-lidded, as if looking inward, searching. They fluttered, showing white. Julie smiled, still searching, then gave a dirty little laugh. Found it.

Paul moaned again and slid into place, getting into the groove. If one of the trade-offs of age was the sheer frequency of passion, one of its overwhelming benefits was its nuance, and he and Julie had long since learned to parlay their intimate energy into a deeper kind of dialogue. With time and guidance Paul had found exactly how to coax her into a state of free-fall abandon, peeling away inhibition layer by mental layer until she was stripped to her pulsating core. And Julie, in turn, knew the rise and fall of Paul's inner rhythms, how to get him hard and keep him that way, how to sustain and forestall the ultimate release through speed and intensity, until it was fleeting, transcendent perfection.

Over the years, Paul and Julie had refined their lovemaking to an art form, a timeless duet of touch and taste, sound and sight and motion. At the moment, they were locked in a slow, steady rhythm, Paul's orgasm a distant, retreating concept, ever slipping over the horizon.

He gazed up at the sight of his wife riding him and felt time slow, go liquid, stop altogether, as the years and layers evaporated: *teacher*, *mother*, *wife*, *mate*, *friend*, all fading away and distilling down to essence, until she became a fecund vision, an eternal force of feminine fury and power. Paul felt himself adrift, cut loose from his own moorings, rooted only at the point of ultimate union. He felt carnally transcendent, as if he could go on like this forever.

But Julie had other plans. She was fully astride him now, his hardness buried deep inside her. Her breasts were swollen, the nipples achingly hard, the soft rise of her belly taut as his cock merged with her, inches beneath its surface. Her features were fierce, languid, feral. His cock felt like a lightning rod driven into the molten core of the earth, Julie's body the roiling storm that billowed around it.

Then she shuddered, as thunderous climax rumbled up like an earthquake shearing a secret fissure, became tsunami piling into an unsuspecting coast. She gasped, arched her back and thrust three times in short, staccato repetition, then three more, instantly and unconsciously snapping Paul back into the heat of the moment. Julie uttered a hoarse, guttural cry and fell forward, instantly smothering him in heat and sweat and soft, musky woman scent. She kept the rhythm, arms wrapped around him, teeth grazing his neck as she cried out, breath hot on his skin, hips furiously pumping, flesh slapping rhythmically against his straining thighs. His own hands hovered momentarily, tracing the contours of her round and glorious ass . . .

. . . then he, too, felt the sensation boiling up like lava inside. She knew instinctively and exactly how to make him come, and she was doing it now, as no one else ever had or ever could, taking him inexorably with her over the edge of her own wanton release. Paul's thoughts dissolved into a blinding wash of wordless love and formless pleasure as bodies, bedroom and world unraveled, became only engorged wet on thrumming hard, again and again and again . . .

. . . and then his own climax surged up, enveloped and absorbed by hers, a bucking syncopated merger of flesh and heart, mind and soul. Paul and Julie emptied themselves into each other, felt the waves of pleasure tumble and wash them together, leave them spent and sweating on a distant, placid shore. As the inner tide pulled out Paul did, too, and they lay, breath ragged, hearts pounding, enmeshed and entwined.

Two seconds later, a car door slammed outside, and Paul and Julie froze.

Busted.

In less than a heartbeat, identity, responsibility, and parenthood slammed back into place, as one thought simultaneously pierced both their brains—Kyra—and Julie instantly grabbed for the bedcovers, pulling them up protectively as Paul's ears tuned to the sound outside, waited for the slap of footsteps on the porch, the click of house keys hitting tumblers.

"I thought you said . . ." Paul began.

"Shhhh," Julie hissed and buried her face in his shoulder, embarrassed. She suddenly wondered if the whole neighborhood had heard them.

They waited. Nothing. A second later, a car engine turned over, and they heard the crunch of wheels pulling away from the curb, rolling away. Paul and Julie let out a collective sigh of relief, then Julie rolled off him, automatically slid her fingers between her legs.

"Shit," she said, reaching for the Kleenex box on the bedside table. Empty. "Shit shit shit." She groaned again and stood, legs unsteady, hand awkwardly stanching the post-coital seminal flow, as she duck-walked over to the bathroom. Paul watched, chuckling ruefully.

"Bite me," she sneered. "You try doing this."

"No thanks," he said, slumping back onto the pillow. "Oh, well," he sighed. "It was fun while it lasted."

Afterwards, they lay warm and quiet and sated, Julie nestling into him, one lithe leg curling over his thighs, her fingers tracing little patterns in the hairs on his chest. Paul stared up at the ceiling, thinking.

"We need to get away," he said softly.

"Away from what?" she asked.

"Everything," he replied. "Take a weekend, run away somewhere, just the two of us. We could get really wasted and make love like crazed weasels."

"What do you call what we just did?" she asked.

"Mmm, I don't know," he replied cagily. Julie dug her nails into his chest. "Ow!" Paul cried. "Okay, I give, it was great!" She relented, pleased. Paul continued. "I'm just saying . . . I was thinking maybe New Hope . . ."

"New Hope . . ." Julie sighed in lewd nostalgia. New Hope was a quaint little berg on the border of New Jersey and Pennsylvania, a picturesque getaway some two hours west, nestled in the deep piney woods of Bucks County, on the banks of the Delaware River. They'd spent their tenth anniversary there, a romantic weekend far from the hectic urban hive. By day they'd hiked and ridden horses and strolled through art galleries and shops, then spent their nights staring up at the stars through a luscious haze of champagne bubbles and hot tub steam, making love with homegrown Kama Sutra glee. They'd always sworn they'd go back. But somehow, life had always intervened. "I wish . . ." she said.

"Why not?" Paul asked. "I mean, what's stopping us?"

"Yeah, right," Julie said, her thoughts drifting off. "Like when?"

"I don't know," he replied. "Next weekend? We'll just go."

"Mmmm," she murmured sleepily. "We'll see . . ." She kissed him goodnight, then curled into the crook of his arm, slipping into dreamland with nary another moment wasted. She had to get up early.

Paul's mind, meanwhile, hummed along, wide awake. For some reason, good sex always left him fully conscious, his intellect striving to reclaim ground so recently ceded to sensation. As he lay on his back, sated and pleasantly numb, Paul's mind turned from thoughts of lusty escape, took stock of other things.

It was okay for Kyra to spend the night at Jennifer's, he decided. And Julie was right, he needed to lighten up. After all, if she hadn't, would they have been able to go at it with such animal abandon? No way; even if they'd wanted to, the parental governors would have gone on autopilot, pinning back the passion, muffling every cry. Stealth sex. Experience had proven that coitus and child-rearing were an uneasy mix, a wet diaper on the fires of frenzy.

Besides, Kyra was a good kid. *Correction*, he amended, *she was the best*. Familial frictions notwithstanding, Paul loved his daughter more than life itself. It continually made him a sucker in the discipline department—all snarl, with very little snap—and while Paul knew that ultimately there was nothing he wouldn't do for her, Kyra knew it, too, and though they both knew where the line was, she pushed it at every available opportunity. And Julie was right—when all was said and done, maybe he was just having a hard time letting go.

That settled, his thoughts drifted over the landscape of his life. All things considered, there was a rhythm to his existence that Paul greatly enjoyed. It was measured not by the ceaseless grind of nine-to-five wage slavery but rather by something organic, almost mysterious. It was unpredictable, yet patterned according to a plan he could not so much see as feel.

Like the cycle of seasons or the ebb and flow of ocean tides, there was always a sense that periods of maddeningly hectic and death-defying pace would invariably be followed by an almost dormant stillness, a time to fall back and regroup, recharge his internal batteries, and tend to loose ends.

Then invariably, just as he began to itch for the moment-to-moment rush of action again, something would come along to jar him out of thinking that things were too easy, that everything was too neatly in its proper place and life was getting stale. Maybe not exactly when he liked, or the way he liked it—but it always came. With time and experience he had learned to watch for clues, to read the lay of things the way a fisherman can assess the surface of seemingly still waters, or a farmer can foretell the coming storm by the way the breeze ripples through a field of wheat long before the first cloud appears.

There were troubles, to be sure. There were always troubles. But Paul had never really expected any different. Trouble was simply a part of the rhythm of things, as inevitable as the changing of seasons or the pull of the tides. He sometimes speculated on different people's order-to-chaos ratio— the relative percentage of stability-to-upheaval in life, both his own and those of the people he loved.

Some people—Julie, for example—were intensely ordered in their worldview, and the first sign of instability or flux would unnerve her to no end, pitching her into control mode. Control was Julie's default setting; it was one of the things that made her a good teacher, as well as a devoted and doting mother, and even a world-class lover, and Paul both admired and depended upon her for it. And he, in turn, became her antidote to becoming too strictured, too anal in her outlook. Paul was Julie's wild card, perpetually full of surprise. Then again, flipping the mental coin, she was perfectly capable of blindsiding him with a thought or a word, knocking him out of his own boxed perceptions when he least expected it. Indeed, she was almost an expert at it. So, in a way, they balanced each other out.

His mind drifted to other people in his life. Like Dondi, the archetypal chaos junkie: thriving on utter madness, most comfortable when things were burning unchecked or careening out of control. With Dondi, it translated into everything from his personal habits—he was a gleeful, unrepentant slob—to his unflaggingly cheerful outlook and almost reckless willingness to dive headfirst into situations where angels feared to tread. It lent him a resiliency and an aura of balls-out courage that Paul both respected and counted on. And Paul was the eye in the hurricane of Dondi's life, centering his best friend's manic abandon, channeling his energy.

Both were comfortable roles, and ones to which Paul felt himself naturally cast. To the best of his knowledge, he was a creature caught somewhere between the two. He knew from experience that he could handle uncertainty and danger seventy-five, even eighty percent of the time, as long as he had that critical twenty to twenty-five percent margin of security. It was his psychological safety net, a fallback mechanism that allowed him to function at his best, and it continually shifted in response to the forces at play.

When the job wore on him too much, he had his family to keep him grounded, seeking refuge in the love and comfort of Julie and Kyra. Paul genuinely loved being a family man. He made a conscious effort to be a good husband to his wife, a good father to his daughter, a good provider and protector, a good man.

This had come as a surprise: years before, Paul had wondered about his own innate capacity for either commitment or fatherhood. His own experiences on the pay-end of bad parenting had been uninspiring: biological pater missing in action since before Paul's birth, stepdad Ken a blue-collar cretin who Paul always felt viewed him as one would an unruly pet—something to suffer grudgingly, and whip when it went on the rug.

Paul's mother, Ellen, was not much better in the nurturing department; she loved him but was too burdened with her own emotional baggage to have much to offer beyond a roof over his head and the most self-serving expressions of affection. She had feared life alone, and so had sought security in the form of a man, any man, only to end up walling herself into a low-wattage domestic hell with a husband whose most sterling character trait was that he was there.

The resulting imprint had left Paul embittered and alienated, high on self-reliance and short on trust. He'd grown up hungering for a sense of home, yet innately distrusting the very concept of such a thing.

But the warm woman sleeping beside him had changed all that. From the first, she was strong-willed, kindhearted, and deeply caring. She was also blessed with a no-nonsense hopefulness that was the natural antidote to Paul's deeply ingrained cynicism. She'd seen through his armor, had known instinctively how to reach through and unlock the fortress around his heart. And, perhaps even more miraculously, she had actually wanted to.

Falling in love with her had been like the climax to their lovemaking tonight—tumbling off a steep cliff, only to find yourself rising. It had been like that from the first and had only deepened over the years. As time went on, he could not imagine a life without her. Julie made it easy for Paul to believe. She made the dream seem possible.

And when she'd given him Kyra, it had become a reality.

Paternal grousing aside, Paul was still astounded by the depth of love he felt for his daughter. It went way beyond the fact that she was his only child and, given Julie's fragile health, the only child they'd likely ever have. It even transcended the anxiety born of a difficult breech-birth labor that had almost cost both their lives.

No, it was a simple truth that had been born the moment he held the blood-smeared, squalling bundle in his hands. Kyra had been borderline preemie, but the power contained in that small form had been immense. As he'd cradled her in his arms and her tiny fingers instinctively locked around one of his own, Paul had felt his entire universe spiral and realign itself, yielding to the life that was its new and unequivocal center.

The old saying went, Any fool can make a baby, but it

takes a man to be a father. It was true. Julie had given him many things, but it was his daughter that made him a man. She was the most astonishing person he had ever known, or ever would—a miraculous baby, a bright and vibrant child . . . now fast becoming a smart and wonderful young woman . . . who still hadn't cleaned out the gutters or raked the yard.

Paul smiled. Domestic bliss was not without its fair share of grief. But when tensions ran high, he would invariably gravitate back to the bustling fraternity of Rescue One, hanging and joking with the guys at the station, playing softball or just kicking back after hours at the Gaslight Tavern.

At the odd times when both work and home were getting on his nerves, he found release in his seemingly inexhaustible roster of projects: teaching at the academy, or public relations in the form of fund-raisers and charity events, or his renovation of the house on Marley Street. It was rare that all three bottomed out at once. In the grand biorhythmic scheme of things, the laws of probability virtually ensured that at least one curve would always be on the upswing when the others were falling. It was a balancing act of sorts, but it worked.

All in all, Paul felt a deep satisfaction with his life. He went to bed at night knowing he had done the best he could and woke up each new day determined to meet the challenge of whatever came his way. He had a job he loved, a wife and daughter he adored, and a funky, comfortable home that he had restored with his own hands. Hell, he even had a nest egg saved up and a pension not too many years down the road, as well as the promise of time to enjoy it while he and Julie were relatively young.

I'm only thirty-eight, he thought. *Thirty-eight is young.* Paul curled into his wife's warm body, spoon-fashion; Julie murmured and stirred agreeably. Paul sighed. All in all, it was as fine a life as a poor boy from the mean streets of Jersey could reasonably have hoped for. Life was hard, but life was good. Life was fair.

Paul drifted off as the tacit fabric of thought unravelled

into sleep. Thirty-eight years to reach a point of sublime balance. Thirty-eight years to build something that was worthwhile. It was a labor of love. The labor of a lifetime.

And it would take less than a night to obliterate it.

7

It was just after nine o'clock on Thursday evening. It had been a slow week, marked by low-level crises: false alarms and fender benders, Stovetop Stuffing fires, people smoking out their homes because they forgot to clean the chimney flue or suburban outlaws burning leaves in flagrant violation of city ordinances.

Even the weather had turned rainy and gray, a depressing pre-holiday gloom. The skies lay heavy and dark over the city; fallen leaves windswept into gutters and mashed into clammy brown paste. A good night to be indoors, a better one to stay there.

Inside the station, the mood was low-key, genial. Rescue One was housed in a two-story building built in 1927, and it still carried a worn Norman Rockwell vibe in its vaulted, embossed tin ceilings, red brick, and black-and-white tile. On the downside, the years had taken their toll, as evidenced by drafts that wormed their way through casement windows and radiators that hissed and gurgled like something out of a bad horror movie.

The first floor was consumed by the huge truck bay that

housed the Rescue One rig and its attendant gear lockers, plus a large common room that functioned as combination dispatcher's office, dining area, and general downtime hang space. In the common room, a twenty-seven-inch Zenith monitor and four-head VCR sat atop a scarred wooden hutch that held videotapes, piles of dog-eared magazines, a stack of equally well thumbed paperbacks, and softcore porno mags. A neat pile of hardcovers were set off from the rest— Paul's private stash, which ranged from gritty nonfiction like Mark Baker's *Cops* or William Dunn's *Boot* to more intellectual fare such as Gavin DeBecker's *The Gift of Fear* or Adam Hochschild's *King Leopold's Ghost*, along with novels by William Goldman, Thomas Harris, and Kurt Vonnegut. Dondi's tastes ran to pulpier fiction and seamy true crime tales, though he could be coaxed into a good Dashiell Hammett. As far as anyone could tell, Tom and Joli read only under duress, apart from training manuals, and were innately suspicious of anything that didn't have pictures and big print.

A bruised and ancient table served as a work surface for the countless hobbies that whiled away downtime. In the opposite corner, a government-issue metal desk sat next to a refrigerator and an old Coke machine. The desk sufficed as the dispatch station, neatly packed with the telex unit, a multiline phone, and the clipboard that held the daily run log. The wallspace above and beside it was plastered with OSHA and FBA bulletins, cartoons from everything from *Firehouse* to *Penthouse*, and yellowed newspaper clippings. One article stuck out from the others, relatively fresh and underscored with Magic Marker; the headline read, "Mystery Blaze Claims One, Leaves Dozens Homeless." It was page-two coverage, not glamorous enough to unseat the ceaseless parade of more press-worthy evils. The origins of the blaze were described as simply "suspicious"; the rescue of the child was mentioned as a highlight. There was an action shot of Paul, holding the bawling baby girl. Across the margin, someone had scrawled a sarcastic message in Magic Marker: "Our heeero!!"

Paul sat with his feet up on the table, reading. Technically, he wasn't even supposed to be in today, had in fact planned on spending the day changing the locks and tackling the boiler from hell on Marley Street. But Tom had called in sick with the flu, and Paul had agreed to cover his tour.

A fire company never rested; even on a slow day, there was still the ceaseless cycle of chores—equipment and apparatus upkeep, housekeeping duties, food prep, and paperwork. By six he had finished doing inventory on the medical supplies, restocking the wagon from the locked supply cabinet in the basement, making his weekly maintenance checks on the battery-powered defibrillator units they kept on hand to jump-start cardiac patients, and putting together a shopping list for their next food run to the Price Club.

He was just settling down to a mountain of technical information in preparation for the upcoming lieutenant's exam. Dondi was out in the bay, making busy with Wallace, the new probationary cadet. Joli was seated at the other end of the long table, absorbed in a bootleg videotape of Tarantino's *True Romance* and absently playing with a latex rubber Freddy Krueger mask. Halloween was on the following Wednesday, and Paul had opted to go ahead with the whole Hell-House thing, with or without Kyra's help.

"Check it out," Joli said. "This is my favorite scene." On the tube, Patricia Arquette's bruised and bloody Alabama Whitman had just gotten tossed through a shower stall by James Gandolfini's pre-*Sopranos* leering Mafia errand boy.

"You're a sick fuck," Paul mumbled, not looking up.

"Seriously," Joli continued, "this is the part where she blows this guy away with his own shotgun and then beats him to death with it." On screen, Alabama brought the gun up and down, up and down, Maidenformed breasts bobbing in slo-mo, face a mask of thespian rage. Joli stuck his hand inside the Freddy mask, working the rubber jaw, the world's worst ventriloquist.

"Great tits," Joli growled. "Whaddayasay Pauleee?? Patricia Arquette's got some happenin' hooters, eh?"

Paul didn't even look up. "Isn't it your turn to clean the crapper, or something useful?" he said.

"Let Wallace do it," Joli said, waving it off. "That's what probies are for. Say, what do think of my mask? Good burn sculpting." Joli slipped it on, immediately became a leering latex monstrosity. He fumbled with the mouth-hole, stuck his tongue out lasciviously. "I'm Miisster Toast!!"

"You're a moron," Paul countered. Insults bounced off Joli as if his ego were Scotchguarded; he shrugged and made an obscene gesture. Just then a blast of cold air rattled the windows; Paul looked up to see a shivering figure push through the front door. The man was thin, fortyish, with thin dark hair and thin, craggy features offset by oddly warm brown eyes. He looked like Crime Dog's distant, rumpled cousin.

"Detective Buscetti," Paul said, mock formally. "What's shakin'?"

"Me . . . s'nasty as a motherfucker out there," Buscetti said, beelining for the coffeepot. He turned and saw the deadpan, molten-faced man sitting silently before him.

"Heya, Joli," he said.

"Shit." Joli pulled the mask off, tossed it on the table. "How'd you know it was me?"

"I'm a trained professional," Buscetti shrugged and filled his cup. He sat, glancing at the spines of Paul's books. *"Fire Stream Management, Principles of Departmental Organization,* and *Protocol of Command."* He rolled his eyes. "Woo-woo."

"Oh, yeah," Paul said. "I'm thinkin' about sitting on the shock paddles, just to liven things up." He closed the book. "So, what's happening in the big bad world of law enforcement?"

"Same shit, different day," Buscetti replied, then added, more seriously, "We're still looking into that apartment fire last weekend."

"Really." Paul's eyebrows arched. "I thought arson was handling that."

"Technically, yes. But there was a body involved, so that makes it homicide."

"No shit." Joli turned away from the tube. Real-life carnage was always more interesting. "Think it's the Toastinator?"

"Dunno." Buscetti shrugged. "Could be anything from an insurance scam gone bad to a pissed-off ex- to some psycho flicking his Bic. We canvassed the neighborhood twice, got nada. I wanted to ask you guys if you noticed anything odd on the scene."

"Not really," Paul replied. "Same m.o. as always: fire starts in the basement, yer basic Charmin starter." Buscetti shrugged. Paul clarified, "Roll of toilet paper unstrung like a big fuse. Probably uses some kind of accelerant, given how fast it travels, but whatever it is, it burns off clean. No residue."

"Lovely," Buscetti murmured and sipped his coffee. The kind of go-nowhere case that could drag on for years, unless the perp got an attack of conscience and fessed up or they caught him in the act. "By the way," he added, "good work with the kid."

"Thanks," Paul replied, slightly embarrassed.

Suddenly a voice cried out from the bay, swearing a purple streak, followed by the clanging of metal on metal and the sound of oxygen bottles pinging off concrete. Paul, Joli, and Buscetti all glanced up, then Paul looked back to the detective and shrugged.

"Probie," he explained.

Dondi entered, still swearing. "Jesus fucking Christ, I tell the kid, fill the tanks to twenty-three hundred psi, so what does he do? He fills 'em to thirty-two. I swear to Christ, that kid is dyslexic and spastic both. He's spaslexic." Dondi spied the lanky detective in mid-rant and beamed. "Stevie! How the hell are ya? And here I was just telling Paulie you'd gotten too good for us." He reached out to the visitor, shook hands warmly. "How's Angela, and the baby?"

"Angela's great," Buscetti said. "Labor was brutal." He smiled. "Twenty-two hours, then the baby pops out like one of the Flying Wallendas." He pulled his wallet out, proudly flipping to a photo of a red-faced gnome with a full head of wispy black curls. "Dana Jean Buscetti, seven pounds, two ounces, lungs like a banshee," he said. "She's already running us ragged."

"She's a doll," Dondi said.

"Liar," Buscetti said flatly. "She looks like Tor Johnson in a fright wig."

"This calls for a toast," Dondi said. He went over to the Coke machine and keyed it open, pulled four cold Budweisers from a stash secreted inside.

"Not in front of the children," Paul admonished. Dondi, who was acting captain on the tour, peeked over his shoulder at the door to the bay.

"Ah, fuck'im," he said, "this is a special occasion." He popped the tops and handed them around. "To kids," Dondi intoned, raising his bottle. "Can't live with 'em, can't leave 'em by the side of the road." Glass clinked, then each took an illicitly celebratory swig.

"Shit, that reminds me," Paul suddenly blurted. "I gotta make a call." He stood and headed for the pay phone in the hall. Buscetti watched him go, then glanced at Dondi questioningly.

"Fam stuff—he's had a bug up his butt all week," Dondi replied. Buscetti nodded; Dondi took another swig. "You just wait," he added sagely, "they hit a certain age and bam—fahget about it. Boys are easy: just one big walking gland, like a hard-on with a learner's permit. But girls . . ." Dondi whistled low, like a prophet of doom. "Girls are a fuckin' mystery. By the time Dana's in high school, you'll be what, in your fifties? You're gonna be up to your eyeballs in estrogen. Shoulda started earlier, while you still had time to recover."

"Thanks," Buscetti lamented. "I feel so much better now."

"Man, I ain't never havin' kids," Joli piped in. "Way you guys talk about it, it sounds like a fuckin' death sentence."

"Nah," Dondi countered. "They're a pain in the ass, but nothin' compares to watchin' 'em grow up and become something."

It was at that precise moment that Wallace Clyburne loped in. He was fair-haired, freckled, and rail-thin, twenty-two on paper, but he looked about half that. "Sorry about that," he said sheepishly.

"On the other hand . . ." Dondi muttered, and the other men snickered.

Wallace looked around, vaguely aware that he'd walked in on a private joke just in time to become its punch line. "Did I miss something?" he asked.

Dondi waved it off. "Wallace, this is Stephen Buscetti, the most badass detective in Glendon PD. Stevie, Wallace Clyburne, our new probationary cadet. Wallace is a Rescue man." He intoned the last part sardonically. Joli scoffed. Wallace turned beet red.

"Uh, hi," he said to Buscetti. "Good to meet ya."

"Likewise," Buscetti nodded. "Listen, don't let these degenerates give you too much guff. They're good guys in a pinch."

"Thanks," Clyburne said, as if waiting for a setup he could only barely fathom. He turned to the other men. "I'm gonna hit the rack now, if that's okay?"

Nobody said anything, but as he started to head for the hall Joli cleared his throat conspicuously. "Oh, *Rescue man,*" he said snidely, "I believe there are some toilets in dire need of rescue." Dondi winked at Buscetti, telegraphing the joke. "You're on shithouse duty, son."

"But . . ." Wallace began, then glanced at the schedule sheet on the wall, saw that that wasn't right. He looked back to Dondi and Joli, saw no mercy.

"Uh, yeah, sure," he finished. "No problem." He looked at Buscetti. "Nice to meet ya."

"Sure, kid." Buscetti smiled. As Wallace left the room everyone waited a beat, then busted up laughing. Buscetti whistled. "Bit young, isn't he?"

"He's a fetus," Joli said. "Straight outta the womb."

"Nah, he's okay." Dondi caught Buscetti's look, then explained, "Earlier this week, we got called out on a bullshit run—somebody scorched their Hamburger Helper and set off every smoke alarm on the third floor. Real no-brainer, right?

"So Engine 13 is already on-site as we pull up," he continued, "and already it's all over. But as they're cleaning up Maytag asks the kid to hump some hose back to the pumper. And the kid says"—Dondi scrunched his features into his best Wallace imitation—" 'I don't hump hose, I'm a *Rescue man*!' "

Joli snorted; Buscetti just winced. "Ouch." Probies were to firefighters what Boots were to cops: two clicks above plankton on the evolutionary scale, until they made their bones. Dondi grinned evilly.

"You got it," Dondi continued. "Needless to say, Maytag about tore him a new hole . . . then Georgie heard about it and damned near stuffed his head up it." Everybody cracked up. "So now our Wally is about the most eager little probie in all of Glendon. But we're still busting his balls, though, on general principle."

"Moral imperative," Joli said, nodding.

"You guys are cold," Buscetti said, but he understood. It wasn't the kind of job that catered to elitists—especially probie elitists. Just then they heard Paul's voice raise a notch in the hall.

"GodDAMMIT . . ." His tone peaked, then notched back down to a tense burble, and the other men exchanged wary glances. A heartbeat later Paul appeared in the doorway, looking decidedly peeved. He shook it off, looked at the guys.

"So what'd I miss?"

"Nothing," Joli said brightly. "We were just toasting fatherhood." Paul laughed ruefully.

"Problem in the nest?" Buscetti asked.

"No, no problem," Paul said flatly. "My daughter's just grounded until she's fifty, the second she walks through the front door." He groaned. "Stevie, you want my advice? Shoot yourself now, get it over with." He swigged angrily off his beer; everybody looked at Paul as though waiting for his head to explode.

But before he could say another word, a piercing bell went off, huge and clanging. The tone of the room changed instantly; Paul's mood evaporated in a blast of adrenaline as they all scrambled, Paul grabbing the call sheet off the rattling telex as Dondi and Joli headed for the bay. Paul paused at the door, looked back at Buscetti.

"Congratulations, dad."

Buscetti nodded, waved him off. Paul followed hot on their heels, all business now, as Buscetti hovered at the threshold and watched. His wallet was still in his hand. Buscetti looked down at the photo of his newborn girl.

He sighed, murmured, "Dad."

The Rescue One bay lit up like a Christmas tree on speed—lights strobing as the men jumped into turnout gear lining a bench on the wall, boots and waders turned out for instant access, coats hanging ready on pegs above.

"Thirty-nine Ramble Street, near Westminster," Paul called out, hauling on his bulky rubberized turnouts.

"Got it!" Dondi yelled back, already at the driver's side, then shouted at the ceiling, "WALLACE, MOVE YER ASS!

"WALLACE!!"

A second later, the probie came sliding down the brass pole behind them, literally caught in the crapper with his pants down. Paul climbed up, slid into the shotgun seat as Wallace grabbed his gear and climbed onboard the rear jump seat, landing so hard he banged his head on the firewall. Paul glanced back. "Easy, boy," he cautioned. "No sense killing yourself before we get there."

His words were drowned by diesel roar as the rig rumbled to life. The garage door rumbled, yawning wide. Wallace notwithstanding, they had done this hundreds of times before, and together they moved swiftly, with an economy born of experience. They were out the door and down the street in sixty seconds flat, sirens howling, lights ablaze. Each feeling that, whatever crisis awaited, they were ready for it.

And never once dreaming of just how wrong they would be.

8

They roared across town, banshee-wailing into damp night as the tinny voice of the radio dispatcher blasted in the cab.

"Rescue One, what's your twenty?"

Paul keyed the handset. "Dispatch, this is Rescue One," he relayed. "We're eastbound at the corner of Clough and Melhorn, ETA five minutes."

"Roger, Rescue One. Will advise." Dispatch signed off. Paul racked the handset a little too hard and sat back. They drove in silence for a good ten seconds, then Dondi couldn't stand it any more.

"So," he said, "you wanna get it off your chest, or should I break out the Prozac?"

"That was Julie," Paul sighed. "Kyra says she needs to go to the library, and Julie tells her to be back by eight-thirty. Like this is news, right? School night curfew is eight-thirty. Not eight forty-five, not nine. Eight-thirty."

"You mean, as in eight-thirty," Dondi said sarcastically. He glanced at the LCD clock on the dash: it read 9:25.

"Oh," he murmured.

"Bingo," Paul replied, annoyed. "I tell ya, there's gonna be some changes around here, starting tonight. I shit you not." The rig hit a pothole, jostled mercilessly. Paul sighed and put it behind him, flipped on the map light, reading the jostling printout.

"So what do we got?" Dondi asked as he nudged through the intersection and gunned it, running the light.

"Thirty-six units," Paul read. "Two floors, brick construction, tar roof, shutoffs in rear, annunciator alarm system."

"How's access?"

"Elevator in the east wing. Stairwells east and west. Service ramp in the back."

Dondi nodded and racked the wheel, ducking around a Ford Fiesta. "OUTTA THE WAY, YA PRICK!" he shouted, sounding the horn. The little car visibly shook, as if the sheer decibel level would blow it off the road. As they raced past, Dondi glanced at Paul. "Anything else?" he asked.

"Yeah," Paul said. "Says here, it's a rest home." Dondi cackled.

"Not for long," he said.

The sign out front read *Shady Acres,* but it was neither. On a good day, it was a low-slung, ranch-style warehouse wedged between a funeral parlor and a low-income housing unit, a Medicare gulag for inconvenient elders. At the moment, it was a circus.

The fire itself was no big deal: some nearsighted oldster sneaking a smoke in his room had tossed the butt at the toilet and hit the trash instead. A lot of smoke, a lot of panic, but no real threat. But by the time they arrived on-site the night staff had already evacuated the building, and by quarter to ten Rescue One was up to its armpits in wheelchairs and walkers: a sea of shivering shut-ins, night of the living dead on Geritol. Everyone was agitated and harassed, the staff fearful of pneumonia and lawsuits, the firefighters almost as overwhelmed as their disoriented charges.

"Hang on, lady," Paul said, reaching down to free spoked wheels from a stray shrub. "We'll get you back inside in a flash." As he stood he caught sight of Joli and Wallace passing out blankets, lost in the shuffling fray.

The woman in the wheelchair was tiny and frail, somebody's forgotten grandma, on the far side of senile. Osteoporosis had bowed her back into a painful dowager's hump; pendulous goiters hung from her shriveled neck like withered fruit. Her eyes were huge and uncomprehending, pupils irised wide and black.

"Eenie-meenie-miney-moe," she murmured urgently, fingers frittering at the edge of her blanket. "Eenie-meenieminey-moe."

"Leggo, ya bastid!!" a voice growled somewhere behind him. "I know all about ya, pricks!!" Paul glanced over and saw Dondi struggling to maneuver a hairless geezer with one leg and the meaty forearms of an ex-dockworker. Huge and leathery hands clutched vainly, locking onto everything in sight: lampposts, bushes, other patients' chairs, the other patients themselves.

"LEGGO ME!!" he growled.

"Relax, pal, I'm trying to help you."

"Bastid!" The old guy took a wild swing, missed by a country mile and almost fell out of his chair. Dondi lunged and grabbed, caught the back of his robe. "Help!" the old man cried, his voice gruff, oddly vulnerable. "He's tryin' to KILL me!! HEELLLP!!"

"Eenie-meenie-miney-moe . . ." the old woman quivered and fretted. "Eenie-meenie-miney-moe . . ." Dondi drew abreast of Paul, and the old man grabbed on to the other chair, pulled with surprising strength. The wheels of the two chairs gnashed and locked, stopped dead. Grandma and grandpa stared at each other blankly, then suddenly grinned gummy grins.

Dondi leaned over to Paul. "Love Connection . . ." he whispered.

Paul managed a rueful grin. "C'mon, folks," he said. "Let's get you inside before you freeze."

They had just separated the chairs and begun to roll them inside when they heard a scream coming from behind. Paul and Dondi turned in time to see an elderly stray stumbling down the drive and onto the rain-slick street, bathrobe belt trailing like a soggy tail. Up the block, a pair of headlights, bearing down way too fast. The old man was oblivious, lost.

Paul and Dondi's hearts ballooned into their throats simultaneously, collision course vectors all too grimly clear. "JOLI!!" they cried in unison.

But Joli had his hands full already. He followed their gaze and started to shout himself, as firefighters and orderlies scrambled, too slow on the pickup. The driver saw him, too late. Brakes locked. The old man froze. There wasn't time. The car screeched and slid. No one was close enough. There wasn't enough time . . .

. . . and that's when the miracle in black canvas flashed past, vaulting the hedgerow, rubber boots slapping the street as he closed the distance like an Olympic track star. His helmet flew off as he scooped the old man off his feet a split second before the car careened past. But Wallace somehow dove clear without falling, without losing balance or crushing his fragile cargo as the car skidded to a heart-attack stop, rear tire grinding the fallen helmet to shrapnel with a sickening crunch. There was an adrenalated beat of silence, then the driver of the car floored it, screeching around the corner of Westminster, and gone.

Wallace Clyburne slid into the curb, the old man slung over his shoulder in picture-perfect fireman's carry. The elderly gent's hair was a tousled white shock, his eyes wide with clueless surprise. Wallace looked up, a little surprised himself.

"Did you see what I just saw?" Paul said, in shock.

"Fuck me," Dondi murmured. "It's super-probie."

Wallace beamed. Suddenly there came a moist, popping sound, and the kid suddenly found himself hosed with waste as the colostomy bag under the old man's robe ruptured and rained down the sleeve of Wallace's coat.

As the nursing home orderlies raced up, Wallace set the old man down as gently as possible, then gazed at the stinking sleeve and groaned. Paul and Dondi approached, laughing in spite of themselves. Paul patted him carefully on the back.

"Welcome to the life," he said. "*Backdraft*, it ain't."

Wallace smiled queasily as the other men grinned and jostled the probie; then together, they turned back to matters at hand. There were still patients to tend to, more work left to do. It took another twenty minutes to finish herding the overexcited residents back to their beds; mercifully, no one else seized up, keeled over, or otherwise jeopardized life or limb. But everyone seemed slightly transformed in the aftermath; as the patients were packed away, some of the nursing staff disappeared into the kitchen, came back with coffee and snacks for the frazzled firefighters.

Wallace himself seemed different; after his amazing stunt the probie's bumbling station-house demeanor was nowhere in evidence. He cleaned himself off, then was right back at it, tackling the rest of the job with gentle efficiency and an understated confidence. Even Joli was impressed; he looked at Paul and shrugged, "Go figure . . ."

As they wrapped things up, Paul laid a brotherly hand on the probie's shoulder. "Way to go, kid," he said. "You did good back there."

"Yeah," Joli chimed in. "Nice save. Where'd you ever learn moves like that?"

"I dunno," Wallace smiled, then added, "my dad had a stroke couple years before he died, came out half-paralyzed, kinda senile. I got used to dealing with all kinds of crazy shit."

"Hey, kid." Dondi came up, holding a handful of donuts. "You saved someone and got shit on. Guess you're a Rescue man after all, huh?" He smiled as he said it, then offered the kid a sugar fix. Wallace grinned and accepted. The men split left and right, heading for their respective seats on the truck. As Paul and the kid moved toward the passenger side, Wallace paused to scoop up the shattered remnants of his wasted headgear.

"Jesus," he said.

"Better that than your head." Paul opened the door. "Hey,

don't worry about it," he added as he climbed onboard. "We'll fix you up later."

Wallace nodded and took his position, one of them now. The dispatch radio crackled to life. *"Rescue One, respond to possible body at Kozy Kove Motor Lodge . . ."*

"Why us?" Wallace asked.

"Availability," Dondi answered. "Well, kiddies, it looks like the weekend rush hit early."

"Figures," Joli groaned. "When it rains, it fuckin' pours."

"You got that right." Paul nodded, then said to Wallace, "Word of advice, kid: hope for the best, but always plan for the worst."

Wallace nodded; it was good advice.

Paul had no idea how true it would be.

9

Joli's voice sounded over the roar of the rig. "Hey, Paulie," he called out. "I need a favor."

"You got it," Paul said, then added, "what is it?"

"I, uh . . ." Joli hesitated, tried to sound casual. "I need to borrow some books, dude."

Tom snickered; Paul and Dondi traded mock shocked glances. Wallace watched as if on the permanent outside of a running joke. Paul shrugged. "Sure," he said. "What kinds of books?"

"I dunno," Joli said. "Big ones. Something to make me look smarter."

"Jeez, Joli," Paul replied. "I don't know if they make books that big."

Everyone cracked up; Joli looked uncharacteristically sensitive. "Fuck youze guys," he growled, then returned to Paul. "I'm serious."

"What's this about?" Paul asked. Tom chimed in, thoroughly enjoying himself. "He's trying to impress Liiiiiza . . ." he chortled.

A collective "Woooooo" sounded in the cab; Paul looked at Dondi, then turned in his seat. "No shit . . . nurse extraordinaire Liza?"

"Yeah." Joli nodded sheepishly, turning noticeably red-faced. "Problem is, she only goes out with, like, geeks."

"Lucky for you," Tom said.

Joli ignored him. "No," he said, "I mean, like, sensitive guys . . ."

"Now you're fucked," Dondi said. Paul smiled ruefully, tried to play it straight. "Seriously," he said, feeling anything but, "what kinds of books do you want?"

Suddenly Wallace spoke up. "How 'bout poetry?"

Everyone grinned; Joli turned to him, deadly earnest. "Yeah," he said. "What's a good poem?"

But before Wallace could answer, Dondi called out, "I do not like green eggs and ham . . ." Tom grinned and chimed in, *"I do not like them, Sam I Am!!!!"*

Gales of raucous laughter sounded; Joli looked flummoxed. Paul explained. "It's Dr. Seuss, dude . . ." he began.

Joli shook his head adamantly. "No doctors," he said. "Bad enough she works in a hospital."

Paul smacked hand to forehead. Hopeless. Just then Dondi got serious. "Heads up, people," he said.

They had arrived.

The Kozy Kove Motor Lodge was one of the endless parade of tacky little no-tell motels that clustered under the refineries along the rim of Route 9 like chancre sores, offering waterbeds, in-room porn, and hourly rates. It was a favored haunt for truck-stop tricks and long-haul drivers, horny businessmen looking to cop a quick extracurricular hump on the way home to the wife and kids, and the occasional underage lovers looking for a place to party, no questions asked.

A pair of black-and-whites and an unmarked unit were already parked in the U-shape courtyard as they arrived, lights flashing ominously. Dondi slowed the rig, reversed and backed in, effectively sealing off access. In the parking lot, a plainclothes officer methodically copied down license plate numbers as venetian blinds parted nervously from room to room, warily watching.

"Management called and said there was a bad smell coming from number 10," the cop explained, leading them in. He was young, Irish; his nameplate read Reilly.

"How could they tell?" Paul grimaced as they trudged up the stairs. Dondi followed behind, smoking a cigarette in purely olfactory defense, a folded sheet of zippered plastic shoved under one arm. Body bag.

The hallway was dark and bathed in a cheesy red glow; budget mood lighting, ersatz erotic. The air was close and hot and reeked of Lysol, cheap perfume, and body funk. As they cleared the landing Paul saw Steve Buscetti at the end of the hall, wrapping up questioning a swarthy Lebanese in a loud polyester shirt—the manager, judging from body language.

The john stood nervously off to the side, hastily buttoned shirt revealing pale middle-aged paunch. A young black TV pre-op with bad implants and press-on nails stood wrapped in a bedsheet, eyes down, teased hair atumble, looking bored and antsy. Her feet shifted nervously, doing the junkie two-step.

Buscetti saw Paul and smiled. "We meet again."

"Yeah," Paul sighed. "What's up?"

Buscetti gestured to the unhappy couple as he led them to the room. "Apparently these two were playing rump ranger when they noticed things were getting kinda ripe. The manager says they clean thoroughly after every guest," he added, emphasizing the last word sarcastically, "but I guess housekeeping missed this." He pulled a kerchief, held it in readiness.

"Brace yourself," he warned. They turned the corner.

The smell was astonishing, weirdly familiar: a moist, fetid tang that clung to the palette as it clawed at their innards. Gag-reflex was automatic, instinctive. The room was tiny, claustrophobic vibe offset by voyeuristic mirrors that lined the walls and ceiling, lending not so much a sense of space as a magnified constriction. A police photographer maneuvered in the tight confines, snapping Polaroids. The mattress and box spring were tipped to the side, leaning against the far wall, blocking the bathroom.

A body, wrapped in garbage bags and hotel towels, lay seeping into the carpet where the bed had been. It was female, five-foot-four, and young, but anything beyond that was a guess. The face was blackened and soft with decay, rigor mortis a distant memory. Tiny skittering roaches had already gone condo in the soft tissues; its features were mashed flat by contact with the box spring, lips peeled back by friction to reveal a frozen, leering grin. It had been there a while.

"Guess all the bouncing popped the bag," Buscetti mumbled through his kerchief. "She sprang a leak."

Paul coughed and choked, eyes watering. "Jesus," he gasped. "Who is . . ." he started, stopped. "Who was she?"

"Good question," Buscetti said. "Murdered hooker, runaway o.d., some kid on a milk carton. She obviously had help getting there."

"How long?" Paul asked.

"Two weeks. Maybe three," Buscetti answered. The detective gazed around at the nightmare tableau reflected off every surface; a dozen disgusted Buscettis gazed back.

Paul noticed that the dead girl had left an indentation on the underside of the box spring, a Turin-intaglio in congealed fluids. He felt ill. "Gonna wait for the M.E.," he asked, "or should we bag her?"

Buscetti looked around and sighed. "Good luck finding a clue in this petri dish." Just then a little *beepbeepbeep* sound trilled at the detective's belt; he reached inside his jacket and pulled his pager free, squinted to read the number.

"Gotta go," he said, then added, "go ahead and bag her. Gonna take an autopsy to determine cause of death, anyway, probably a dental to establish positive ID, if we ever do." He shrugged. "Either way, she's Forensics' problem now."

Paul nodded, and Buscetti excused himself, exiting into the hall. Paul and Dondi followed, and as they cleared the door Dondi took a great, heaving breath. They both pulled out cigarettes and lit up. Dondi sucked in a deep drag, blew it out slow.

"Whew," he gasped. "That was festive. I don't know about you, but I ain't going back in there without a full tank and a respirator, maybe break out the Hazmat gear. Christ . . ."

Paul looked rattled, as though tuned to another channel. He fumbled inside his coat, pulled out his Nokia cellphone. "Tell Joli and the kid to get up here with the gurney," he said quietly.

"Excuse me?" Dondi looked at him strangely; technically he outranked Paul, and it sounded too much like an order. Paul snapped back into focus.

"Sorry," Paul said. "Dondi, please. I gotta make a call."

Dondi picked up on the vibe, nodded. "Yeah, sure," he said. "I need the air anyway." He started down the stairs; Paul waited, then walked in the opposite direction, squeezing past the uniformed cops, the doorway, the dead girl still inside. Buscetti had already left; they were stuck with the leftovers.

Paul glanced at his watch, fought a queasy feeling rising in his gut—sub-rational, beyond reason—like a cold breeze of ill intent. He found himself suddenly gripped by a dread that transcended images of missing girls and dead bodies under beds. He wanted to talk to his family, to hear Julie tell him that Kyra was back home and safe and deep in a world of sixteen-year-old hurt, fretting over the inevitable grounding or passing loss of privileges that were the worst a kid should ever have to expect.

At 10:02, Paul was suddenly overwhelmed with the irrational need to talk to his daughter, not to bitch or vent or play hell-dad, but simply to hear her voice.

He punched his number on the speed dial. Waited for it to connect.

And that was when the other call came in.

10

Dondi was strong-arming him toward the truck, fingers vice-gripped onto Paul's sleeve. Paul didn't know what was happening, but something was terribly wrong.

"Just get in," Dondi told him. "We gotta move."

But Paul was already moving, driven by the cold feeling in his gut. He saw the confusion in the other men's faces, felt his blood chill until his pallor matched their own. Paul and Dondi threw open the doors, vaulting into the cramped cab. They were off and running before his ass hit the seat cushion, siren winding up like a lost soul's lament, lights strobing seizure-patterns off the blur of buildings racing by.

The siren howled, drowning out their words. "A call just came in," Dondi explained, eyes fixed on the road. "Domestic disturbance, officers on the scene. There's been an injury."

Paul's head was spinning, free floating anxiety waiting to ignite. "Yeah? And?"

Dondi's features were pale in the dim dash lights. He wracked the wheel and sliced across the intersection, blatting the horn at anything that even looked like it might want to get in the way.

Paul saw they were heading for the west end, away from his home, from Dondi's, Joli's, even the new kid's. A fleeting rush of relief fueled the anger and confusion.

"What's going on, Dondi?" Paul barked. "Why are you flipping over a goddamned domestic?"

"It's the address," Dondi said, white-knuckling the wheel and downshifting. The big rig roared, gear teeth gnashing beneath their feet. "It's Marley Street, Paul. 514 Marley Street."

"What are you saying?" Fear spread, mental kindling crackling. Paul was sweating now. "Dondi, did somebody break into my house?"

"We got a description . . . Caucasian female, multiple blunt trauma to the head . . ." Dondi paused, throat constricting, his face a mask of dread determination.

The logical part of Paul's brain tried to make a connection, failed. "Who is it, Dondi?" Dondi said nothing.

And just like that, it all clicked nightmarishly into place.

The front of the house was bathed in a wash of frantic red lights; searchlight beams slashed white across the facade and lit the narrow alley on the side of the building, casting ghostly shadows through rain-spattered glass. Newsvans lurked on the periphery, minicam arclights giving everything a harsh, surreal aura. Neighbors hovered in doorways and peered out windows, feeding on the spectacle of a half-dozen police cruisers and unmarked units parked at odd angles in the street, on the curb, everywhere. Cops were crawling all over the place, combing the scene. Searching for someone, or something.

But Paul couldn't think about that. His attention was wholly focused on the ambulance, its doors open, waiting at the gate. The world around him strobed red and white and black as Paul leapt from the cab before they had even stopped, pushing his way through the knotted throng. He saw Buscetti, already on the scene. The detective's presence served to further unnerve and disorient him; Buscetti didn't belong there. He belonged back at the flea-pit motel, back where things, ugly as they were, made sense.

"Stevie!" Paul cried.

Buscetti turned. "Paul," he said, "what the hell are you doing . . ."

But before he could answer, the front door opened. Paramedics emerged, wheeling a gurney. Paul caught a glimpse of dark hair, done in rows of tight little braids.

"Oh, God," he stammered. "Kyra . . ."

He pushed his way past the detective, ducking under the span of yellow crime scene tape already stretched across the perimeter. "KYRA!" he cried.

Paul caught up just as they were loading the gurney into the ambulance. He started to follow, but the medics stopped him. They were a crew from a neighboring township, one of the sister-city resource agreements that Glendon had signed on to in the face of budget cutbacks and personnel shortages. Paul had never seen either of them.

"She's my daughter," Paul said. The two men looked at each other and nodded, and Paul climbed aboard, heart pounding, hands trembling with terror. The doors slammed shut.

And that was when Paul got his first real look.

11

aul had seen a hundred times worse, a thousand times before. That wasn't the point. This was *his* child laid out on the gurney, *his* flesh and blood at the center of the howling siren storm. Paul hunkered down next to the cold metal cart and started to cry.

She had been beaten savagely, a deep gash across the forehead marring her once porcelain and delicate features. Her eyes were black and bruised, her nose mashed flat, broken. Deep purplish indentations marred the soft skin of her throat. Someone had tried to strangle her. God only knew what else they'd attempted to do. But from the bloody laceration on her forehead, it was clear they had tried to bludgeon her to death, too.

But she was still alive, he told himself. *My baby is alive, she's a Kelly and that means she's a fighter, she's gonna make it . . .*

Her arm dangled as one of the medics began taking her blood pressure; Paul reached out and took her hand in his own. Her skin was cool, the knuckles abraded, one of her nails broken off. Her breathing was shallow, irregular. The medics worked quickly and professionally in the jostling confines. They pulled open her shirt, his daughter's breasts suddenly, rudely exposed as they hooked her up, got readings on the monitors. Paul winced and leaned close.

"I'm here, baby," he whispered. "Daddy's here." Her hand squeezed his, ever so weakly. "She can hear me," Paul informed the medics urgently. "She's still conscious."

"Talk to her," the first medic, a burly man named Jorgensen, said as he glanced at Paul. "Keep her focused."

"You're gonna be all right, honey," Paul told Kyra softly. "We're taking you to the hospital. You're gonna be fine."

"Pulse one-forty," the second medic, a man named Scully, called out. "Blood pressure, ninety over palp." He glanced at Paul, worried. "Is she on any medication that you know of, any drugs?"

"What??" Paul said, shocked.

"Her heart's working way too hard," Scully said sternly. "She's either on something or bleeding internally. Now, to the best of your knowledge does your daughter use drugs?"

"No," Paul said adamantly. "No."

The heart monitor was spiking wildly, cardiovascular rhythm horribly out of synch. "Notify Bergen County ER," Scully yelled to the driver, a woman named Ellis. "Tell 'em we got an internal bleeder coming in."

Paul looked up, alarmed. "St. Anthony's," he countered. "Bergen doesn't have trauma, they can't handle this."

"Bergen is closer," Scully argued.

Paul shook his head adamantly. "Take Glendon Boulevard to Covington, Covington to Mansfield," he said. "Three minutes, tops."

"What's it gonna be?" Ellis yelled over the siren's blare. Scully started to say something, but Jorgensen cut him off. "He's right." He looked at Paul, then called out, "You heard the man! St. Anthony's!"

"You got it." Ellis nodded and radioed in the change, then floored it.

Suddenly Kyra sputtered and coughed violently. Her chest hitched in ragged spasms. Jorgensen bagged her, trying desperately to regulate her breathing. "Pulse one-sixty, b.p. eighty-five and falling," Scully warned. "She's slipping!"

"She's got fluid in her lungs," Jorgensen said. Paul looked at the man. Jorgensen desperately tried to intubate her, pressing the rubber tube past swollen and bloody lips. As he got it down her throat Kyra suddenly coughed, spraying bloody froth. "Shit, her trachea's collapsed," he hissed.

"Do something, dammit!" Paul cried.

Kyra's chest was bucking and heaving now, her heart monitor beeping madly. The men watched in horror as her flesh took on a mottled, blue-gray hue and a clammy sheen of sweat broke out.

"Shit, she's going dusky."

"Move!" Paul roared into action, pushing the men out of the way, stripping off his coat and grabbing the intubation tube. His mind pushed aside the fear as he set to work, carefully worming the plastic nozzle past savaged tissues, deep into her larynx. Suddenly it stuck, would go no further. The monitors keened. Paul cursed, biting back panic. "We gotta do a trache," he said.

"Here??" Scully countered. "We can't—" Paul shot him a lethal glance, and Scully shut up.

Jorgensen moved in as Paul extubated the tube then grabbed cotton gauze and a squeeze bottle of betadine from the medbox, spritzed the soft hollow of his daughter's throat with disinfectant, stray red trickles staining milk skin jaundiced yellow. Paul handed off the intubation tube as Jorgensen passed him a swiss army knife, opened to a razor-sharp two-inch blade. Ambo crews carried no scalpels by law, but a well-honed pocketknife had sufficed more than once, becoming standard unofficial issue.

The ambulance bounced and surged. Kyra's eyes rolled back, her body convulsing. Performing a field tracheotomy in a careening vehicle was like trying to thread a needle in a hurricane. But he had no choice.

Paul blinked back sweat and steadied himself, the blade's tip poised on the surface of her skin. He punched down—a short, sharp jab. There was a wet pop, then a burbling noise like a straw sucking the bottom of an empty cup. Kyra's chest heaved up and down again, air flooding starved cells.

She could breathe.

"Got it," Paul said, then, to Jorgensen, "tube." Jorgensen quickly handed off the nozzle of the intubation tube; gingerly, Paul worked it into the wound, then taped it off. His heart was pounding almost as fast as the rhythm of the rig. Kyra hitched again, her tortured breathing giving way to a wet regularity. The monitors calmed. They were going to make it.

Paul glanced up, saw the glow of St. Anthony's dead ahead. "Hang in there," Ellis called back as they pulled into the bay. "We're almost home."

Kyra's eyes fluttered open, gaze swimming. She saw her father hovering above her, tried to speak, voice rasping.

"Daddy . . . ?" she whispered, barely audible. A thin froth of blood graced her lips.

"Hang on, baby," he told her. "Hang on."

Paul gripped his daughter's hand. He gave her a reassuring squeeze. For one brief, elongated moment, it seemed like the worst was behind them. She squeezed back, once. Then her fingers went limp.

And just like that, she was gone.

PART | TWO

Darkening Down

Office of the Glendon County Coroner

Post Office Box 27 • Glendon, NJ 08840
5467 Main Street • Glendon County Justice Center
Glendon, NJ 08840
(908) 555-9083

AUTOPSY REPORT

NAME [L/F/M]:	Kelly, Kyra, Ann	**AUTOPSY NO:**	00-A-012
DOB:	12/23/84	**DEATH D/T:**	10/21/00 @ 2145
AGE:	16Y	**AUTOPSY D/T:**	10/22/00 @ 0725
PATH MD:	M. WRIGHT, M.D., M.E.	**ID NO:**	217731
TYPE:	COR	**COR/MEDREC#:**	1417-00-A

FINAL DIAGNOSIS

Manual strangulation
Circumferential ligature with associated manual furrow of neck
Abrasions and petechial hemorrhages, neck
Petechial hemorrhages, conjunctival surfaces of eyes and skin of face

Scalp contusion
Linear, comminuted fracture of right side of skull
Linear pattern of contusions of right cerebral hemisphere
Sebarachnoid and subdural hemorrhage

TOXICOLOGICAL STUDIES
blood ethanol ñ concentration .02% by weight of alcohol in blood

CLINICOPATHOLOGIC CORRELATION
Cause of death of this sixteen year old female is asphyxia associated with craniocerebral trauma. Homicide.

The body of this sixteen year old female was first seen by me after I was called to the hospital on 10/22. I arrived at the scene approximately 0645 and entered the hospital morgue. I initially viewed the body in the morgue. The decedent was laying on her back, in a hospital body bag. The decedent was wearing a jacket and scarf, sweater and t-shirt and blue-jeans. A brief examination of the body disclosed a ligature around the neck. Also noted was a small area of abrasion or contusion below the right ear and on the lower left neck. After examining the body I left the hospital at approximately 0925.

EXTERNAL EXAM
The decedent is clothed in a black button down sweater over short sleeve white knit colorless shirt, containing no designs or markings. The shirt was torn down the center line by EMT personnel while attempting treatment during transport. The upper anterior right sleeve contains a dried brown-tan stain measuring 2.5 x 1.5 inches, consistent with mucous from the nose or mouth. There are short white underwear with an elastic waist band. The underwear are urine stained anteriorly over the crotch area and anterior legs. Decedent was menstruating at TOD; vaginal examination revealed OB style sanitary napkin containing 6 ccs decedent's menstrual blood type A+, mixed with urine. Decedent was administered emergency tracheotomy en route to hospital by paramedic personnel, accounting for small puncture wound at base of throat. Decedent D.O.A.

EXTERNAL EVIDENCE OF INJURY
Located just below the right ear at the right angle of the mandible, 1.5 inches below the right external auditory canal is a $\frac{3}{8}$th inch area of rust

colored abrasion. In the lateral aspect of the left lower eyelid in the internal conjunctival surface is a 1mm in maximum petechial hemorrhage. Very fine, less than 1mm petechial hemorrhages are present on the skin of the upper eyelids bilaterally as well as on the lateral left cheek. On averting the left upper eyelid there are much smaller, less than 1 mm petechial hemorrhages located on the conjuctival surface. Possible petechial hemorrhages are also seen on the conjunctival surfaces of the right upper and lower eyelids, but livor mortis on this side of the face makes definite identification inconclusive [see attached photographs].

A deep manual furrow encircles the neck. The width of the furrow varies from 3 inches to 1 inch and is horizontal in orientation with little upward orientation. The skin of the anterior neck above and below the manual furrow contains areas of petechial hemorrhage and abrasion encompassing an area measuring approximately 2 x 1 inches. The manual furrow crosses the anterior midline of the neck just below the laryngeal prominence, approximately at the level of the cricoid cartilage. Fibres and abrasion pattern along furrow mark consistent with fibres of decedent's scarf [lab analysis pending]. The remainder of the abrasions and petechial hemorrhages of the skin above and below the anterior projection of the manual furrow are non patterned, purple to rust colored, and present in the midline, right and left areas of the anterior neck. The skin just above the manual furrow along the right side of the neck contains petechial hemorrhages as well as several larger petechial hemorrhages measuring up to one-sixteenth and one-eighth of an inch in maximum dimension. Similar smaller petechial hemorrhages are present on the skin below the ligature furrow on the left lateral aspect of the neck. Located on the right side of the chin is a $3/16$ths by $1/8$th inch area of superficial abrasion. On the posterior aspect of the right shoulder is a poorly demarcated, very superficial focus of abrasion/ contusion which is pale purple in color and measures up to $3/4$ by $1/2$ inch in maximum dimension. On the left lateral aspect of the lower back, approximately $16\frac{1}{4}$ inches and $17\frac{1}{2}$ inches below the level of the top of the head are two dried rust colored to slightly purple abrasions. The more superior of the two measures $1/8$th by $1/16$th of an inch and the more inferior of the two measures $3/16$ths by $1/8$th of an inch. There is no surrounding contusion identified. No overt evidence of vaginal laceration or abrasion.

REMAINDER OF EXTERNAL EXAMINATION

The unembalmed, well developed and well nourished Caucasian female body measures 66 inches in length and weighs an estimated 117 pounds. The scalp is covered by long brunette hair which is fixed in a series of tight knit braids. No scalp trauma is identified. The external auditory canals are patent and free of blood. The eyes are green and the pupils equally dilated. The sclerae are white. The nostrils are both patent and contain a small amount of tan mucous material. The teeth are native and in good repair. Mucus membrane of upper lip lacerated consistent with contusion to mouth; lips and external tissue surrounding mouth swollen and bruised, indicating blunt force trauma to face and mouth. The tongue is smooth, pink and granular. No buccal mucosal trauma is seen. The frenulum is intact. On the left cheek is a pattern of dried saliva and mucous material which does not appear to be hemorrhagic. On the right cheek is a small amount of decedent's blood type A+, consistent with bleeding from tracheotomy. The neck contains no additional palpable adenopathy or masses. Trachea and larynx are crushed.

Breasts are adolescent and well developed. The abdomen is flat and contains no scars. No palpable organomegaly or masses are identified. Examination of the extremities is unremarkable. The fingernails of both hands are of sufficient length for clipping and coated with clear lacquer; the right index and left middle fingernails are broken. Examination of the back is unremarkable. There is dorsal 3+ 4 livor mortis which is nonblanching. Livor mortis is also present on the right side of the face. At the time of the initiation of the autopsy there is mild 1 to 2+ rigor mortis of the elbows and shoulders with more advanced 2 to 3+ rigor mortis of the joints of the lower extremities. Post mortem lividity present in back, buttocks and lower extremities. Rectum is intact. No traces of semen/ejaculate found in vaginal area, mouth or digestive tract.

EVIDENCE

Items turned over to the Glendon Police Department as evidence include: fibers and hair from clothing and body surfaces, ligatures, clothing, vaginal swabs and smears, rectal swabs and smears, oral swabs and smears, paper bags from hands, fingernail clippings, jewelry, paper bags from feet, white body bag, sample of head hair, sample of pubic hair, eyelashes and eyebrows, swabs from right and left thighs and right cheek, red top and purple top tubes of blood.

Signed:

Dr. Marcus J. Wright

Marcus Wright, M.D.
Pathologist

END OF REPORT

13

Beyond paramedics and police, hard-lit corridors sharp with stainless steel echoes and the stench of human suffering; beyond priest and paperwork, the scrape of ballpoint on paper and click of silicon keys; after the tears and howls of grief and rage; beyond the great shameless whirlwind of death in the belly of the machine, one thing remained.

Paul had seen it a thousand times before, from the cool distance of the professional. After a big fire, there was always something left: a scorched bit of wire or faint chemical residue to explain its origins; a photograph unscarred, some memento mercifully unsinged by the flames. And no matter how total its fury, or how far the pyre clawed into the night, the morning after always came.

And with it, the survivors: victims, shell-shocked and reeling, adrift and isolated in a nightmare from which there was, and would be, no waking. Shambling like zombies, sifting acrid wreckage, searching for some fragment of the life just lost.

The weaker ones clung to cindered shards and pitiful

remains, unable to process the sheer magnitude of their immediate suffering or imagine any future beyond its blackened borders, no less the long road that lay ahead.

But the strong ones . . .

The strong let the weight of it fall fully upon them. They squinted through the smoke and ash, picked and prodded smoldering debris, searching the rubble for something, anything, that might somehow be saved. Fighting back tears, muzzling their emotions, they kept going. And in so doing, ultimately found that upon which they might build again.

But strong, weak, or in between, they all shared one common element at the molten core of their experience, one tie that inextricably bound them. Paul had seen it before, but it had never been truly his. Until now.

That thing was pain.

And, as with them all, Paul's had a name.

14

Daddy . . . ?

Paul jerked awake in the darkened living room. For the moment it took for consciousness to bleed through the last tortured fragments of dreaming, it was possible to believe Kyra was there. He didn't want to wake up. Kyra's voice chimed again, mischievous.

Daaa-deee . . . wake UP, Daddy!

Paul opened his eyes. Kyra's digitized voice peeled girlishly from the little travel alarm clock on the table. It was a Father's Day present, all sleek black portable LCD wizardry. It could record a ten-second sample and store it on a little chip, then play it as an alarm. Paul had first seen it while cruising the Sharper Image store at the Glendon Galleria and had commented to Julie that it was just the ticket for sleepover shifts at the station. But it had been Kyra's idea to go back and get it and to record her own special wake-up call. That was Kyra for you. She remembered.

Daaa-deee . . . Kyra's voice peeled again, singsong, a little silicon ghost. Forever sixteen. Forever impatient.

Paul sat up, started to reach for the snooze button,

stopped. He couldn't bring himself to turn it off. Kyra's voice sounded again, looping.

Daddy . . . ?

Paul shut the clock off. He had passed out fully clothed in his black velour recliner, the VCR remote control clutched loosely in one hand. Across the room, the TV was still on, screen glowing blue, volume mercifully muted. At his feet lay an empty bottle of Jack Daniel's and a pile of videotapes, splayed randomly across the floor. Their titles were rendered in Julie's tidy handwriting . . . *Kyra's first Christmas!!, Trick or Treat!, Kyra's 3rd birthday, Kyra gets her license!* Easily a hundred more stood behind him, stacked in a six-foot-high glass-doored case. The Kelly family history, on high chrome VHS—every holiday, every birthday, a thousand fleeting moments—all filed, compiled, and neatly indexed.

All that remained.

Just then Spock came over and nudged him, long canine snout prodding his knee. Behind drawn blinds, the first cold tendrils of sunlight reached through an exposed gap between sash and frame, crawled inexorably across the rug. Dawn. Paul dreaded it.

Night was somewhat more merciful, the only mercy left. His eyes were sunken pits, the tender flesh beneath revealing a deeper darkness, almost bruised. A crust of stubble coarsened his features. His throat was hoarse, pasty. He had to remember to swallow. Pain as if from a great weight hung on his every breath, like some unseen force bearing down on him, pressing the life out. His vitals had been wrenched screaming from form, mangled and poured back in. Everything inside him fit wrong, bled, burned.

But he still had to walk the dog.

Spock squirmed in place, the dobie's eyes balefully focused on his master. "Hey, boy," Paul said softly. "We forgot all about you . . ."

Spock wagged his stubby tail gratefully, ever forgiving, snout still planted on Paul's leg. He had to pee, bad. Spock disengaged as Paul sat up. The easy chair groaned under his weight. The rest of the house was utterly still. Downstairs, the boiler kicked on with the sub-audible thump of gas flame igniting.

Upstairs, in another universe, Julie stirred in narcotic release. They'd had to sedate her, so frenzied was her grief upon hearing. Paul had never seen her that way; in a billion nightmares he could never have imagined seeing her that way. But his universe had shattered into a billion bleeding shards, re-formed into the image of his wife, screaming, tearing her hair, clinging to and clawing at him, as if he might somehow make this all not be happening . . . re-formed, into the image of his daughter, cold and lifeless in the morgue . . . gone . . .

Paul stopped, started choking up. Upstairs, Julie murmured; inchoate, subconscious torment. Her parents, up from Atlantic City in the wake of the tragedy, were sleeping in the guest room. Paul heard her father hitch and snore, vaguely resented it. Somewhere in his mind he knew that wasn't fair. The truth be told, they had done their best, arriving at their door within hours of getting the call. Eleanor, Julie's mom, had again proven herself to be the source of her daughter's control streak by immediately setting about cooking and cleaning, as if the raw hole in their lives could be magically filled with food, order restored with Formula 409. Under ordinary circumstances she was a forcefully cheerful woman who spouted quasi New Age self-actualizing platitudes and wore her smile like a cross to ward off vampires, but her heart was in the right place. These circumstances were not ordinary. And Paul could not fault her for it.

And as for Ted, well . . .

To his credit, the trauma had seemingly forced a truce in the decades-long rift between Paul and his father-in-law. They had never been close; Ted telegraphed passive contempt to the man he judged unworthy of marrying his only daughter, which had mellowed into a sort of grudging acceptance with the passage of years and the birth of the granddaughter he cherished. Kyra was the only grandchild they had, the only one they'd ever have. She had brought the two men as close as they'd ever come to accepting each other as family.

And now she was gone.

The tears in the older man's eyes had been unmistakably genuine, the embrace he'd offered Paul no less so. Paul had hugged him back, felt him shudder in anguish, in the most fleeting moment of vulnerability, of connection. "How could this happen?" Ted had asked quietly. Then they separated, and Paul caught a glimpse of the older man's eyes. And he saw the answer, cold and clear as the encroaching dawn.

Your fault . . . I blame you . . .

The kitchen was dimly brightening as Paul shuffled through the doorway, squinting. The intrusive sun offered light but no warmth, obscenely clear and crisp. The Felix the cat clock waved its tail and rolled its eyes from side to side, marking time, the same sly grin on its plastic face. An oil slick sloshed in Paul's gut as he moved. Spock followed obediently beside, toenails clicking on terra-cotta tiles as he kept pace. Something in his primitive doggy hindbrain had picked up on the vibe, warned him not to be too anxious. They moved through the mudroom and Paul undid the deadbolt.

"Sorry, boy," he murmured. "Good dog." Spock wiggled impatiently as Paul opened the door, felt a stinging waft of chill air. Spock wormed his way past, slipped through the crack and bolted into the yard. Paul watched blankly as his pet went about his doggy business, sniffing and squatting and loping across the lawn. Yep, a good dog.

He was eight, Paul thought. Past and present met, instantly collided in his mind. He remembered Spock the puppy, a gangly furball birthday present for Kyra. She was eight, too, the same age as the photo Paul kept in his helmet liner, the lucky photo that had seen him through countless disasters.

Coincidence? His mind struggled to find a pattern. He remembered the trip to the vet to clip the dog's ears and tail, the stiff white bandages that invoked his pointy-eared namesake. He remembered how Kyra had asked Paul if it hurt much, how pleased she had been when he'd said no. Then she'd said, "He looks like Spock!"

And it had stuck.

Kyra and Paul had loved *Star Trek;* they'd watched the old episodes in syndication each weekend on Channel 11. Which had been their favorite episode—the one with the gunfight at the imaginary OK Corral? Yes, that had been it. Paul had loved it because it was surreal, dreamlike, with phantom constructs of Wyatt Earp and Doc Holliday and the others, all culled from their own imaginations, trying to kill them, the product of some superior alien being or another. It had scared eight-year-old Kyra half to death, and she had curled into Paul on the big sofa, safe in Daddy's arms, eyes wide and rapt as Paul had explained that they could only die if they believed the illusion, that it was all a dream . . .

. . . and Paul remembered even further back, to the first time he had ever seen the program, this very episode, when he was eight, and wasn't that a coincidence, too . . .

. . . and Spock had hypnotized them with his handy Vulcan mind-meld, so cool and logical, telling his frail human counterparts the revelation that logic had given him: that they had nothing to fear, that the figures were illusions, the bullets mere shadows, ghosts . . . spectres . . .

. . . and there was a logic here, he thought, there had to be, if logic could save William Shatner and Leonard Nimoy on a fucking TV show it should work here in the screaming real world, right? I mean, is that all logic is good for . . .

. . . as one by one, a make-believe character named Spock worked the magic: coming alive in his daughter's mind just as he had in eight-year-old Paul's some twenty-two years before, placing long and graceful fingers on the key mind-meld points—forehead, temple, under the eye, under the jawline . . .

. . . and Kyra had deep purplish bruises under her jaw, indentations from fingers pressing, crushing her windpipe, ligature marks, strangulation . . .

And that was when logic failed him and the desperate pattern dissembled into nothingness. The oil slick in Paul's belly suddenly came roaring to life, sluicing up from deep within as he bolted and lurched for the bathroom, realized in a heartbeat he would never make it, beelined for the kitchen sink instead. The bile rushed out in a scalding, bitter torrent as Paul gagged and vomited, took a heaving gasp of air, then threw up again. His knees wobbled, and he clung to the edge of the counter, heaving until there was nothing left, until it felt like he would turn himself inside out. With every next spasm the void grew darker, deeper, until by the time it subsided he was utterly empty, clinging to the sink like a shipwreck survivor, drained, spent.

Paul looked up. A little wooden placard hung over the window, a present from Eleanor's mental storehouse of cheery affirmation. TODAY IS THE FIRST DAY OF THE REST OF YOUR LIFE, it read. The words sank in.

Paul heaved again.

15

Over the next days the Kelly home reeled, under siege. The telephone rang every few minutes from dawn to midnight—well-wishers and bereaved friends tag-teaming with mainstream media and freelance stringers vying for scraps. The message tape filled to overflowing, was not replaced.

Outside, news crews hovered, noting every rustle of blinds and car in the driveway; the Halloween decorations became the focus of many the ghoulish lead-in. Link Lenkershem preened and intoned forebodingly at regular intervals, all prime-time grief and pre-chewed emotion. In a grim bit of abattoir opportunism, the tragedy got picked up during an otherwise slow news week and became filler for the wire services; within twenty-four hours Kyra's beaming high school yearbook photo was splashed luridly across the tube on the local channels, picked up as a drive-by media blip for the network affiliates. Pundits waxed prophetic about yet another sad reminder of the violent times in which we live, bemoaning the breakdown of family values and Western civilization while heedlessly cannibalizing Kyra on behalf of ratings and an insatiable public's presumed need-to-know. It seemed everyone had an agenda or a sociopolitical ax to grind, and most were happy to sharpen their edge on the murdered child's memory.

The *Post* and the *Daily News* followed suit, hawking gory details in grainy black-and-white. Glendon's local paper, the *Herald Examiner*, took the merciful high road, giving Kyra page one coverage with an inside spread. They had lost one of their best and brightest, and her murder only fanned the flames of public outrage. Kyra's death sent shock waves through every parent's psyche; within thirty-six hours there were plans for both a candlelight vigil and a manhunt.

The house on Marley Street was combed again and again, sifting for anything that would constitute a clue. The impromptu crash pad upstairs pointed an accusing finger at the indigent; within seventy-two hours every vagrant and shambling wino in the greater Glendon metropolitan area had been swept in for questioning, grilled relentlessly. It all went nowhere. The public clamored for an arrest, a suspect, something—anything—that would substitute for justice . . . or payback.

The political fallout was just as obvious and equally intense. Howard Haims, Glendon's waxy, posturing mayor, had ridden his recent reelection bid to victory on a hard-line, get-tough-on-crime platform, and he could hardly appear weak or ineffectual now. Registered voters were in a panic, the aggrieved family a decorated civil servant and a local teacher. Haims made a big show, promised that he would not rest until Kyra's assailant had been brought to justice, and he looked suitably grievous at every photo opportunity. St. Anthony's Medical Center likewise decided, in a stunning display of politically motivated empathy, not to penalize Paul for his unauthorized medical procedure en route to the hospital, partly because the M.E. ruled it did not contribute to Kyra's death, mostly because they reasoned it would be difficult, legally speaking, for Paul to sue himself for malpractice, but also because it made for hideous headlines. The Fire Department agreed. Small comforts.

It was a smart move. Paul was known and liked in the

trenches of city government, Julie no less so in her own, more academic, milieu, and public sympathy was clearly on their side. From the D.A.'s office to the medical examiner down to the greenest rookie on the beat, everyone was deeply committed to finding Kyra Kelly's murderer. Steve Buscetti combed the roster of known sex offenders, pedophiles, and perverts, but whether guilty of past or planning future depravities, Kyra's murderer did not appear to number among them. Nonetheless, every shred of information, no matter how unlikely or obscure, was scrutinized for clues.

For all the good it did.

There was a knock at the door.

Paul pried it open, one sunken eye peering through the crack. Stevie Buscetti huddled on the porch, his collar flipped up against the wind and the snick of autowinders. It was just after five o'clock, and the setting sun cast everything in burnished, shadowed hues. The golden hour, photographers called it, one of the most optimum times to shoot. Even in this most flattering light, Paul looked about three million years old.

"Hey," Stevie said softly.

"Hey," Paul replied. The conversation faltered, stillborn. Buscetti held a large manila envelope in his hands, hovering at the vestibule like a plague bearer. "Can I come in?" he asked.

Paul nodded, and the door swung back. The detective stepped into the foyer, in the process doing his best to obscure the view from prying eyes. Paul closed the door behind him, throwing the deadbolt.

The interior was warm and cluttered with the detritus of family life, rendered subtly poignant in the wake of the tragedy. Kyra's big overstuffed coat hung on a peg, sandwiched between Paul's bulky leather bomber and Julie's more conservative Land's End gear. Kyra's daypack sat on the little hardwood chest beneath, as if she were off in another room somewhere, about to come bounding in. An oppressive stillness permeated the air, as though her absence had somehow registered on the molecular level, a palpable flaw in the Kelly family DNA.

Buscetti unbuttoned his coat but did not take it off. He hated this moment, though he, like Paul, had weathered it scores of times before. They both knew the drill. Informing the bereaved of the gruesome particulars on a case simply came with the job, along with toe tags and body bags and the stench of violent death; over time one simply acclimated, did what had to be done, and got the hell out. You wore your professionalism like body armor, cumbersome and uncomfortable but essential. You kept a distance. You simply couldn't afford to feel their pain. But this time there was no avoiding it.

"How's it going?" he asked.

"A minute at a time," Paul replied, his voice low, stoic. "I figure if we can make it through this sixty seconds, we'll be ready to try for the next." He shrugged and laughed, dry and humorless. "Repeat as necessary, a few thousand times a day."

Buscetti nodded. "How's Julie?"

Just then Julie appeared in the living room doorway. She was visibly shrunken, her natural beauty eroded by grief. If Paul was a husk, loss had transformed Julie into a pillar of salt—the normally pleasant laugh lines around her dark eyes now deepened into fissures, her features stark and haunted, her shoulders caved in to cover the hole in her heart. She folded her arms across her chest, leaned against the door frame. She tried to smile, managed a grimace, nothing more.

"Stevie," she said softly, then stopped, as though she couldn't think of another thing to say. He leaned forward to hug her, and she drew back. He stopped. "You, uh, you want some coffee?" she said.

"Thanks," Buscetti murmured. "Coffee would be great."

Julie nodded and pushed off from the wall, heading down the hall, a grim automaton. Spock appeared behind her, pressed past and nuzzled up to the detective.

"Hey, fella," Buscetti murmured, scratching the dog's

ears. Spock wriggled, relieved to see a familiar, friendly face. Even he seemed to sense the eggshell vibe, the brittle click of his toenails on the floor underscoring the fragility of the mood. Spock gazed dolefully at Paul and hunkered off, looking for someplace warm to hide. Buscetti knew the feeling.

Paul gestured, and the two men followed Julie to the kitchen. Julie's parents were already there; Eleanor was puttering at the sink, rinsing barely touched dinner plates. Ted, at the table, was reading the sports page—an absurd parody of normalcy that masked his insistence on prescreening the headlines lest his daughter be blindsided by some wayward hindbrain's reportage. His silver hair was mussed; a patina of gray stubble stippled his jowls.

"Mom, Dad, this is Detective Buscetti," Julie offered. Buscetti stiffened somewhat, at the presence of the elder folk as well as at the demotion from family friend to public servant. He nodded to Eleanor, offered his hand to Ted.

"My deepest sympathies," he said.

Eleanor nodded, eager to take the edge off the tension. Ted just eyed him skeptically. "So," he said gruffly, "do you know who murdered our little girl yet?"

"Uh, nossir, not at this time," Buscetti said uncomfortably. The tension between the two men hummed like freshly plucked piano wire. "But I want you to know we're doing everything we can."

"Hmmph," Ted grunted, then picked up the paper and exited the room. As he left, Buscetti whistled soundlessly. Eleanor interceded.

"Please excuse my husband, Detective," she said. "This has been a terrible strain on all of us."

Buscetti nodded thanks, then took a seat as Eleanor fetched four steaming mugs of java. When it became apparent that she intended to join them, Buscetti leaned toward Paul. "Um, can we talk?" The look in his eyes said, parenthetically, In private?

Eleanor got the hint. She rose, motioned to Julie. Julie didn't budge. "Anything you've got to say, I can hear," she said.

"This might be unpleasant," Buscetti warned.

"This is already unpleasant," she countered.

Buscetti sighed, then the three of them watched as Eleanor smoothed her apron and retreated. Buscetti waited until she was safely out of earshot, then turned his attention to the task at hand.

"I, uh, thought you might want these." He handed Paul the envelope, still bearing the stamp of the Glendon PD forensics department. "I'm bending the rules a little," he continued, "but we've already determined that robbery wasn't the motive. Her clothing is still in the system—we're analyzing it for hair, fibers, anything that can help us nail this bastard."

Paul and Julie nodded wordlessly as Paul slid the contents out onto the table—a pair of dangling silver earrings in the shape of a pair of hands; a tiny, delicate bracelet with chains like gossamer thread linked to an equally delicate silver heart; and the guts of Kyra's shoulder bag—wallet, hairbrush, makeup, assorted accouterments of girl-tech. The mere sight of it caused Julie's eyes to well with tears. As she fingered the bracelet, Paul picked up Kyra's wallet; it fell open to reveal school ID, an AT&T calling card, a brand-new driver's license, youthful beauty shining through holographic tape. Inside were four crisp twenties in cash. Paul looked at the envelope, as if hoping to see something else. But that was all.

Buscetti cleared his throat and drew a little notebook and pen from his pocket. "The M.E.'s report came back," he told them. "Based on the ligature marks and the amount of carbon dioxide in her blood, the official cause of death is listed as strangulation." A deathly silence hung in the air, as each next word seemed to settle onto them like a cinder block.

"I just have a few questions." Buscetti flipped open the notebook, clicked the pen. "Was she seeing anybody? Steady boyfriends, anything like that?"

"No," Paul replied.

"She was dating Kurt Wheeler for a while," Julie added softy, "but they broke up, maybe four months ago."

Buscetti nodded corroboratively. "We checked the Wheeler kid out on the first canvass, and he's clean—he was home watching reruns of *The X-Files* on the tube when it happened. Did you notice anyone suspicious hanging around lately?" They both shook their heads. "Any unknown numbers show up on your phone bill? Hang-up calls?"

Paul thought back. "We had one a couple of nights ago," he said. "Some mouth breather, nothing to it."

Julie looked at the detective. "Why? Is it important?"

"At this point, anything could be," Buscetti replied. "Why do you ask?"

Suddenly Julie looked vexed, anxious. "We had a few more than that," she confessed. Paul looked at her, surprised and angry.

"A few *more*?"

"So what?" She went defensive. "I mean, there were a couple in the past week, and maybe about a month ago, but that's it." Both Paul and Buscetti were looking at her now; Julie pulled back defensively.

"Jesus, babe, why didn't you say anything?" Paul snapped.

"I didn't think it was important!" she snapped back, then added, lower, "They were hang-up calls, no voice, no nothing. What was I supposed to say?" She looked at Buscetti guiltily, as if he had the power of absolution. "Stevie, do you think it was? . . ."

"Probably not," he said, but he scribbled something down just the same. He shifted gears. "To the best of your knowledge," he asked, "was Kyra sexually active?"

"What the hell kind of question is that?" Paul responded angrily. He looked from Buscetti to Julie, who looked away.

"I'm sorry, Paulie," Buscetti replied. "I gotta ask." The two men eyeballed each other for a moment, then Paul sighed, shaking his head. "No," he said heavily.

Buscetti nodded, scribbled some more. "Okay. Do you know what she was doing in the house? Did she have keys? Was she expecting to meet you?"

"No, no, no," Paul said. "She wasn't supposed to be

there." Paul's tone was aggrieved, exasperated. "Christ, she was coming home from the library. The house was on the way. I don't know, maybe she saw someone inside and thought it was me."

Buscetti nodded. "Had you been getting along all right with her? Any fights lately, arguments, stuff like that?"

"No," Paul said defensively. "We argued some, sure, but it was bullshit, standard-issue teen-angst. No big deal." He looked to Julie and she nodded; the grieving parents drew together instinctively, a psychic circling of the wagons.

"Where are you going with this?" Julie demanded. "Why don't you tell us something?"

"Sorry, Julie. You, too, Paulie." Buscetti sighed and closed his notebook, ran a hand across his hangdog features. "Okay," the detective said, "here's what we got so far. As near as we can tell, she was heading home, and wandered into this dirtbag's sights. What we don't know," he continued, "is whether this was random, or whether the perp targeted her, which is why I have to ask so many questions." He shrugged. "Maybe he set her up. Right now, we just don't know."

"There's a lot you don't know," Julie said bitterly.

"True," Buscetti confessed. "But at this point, we've ruled out the junkie theory, because any of the local skels would've taken the money. So, we're thinking it was some deviant." A visible shudder rippled beneath the surface of Paul and Julie's composure. "We ran the m.o. through the computers, to see if we get a match," Buscetti told them, "but so far, nothing."

"So you've got nothing," Paul said.

"Not exactly," Buscetti corrected. "One of the neighbors said she saw a lone male, slight build, leaving the scene shortly after it happened. We know he's white. And he got scratched."

"Scratched?" they both said, almost in unison. Paul leaned forward, unconsciously shielding his wife from the information. Buscetti paused, squirming like a worm under a magnifying glass. He was dangerously close to crossing the line, but the Kellys were practically family, and he knew

Paul would find out eventually. "The M.E. found evidence under her fingernails," he said as gently as possible.

"What does that mean?" Julie asked.

"It means she fought him," Paul said flatly. His thoughts instantly spun back to the ambulance, Kyra's torn fingernails . . . any illusions, however fragile, of their daughter's suffering being somehow mitigated were instantly shattered like crystal on concrete; the jagged truth of it now lay before them. Kyra had been beaten, had been violated. Had been murdered.

And she had fought her killer every step of the way . . .

That was when Julie snapped, standing and pacing the room in tight circles, a caged animal, trapped in the unspoken ugliness of the truth. "Oh, God," she said. "Oh God, oh God . . ."

Paul and Buscetti watched her, afraid to breathe or move. They were each in their own way willing supplicants to a battle-weary belief: that in a world full of bad guys and bullshit, the innocent would be saved. The guilty, punished. The system would work. And justice would somehow prevail. "We'll get him, Julie," Stevie said. "I promise."

"Yeah," Julie snorted bitterly. "And then what?"

"He'll go away for a long, long time."

"Sure he will," Julie murmured, looking right through them. "But that won't bring my baby back, will it?"

Buscetti met her gaze, then looked away. "No, it won't."

Julie nodded. It was too much. She withdrew from the room. A moment later they heard her sobbing in the living room, Eleanor murmuring vain comfort.

"I'm sorry," Buscetti murmured to Paul. Paul nodded as Buscetti closed his little notebook. They rose and moved toward the rear door, through the mudroom. The space was small, a bulky washer and dryer squatting along one wall; the air chill and dark, an icy draft pressing through the weather-stripping surrounding the back door, making the plastic lining the glass expand and contract, as if breathing. Buscetti shuffled, not entirely from the cold.

"Look," he said at last, softly, "I didn't want to bring this up in front of Julie, and we haven't made this public, but there was alcohol in her system."

"Meaning what?" Paul asked, indignant.

"Meaning nothing, except she'd been drinking shortly before it happened."

This was news to Paul. He looked at Buscetti questioningly, hackles rising. "So what are you saying?" he asked. "My daughter engages in a little underage drinking, and for that she gets the death penalty?"

"Whoa," Buscetti put his hands up, backing off. "I'm not saying anything like that. Kyra was a good kid. This guy's a fuckin' sicko, and swear to Christ, I want him as bad as you do," the detective said. "But I need to know, is there anything else you can tell me?"

"Like what?"

"Like anything," Buscetti said. "Son of Sam was nailed from a parking ticket, Paulie. Right now we're looking for anything that might help us catch this guy." Paul shuddered, pulled himself together. He shrugged—there was nothing.

"Okay," Buscetti said. "You think of anything, you call me."

"Yeah," Paul said, utterly miserable. "Sure."

There was nothing more to say. Outside, the night was brutally cold, starless. Wind whispered through naked branches. The detective flipped his collar up and walked off, into the shadows. Paul heard receding footsteps crunch on the crushed stone of the driveway. A car door open, then shut. An engine, grunting and rumbling to life. Only then did he lock and double-lock the door, make his way back inside.

Back in the relative warmth of the kitchen, Paul glanced over to the table, saw Kyra's things, splayed out like a second autopsy. Scattered remnants, leaving many questions and precious few answers. *Anything,* Buscetti had said.

But Paul didn't know anything. Which was worse—the knowing or the not knowing? Impossible question, begetting impossible answers. He looked around the room, heard Julie crying in the background. He decided not to tell her about the drinking—not now. What purpose would it serve?

On the refrigerator, Kyra's picture stared back, her whole life ahead of her—what little had remained of it. Now, gone.

Paul stared, his thoughts spinning.

Then he cried, too.

16

The morning of the funeral rose, slate gray and damp. Mourners turned out by the hundreds: crowding the pristine grounds of Glendon Gardens cemetery, encircling the mound of freshly turned earth, rendering it tiny in perspective. The sun was a pale and distant ball of fire, obscured by heavy cover; low overhead, a News Four helicopter made slow, looping passes around the perimeter, providing channel-surfing filler for that night's update. Marginal consciences prevailed, and the chopper kept just enough distance to avoid drowning out the services in prop-wash.

On the ground, the assembled milled in loosely concentric circles, ranked according to proximity to the deceased. On the outermost edges were news crews and reporters, followed by concerned citizenry and nearly the entire student body and faculty of Glendon Hills High. The school had taken the day off in observance of the tragedy, transforming Kyra's burial into a kind of macabre field trip. Each student in attendance held a tethered helium balloon with a personal message scrawled in Magic Marker, courtesy of a crack psychologist called in to do emergency bereavement counseling. The brilliant idea had been advanced that each child should write their wishes for Kyra on the colored rubber skins, then release them to fly up to heaven. It gave the scene an absurdly cheerful air; indeed, the whole affair had taken on a pomp and circumstance reserved for dead celebrities, which, in a way, she had inadvertently become.

Still, a charge of genuine emotion telegraphed through the throng. Dozens of wreaths and bouquets of flowers rimmed the headstone, irises, lilies and pink roses, Kyra's favorite, pale colors splashed on a gray tableau. Teachers and students who had never known Kyra openly wept alongside friends and family, and it seemed everyone was swept up in the swelling gestalt of grief.

Closer in, the Glendon Fire Department had sent an honor guard, which was unheard of for the death of a family member. The Police Department had similarly volunteered a contingent, headed by Steve Buscetti, in a stunning display of interdepartmental solidarity.

At the inner circle, family and close friends huddled. Dondi, Tom, and Joli were there in their dress blues, according their friend's daughter their every measure of respect. Their loved ones clustered beside them, shivering with cold and palpably crushing waves of pain. Even Wallace Clyburne was on hand, looking genuinely aggrieved.

Paul and Julie stood closest to the grave, flanked by a stoic Ted and Eleanor. Julie's black and diaphanous veil did little to conceal her ravaged emotions; she looked brittle, drained. As the priest delivered the liturgy, she shuddered and wept bitterly.

Paul held her, felt her anguish meld into his own. His thoughts scattered at random, shock and grief coursing narcotically through his veins. He felt like a perfect replica of himself fashioned entirely of sand, inwardly crumbling against some dark, leeching tide.

A neat apron had been laid on the ground surrounding the grave, to mask the brutish truth of its purpose. Father Riley, a stately and laconic man not much older than Paul, was saying how God, in His infinite wisdom, had decided that He needed Kyra in Heaven. Paul gritted his teeth.

As Father Riley spoke, Paul stared, transfixed, at the mahogany casket hovering above the mouth of the moist and neatly excised hole. Pictures came: unbidden, psychic snapshots, flash-frozen in time. Dreams and fears, intertwined and grown together, feeding on desires, on deepest feelings of the essential rightness—or wrongness—of life. Gossamer things; fleeting, ethereal. Yet powerful, singular. Epiphanous. Images, of how things were. And how they were meant to be.

Seventeen years ago. The word still fresh from Julie's lips, echoing over a supper of pasta and cheap Chianti. Pregnant. Paul's heart had skipped and halted, as if some unseen hand had just hit the pause button on his life, waiting to see how everything would shake out. Or at least, how he would.

"Are you sure?" he had asked, and she'd nodded. Her eyes had been full of expectation. It had been different for Julie. Somehow Julie had just known, like it was encoded into her DNA, secreted on some cellular level, passed telepathically from generation to generation. But for Paul, the wisdom had been harder to come by.

To his eternal regret, his immediate reaction had been unmitigated selfishness. Paul had felt not joy but dread, the imminent loss—of youth, mobility, freedom. Choice. A dozen desperate arguments had sprung to his defense. It wasn't a good time for kids. They were too young, too broke, too unsure of themselves, their futures, each other. He couldn't imagine being a father. He just wasn't ready yet.

The moment had lasted barely a second, and he had masked it as well as he could, which was not very. But it had been enough. Julie's gaze had lowered. She'd gotten up and left the room.

The shame of it still stung.

Later, after much groveling and apologizing, Paul had come to bed. Laying in the dark, he'd placed his hand against his wife's belly, felt the gentle cadence of her sleeping breath. Something was dreaming there, just beneath the soft surface of her skin. Becoming someone. Waiting for its moment to arrive. And he'd known then that all the love he felt for this woman had taken root, was now personified in the tiny bit of matter growing in her womb. It was then that Paul had realized that he could embrace this as a blessing, or reject it as a burden, or run from it altogether. They could grant it the chance or erase it outright. But there was no escaping the truth: that whether they had meant to do this or not, from this moment forward— no matter what else happened—his life would never be the same.

And he'd damned well better get used to that.

Paul had changed that night; from then on, he embraced impending fatherhood with the fervor of the true penitent, as though his zeal could wash away his shame. He did Lamaze classes, scored an antique crib at a Jersey City junk shop and meticulously sanded and refinished it to glowing perfection, bought a secondhand camcorder and stuffed animals by the fuzzy dozens. Before he caught the first grainy glimpse of his daughter courtesy the ultrasound screen, he loved her beyond measure or belief. By the time he held her in his hands, Paul could not imagine a life without her. He swore to make the world perfect for this little stranger, his baby girl, his Kyra. He had always pictured a world of possibility for her.

But he had never pictured this . . .

A box. A dank and open hole, into which his hopes and dreams were about to be laid to untimely rest. His little girl was in there, just behind that polished veneer. Just before they'd closed the lid at the funeral home, Paul had kissed her cheek, saying one last good-bye.

"Sweet dreams, baby," he'd whispered. "Daddy loves you."

A tear had fallen, stealing through a stray chink in his

armor; it touched her cheek and trailed down, so that it almost looked as if she were crying, too.

How much he wished, in that final parting moment, that he could have awakened her with that kiss, like some secondhand prince in a cut-rate fairy tale. And maybe then she would have told him that she loved him, too, and always would. Maybe she would have said that she forgave him for not being able to save her, for not protecting her from the real monsters that prey on the innocent.

Or maybe, at least, she would have been able to tell him the answer to the one question that burned in his heart.

Why?

Father Riley was wrapping up the sermon. "Ashes to ashes," he intoned, genuflecting over the grave. "Dust to dust . . ."

He glanced to Paul and nodded ever so slightly. A cue. Cupping his wife's arm, Paul and Julie stepped up, laid fresh white roses on the immaculate, polished lid. The inner circle followed suit, stepping forward to lay their scented offerings in kind, then turning away to join the other mourners. As the flowers landed, beads of dew struck the smooth surface of the coffin and skittered off into the waiting earth.

Julie turned to her waiting parents, sank into their embrace. Paul stood, staring at the box. He could see his reflection, skewed in the casket's gleaming curves, distorted and grotesque, a ghastly fun house refraction.

The casket creaked on the winch, began its final descent into darkness. The milling throng rustled like a breeze through autumn leaves; and with a shared murmur the balloons were released, dots of color drifting into leaden sky. In the distance, someone cheered, and Paul wanted to kill him.

With every winding click of the gears Paul felt his soul constrict like a tightening coil. As the coffin passed his sight line and was absorbed by shadow, the mourners turned away, the crowd breaking ranks to offer last bits of comfort. Paul glanced past the black-garbed gatherers; past the gravediggers, quietly smoking by the backhoe and awaiting their turn.

His gaze skimmed blankly across acres of neat granite, arcing out and up the low hill that marked the southern edge of the cemetery.

And that was when he saw him.

The dark figure hovered by an outcropping of statuary, some three hundred yards away. He was conspicuous in his distance, even more so by his apparent interest. Even from so far away, it seemed that he was no mere passerby, but a watcher, intent. Paul caught a glimpse of slight build in jeans and leather, a dark mass of hair obscuring pale features. Though it was too far to tell, it seemed the stranger's eyes met his and held, then . . .

"Paul," a gentle voice said, behind him. A gentle hand on his shoulder. Paul turned to find Dondi, Stevie right behind him, concern etched deeply across both their features. "Hey, pal . . ."

"You see that guy?" Paul asked, his voice low and urgent.

They stared at him uncomprehendingly. "What guy?" Buscetti asked.

Paul gestured back to the crest of the hill. "There's somebody up there." He pointed. "Right there . . ."

But the stranger was gone.

"Well, he was there not two seconds ago," Paul insisted, neck craning as he scanned the horizon. "He was watching us."

Dondi and Stevie traded uneasy glances. "Paul, there must be five hundred people out here today," Dondi said.

"Yeah, well, I don't know this guy."

"You don't know half the people here," Dondi said, appealing to his reason. "Whoever he was, he was probably just paying his respects."

Paul paused, pulling himself together. "Yeah," he said, sighing heavily. "I'm sorry. Just having a lousy day, I guess."

Dondi and Paul embraced, and Paul clung to him briefly, a shipwreck survivor clutching a passing life-ring. Dondi patted his back, murmuring, "We're here, buddy. We're here."

"I know," Paul whispered. "I know." The two men disengaged, and Paul glanced at Steve Buscetti, who was watching the crowd of mourners disperse and stroll through the rows of stone. For a moment it seemed that he, too, was looking for something.

Buscetti glanced back to Paul and Dondi. The three men exchanged a wordless nod of understanding, then turned their attentions to their loved ones.

And got on with the business of burying the dead.

17

Life, such as it was, went on. The days went by. The crime faded in the public eye, subsumed by the endless parade of fresher horrors. Wars and rumors of wars rumbled in far-flung lands; disasters, natural and otherwise, claimed their hapless human toll. Glendon made its own contribution to the body count, via disease, old age, drug o.d.'s, gang drive-bys, domestic disputes, shootings, stabbings, DUI crackups, and just plain bad luck. Just as it always had.

On the flip side, babies continued to be born, new life entering to replace that which had shuffled off this mortal coil. The earth stubbornly continued to circle the sun. Just as it always had.

But for Paul, it might as well have stopped entirely.

The time immediately following the funeral was punctuated by well-meaning friends and neighbors appearing at the door, bearing sympathies and casserole; by fitful nights giving way to shell-shocked awakening. Julie's grieving had become numbness, settling like a leaden cloud, going through the motions of each new day like an automaton. Ted and Eleanor stayed through the week, running block and generally being supportive.

But by week's end, the flow of human kindness began to recede: tragic as it all was, there were still bills to pay, mouths to feed, lives to live. Halloween came and went with porchlights off and curtains drawn: neighborhood parents accompanying eager trick-or-treaters whispered and steered clear; even the youngest Power Ranger or friendly Casper seemed to pause in mid-sugar high to give the house wide berth, the spectre of real ghosts all too painfully apparent.

On the first of November, the local Hispanic community celebrated *El Dia de los Muertos*, the Day of the Dead. Area residents danced to Latin grooves and dead relatives as their children munched traditional candy skulls, tiny faces painted in garish reaper hues. Later in the day, after the traffic had died down, Ted and Eleanor packed their bags and bade their reluctant farewells. In the end everyone knew that some damage could only be healed from within, some could never, and the mere presence of such heightened compassion had become almost as burdensome as the pain that inspired it. Julie's parents left amidst many tearful embraces and promises to stay in touch, along with assurances that, somehow, everything would be all right.

Leaving Paul and Julie to what was left of their home. To pick up the pieces.

It was all about control.

Paul strained, exhaling through gritted teeth. *One twenty-three, one twenty-four, one twenty-five* . . . Sweat beaded off his forehead, soaked his back until it stuck to the black vinyl surface of the slantboard. Dank heat filled the claustrophobic confines of the basement, fogging the tiny windows, making it hard to breathe; Paul ignored it, his arms folded over his chest, his face a mask of iron resolve. *One forty-six, one forty-seven* . . .

Pain laced through his abdominal muscles, knitted into the burn in his lower back. *One forty-eight, one forty-nine* . . .

". . . one fifty," he said, then exhaled heavily and lay back. The board was black steel and foam-padded, the words LifeGear stenciled in jaunty blue letters on the cover. It had been a birthday present, a dry holiday poke in the love handles, though, given his physique, it had been more symbolic than actual; underneath the brand name was the over-achieving slogan GET YOUR LIFE IN GEAR!

That was the general idea.

"One . . . two . . . three . . . four . . ." Paul laced his fingers behind his head and started again, twisting from side to side as he came up, blood thudding in his temples, heart pounding in aerobic overtime. The board had been in the basement storage for months, forgotten in the press of day-to-day life. After the funeral, Paul dragged it out of its hiding place, blew the dust off, and began.

"Seventeen . . . eighteen . . . nineteen . . . twenty . . ."

Paul grimaced, his body in agony. It wasn't vanity that drove him. What Paul sought was deeper, more amorphous. Pulling himself up each time, mental knives driving through his torso, Paul felt a pain infinitely preferable to the devastation that awaited each waking moment. When the endorphins kicked in, nerve endings numbed into obedience by repetition, he simply pushed harder, upped the number, drove himself to the brink of exhaustion.

Control.

The numbers blurred, ran together, became meaningless markers extending into oblivion. A dark cloud rippled in his mind's eye, threatening to overtake him. A crazed heartbeat before blackout. Paul fell back, let the waves of release wash over him. He was spent.

Only then might he hope to sleep.

Paul sat up, looked at his surroundings. The basement had always been his sanctum, the one part of the house he had always set off for himself. When they'd first bought the place, Julie had been more than happy to make the concession: it was, frankly and almost literally, a pit. A poured concrete floor, raw cinder block walls, exposed ceiling staring up at the kitchen subfloor, pipes, boiler, furnace, and dirt. Not exactly a going concern.

But that was before Paul got hold of it. Over the years he had painstakingly tweaked and fiddled with it, transforming raw space into a finished and funky place to hang, guy-style. A false wall had been constructed, separating the boiler and furnace from the room proper. The floors and walls were covered and paneled via a connection he had with Big Bobby's Karpet Kingdom after they'd saved it from becoming Bobby's big burnt livelihood; Big B had sworn eternal gratitude, plus ten percent above cost. The resulting paneling was real wood, not fake cheesoid Home Depot crap; the subfloor state of the art, the floor tile some new polymer hybrid that could take a licking and keep on ticking, and all on a fireman's budget.

Shelves on the back wall rimmed a prodigious workbench, where Paul worked downtime magic on electrical appliances and assorted other pet projects. A huge black metal rack housed his old stereo components and the manly speakers with fifteen-inch subwoofers that Julie had steadfastly refused to allow in the living room, instead favoring a compromise of small, tasteful Polk Audios that sounded just as good but didn't trash the décor. A set of cabled Sony headphones hung over the top of his big black velour recliner, which was hugely comfortable but similarly consigned to the testosterone-ridden hinterlands, along with his black hi-tech halogen reading light.

And then there were the books: virtually every volume he had ever laid hands on since birth, a lifetime of accrued knowledge neatly packed and stacked into handbuilt floor-to-ceiling bookshelves, completely lining three of the four walls. There were hundreds, even thousands, of titles, ranging from history to how-to books to philosophy, from science fact to science fiction, plus an assortment of thrillers, horror, and mysteries.

Paul was not an educated man by any traditional definition; indeed, it had been all he could do to graduate from the lemminglike assembly line of high school, where success had been measured less by intelligence than by the ability to follow orders. And college, once a distant dream for a working-class lad without benefit of scholarship or trust fund, had quickly become a forgotten one as the grim Darwinism of life in the real world kicked in. But none of that precluded his educating himself, and that he had done with determination, reading voraciously, constantly trying to open his own mind to new ways of thinking. He read for passion and pleasure as well as edification, often five or six at one time, tagging back and forth, channel-surfing the printed page.

It was more than habit, more like a way of life, and it filtered into every aspect of his world. Where some guys got ties on Christmas and birthdays, Paul got books. And whenever he was on a call, he would instinctively note the presence—or more often the absence—of books in the homes of those he served. It was usually the latter, and while the bookless homes lacked the extra flammable material, they seemed incrementally more emotionally scorched—more domestic calls, more pointless tragedy. He didn't know why.

All he knew was that his basement contained worlds within worlds, and he had always relished the time he spent there. It was a passion he had shared with Kyra, who had in turn become an avid reader herself, actually teaching herself to read a year before she had entered preschool. Paul remembered her sitting in his lap, her curly hair tickling his nose as she'd sounded out the caption to a Time-Life Science series photo caption with four-year-old determination that had both amazed and astounded him. That had happened in this very room.

And now it meant nothing.

Paul dragged himself up the stairs, padded through the darkened house. It was cold upstairs, a vague draft from the dormer window at the end of the hall making his flesh prickle and crawl. As he creaked up to the second-floor landing he purposely avoided looking at the door to Kyra's room, sealed sarcophagus tight. He shuddered as he passed it, as yet unable to face the emptiness there.

Julie lay sleeping in the master bedroom; buried under the covers, she seemed very small. Paul's regimen was just one more irony in the grand scheme of things; in the wake of things, her own had evaporated to nothingness. She drifted from day to night to day again, the emotional cauterization of grief flattened by the psychiatric cocktail of Valium and Prozac, which she took at alternating intervals—mood levelers and antidepressants. Pharmaceutical communion. Better living through chemistry.

Paul sat on his side of the bed, which was uncharacteristically expansive. In happier times, he would have retired only to find Julie sprawled well across the imaginary dividing line that demarcated his from hers, tumbleweeds blowing across the vacant plain of her side, with only a jumper's-ledge worth of sleeping space on his. He would curl into her huddled warmth and gently push her into an equitable middle ground, until their bodies melded together in intimate familiarity. He bitched about it every other day, but he wouldn't have had it any other way. It was weirdly endearing.

But this, too, had deserted them, along with every other semblance of normalcy. As he slid between the sheets she stirred and moved away.

He wondered if she would ever come back again.

Six o'clock, Tuesday morning. All quiet at Rescue One. The night shift snoozed upstairs, a nasal concerto. Downstairs in the kitchen, a timer clicked; hot water burbled through the battered Mr. Coffee maker, making a horrible sucking noise. One of the night shift crew, Andy Vasquez, was sitting in a chair by the big worktable: feet up, head tilted back, a rumbling snore emanating from his powerfully compact form. A baseball cap perched on his buzzed black hair, the brim pulled low to touch the tip of his nose. A copy of *Soldier of Fortune* magazine splayed across his chest, open to an article on Navy Seals. Andy was a jovial, good-natured Puerto Rican in his forties, an ex-military man from Sunset Park who'd done two tours in Nam as a Ranger; if you added up all his mission stories it seemed he was there for one hundred and twenty years.

The front door clicked and opened; Andy stirred, sat up. Magazine and cap slid off and hit the floor. He bent to retrieve them, then looked up, surprised.

"Paulie," he said, accent thick Brooklynese. "What are you doing here?"

"Working," Paul said. "What does it look like I'm doing here?" Paul peeled off his bomber and slung it on the rack, revealing his work blues. He went to the duty desk, scanned the teletype. "Slow night?"

"Dead," Andy replied, instantly regretted it.

Paul said nothing, just moved toward the coffeemaker and poured himself a steaming cup. The coffeemaker hitched and sucked like a straw hitting the bottom of an empty cup. Paul paused in mid-pour. His hand trembled.

Andy sat up, shaking off sleep. "So you back on rotation?"

"Half shifts," Paul said. His hand stopped shaking. "Problem?"

"No," Andy said. "I'm just—we just didn't figure to see you so soon. Thought maybe, you know," he fumbled, "thought maybe you'd wanna take some time."

Paul finished pouring, turned to the firefighter.

"Thanks," he said. "But what I really need is to get back to work, ya know?" Paul gave him a tired smile. "Don't worry, I'm good. Department shrink even said so."

Andy looked at him and nodded. He'd seen enough death in his day, even before the job, to know that everybody took it a little differently. Some guys ran from it. Some faced it down and fought. And some needed to just ruck up and carry on.

Paul moved between Andy and the wall, carrying his mug, heading for the truck bay. Andy called out softly as Paul reached the door.

"Hey, Paulie? We're all real sorry for your loss," Andy said.

Paul nodded. "Me, too."

* * *

Paul stood in the bay, clipboard in hand, meticulously checking his gear. Oncoming shift duties: place coat, boots, helmet, mask in assigned positions; check airtank, flashlight, charge radio battery; check assigned and sundry tools—mini-Haliburton, axe, pike pole, bolt cutters, tin snips, clamps, d-rings and ropes.

Check.

Paul opened the metal side compartments on the rig, pulled out the saws and power tools, the big nutcracker vise-like Jaws of Life, made sure everything was gassed up and good to go. He fired up each piece and revved the throttles. Motors blatted harsh in the cavernous space, like angry animals fighting in a cave. Paul shut them down and stowed them back.

Check.

He climbed into the back of the truck, grabbed his med-box and the portable difibrillator unit from their resting places in the stainless steel confines. Paul hauled them down, made his way to the back of the bay, where a narrow steel cage stood, secured by a padlock. Inside stood an old wooden table and a locked steel supply cabinet. The table had just enough room for the two defibs—one onboard, one spare, hooked to its charger. Paul unlocked the gate and entered, racking the one he was carrying and plugging it in, then pulling the second one free. He flipped it on, saw the power meters surge. Full charge.

Check.

The routine was long practiced, oddly comforting. Its ordered familiarity put him on autopilot, helped take his mind off the fact that every breath he took felt like inhaling ground glass. Paul shut the fresh defib unit down, then turned to the locked metal cabinet.

Inside resided the house's secret stash—ampules and pills, assorted painkillers, pharmaceutical samples tendered to docs at the hospitals they serviced. Paramedics and emergency medical technicians were legally not allowed to administer drugs, but everyone in the frontline trenches of human suffering knew from experience that pain sometimes needed to be suppressed, and well before the patient arrived at the ER gates. So with a wink and a nod, various sympathetic physicians looked the other way or surreptitiously provided that which bureaucracy could not.

There was an inventory sheet in the cabinet. Paul grabbed a few ampules and vials, noted the withdrawal, then packed them in the bottom of the medbox. As he closed the lid, he reached into his pocket, withdrew a vial of little blue-and-white pills. The label read SECONAL SODIUM 50 MG. PULVUL., and beneath, in tiny computer printout, TO COMBAT TENSION, NERVOUSNESS, SLEEPLESSNESS AND ANXIETY. Paul sighed. A bit more heavy duty than Valium, to be sure. But this was a heavier than normal situation.

Grief counseling with the Department shrink was standard procedure after a really bad death on the job, and though this was a bit of a gray zone, Battalion Chief Davie had thought it best Paul go and get checked out. This he had done, pro forma, dutifully logging his emotional wreckage for the Powers That Be. The shrink was a fiftyish pinhead named Weinstein, who had probed his defenses with clinical aplomb—Are you eating? Sleeping? Having nightmares?—then gone on to explain, with some vaguely New Age verbiage, how it was okay to feel bad when bad things happened to good people.

Paul had nodded obediently, innately sensing the session was less for his benefit than theirs—the city feared public servants going postal—and more like probing his defenses for hidden trip wires than actually seeking to ease his suffering. He'd said all the right things at all the right places, walked out with a clean bill of health and a scrip for sedatives to ease him through sleepless nights. Additional psychological counseling had been both offered and recommended; Paul had said he'd think about it.

Paul now looked at the vial in his hand. Sleep had mutated in the days since Kyra's funeral: a cold descent into nothingness when wakefulness became too black to bear, then popping out like a pilot hitting the ejector seat when the dreams became too brutal to endure. And the dreams—the

ones he hadn't shared with the estimable Dr. Weinstein—
were always the same . . .

*A burning building. Poisonous smoke. The sound of
his own heartbeat. Regulator hiss. The fire was in
there somewhere, lurking in the blackness, feeding,
growing stronger. He came to a doorway, locked, stuck
shut. The fire crackled in the background. He could
feel its presence. He forced the door open . . .*

*On the floor, the woman, huddled, fetal. He reached
down, rolled her over, saw the small form hidden
beneath her. But as he scooped up the tiny bundle, he
heard her voice.*

"Daddy . . . ?"

*Heart pounding, Paul looked at the woman on the
floor. It was Kyra: face smudged black with soot, eyes
open, milky. Her face tilted toward him, a thin trickle
of blood oozing from her lips . . .*

"Daddy . . . ?"

Paul snapped back: to reality, the cage, the bay, the firehouse now stirring to life. From the ready room he heard
men's voices, muted strains of conversation, laughter. It was
six-forty-five, and the relief shift was starting to arrive. A
new day dawning.

Paul shuddered. He had to get a grip somehow. He looked
at the pills, thought, *Not like this.*

Control.

Paul placed them on the shelf and closed the door.

18

The house was dark as Paul arrived home, cold November sun sinking in the sky. Julie's car was gone, the garage yawning like an empty mouth. Paul felt a stab of irrational anxiety twist in his belly—she should be home. Where was she? Was she safe? He moved up the walk, went to unlock the back door . . . then noticed it was already unlocked.

Paul's hackles instantly rose. He opened the door, stepped inside. The house was still, lifeless.

"Julie? I'm home."

No answer. He called again, louder.

"Jule?"

Spock poked his head around the corner, loped up to him. "Spock, where's Julie?" he said, felt instantly stupid. The dog just stood, head down, stumpy tail wagging. Paul petted him perfunctorily and let him out into the yard, then moved into the kitchen.

He surveyed the room; sans Julie's mom, it had descended into post-traumatic disarray. Pots and pans covered the stovetop; dirty dishes clogged the sink, the faucet leaking a steady drip, drip, drip. Paul tightened down the knob, saw a juice glass broken amidst forgotten crumb-strewn plates. He picked up the shards, turned toward the trash can by the fridge. As he bent to raise the lid he came eye-to-eye with Kyra's smiling yearbook picture. Paul glanced away.

He made his way through the hall, headed up the creaky wooden stairs. The top floor, too, was eerily quiet. Paul passed by the guest room, bathroom, down the hall to their bedroom, saw the big brass bed rumpled and unmade, empty . . . then turned back. Only then did he dare pause and look at the door to Kyra's room.

The door was closed, had been so since the night she left. Privacy was a big thing in the Kelly house, particularly for Paul in a house full of women—he'd learned early on to knock before entering, and wait for permission before venturing further. Kyra had always closed the door to her sanctum sanctorum and had responded with nothing short of full-blown theatrics when that sanctity was breached. But adolescent boundaries notwithstanding, Paul had relearned the hard way, some months back, when he'd unceremoniously popped his head through the door . . .

It had been dinnertime, and she'd been up in her room, Alanis Morissette blasting on her boom box. The food was getting cold, and he'd called three times—twice from the kitchen, once from the foot of the stairs. Finally, annoyed, he'd bounded up, knocked once, then thrown open the door, only to find his daughter clad in panties and a baby tee, standing side-ways before the mirror, looking at herself: hands trac-ing the contours of her belly, her willowy form surprisingly verdant, graceful legs and breasts and hips having somehow and dramatically crossed that imperceptible line between girl and woman.

Paul had gulped as Kyra had screamed that pierc-ing cry unique to teenaged girls that arcs into registers only dogs can hear, and Paul had beat as hasty a retreat as he could possibly muster.

She'd sulked all through dinner, wounded and affronted. Julie had been sympathetic, assuring Kyra that Paul hadn't meant to embarrass her while shooting him a bemused look that said, That'll learn ya. Paul had murmured mortified apologies and generally felt like hell. But it hadn't been until they talked later that night that she'd really nailed him. Again he'd fumbled apologies, but this time Kyra had met his gaze and had said, very simply, "Dad, a closed door is closed for a reason."

Paul stood before her door now. A closed door is closed for a reason. This one had reasons in abundance—her room had become part crypt, part shrine: untouched, unexamined. His hand hovered at the knob. Suddenly Julie's voice sounded beside him.

"What're you doing?"

Paul's heart skipped a beat; he turned to see his wife standing at the head of the stairs. She was still in her coat and scarf, looking as surprised to see him as he was to see her. "Nothing," he said, hand recoiling, then added, "you weren't here . . ."

"I was out," Julie replied, then turned and headed down the stairs. Paul followed her into the foyer. "The back door was unlocked," he said.

"Mmmm," Julie monotoned tiredly, slipping out of her coat and hanging it on the rack. No explanation was forthcoming. Paul caught a glimpse of a piece of paper protruding from the pocket of her coat, then watched as Julie moved away from him, into the kitchen. He followed; saw her pour a glass of wine from a half-opened bottle on the counter. Her movements were vacant, distracted. "How was work?" she asked absently, gazing at the middle distance, at nothing.

"Work was work," Paul said. "Jule, where'd you go?"

"What do you mean, 'Where'd you go'?" She shot him a

defensive look, her tone both weary and caustic. "What are you, my keeper?"

"What do I mean?" Paul said, on edge now, as concern polluted, turned ugly. He didn't understand, she wasn't helping, and it was pissing him off. "Jesus, Jule, I come home, you're gone, no note, the back door is wide fucking open. I'm just asking . . ."

"I was at *church*, okay?" she suddenly blurted, cutting him off. Paul stopped. She sighed, reiterated, "I went to church . . ."

Paul was shocked—whatever he'd expected to hear, that wasn't it. Julie was beyond lapsed Catholic, clear into *renegade*; she'd long ago rebelled against and abandoned what she'd always viewed as the hypocrisy of the Church. His reaction was as immediate as it was unchecked. "Mass?!" he said incredulously. "What the hell for?"

"You figure it out," she hissed, then put the glass down and stalked off. Paul watched, momentarily stunned, then followed her into the living room. Julie sat on the couch, elbows to knees, fingers steepled to forehead, tense and pensive. Paul stood before her.

"I don't get it—you go to church, and suddenly *I'm* an asshole?" he asked. "What's that about?"

"I don't want to talk about this," she said flatly.

"Why not?" Paul demanded. "Why not talk about this?" Cold fury uncoiled inside him, snaking through his guts. He felt it rise, wanted to unleash it—not at her, but at the world, at the universe . . . at God. "What good is the Church gonna do us, babe? You heard that jerk priest at the funeral . . . 'God needed Kyra in Heaven' . . . well, *we* need her *here*! The Church is full of shit!"

"It's not about the Church," she countered. "It's about God . . ."

"Oh. God . . ." Paul scoffed bitterly, and something inside him snapped. "Where was God when all this happened? What does God have to do with any of it?" He was pacing now, stalking the room like a chained dog. "I was there when Kyra died, Julie . . . God wasn't! I see people die every day—their houses burn up, their lives burn up, their families . . . they're all looking for God, too. But He's not there, either!"

"No." Julie shook her head, her gaze casting wildly. "No."

It just pissed him off all the more. The anger was subrational, feeding off itself. "You think you can go and light a candle, and God is suddenly gonna give a shit?" Paul spat. "It's been, what—fourteen, fifteen years?"

"Sixteen," she said, then looked up, her eyes piercing him. "Sixteen years, Paul. Since Kyra—" She stopped suddenly.

Paul looked at her, then realized. . . . Since Kyra was born.

And then it hit him.

His mind tripped back to the battle: Julie's folks on one side, Paul and Julie, the good girl gone bad and the bad boy made good, on the other. Her parents, however absent in their attendance, were still stalwart Catholics, and baptism was a must; Paul was just as obstinately agnostic, wary of in-law intrusion into matters of how they would raise their daughter, resentful of forced subscription to any belief whose credo was Give them your children till they're six and they were the Church's forever. Leaving Julie, poor Julie, caught in the middle, feeling emotionally hijacked by the mother of all parental guilt trips on the one hand, torn about her own misgivings on the other.

The harder her folks had pressed, the more bitterly entrenched things had become . . . until Paul and Julie had finally snapped, and she'd told her parents in no uncertain terms that they had decided to let Kyra decide for herself, when she was old enough to comprehend exactly what she wanted to do about her own immortal soul. It had been, for Julie, a stunning display of self-individuation. It had not gone over well.

But Paul and Julie had stuck to their guns, fully intending that, in the fullness of time, they would grant Kyra the right to determine her own spiritual fate. And they would be there to guide her, should she so require. It had been a great and noble plan.

But somehow, they had never gotten around to it . . .

Paul looked at Julie, the shared history flashing before them. Tears welled in her eyes. "She wasn't baptized, Paul . . ." Her voice was aching, poignant. "We always said we'd let her make up her own mind, but she never did, and we never did, and now . . ." The tears came, spilling down her cheeks. "So where is she now? Where is her *soul*?"

Paul felt the anger dissipate as quickly as it had flared— suddenly he felt shitty, exposed, vulnerable. He went to her, and they hugged, clinging to each other, seeking sanctuary in each other's arms. But there was none to be found.

"Where is my baby?" Julie whispered, a lost lament. *"Where is she now?"*

Paul just hugged her tighter. He didn't know. He couldn't say. He wanted to believe she was in a better place. He wanted to believe that there was a God who watched over the innocents of the world and kept them safe from harm. But he couldn't. As many times as he had walked willingly into mortal peril, Paul had always thought that wherever and whatever God was, they had a deal—whatever happened to him, God would take care of Julie and Kyra. The picture in his helmet was more than a talisman or good luck charm—it was a covenant, an unspoken agreement that Paul would watch God's back in the trenches, as God watched his above.

But now God had gone and broken the deal.

"Where is she?" Julie whispered, and began to sob. *"Oh, God . . . oh, God, please . . ."*

Paul held her, feeling utterly powerless, utterly wretched. Frustration and fury swelled and swirled inside him, laced with a sad and bitter pathos. Julie needed to believe. He could not. Miracles were beyond all hope or imagining; beyond burning bushes or parting seas or cheap wine transubstantiating into blood; as unlikely as his murdered girl walking through the front door. *If God was real,* he reasoned bitterly, *where was the proof?*

And that was when the telephone rang.

19

"**P**aul, get down here right away. We got something."

Buscetti's words were still ringing in Paul's ears as he arrived at the three-story brick building that housed Glendon PD, downtown division. He had come alone, Julie being in no condition to face whatever news awaited; Paul had left her with a lie offered only in mercy, a mumbled something about urgent business at the firehouse. Julie had accepted it without question and repaired to the scant comfort of weary sleep.

It was shortly after dark as he pulled into one of the diagonal parking slots lining the curb, jumped out and took the stone stairs two at a time. The darkened sky hung low and oppressive with heavy clouds, distant thunder rumbling like a rumor.

The detective was waiting for him on the second-floor landing as Paul bounded up, wired and winded. "Stevie, what's going on?" he asked.

"C'mon," Buscetti said, low, clearly not wanting to talk

yet. He led Paul through the cluttered confines of a once large and high-ceilinged room later subdivided to accommodate space for Homicide, Robbery, and Grand Theft Auto, with Narcotics, Vice, and Bunko residing in similarly cramped quarters upstairs. The resulting renovation managed to eradicate all the charm of the original architecture while creating a series of improbably truncated offices, all joined by a narrow hallway, each crammed to capacity with gray government-issue metal desks, gray metal filing cabinets, and gray metal chairs with gray vinyl cushions. The walls themselves were half wood, half wire mesh safety glass, presumably designed to lend an airy nature to the proceedings but which had the net effect of making everyone who worked there feel like something in a Kafka science project. The wood trim was painted gray. Buscetti once joked about how, if the city could figure out how to install gray air, they'd jump at the chance.

The two men headed down the row, past a half dozen denizens of the department's 4-12 shift engaged in the act of keeping the forces of evil at bay. Assorted others—victims, P.A.'s, uniforms, and perps—went about their business on the respective ends of the legal machine, giving information, filling out reports, taking or making phone calls, or sitting cuffed to a chair, awaiting their sorry fates.

There was another hallway at the end of the room, a perpendicular offshoot leading to an older and unmolested part of the building, which housed the euphemistically named interview rooms. Buscetti brought Paul up to speed as they turned the corner.

"This is an unofficial heads-up," he explained. "We picked him up about two hours ago. Figured better you hear it from us than off the news."

Paul nodded, his heart racing. Roughly twelve billion questions gridlocked his mind at that moment, but only one made it out.

"Who is he?" Paul asked, voice tight and dry.

"Wells," Buscetti told him. "His name is William Wells."

They arrived at a pair of wooden doors, set side by side. Behind one Paul could hear voices: muffled, angry. Buscetti opened the other one, revealing a small, darkened room the size of a walk-in closet. A two-way mirror loomed on the wall. Paul hesitated, looked at Buscetti. "Has he . . ." Paul began, ". . . has he admitted anything?"

Buscetti shook his head. "So far, he's been less than cooperative," he said sardonically, adding, "he did tell us to go fuck ourselves a couple of times."

Buscetti ushered Paul in, gestured to the glass. Paul stepped up to the window, his palms suddenly moist. Everything felt hyper-acute, oversaturated: the shadows deeper, the close confines of the room even more claustrophobic. His heartbeat thudded in his skull, his breath a staccato counterpoint. Since her death, Kyra's killer had taken a million different shapes in his mind, each more lurid than the last . . . *slavering wild-eyed crackhead dope fiend . . . lunatic escaped asylum inmate . . . sociopathic homicidal maniac . . .* and beyond, to forms inhuman, indescribable, nightmarish. But whatever shape they took, they all shared a common theme. All were brutish. All were savage. All were incalculably, irredeemably evil.

Paul stared, in shock. Through the looking glass he saw two detectives—a thirtyish black woman named Gardner and an older white guy named Parrish—circling a figure seated at a table. The suspect was clad in a battered black leather biker's jacket, his slightly built frame slouched in the chair. His T-shirt was dirty, as if from a scuffle, and torn at the collar, revealing a neck Paul instinctively felt like snapping. His face was downturned, pale and lupine features obscured by a shock of thick black hair.

The cops stalked the table, tag-teaming intimidation, their voices projecting muffled threat. Wells said nothing, kept looking at the floor. Parrish slammed his fist down on the table. Wells looked up.

And Paul got his first good look.

"Jesus," he gasped. "He's just a kid."

And it was true. William Wells, the monster at the heart of his darkest nightmare, Paul's very own angel of violent, untimely death, was barely old enough to shave. And not even old enough to vote.

His face was a paradox of angled bone and soft skin, youthful and hard by turns—a face caught in the crossfire between boy and man. A wispy bar of stubble graced the skin below his lower lip and down to his chin, the barest beginnings of what jazz musicians called a soul patch. As an attempt to project toughness it failed miserably, but it was not necessary: Wells's real edge was in his eyes. Dark, deep, heavy-lidded, his eyes stared at no one and nothing, radiating practiced indifference. They flared for the tiniest fraction if one of the detectives got too much in his face, like shades rustling in an abandoned building, revealing . . . something else. Then the blinds would go down again, revealing nothing. And, arcing across his left cheek, three faint furrows raking diagonally downward. The receding remnants of scratchmarks.

"Sixteen," Buscetti said. "We got his name off a second canvass at Kyra's school. First one turned up zip, but we went back and checked absences the day after . . ." He stopped, let the sentence trail off. "Anyway, his name was on the list."

Paul gulped. "He went to school with her?"

"Technically," Buscetti replied. "More like they sometimes occupied the same building with a thousand other kids. Judging from his file, school for him is just one more institution to go through before landing here. That's why it took us so long—we were looking for unusual absences. For him, it was just another day in the life."

"How do you know it was him?" Paul asked, still unable to comprehend.

"When we went to his house, he ran," Buscetti said. "Always a good sign. Had to chase the little bastard for a block and a half. Took a swing at us when we caught up to him." He paused, watching Paul watch the boy. "You recognize him? Maybe from the neighborhood, anything?"

Paul shook his head. He'd never seen him, never even heard of him. He regarded the boy slouched at the table as one would some rare and poisonous bug. "Does he have a record?" he asked.

"Dinky shit." Buscetti shrugged. "Shoplifting, curfew, misdemeanor possession, vandalism . . . regular upstanding little citizen in training. We went back and ran his prints off the squat in the Marley Street house," he added. "Got a hit off a beer bottle."

Paul looked from Buscetti to the kid and back. "So he did it," he said.

"Allegedly," Buscetti cautioned. "So far, we can put him at the scene, but we can't link him definitively to Kyra. He could have just been crashed there."

"But you think—"

"We like him for this," Buscetti said. "We're checking phone company LUDs to see if any of the calls to your house trace to him. Now we just gotta get him to give it up, preferably before he lawyers up."

"And how do we do that?" Paul asked.

Buscetti shook his head. "You don't do anything," he said adamantly. "This was a courtesy, Paulie, 'cause you're a stand-up guy, and we thought you oughta know. But anything beyond this is our job. Let us do it. You know the system. You gotta let it work."

It was an odd beat between the two men, a sudden underscoring of the dividing line. Paul's firefighter status meant nothing—he wasn't cop, thus not part of the empowered forces of justice. And his role in whatever happened next would be that of civilian, of spectator.

Buscetti put a reassuring hand on Paul's shoulder, feeling his friend's pain. "Go home, Paul. Get some rest. Be with your wife."

Paul nodded, thought of Julie, and how—even what—he could tell her of the sullen creature on the other side of the glass. Of how she would take it when she learned that their child had died at the hands of, however feral, another child.

In the interview room, Wells looked up, staring deadpan into the reflective surface of the glass. Though he could not see Paul, for a moment it seemed their eyes met. And there Paul saw not mystery but enigma. If the eyes were the windows to the soul, William Wells was not an empty house.

Something was in there, lurking in the shadows, like staring into the abyss only to find the abyss staring back.

Paul felt his blood run cold. His hands clenched into fists, unclenched again. He turned away. "I've seen enough," he said softly.

Just then, another detective entered, handed Buscetti a file folder. The label read *H4687 Kelly, Kyra LAB*. Buscetti nodded thanks, then opened it. "Lab analysis of tissue samples," he explained to Paul. Buscetti scanned the contents, nodded grimly.

"AB negative," he said. "It's a match." He looked at Paul. "We got him."

Paul's heart raced as Buscetti reached up and rapped the glass. The detectives in the room stopped talking. Paul watched as Buscetti exited, appeared a heartbeat later on the other side of the glass. He nodded to Gardner and Parrish; they hauled the kid up and cuffed him. Paul heard Detective Buscetti's voice in the tinny speaker . . .

"William Wells, you're under arrest for the murder of Kyra Kelly. You have the right to remain silent. If you give up that right, anything you say may be used against you in a court of law . . ."

They started to exit; Paul moved to the door. He made it just as they came out, Wells sandwiched between the interrogating detectives as Buscetti continued the Miranda.

"You have the right to an attorney," he said. "If you can't afford one, one will be appointed for you . . ."

They pushed past, heading for a stairway leading to booking; as they did, William Wells looked up, saw Paul staring at him. Though the boy's eyes remained flat and dead, his upper lip curled ever so slightly, into a faint but unmistakable sneer.

Then they turned the corner and were gone.

Paul made his way back to the outer stairs, feeling both chilled and weirdly elated. Buscetti appeared behind him just as he was descending. "Paul," he called out.

Paul turned. The two men shook hands. "Thanks, Stevie," Paul said.

"Glad you got to see it," Buscetti replied, then added, "he's being booked as we speak. You might wanna beat it before the vultures come." Paul nodded, pensive. Buscetti picked up on it.

"We'll nail him, Paul," he promised. "Right to the wall. Just give it time."

"Sure, Stevie." Paul smiled wearily, a thin and humorless gesture. "Sure." He gave one last baleful glance, then turned and went down the stairs.

Outside, Paul opened the truck door, paused. A chill wind had picked up, parting the gray cloud cover; the moon shone through, hanging high and silvery above the old brick building where monsters and their keepers dwelled. He shuddered and flipped his collar up.

Just give it time, he thought coldly. Of course. It was the only logical thing to do.

But as it turned out, it would take a little more than that.

PART | THREE

Smoldering

20

nd thus did the wheels turn.

For thousands of years, societies viewed murder as a fundamentally personal crime, justice belonging first and foremost, if not to the victim, then to the family of the slain. If the killer's family was not forthcoming—if members resisted or failed to act in accord with the needs of the aggrieved—a vendetta would ensue, a blood feud that could last untold generations.

As civilization matured and populations grew, it became in the best interests of all to find more civilized solutions. Tribal elders interceded on behalf of kith and kin, mediating the warring parties, seeking equitable resolution. If negotiations broke down, the feud would resume. Not just the murderer but the accused's entire clan was held responsible for upholding the conditions of a settlement, be it payment, in the form of gold, land, perhaps a virgin daughter offered in marriage, or other steps to ensure the future peace. A murderer who broke such a vow might well be slain by his own clan, for the common, if not greater, good.

As civilization progressed, systems inevitably evolved to codify and ascribe order. Under Anglo-Saxon law, a ninth-century code known as the *Dooms of Alfred* specified the actual price of a human life, as the killer paid a fine, or *wergeld*, to the victim's family, the exact amount arrived at through complex equations based on social status of the deceased. If the accused failed to pay, they were judged as demoted to outlaw status—rejected by all in the community, and fair game for any who would seek either bounty or blood vengeance.

In addition to the wergeld, the murderer was levied a separate sum, the *wite*, payable directly to the governing noble. In time, the wite outweighed the wergeld, so much so that by the twelfth century the reigning noble took the entire payment, sublimating any claim by the victim's clan. Murder was thus redefined, deemed a violation of the King's peace: a crime not against persons or family, not even against community, but against the ruling monarch. In so doing, the centuries-old relationship between killer's clan and victim's clan was destroyed—the bereaved held no special status, no right to compensation, nor had they any say in determining the killer's fate.

With the Industrial Revolution and the advent of the modern city, power to enforce the law, and indeed whom the law served, was increasingly transferred from ordinary citizen to paid professional. Police forces, prosecutors, judges, and penal systems inherited the right of action as the state became the offended party, solely entitled to seek and secure justice on its own behalf.

And here is what the loved ones of the murdered became entitled to as a result: exactly zip. Zero.

Nothing.

Click.

"*. . . Shock waves rocked the town of Glendon tonight, as authorities arrested a suspect in the murder of Kyra Kelly, a popular local high school student. The suspect, William*

Wells, was detained after fleeing from police who sought him for questioning in the death of Kelly, who was viciously murdered on Oct. 22 . . ."

Click.

". . . Wells, a student at Glendon High, was charged with the brutal slaying of the Kelly girl, after blood analysis provided a match to blood found at the crime scene . . ."

Click.

". . . Authorities as yet have no motive for the slaying. Sources close to the investigation report that Wells has refused comment on the charges leveled against him . . ."

Click.

"Tonight on Action 9: *'When Kids Kill Kids' . . ."*

Click.

The feeding frenzy churned. Carefully coiffed anchormen and pert anchorwomen projected ersatz earnestness, eyes flitting to teleprompters as they reported and opined, dutifully regurgitating factoids against boxed video graphics of chalk-lined silhouettes, pausing occasionally, post delivery, to add a woeful headshake or cluck of tongue.

It was the kind of crime hungry media types lusted for: smart, pretty, middle-class white girl cut down in the flower of her youth by bad boy loner from the wrong side of town. But as the story heated up, Kyra's image, already reduced to cipher or pre-broadcast lead-in tease, was increasingly pushed aside to focus on the new center of the unfolding drama: sixteen-year-old William Wells.

The *Post* screamed WILL KILL!, the *Daily News* trumpeted KID KILLER CAUGHT! Video vultures circled as Wells was hustled through the system, as arrest begat grand jury begat indictment, and on. Silent, sullen, and oddly photogenic, Wells was a perfect blank upon which to project an audience's deepest trepidations. And project they did, rendering him everything from soulless psycho to black leather Jekyll and Hyde, a symbol of a society increasingly afraid of its own progeny. Glendon collectively shuddered as it joined the sad ranks of places distinguished mostly by the spectre of violent and senseless death . . . humble places with humble names like Littleton and Jonesboro, Pearl and Padukah, Edinboro and Springfield, Bethel and Moses Lake. But what the crime lacked in body count or sheer spectacle of lurid firepower it made up for with brute intimacy—the deed had been done with bare hands—and a mystery compounded by the lack of easy answers . . . or any answers at all.

Preliminary psychiatric evaluations only deepened the enigma. School records indicated Wells was intelligent, with an IQ of 134, though he consistently had poor grades, even poorer attendance, and an almost pathological aversion to authority. Other diagnoses offered a host of criteria from the American Psychiatric Association's DSM-IV guidelines: 314.01, Attention Deficit Disorder. 312.8, Conduct Disorder. 313.81, Oppositional Defiant Disorder. 301.07, Antisocial Personality Disorder, and on. A mix 'n' match smorgasbord of dysfunction, and a perverse inversion of the maxim once popularized by a president's wife: It takes a village to raise a psycho.

Still, Wells did not fit the stereotypical profile of a teen killer. He was not addicted to drugs, not a gang banger, not the victim of sexual abuse, not the product of a broken home. Indeed, Wells's parents were cut from much the same blue-collar cloth as the Kellys: God-fearing, hardworking, frankly horrified at their only offspring's alleged crime, and unable to accept that their boy might be a stone-cold killer.

Equally mystifying was the fact that repeat canvasses of the neighborhood and interviews with Kyra's teachers, counselors, and classmates revealed very little that wasn't already common knowledge. Kyra was bright, pretty, a bit on the quiet side. A good student; honor roll, college bound. Lots of friends and acquaintances, no serious boyfriends, and no one who could rightly be called an enemy. Mildly rebellious of late, but nothing that didn't come with the territory of being sixteen. In a student body stratified into the usual grab bag of brains, jocks, stoners, bangers, dweebs, feebs, goths, and phreaks, Kyra Kelly was the oddest of social anomalies: a good kid, liked by all who knew her, able to transcend the social cliques, very much her own person, choosing her own path.

By contrast, Wells was the embodiment of nonachievement and poor social integration. A loner with no close friends, no compelling goals, no visible hopes or dreams, he seemed most noticeable by dint of just how *unnoticeable* he had been. There were no handy signatures to sharpen the collective hindsight on—Wells had no computer at home, nor had he demonstrated any capacity to cruise the Information Superhighway, thus no trail of Internet websites full of pornography and hate cults to pollute his impressionable mind; his CD collection was sparse and sporadic, with nary a Marilyn Manson or gangsta rap album in sight; no visible video game addiction, sodden with virtual violence and imaginary, media mayhem; not even a black trenchcoat to telegraph *troubled teen* to the masses. In all, a forgotten and forgettable kid, seemingly destined to grow up hard, go nowhere fast, and end up bad. Wells and Kyra were as different as night and day, and ran in different circles, with no overlap.

But there was the *fire* . . .

A small detail, disgorged by neighbors some seventy-two hours after his arrest. It seems William Wells had lit a trash barrel blaze the afternoon of Kyra's murder. The fire itself had been no big deal—papers burning in a backyard ashcan—and had been easily doused by the elder Wells without need of departmental assistance. But the ensuing argument between father and son had been bitter and divisive, and had ended with the younger Wells storming out into the coming night. No one knew what he had burned, or why. But the simple fact of it seemed proof enough of an unstable psyche.

As for William Wells—he offered nothing. No explanation. No confession. No denial. Not a word. It was not that he didn't comprehend his circumstances. Just that he didn't seem to care.

But unanswered complexities did not make for good copy, nor did ambiguities sit well with broadcasters accustomed to feeding pre-chewed sound bytes to a public weaned on getting the world in twenty-two minutes, sans commercials. People needed a ready answer, a slot in which to neatly fit the William Wellses of the world. And a week later, it came.

Click . . .

"*. . . shocking videotape uncovered in the tragic murder of Kyra Kelly. The* Action 9 *news team now takes you to Link Lenkershem, outside Glendon Hills High School . . .*"

Cut to Lenkershem, standing on the football field of the school, intoning dramatically. "*Concerned citizens of Glendon have puzzled over the death of Kyra Kelly since October 22, when Kelly's bruised and battered body was discovered barely clinging to life in a vacant house not far from here. Her senseless death has rocked this peaceful bedroom community, and everywhere, parents, authorities and educators ask . . . why? Now, a just discovered videotape may provide insight. . . .*"

Cut to jangly home camcorder footage of the same football field, at night, a home game in progress. A time/date stamp in the corner reads 10/15 8:37 P.M., one week before the murder. As the team huddles, the camera zooms and pans across the crowd in the bleachers. It zeroes in randomly on Kyra, cheering the team. Two rows back, William Wells watches her watching the game. Wells moves forward, touches her shoulder. Kyra turns and pushes him away, as the team breaks, and the focus shifts, and the game goes on . . .

Click . . .

The footage was recycled again and again, cropped and highlighted like Bill and Monica's beret-festooned hug, a moment in time, distilled to its visual essence: He reaches

for her . . . she pushes him away . . . . He reaches for her . . .
she pushes him away. . . .

He wanted her. She rejected him. He killed her.

Bim. Bam. Boom.

The media had found a neat label to hang upon William
Wells: *stalker*. The implied answer seemed to satisfy most.

With one notable exception.

Paul and Julie were in the kitchen, making food neither of
them would eat. A hollow gesture, born more of habit than
hunger, the meal would go from counter to table to trash,
flavorless, pleasureless, largely untouched. As it had the
night before. And the night before that. And the night before
that.

Paul placed a stir-fry pan on the stovetop and poured a
dollop of oil into the bowl. Julie stood at the counter, wielding a sharp paring knife in one hand as she sliced through
red bell peppers, making a neat little pile of moist slivers.
They worked in a robotic and concerted silence, driven by
little more than force of habit, the clatter of cookware and
rustle of foodstuffs deafening in the hyper-attenuated
silence.

Just then, the doorbell chimed. Paul and Julie looked up
and at each other—neither was expecting company. Paul
started to move first, but Julie waved him off.

"I'll get it," she said, putting the knife down and wiping
her hands on a dishtowel. Paul watched as she exited, then
turned his attention back to the stove. A blue gas flame lit
with a soft hiss, heat licking the curved steel surface of the
pan. He heard Julie's retreating footsteps in the background,
the sound of the front door opening. Then, nothing.

"Jule?" he called out after a moment. "Who is it, babe?"

No answer. Paul suddenly felt an irrational stab of anxiety. "Julie?" He stepped away from the stove, craned his
neck to peer around the hall door.

The front door was ajar, but no Julie. Paul felt his hackles
rise, moved quickly out of the kitchen and into the hall—but

as he closed the distance he saw first her hand, delicate fingers clinging to the edge of the door, tight gripped and white, then her body, slight frame hunched protectively in the space between door and jamb, as though trying to block the space.

"Jule, is everything okay?" he asked.

Then he was behind her, and saw that indeed it was not.

A man and woman stood on the porch, huddled against the evening chill. He saw the woman first—middle thirties and slender in a cheap Burlington overcoat, once pretty features rendered careworn, weighted with sorrow, skin pale and fair. A woman quickly being made old before her time.

The man stood behind her: maybe late forties but with a demeanor easily a decade older, gruff and working class, swarthy and craggy, a black and white man in a world of gray. His body language telegraphed extreme discomfort, like he'd rather be anyplace else; it was clear even at a glance that their presence was entirely her idea. It took Paul a moment to recognize them. Then his eyes widened with shock.

"Mr. Kelly?" the woman said, meeting his surprised gaze. "I'm Kathryn Wells. This is my husband, James."

The gruff man nodded, shuffling his feet. Paul stared, still in shock. Kathryn Wells took a tentative step forward and held out her hand; Paul felt Julie bristle before him in purely animal alarm. Kathryn sensed it as well, and halted. Her hand withdrew to smooth away strands of chestnut-colored hair threaded with premature gray.

"What . . ." Paul began, then stopped as colliding questions—*What are you doing here? What do you want from us? What the fuck is wrong with you?*—all came screaming to mind. But what came out instead was an absurdly polite "Can we help you?"

Kathryn Wells smiled wanly, thankful of even the most hollow civility. She looked from Julie to Paul. "We're very sorry to intrude," she said haltingly. The elder Wells shuffled in mute and grudging assent as Kathryn continued. "I just wanted . . ." She paused, rephrasing. "My husband and I wanted to let you know how sorry we are for everything that's happened."

"Really," Julie snorted derisively. "Feel better now?"

Paul winced as the words flew like poisoned darts, aimed straight at the Wells woman's heart. She took the hit and stood her ground, summoning every ounce of courage in her being. "I understand," Kathryn replied. "I know how you must be feeling . . ."

"I don't *think* so," Julie snapped, grievously offended. She drew herself up tight, arms crossed in defiance, bristling with barely repressed rage. "I don't think you have the slightest fucking clue how we're feeling right now."

"Please," Kathryn Wells started to say. "I didn't mean anything by it. I just meant to say—"

"I don't care what you meant," Julie said bitterly, cutting her off. "Just leave us alone, all right? Just go."

With that, Julie turned and slipped past Paul and into the house, leaving him standing there. Kathryn looked downward, and it struck him that it had taken a lot for her—for them—to reach out like that, offering solace, however misplaced, through their respective pain.

James Wells, on the other hand, felt otherwise. "C'mon, Kathryn," he said. As they turned away Paul heard him grumble, "Told ya this was a bad fuckin' idea."

Kathryn nodded dejectedly, and as she looked up Paul found himself suddenly struck by the resemblance between mother and son; but where the boy's eyes were hooded and distant, Kathryn's were wide and sensitive, brimming with tears. Their eyes met fleetingly. Then Paul closed the door, catching another glimpse of her through the laced curtain panel. And then they turned and disappeared into the night.

Inside, he could hear Julie in the living room, softly crying. The faintly acrid odor of smoke wafted from the kitchen, and Paul suddenly realized something was burning. *The oil,* he remembered, then raced back to the kitchen just as the smoke alarm triggered, a high, peeling tone filling the clouded air. Paul hit off the stove and grabbed a dishtowel, fanning madly at the air until the screeching stopped. The pan was blackened, burnt and spattered. Paul cursed and cracked open a window.

"Fuck," he hissed, glancing back at the counter, the waiting food. *The hell with it*, he thought disgustedly.

He wasn't hungry, anyway.

21

"So, we get this call last week," Dondi said over his beer. "Woman with chest pains on a third-floor walk-up."

Paul nodded, listening. "Then we get there," Dondi continued, "and she's *huge*. We're talking Jabba the Hut in a housedress: four-fifty, five hundred pounds, easy . . ."

Paul looked across the booth to Tom and Joli, who were sandwiched together like muscle-bound sides of beef. They nodded ruefully. Wallace the probie was there, too, relegated to a chair pulled up to table's edge. Dondi continued.

"She's sitting on this big sofa, and it's bowed in the middle, from the weight," he said. "She's got asthma, and tells us she's having trouble breathing. So I ask her, where's her inhaler? But she don't know. Says she hasn't seen it since yesterday."

The others snickered. Paul sensed a punch line coming; Dondi grinned wickedly. "So, we gotta get her outta there, right? But we can tell by just looking at her that if we lay her down on the backboard, we'll never get her up again." He took another sip of beer. "So, we grab her arms, figuring we'll get her standing, then slide the board between her and the couch and ease her back." He paused. "But when we go to lift her, out pops the inhaler from under her armpit. And she's like, 'That's where it went!' "

Everyone cracked up. Paul shook his head in amazement.

"Wait, wait," Tom chimed in, "it gets better. We're all standing there heaving and ho-ing, getting her on the board, and the TV keeps changing channels all by itself. But there's no remote—"

"So we're moving her out the door," Joli jumped in, "and Wally and I are on the down side heading for the stairs, trying to keep her steady, right? And the whole time her legs are rubbing together, making this *whuff, whuff* sound, and the TV's flipping back and forth, back and forth . . ." He gestured to the probie. "Then he looks up and shouts, 'There it is!' "

"There what is?" Paul asked.

"The remote," Dondi answered.

"Where?"

"Between her THIGHS!" the men shouted in unison, and lost it altogether. Wallace blushed; Joli slapped him on the back. Dondi added, "I swear to God. The top of it was sticking up like a little red eye between two canned hams. She thought something was wrong with her cable . . ."

Another blast of raucous laughter; Joli banged the table, made empty pitchers shimmy. Paul just groaned.

It was just after eight in the evening. They were esconced in a booth at the Gaslight Tavern, a bar and grill located some four blocks west of the Rescue One station. Situated in a former residential house rezoned for commercial business, it was dark and smoky and built for the business of helping cops and firefighters let off steam after a hard shift.

Mickey D., the Gaslight's owner and reigning presence, was a barrel-bellied lifer who ruled over the establishment with gruff efficiency. Amenities were basic—pool table, video poker, jukebox, a TV over the bar—as was the food, which featured hoagies, deep fried cardiac fare, and perhaps the worst pizza in the tristate area. But the booths were private, the bar honest to God mahogany with a real brass railing, and the drinks were both cheap and plentiful. Mickey kept a generous last call policy, especially to those on the job. And when non-smoking legislation threatened to snuff out butts in bars across the state save for private clubs, he sold memberships for a buck and renamed the joint the Gaslight Tavern Social Club.

At the moment, Paul was feeling pretty social. The beer was flowing. Johnny Lang was pumping on the jukebox. It was the first time he'd been out with the guys since it happened, and it felt almost like normal, his mind drifting for ten, even twenty seconds at a time without thinking of Kyra.

A dark-haired, full-hipped waitress brought a fresh pitcher, carted away the empties sprawled before them. Dondi winked at her.

"Thanks, Angie," he said, then hoisted the sloshing pitcher to fill everyone's mugs. "A toast," he said, raising his. "To Paul . . . good to have ya back, man."

"Fuckin' aye," Tom said. The others readily agreed, clinking glass with rousing good cheer.

"It's good to be back," Paul confessed. "I don't know how much more paperwork I could take." The others nodded. He had been on 9-to-5 in-house admin duty—filing and collating house reports, doing general scut work—since the funeral. Now he was back on full rotation—two days on, one day off, two days on, two days off. The first two were day shifts: 7 A.M. to 7 P.M.; the second set, nights—7 P.M. to 7 A.M., a total of forty-eight hours per. They had just completed the first round; the shifts flipped every other week. It was a crazy-making schedule, guaranteed to wreak havoc on personal lives.

But given where Paul's personal life was, it was almost a relief.

"You haven't missed much," Joli assured him. "Mostly more proof that Darwin was right." He nodded to Dondi. "Tell him about the plaster casters . . ."

Dondi grinned. "We go on a run, kitchen fire," he began. "We get there, and it's two old alkie queens making dinner. We put it out, no biggee. But then one of 'em starts in with abdominal pains. Turns out they were messing around with plaster of paris before dinner and one of 'em got the bright idea to take a funnel and pour it up his buddy's butt. But then it hardens, right? So we gotta take him to County, and they surgically extracted a perfect cast of his colon . . ."

Joli almost blew beer out his nose. "So the ER resident asks us what happened," he said, then pointed to Dondi. "And he says . . ."

Dondi replied, deadpan, "Guess he got more than his stovetop stuffed."

The others guffawed caustically. Wallace shook his head. "That was really bad," he said.

"That ain't bad," Tom countered, then looked at Dondi. "Tell him about Mr. Lucky." Everyone but Wallace started to laugh. The probie looked around, perplexed.

"Who's Mr. Lucky?" he asked.

Dondi wiggled his eyebrows and nudged Paul. "You tell him." Paul groaned; the others hooted and cheered him on. Finally he relented, leaning in seriously.

"About a year ago," he began, "the guys up at Iselin Rescue had this run: some guy was working on his motorcycle on his patio while his wife was in the kitchen. The guy was racing the engine, and somehow, the throttle sticks and the bike slips into gear."

The probie's eyes widened; Dondi jumped in. "So the guy grabs onto the bike, but it won't stop. And it drags him right through the patio door and dumps him on the floor inside the house. His wife hears the crash and comes running in, and she sees him on the floor, all cut and bleeding, the bike laying next to him, and the patio door smashed all to shit. So she runs to the phone and calls 911."

Paul picked it back up. "They lived on a fairly large hill, and the wife had to go down several flights of steps to the street to get the paramedics to her husband. The Iselin crew shows up, but there's too many steps to use the gurney, so they gotta use a stretcher. They haul him down and transport him to the hospital, while the wife stays home and tries to clean up the mess. She sweeps all the glass up, but then she sees all this gas spilled on the floor. So she gets some paper towels, blots up the gasoline, and throws the wad in the toilet."

The whole table snickered; Wallace was nodding like a dashboard doggie. Paul paused to sip his beer, and Joli jumped in.

"So this guy gets treated at the hospital, and gets released to come home. But when he gets home all of a sudden he's gotta take this horrendous dump, right? So he goes to the bathroom and sits on the crapper, and while he's there, he lights a cigarette. And he drops the match into the bowl."

It was Tom's turn. "Meanwhile, the wife's in the kitchen," he began, "when all of a sudden: Ka-BOOOSH! She comes running in and sees her husband lying on the floor, his pants blown clean off, and his butt roasted bright red. So she calls 911 again!"

Joli tag-teamed off him. "But the same crew ends up getting dispatched!" he said. "The ambo gets there, and they go all the way back up the steps, load butt-fried hubby back on the stretcher, and start hauling him all the way back down. And while they're going down the stairs, one of the guys asks the wife how the husband burned himself."

He paused; Wallace was transfixed. "What happened then?"

"She told 'em," Paul shrugged, deadpan. "And they started laughing so hard, they tipped the stretcher and dumped the husband out. He fell all the way down the steps and broke his arm in three places."

The four firefighters looked at the stunned probie. "Now THAT'S a bad day!" they cried. Wallace stared for a moment, then sneered.

"You guys are full of shit," he said.

Joli slapped him on the back; everyone joined in the raucous reverie. Everyone but Paul, who suddenly was no longer laughing. He was staring at the TV over the bar.

Dondi followed his gaze. On the tube, the fateful clip of Kyra and Will at the football game was broadcasting, sound off, the jukebox playing Lang's "Lie to Me" in accidental accompaniment. A beat later it cut to an image of Wells, handcuffed in County orange jail togs, being led to a waiting van.

"Jeez, Mickey!" Dondi called out to the bartender; Mickey D. looked up, saw the image, quickly flipped the channel to ESPN. He shrugged: Sorry.

But it was too late; Paul's mood was gone. The days since Wells's arrest had become a Skinner box of avoidance—avoid the TV, lest he be assaulted by video voyeurs; avoid newspapers and radio lest he fall prey to ambush by print or sound. He felt increasingly like a rat in a maze, turning endless blind corners, with nowhere to run, nowhere to hide.

Paul looked at his half-finished mug. "Son of a bitch," he sighed. The booth grew quiet. Dondi shook his head.

"Not for nothing, buddy, but somebody oughta whack that little fuck."

The others nodded in grim assent. "Fuckin' aye," Tom said. "Shrinks and dipshits all moaning about his problems, and the system's so fucked even if he does get nailed he'll probably do juvie time and be back on the streets, just as fucked up as ever. I'm sorry, Paulie, but it ain't right."

"Seriously," Joli offered. "Remember those little creeps in Jonesboro? Eleven and thirteen, they killed four students and a teacher, and they're gonna get released when they're what, twenty? Twenty fuckin' one? Records sealed, no hard feelings, have a nice fuckin' life, right?" He swigged his beer, and Tom took over.

"Yeah," he said, "I heard their shrinks said they're 'model' prisoners now, making the honor roll and everything. They just needed *help*. Well, whoop dee fuckin' *doo*. Nothing going on there that a dark room and a two-by-four couldn't fix."

"No." It was Paul's turn to shake his head. "No."

They all looked at him. "It wouldn't do any good," he explained. Paul glanced up, his gaze searching for someplace safe to land, found none. He realized they were just trying to help, but he couldn't go there. Couldn't allow himself to. "What gets me," Paul confessed, "is that it's all about *him* now. *His* problems, *his* rights, *his* needs. What *we* want or need doesn't matter."

"What *do* you want?" Dondi asked, suddenly sobered. It was a serious question.

"I want my daughter back," Paul said flatly. "I want to be able to tell her that I love her one more time. I want for none of this to ever have fucking happened. I want—" He stopped, features darkening as if overtaken by some sudden inner storm.

"I gotta go," he sighed. Paul drained his mug, then grabbed his jacket and scooted out of the booth. The men looked up at him.

"You okay?" Dondi asked.

"Yeah, I'm good," Paul smiled wanly. "See ya Thursday, bright and early."

They all nodded sympathetically. Paul zipped up his jacket, then turned and headed out, heading home.

But somehow, he never made it.

He meant to go home. He truly did. As he climbed into his car and started to drive, home was the destination in mind. Home to his wife. Home, even, to his goofy dog. Home to the life that was all that was.

But somehow he ended up on Marley Street.

Paul had no clear recollection of deciding to go there, no definitive moment of turning the wheel and steering toward it. It came almost as he was thinking of something else entirely. What was the saying? Life is what happens while you're busy making other plans. Indeed.

One moment Paul was in his truck; the next, he was standing on the dark, quiet street, tattered remnants of yellow crime scene tape still tied to the telephone poles, wafting in the breeze. One moment, he was telling himself, *You should go home, you should go home right now*; the next, he was on the porch, staring at the faded orange police sticker taped to the seam of the front door. One moment he was reading WARNING: DO NOT CROSS, spelled out in bold, black type.

The next, he was inside.

Strange, how quiet it was, it occurred to him. The interior

was as dark and chill as a crypt. Dozens of dusty footprints marked the floor, leftovers from police and crime scene investigators, like an army of ghosts or a diagram for some manic dance step since fallen from fashion. Paul looked beyond them, saw the Sheetrock, the plywood, the beams and nails and bales of insulation still stacked in the living room, the dining room, the hall. He flipped on a work light, hanging off a two-by-four stud. The exposed walls loomed: naked, ragged. Evidence of a job half finished. Paul moved through the house, through the living room Kyra would never see completed. The fireplace was dark and cold; Paul glanced at the mantel that Christmas stockings would never hang from, then moved on into the gutted dining room that would never host holiday dinners.

Paul came to the kitchen Kyra would never make meals in. In the corner, the basement door hung ajar. Paul pulled it open with a squeak, descended on rough and creaking steps.

Downstairs, in the belly of the house, more building materials lay stacked and sprawled across the cold concrete floor—plumbing and pipes, lumber, gallons of stain and paint and thinner. Paul had hoped to one day build a play room here, a family room. Now it lay inert. Useless. Paul sat on the wooden steps and stared into darkness, as snatches of conversation came back to haunt him.

"What do *you want?" Dondi had asked.*

"I want my daughter back," Paul had replied. "I want to be able to tell her that I love her one more time. I want for none of this to ever have fucking happened—"

Paul stopped. This was Kyra's house. It was meant for her. She was gone now, and forever. He couldn't do anything about that. But he could do something about *this*.

One moment, Paul had been driving home. *Life is what happens while you're busy making other plans.*

Paul stripped off his jacket, and started to work.

And so it began.

22

Over the next days and weeks, Paul seemed to all the world a changed man. Not happy—happiness would have been an unreasonable expectation—but less tortured, resolute, like an earthquake or hurricane survivor emerging from the wreckage to rebuild. On Thursday morning he arrived at the firehouse bright and early as promised and worked his shifts with patience and diligent good humor.

To the world at large it seemed that perhaps the brunt of the storm had been weathered. And should anyone ask, Paul would be the first to admit that it felt good to be back in the swing of things. We all live with the illusion that life is certain, he would say to any who seemed concerned, but deep down, we know it's not, and all we really have is today, and a dream. So we should live every moment like we mean it. If pressed—which he hardly ever was—he would confess that the source of his newfound strength was his love for his wife and daughter, and the need to honor Kyra's memory. He had become a veritable pillar of strength, quietly determined to make sense of the senseless, the only way he knew how.

On the job, this translated into a willingness to help, above and beyond the norm. When not actively engaged in the business of safeguarding property and saving lives, he was a figure in calm but constant motion, volunteering himself for the most onerous or mundane of chores without fanfare or complaint. He compiled work schedules, hydrant reports, training and NIFIR reports, monitored sprinklers and alarms out of service, took care of heating oil and supply deliveries, and managed administrative duties like a Fortune 500 exec. He polished company brass and chrome until it gleamed, cleaned kitchen and bathroom areas down to the smallest tile, became a demon for minutiae and care.

On the home front, his energies redoubled, covering both his and Julie's share of the myriad domestic mundanities with humility and grace, the depressive neglect quickly evaporating under his seemingly inexhaustible efforts. Even the Thanksgiving decorations emerged from storage, little pilgrims and turkeys popping up on the front lawn as if by magic. When a package arrived from Julie's mom—a little plaque that read GOD, GRANT ME THE COURAGE TO CHANGE THE THINGS I CAN, THE SERENITY TO ACCEPT THE THINGS I CANNOT, AND THE WISDOM TO KNOW THE DIFFERENCE—Paul called to thank them, and hung it in the kitchen over the sink.

As for Julie, while the passion in their union seemed guttered and dwindling in the wake of tragedy, Paul seemed just as intent on demonstrating that the home fires, though banked, still smoldered and would one day burn again.

And then there was his other project: the house on Marley Street. When not at work or tending to home, Paul returned, sans Dondi, spending every day off, every spare hour behind closed doors, laboring in solitude, occasionally emerging sweat-streaked and grimed to procure new building supplies. He removed the remnants of past violation, installed heavy-duty locks on doors and windows. Ordered some new how-to books. And began to build.

When Dondi offered to help, Paul smiled and thanked him but said no—this was something he had to do himself. It had become more than a simple restoration, more than protecting an investment or preparing a property for sale. It had become something both symbolic and personal. Something he was doing for Kyra. And for his own private need to restore order to chaos.

Dondi understood. Everyone understood. As the wheels of justice in what had become known as the Wells case ground inexorably on, Paul's actions were as understandable as they were ennobling. He was a survivor, valiantly attempting to rebuild his life. Everyone was rooting for him.

And no one dared dream of the wrecking ball coming.

Julie was screaming as Paul walked in: a wordless shriek of rage and lament that sent a jolt of adrenaline pounding through his system. Paul dropped the bag of groceries he was carrying, was running down the hallway before they even hit the floor, splattered eggs and squashed fruit rolling in his wake. It was just after four o'clock in the afternoon.

From the living room, a crash: a glass ashtray hitting the wall. Shrapnel clattered as Paul rounded the corner, saw Julie and Detective Buscetti standing, a stark tableau—one manic, one frozen in place. Julie's eyes blazed with fury. Buscetti looked at Paul, heavy with guilt.

"Paul, I'm sorry," he said. "We just got word."

"Word of what?" Paul demanded. His blood ran instantly cold.

Julie whirled. "He's *out!*" she spat. "He made *bail!*"

"WHAT?!!" Paul cried. "But the arraignment isn't until tomorrow!!"

"It got moved up," Buscetti confessed. "Some screw-up shuffle in the docket . . . we didn't even know until just before—"

"Fuck!" Paul hissed. "Are you telling me we just got screwed by a goddamn clerical error?" He was livid. He had come to know just how irrelevant the victim's family was at such proceedings, even when the accused's kin would be present, looking somber and well-dressed and playing to maximum empathy. The D.A.'s office had tried to keep them informed, even after the initial spate of headline-grabbing concern had ebbed. Paul had vowed to attend, no matter the abuse and added wound salt, just to represent his daughter, and perchance to look her killer in the eye. But these things happened. Now he had been cheated of even this moment, and by what? By clerks. By chance. By faceless bureaucracy. By the very system he served . . .

And that was when Julie started to cry—bitter, gut-wracking sobs. She stormed from the room, ran up the stairs. The bedroom door slammed, her torment continuing, muted, relentless.

Paul turned to Buscetti. "When did this happen?"

"About an hour ago," Buscetti said. "I tried to call you—"

"I was at the store . . ." He glanced at the table, saw his Nokia lying inert, turned off. He'd forgotten it. "God DAMN it!"

Paul shook his head, temples throbbing. The world was spinning. He could barely speak, barely breathe. He fumbled for a seat, head still shaking. "But how? . . ." he croaked.

Buscetti sighed deeply. Then he tried to explain . . .

It was not supposed to happen; in a just world it never would have. To Paul, the details were a swirling blur, as useless as they were labyrinthine . . . smart lawyer, stupid judge, youthful offender with no prior acts of violence and family ties to the community, charges knocked down from murder two to man one on the basis of evidence just circumstantial enough to foment reasonable doubt, overcrowded jails, parents who hocked the ranch to secure his five hundred thousand dollar bond . . . and on . . . and on . . .

It shouldn't have happened. It had. And William Wells was out . . .

He looked at Buscetti. "Let the system work, you said," Paul told him. "You call this working?"

Buscetti grew defensive. "I'm on your side, Paulie. This is totally fucked. But you know the drill."

Paul scoffed bitterly. "Yeah, right . . ." he hissed. "So, what's to stop him from just hiking off into the sunset?"

"He ain't going anywhere," Buscetti assured Paul. "He's gotta wear one of these." He reached into the pocket of his overcoat and handed Paul an odd little device, a heavy canvas strap with a cigarette pack–sized black box attached. A tiny row of LEDs ran across the face of the box. Paul regarded it skeptically.

"Tracking device," Buscetti said. "LoJack for scumbags. We lock it to his ankle, and he's got to wear it twenty-four-seven, and call in at least three times a day. He can't go more than three hundred feet from his house without us knowing about it."

"And if he does?" Paul asked bitterly.

Buscetti took the device back, flipped a little switch. Immediately the LEDs started to flash; a piercing trill filled the air. Buscetti shut it off.

"Tracking signal. He triggers the system, and we're on him in ten minutes, tops. Even if he tried to run, he wouldn't get far."

Paul scowled and lit a cigarette, blew an angry plume of smoke, tendrils curling from his nostrils as if he were about to breathe fire. "I feel better already," he said sarcastically.

"Look," Buscetti said, trying hard to assuage. "This is a raw deal, I know. And I don't blame you for feeling how you do. I just wanted you to know that we're doing everything we can. This ain't over yet." He paused. "What I need to know from you is, are you gonna be right with this?"

Paul turned and looked at him, sensing the double-edged tone of the question. "Is this two friends talking," he asked, "or is this a departmental concern?"

Buscetti looked hurt. "Friends," he said, then cautioned, "but also some friendly advice. I wouldn't want to see anything happen, make things worse than they already are."

"Worse?" Paul said flatly, then paused, looked Buscetti right in the eye. "Point taken, Detective." He underscored the D-word, then said, softer, "Don't worry about me, Stevie. We're the good guys, remember?"

His tone was flat, without warmth or friendship. Paul looked wounded and sad. Buscetti stood and turned toward the hall. Paul walked him out. As they parted, Buscetti paused, as if he wanted to say something else. But Paul cut him off.

"Just go," he said, low and cold.

Buscetti nodded. As he closed the door, Paul heard Julie

upstairs, crying inconsolably. He turned and started up, but as he was ascending, he caught sight of Julie's coat hanging on the rack. The piece of paper protruding from the pocket was still there, like a forgotten clue. Paul hesitated a moment, then crept down, gingerly withdrew it.

A pamphlet—dog-eared, one color, heavy stock. Across the top was the name Our Lady of Sorrows, and an address on Elizabeth Street. Beneath was an acronym, *F.L.A.M.E., Glendon Chapter.*

"Families of the Lost And Murdered, Empowered," he read, then, "Grief Counseling, Survivor Outreach, Welcome All." There was a list of meeting times and dates, some underlined. It took a moment for him to recognize that the underlined times coincided with his shifts.

Paul put the pamphlet back as he'd found it. He suddenly understood why she was going to church so much, and in a whole new light. She went without him; she went when he could not go. Grief had pulled them apart, swept them along on different currents—one washed on rivers of tears into the arms of sympathetic strangers; the other, swept just as surely into a more solitary place. She hadn't told him, maybe couldn't tell him, but he understood. Perhaps it was for the best.

There were things he couldn't tell her, either.

23

I t was exactly one week later, at 7:32 P.M., that all hell broke loose.

At 7:26, Dondi and Tom were upstairs at the station house, gearing up for the seven to seven night shift. Joli and Wallace were down in the ready room watching *America's Funniest Car Crashes* on TV. It was already dark out, the end of daylight savings having rolled back the days into premature night.

The bunk room was large and ordered, with a row of neatly made single beds on one side, a row of tall steel lockers on the other. A manhole-sized opening dominated the center of the room, from it protruded an old-fashioned brass fireman's pole, rarely used, but maintained in tribute to the house's history.

Andy Vasquez emerged dripping wet from the bathrooms, freshly showered and ready to rotate off, a towel wrapped around his thick waist, another draped over his head. Tom saw him and wolf-whistled. "Yo, Vasquez," he called out sarcastically. "When you gonna lose that gut?"

"Yo, DeAngelo," Andy mocked back. "When you gonna grow a brain?" He wiggled his ass provocatively.

Just then Paul entered, running late, looking pissed and winded. He was carrying a nylon ditty bag and cursing under his breath.

"Goddamn it," he muttered, angrily thumbing the combination to his locker. "Goddamn motherfucking son of a *bitch*." Conversation in the room abruptly ceased; everyone watched as Paul opened the locker, stuffed the bag in the bottom, then peeled off his coat and hung it on the hook.

Andy stopped towling his bristly hair. "What's hobblin', goblin?"

Paul shook his head. There were streaks of oil and dirt on his uniform. He grabbed a clean shirt from inside the locker, stripping off the old one. "Ah, nothing," he groused. "Just that I'm driving along, minding my own business, and all of a sudden my truck starts chugging like it's about to blow a rod. Fucker died on me." He looked down, saw spots of grime on his pants. "Shit," he hissed, then unbuckled his belt, stripping them off, too.

Across the bunk room, a palpable sigh of relief—this time, at least, disaster was of less than mortal scope. "You want me to call my cousin Julio?" Andy offered. "He's got a shop over in Elizabeth."

Paul shook his head. "Thanks, anyway," he said. "Triple A already towed it to a shop here. Mechanic said the goddamn oil plug was loose . . . engine was running almost dry. It's my fault—I should have checked it."

"Ouch," Dondi winced. "Is it gonna be okay?"

"Yeah." Paul sighed. "But they gotta keep it overnight. I had to rent a car to get here."

Andy glanced out the back window—sure enough, a dark Ford sedan was parked in Paul's slot.

Paul looked at the clean shirt, his dirty hands. He placed the shirt back in the locker, grabbed a towel. "I gotta shower," he said. "Sorry I'm late."

"Shit happens, bro," Tom said and patted Paul on the back. Paul headed off to the showers. The men waited until they heard the water running, then Andy whistled, low. "Had me worried there for a second," he muttered. "Never mind the truck—I thought *he* was gonna blow a hose."

Dondi and Tom shrugged. "Can you blame him?" Dondi countered. "Little bastard back on the street like that? I'd be fuckin' nuts."

"Fuckin' aye," Tom said. "I'd be on his doorstep with an axe handle."

Andy nodded. Point taken. In all honesty, he probably would, too—at least, he'd want to be. In the week since Wells's release, the house had watched as Paul bore the news with stoic resolve. People had stopped mentioning Kyra's name, subconsciously editing conversations about their own kids and families in his presence, lest they inadvertently trigger some buried trip wire. But Paul had been cool, enduring the injustice—only to blow up over a minor malfunction. "Guess it's gotta go somewhere," Andy said.

"Guess so," Dondi and Tom said, almost in unison. They turned and went down the stairs, leaving Andy standing, still wet. He opened the locker immediately adjacent to Paul's, started changing into his street clothes; the door swung back, obscuring the view to Paul's locker, as well as the fact that it was locked.

Suddenly, a commotion sounded downstairs. Three seconds later, Dondi bounded into the room, pale and distressed. Andy looked at him, confused. "What the—"

"Paul—" Dondi stammered. "Is he still? . . ." Then Dondi heard the water running, beelined for the bathroom. A beat later, the two men came out, Paul pausing just long enough to pull on his pants. Then he and Dondi took off down the stairs.

"Hey!" Andy called after them. "Will somebody please tell me what the hell is going on?" It was 7:31.

Sixty seconds later, they'd all know.

Click.

"*. . . Shocking new developments in the Wells murder case.*"

Link Lenkershem stands in a deserted warehouse district,

a graphic superimposed that promises *ACTION 9 BREAK-ING NEWS*. As the camera racks in he announces urgently, *"Action 9 has just learned that a manhunt is currently under way for accused teen killer William Wells. . . ."*

Pause for dramatic effect, as the camera pulls back to reveal police lights strobing red and blue in the background, uniforms and K-9 sweeping the darkness on foot.

". . . Wells apparently cut through the court-ordered elec-tronic monitoring device he has worn since his controversial release from jail last week. The alarm triggered approxi-mately one hour ago, when Wells violated the one hundred yard security perimeter of the device."

The camera centers on Lenkershem.

"Police tracked the signal to this empty lot on a barren stretch of Glendon's waterfront. State police have been noti-fied, and checkpoints are going up on all main roads. But for now, the question everyone is asking is, Where is William Wells?"

Click.

The room exploded with cries of shock and stunned disbe-lief, a swirling sea of anger and outrage.

"What???" Andy gasped.

"I don't fucking *BELIEVE* this!" Dondi cried out, fist pounding the table. Everyone looked to Paul.

But Paul just stood in the middle of the room, barefoot and shirtless, still dripping from the aborted shower. He stared at the TV screen. "Jesus . . ." he gasped. His hands started to tremble, not entirely from the cold.

On the duty desk, the telephone rang. Wallace the probie picked up. "Rescue One . . ." he said. He listened for a moment, then looked at Paul. "It's for you," he said. "Your wife."

Paul grabbed the handset, sighing deeply. "Julie?" He lis-tened, answering low. "I just heard . . . it's gonna be okay, baby . . . calm down, I'll be . . . okay . . . okay . . ." He nod-ded a couple times, then hung up.

His friends hovered worriedly. "Paul, buddy, you okay?"

Dondi asked gently. The others nodded, echoing concern. Paul shook his head, murmured, "I gotta go." He looked at the men. They all agreed; it went without saying.

Paul turned and walked toward the doorway leading to the stairs.

Pausing just once, to punch the wall.

24

Over the next twenty-four hours, press and TV crews again converged on the Kelly house like sharks scenting blood in water, barraging the already fragile couple with more lights and cameras and questions. Genuine anguish made good copy, a glimpse of real tears even more so: the if-it-bleeds-it-leads credo of news teams seconded only by if-it-cries-get-the-eyes. Wire services and networks picked it up, vaulting the scandal into fleeting but fervid national consciousness. But by seven o'clock the next evening, Paul and Julie were again left by the media wayside, their pain, like Kyra's death, having served its purpose.

The publicity reignited a firestorm of pressure as authorities mounted a manhunt that spread across the tristate area. William Wells's haunting features were plastered on wanted posters and beamed into living rooms from coast to coast. When the Fireman's Benevolent Association announced a five-figure reward for information leading to Wells's recapture and arrest, it was like dousing hi-test on a trash fire. False sightings and random rumors choked the Glendon PD switchboards, adding to the burden of an already beleaguered force. They were not alone; in nine separate incidents as far north as Greenwich, Connecticut, and as far south as Atlantic City, police cuffed and questioned suspected youths only to discover that, alas, they were not Wells but merely some other luckless teen loner.

It did not quell the fires. It seemed everyone was on the lookout for William Wells. But Wells was nowhere to be found. It was as if he had dropped off the face of the earth.

And in a very real sense, he had.

Cigarette smoke: blue and acrid, uncoiling toward the ceiling to join a haze that hung over the group of men and women who sat clustered together on folding metal chairs. They were young and old, working class and well-to-do, white, black, Asian, and Hispanic. Their commonality was manifest by shoulders hunched as though each alone was bearing the weight of the world, and the need of each to somehow talk about it.

"My name is Helen," a small blonde woman began, in a voice so quiet it barely registered. "And today is my daughter's birthday."

"Hi, Helen," a gentle chorus replied.

She was in her mid-thirties, once pretty, but with features rendered hard by regret and eyes that looked easily a decade older. She clutched a photograph of an adolescent girl who looked like a younger, more innocent version of herself.

"Three years ago," the woman continued softly, "she was raped and murdered by my ex-boyfriend." She paused, as though dredging up the words from some distant inner space. "He was addicted to methamphetamines, and she had told me he had started touching her, but I didn't believe her. I couldn't . . ."

Helen's voice cracked, eyes moist and glistening; as hands reached out to touch her shoulder she sighed deeply, as though willing herself to go on. "One night, I came home late from work. He had . . ." She paused again, shuddering. "I found her head in the freezer. He wrote the word 'bitch' on the wall in her blood. Her name was Amy. She was my baby girl . . ."

The woman lost it then, her grief overflowing into the smoky air. Some shuffled, moving to comfort her; others hung back, reluctant voyeurs. But they all knew the feeling.

Paul watched from a chair at the outermost periphery of the circle. The meetings held in the basement rectory of Our Lady of Sorrows were part liturgy, part recovery, a way for survivors to attempt to fathom the unfathomable. A hand-stitched banner hung on the cinder block wall, colorful cloth bearing the F.L.A.M.E. acronym, and the legend Better to Light One Candle. A long table sprawled before it, every square inch covered with photos, mementos, toys, and keep-sakes. Interspersed among them were little votive candles, shimmering in little glass holders, one for each victim. There were dozens.

An attractive woman sat at the center of the loose circle. She was a trim and indeterminate forty-something, clad in jeans and a loose black sweater, no makeup, dark hair swept back into a ponytail. "Thank you, Helen," she said, then addressed the room. "For those of you who are new, wel-come—for those who've been here before, welcome back." The others murmured hellos.

"My name is Nina," she went on, "and my son Trent was killed five years ago in a convenience store holdup. Families of the Lost And Murdered, Empowered, was founded in the hope that we, the survivors, might help each other to cope, to help, and to heal. Our motto is "Better to light one candle than to curse the darkness," and it is in that spirit that we invite Helen to light a candle in memory of her daughter."

Paul watched as Helen stood and made her way to the impromptu altar; he watched as she placed the picture of her dear dead daughter named Amy amongst the others, then lit a candle to join the pyre. As she returned to her seat and sup-portive hugs, others came forward, each sharing their night-mare, each more horrifying than the last . . .

There was Cindy, the lovely blonde NYU graduate, shot dead in a Jersey City carjacking, her brilliant brains splat-tered across the windshield of her candy apple red graduation present. There was Donald, the successful young lawyer from downtown, brutally murdered by a secretary turned closet crackhead who had stolen office equipment from the firm. There was Jason, who had picked up a hitchhiker on his way home from work, found days later with his throat slit, the transient having helped himself to Jason's car, his wallet, and his life . . . and on, and on . . .

. . . and with each tragedy came the tales of injustice compounded: of killers jailed or free, or never found at all; of victims whose final, fatal price had been but downpayment on further degradation as their memories were sullied and slighted by bungled prosecutions or crafty defenses . . . of the reasons offered, be they drugs or bad tempers or bad mommies or inflamed passions . . .

. . . and Paul listened as, through it all, one question burned bright in his mind. The question he had in mind as he cleared his throat and began to speak.

"My name is Paul," he said, noting how eyes widened as they recognized it. "Four weeks ago, my daughter was murdered. Last night, the . . . person . . . accused of killing her escaped. The police are searching for him now."

Across the room, nervous whispers and shuffling of feet. Paul continued. "My wife can't stop crying," he said, "and I lay awake nights thinking that there must have been something I could have done . . . to protect her, to prevent it, something. I keep looking for the answer . . ." He paused. "But I haven't found it yet."

Across the room, heads nodded. Neither had they.

Paul ran out of words then; he looked to Nina, who directed him to the table, where a virgin candle awaited. As he touched flame to wick, he wished a wish so deep it might have been a prayer: Let me find it, please . . . Let this show me, somehow . . .

The candle flared. Paul saw its light reflected in the eyes of the others, knew that their pain was his pain, their anguish amplified in his own. But the candle was just fifty cents of wax and string in a cheap glass holder, from the housewares section of Target. There were no epiphanies there.

He'd have to find them elsewhere.

* * *

Outside it had started to snow, a fine white dusting, luminous in the streelight glare. Paul drove carefully, keeping to just under the posted limit. Making his way not home but to Marley Street. It was just after nine.

He had stayed to the end of the meeting, sharing tears and hugs with the other grieving souls, promising to come again to those who'd asked, accepting telephone numbers from those who'd offered, should he need to talk.

Nina, in particular, had wished him well. "You're a good man," she'd said and given him a hug. He had thanked her, and meant it. The tears and hugs had been genuine enough; his reasons for staying, slightly less so. He had waited with engine running as the last of the group had piled into their vehicles and pulled away. He had done what needed to be done in public.

And now it was time to do the rest of it.

Darkness. Silence. The sound of ragged breathing.

The boy stirred, eyes fluttering open, then coughed violently. For a moment, he thought he was dreaming. It took him another four seconds to figure out that, though his eyes were open, he could not see.

"Wha—" He began to sit up. His head throbbed; his brain felt like cotton gauze soaked in tar. "What the fuck? . . ." he managed, tongue thick and swollen. Groggy, disoriented, he tried to piece memory together.

He'd gone outside, was walking to the bodega two doors down, to buy some smokes . . . still within the hundred yard limit . . . suddenly an unmarked sedan, dash light strobing . . . pulled up beside him . . . cop . . .

The boy reached out, felt a rough wooden bunk beneath him, solid and unyielding. He stood, legs weak and wobbly; as he did, he realized that the ceiling was close enough to touch.

The driver motioned him, get in . . . getting roused, fucking pigs, whatever . . . he climbed inside . . .

The boy reached for his shoulder, felt it throb; suddenly, he realized the walls were close, too close—with arms spread he could almost touch either side. Pitch black space, surrounding, confining.

A moment of shocked recognition . . . not a cop, not at all . . . struggle . . . sudden jab of pain . . . rush . . . burning . . . blackness . . .

"What the fuck??" he said again, louder, his heart starting to pound. He took a blind step forward, banged his shin on something hard. The pain jolted him even as he lost his balance, toppled forward.

The crash was deafening in the tiny space; the boy reached out, felt stout wooden legs: a chair, secured to the floor, thick leather straps attached to its arms and legs. Panicking now, the boy crawled forward. His head smacked something cold and ceramic: desperately he clawed at it, adrenaline flooding his consciousness. He recognized the shape—a toilet. Lidless. Sloshing.

"Hey!" the boy cried out. *"HEY!!!!!"*

His own voice battered his ears. He turned and felt his way, Braille-like, in the opposite direction, past the chair and the bunk, until he came to another wall. Like everything else, it was solid, unyielding. He could vaguely make out the seam of a door, but no handle. He pounded it with his fist, tried to kick it. As his foot reared back, the thing on his ankle he thought was the tracking bracelet clattered. He reached down and felt his naked leg, a cold metal shackle secured to a length of chain against his skin.

And that was when William Wells fully woke up.

"Where am I?" the boy yelled hoarsely. "Somebody? Anybody!!!" He pounded the walls.

"Where the FUCK am I????"

Paul Kelly stood in the red brick bowels of 514 Marley Street. There was a small sink before him, a sooty mirror hanging over it. He felt bad about the lying, the inevitable deception to his wife, his friends, the world at large. Everything had worked so far; it was surprising how people saw what they wanted or needed to see. But it was all necessary, under the circumstances—terribly, regrettably necessary.

Paul ran some cold water, leaned down to splash his face. As he came up he caught a glimpse of his reflection. The face staring back through murky glass looked the same as it had the day before, and the day before that, and the day before that.

"A good man," he murmured. "You are a good man." His reflection offered no argument.

Muffled rage sounded in the background. Paul glanced at his watch—9:23. *Coming off the drugs, right on schedule,* he thought.

Paul turned and gazed at his creation. Standing amidst the crumbling brick and exposed wiring of the basement was a box, sitting nearly a foot off the ground, measuring some eight feet wide by ten feet long by six feet high. Sturdily built, heavily reinforced, sheathed in insulation and ventilated, the box was soundproof, lightproof, completely impenetrable. A door was cut into the side facing him, snugly fitted with recessed hinges and a slot through which food might be passed. Power lines and plumbing snaked from the basement proper up through the box's raised subfloor. It was a sensory deprivation prison, a self-contained universe for one.

And William Wells was trapped inside it.

Paul stepped up to a little control panel, pushed a button neatly marked mic. Wells's muted voice instantly blared from a mounted speaker. *"HELLLLP!!"* he cried tinnily. *"LEMME OUTTA HERE!!!!"* Paul flipped the intercom off. Sans amplification, Wells's cries and thrashing were tiny, distant things. He would not be heard from the street, not be heard by anyone but Paul.

He looked down, saw his abraded knuckles. Punching the wall at the firehouse had been a bit over the top, but what the hell—he'd read it in a novel, once upon a time, and it had seemed an appropriately dramatic touch.

It had been surprisingly easy, in retrospect—once you made up your mind, the rest was mere choreography. Faking a breakdown. A rented sedan. A portable dashboard fire chief's light. A hypo of sedative pilfered from the firehouse's med stash. Dumping the tracking bracelet had been the trickiest part, because of the time factor, but Paul had cut it off Wells's ankle and tossed it into the lot with mere minutes to spare. Again, necessary. To throw them off the scent. So far, it appeared to have worked.

And now, here they were.

Paul turned; his tools were laid out on the workbench. He had his spare medbox, books on psychology, medical and psychopathology texts, and the how-to books he'd ordered, which inclined toward other types of projects entirely: cheaply reprinted bootleg manuals on CIA and KGB interrogation techniques, courtesy of an obscure press in northern California that expressed its First Amendment imperative by publishing things like manuals for hit men and mercenaries.

Paul smiled grimly, not from joy but from a sense of renewed purpose. As a firefighter and paramedic, he had years of experience bringing people back from death's door; taking someone there would not be a problem. Again and again, if need be.

We're the good guys, remember? he had told Stevie Buscetti. *You're a good man,* Nina had told him.

And it was true. Paul didn't want to punish. He didn't want blood, or vengeance. He wanted the answer to the question that had seared his mind since he watched his daughter's casket being slowly lowered into the earth. He wanted to know *why*.

And Paul was willing to do anything to find out.

Anything.

PART | FOUR

Controlled Burn

25

CHAPTER III: BASICS

Though the following chapters deal with interviews necessarily conducted outside the scope of recognized legal authority, all points reflect back to one major theme: control. It is imperative that the interviewer establish absolute control immediately and decisively over the subject, and seek to reinforce or enhance control at all times as the interview progresses. The exact amount necessary will vary greatly from subject to subject: pain thresholds, fear of bodily harm, and overall unwillingness to cooperate can greatly influence the duration and severity of the interview.

Time is also a factor: longer captivity allows for greater ability to "build" the requisite atmosphere; shorter sessions often require a more immediate escalation to achieve peak cooperation. But proper establishment of initial dominance assures the interviewer the best possible chances of success, and must be achieved without fail.

* * *

Paul stood over his daughter's grave. "Hey, kiddo," he said softly. "How's it going?"

It was a cold day, a thin crust of snow softening the rolling mounds of granite that comprised the cemetery. Paul knelt and placed a bouquet of fresh cut flowers into a little holder at the base of her stone, gently removing the now dead ones left by Julie. He stood and surveyed the effect: improbable color in a bleak landscape, a rumor of spring against impending winter. Distant traffic hummed in the background, but as far as Paul could see, he was the only living soul there.

"Sorry I didn't come sooner," he said to the stone. "I think of you all the time . . . I guess I just didn't know what to say."

Paul stopped, fighting back emotion. Kyra's grave seemed small, somehow—a narrow plot of sodded-over earth sandwiched between older, more established plots. The sod had not taken root, and wouldn't for months. It made her grave look unfinished, almost temporary . . . along with her temporary headstone, a small, flat, granite marker set into the chill, unsettled earth. *Kyra Anne Kelly, Beloved Daughter, Forever Missed* was carved in its polished surface with mute finality, along with the dates of her birth and death.

Paul winced. He could barely bring himself to look at it. They had never really thought about family resting places to begin with, had certainly never considered the ghoulish logic of where to bury their child. You worried about planning for a thousand other things—about health care and day care and summer camp and college scholarships. In fitful midnight panic attacks, you lay awake stressing over crib death and poisoned Pedialyte and stranger abductions and hit-and-run accidents, about drug dealers or satanic preschool cults or gang drive-bys, or any of the thousand and one mundane disasters Paul saw every day. In the absence of catastrophe, you worried about whether she'd be happy in the fullness of her life, whether her deepest, dearest dreams would one day come true, or what kind of creep she'd eventually bring home and call her one true love.

But not this. Never this.

So, when it had happened, they had acted in desperation, finding the nicest place they could afford, on a scenic bit of hill at the outer edge of the cemetery. The staff at Blessed Rest Funeral Home had done everything they could to ease the trauma, getting a temporary stone carved, even though Kyra's final headstone wouldn't be ready for months.

"We, um, got a place near you," he murmured, pointing back to the edge of the ever-expanding rows. "So we'll always be close." It struck him then that all fanciful notions of retirement to the Keys, or taking that mystical cross-country road trip, or ever leaving this place, were gone—the future, in all its unwritten mystery, had winnowed down to this. Eternal rest on the installment plan. Paul sighed and shook his head.

"There are so many things I wanted for you," he said, ephemeral wishes for school and college, career and marriage, children and grandchildren, all wafting away in the chill fall air. "I wish . . ." He paused, voice choking. "I guess I just wanted to say that Mommy and Daddy love you very much."

Paul stopped speaking, listened to the hum of heedless noise. He brushed stray snow from the surface of the stone, mindlessly tidying the memorial, then turned and walked away.

He never mentioned Wells, or the box.

Some things he couldn't tell even her.

CHAPTER VI: SIGHT

Light is an easy stimulus to control. Subjects can easily be kept in total darkness in actuality, or by use of blindfolds, heavy canvas bags (such as a mail sack), or hoods. In any event, one clear benefit is that total deprivation provides the interviewer with the option of revealing his identity, and prohibits the subject from later identifying either his questioners or location. But light deprivation is also valuable for heightening disorientation and general sense of vulnerability. Penal systems worldwide regularly employ use of solitary confinement, aka "the hole," for just such a purpose.

Similarly, intensely bright light can be equally disorienting and intimidating. "Spotlighting" subjects by use of bright lights in the face is a common feature of interviews, and intensifies the notion that the victim is both controlled by the interviewer and the center of the interviewer's attention. Flashing lights, such as strobes, can increase disorientation, and if properly timed, can induce headaches and even seizures in certain subjects.

Alternation of periods of total darkness and very bright light can often work where one or the other does not. Irregular alternation over long periods of time further disrupt the subject's circadian rhythms—the natural sleep cycle—leading to intense disorientation, paranoia, and fear.

In extreme cases, where temporary physical blindness is desired, the subject can be disabled by suturing of the eyelids. Where permanent loss of sight is not an issue, there are a variety of techniques that can be employed, ranging from chemical to thermal to surgical. See Chapter IX for details.

There were rules, he decided. There had to be rules.

Paul had wrestled with this more than anything. While the building of the box could almost have been considered an elaborate fantasy, done in a virtual fugue state of grief, Paul had taken a step that could not be taken back. The list of crimes he had already committed boggled the mind—assault, kidnapping, reckless endangerment, and a D.A.'s wet dream of other offenses—but the awareness only served to underscore the seriousness of his quest.

Indeed, it was weirdly clarifying. Paul was a man accustomed to dealing with situations, never one to shy away from a difficult or dangerous task. His entire life had been dedicated to helping others, putting his own life on the line for people he didn't even know, often didn't even want to know. He accepted the risks willingly, even eagerly, for as much as it was due to any notion of altruism it was the chance to test his own limits. To push himself, even to the breaking point, in pursuit of something worthwhile. And what, he reasoned, could be more worthwhile than this?

Paul descended the basement steps, a tray of food in hand. For the first time since Kyra's death, he felt something approximating control. It was an emotional high-wire act, and, paradoxically, the only way across was to remain as unemotional as possible. It couldn't be about mere vengeance, he told himself, not some Charles Bronson *Death Wish* fantasy writ large. Vengeance would not give him what he sought. And what Paul hungered for was something altogether harder to come by. He would find it.

But there had to be rules.

First, the simplest and most obvious. No one must know. No one must even suspect. Not as hard as it might seem, given the devastation of normalcy in the wake of the tragedy—no one really expected Paul to behave "normally," or even presumed to know what such a thing would be under the circumstances.

Public furor had largely and gradually dissipated after Wells's disappearance. The manhunt—for all its best-laid plans and honorable intentions—had gone nowhere, Kyra's killer proving more elusive than anyone had hoped. After a week, it was quietly decided that one dead girl, however popular, simply could not warrant the ongoing allocation of already limited resources; there were budget cutbacks and manpower issues to deal with. The case was left open; Detective Buscetti alone was left to carry the torch.

Deprived of a neat finish, the news media packed up and headed off to redder pastures, drawn to the next exciting installment in the ongoing cavalcade of atrocity that was its sustenance. Indeed, it was possible to watch Kyra's memory slip from public consciousness like a ship sailing over the horizon, as column inches gradually shrank into oblivion and TV coverage was back-burnered into the *America's Most Wanted*-style unsolved mysteries.

Paul divided his time between work and home and the house on Marley Street, just as he had before. The emotional gulf between him and Julie had become a chasm: lost in her own turmoil, she rarely questioned his departures. Which left Paul that much more time to concentrate on the task at hand.

The next part was considerably more complicated: a step-by-step wearing down of psychological walls. Paul knew from observation at the police station that Wells was well armored against mere intimidation. So he had resolved to break him the old-fashioned way: bit by bit. The drugging, while effective at first, was a short-term solution—a drugged Wells might be pliant, but Paul required full participation from his subject. And there were other ways to achieve that.

There was sensory deprivation, to keep Wells off balance. Inside the box, there was no day or night, no clocks or way of marking passage of time. Nothing but maddening blackness. The bunk was short and narrow, to keep whatever sleep he could manage uncomfortable and fatiguing. Deprived of REM sleep, the boy would become malleable; likewise with the anxiety and fear. All designed to break through resistance. Or so the theory went.

And then, there was hunger.

Paul moved toward the box, set the food down on the workbench. There was a control panel mounted near the intercom button on the outer wall, a series of single pole throw switches, along with common household timers. A tape deck was wired into the system. Paul pressed the com button. From inside the box, a hiss of silence. He listened a moment, ascertained that the boy was sleeping.

It was showtime. Paul took a deep breath, steeling himself. Then flipped the switch.

*   *   *

CHAPTER VII: SOUND

Do not underestimate the efficacy of sonic disruption on the subject, especially in conjunction with other deprivation techniques. While somewhat more subjective than other sensory stimuli—e.g., loud noises may not disturb a city dweller as much as a rural subject, or a young rock music enthusiast may not be as susceptible as an elderly subject— proper use of varied wide spectrum sound and noise can be an important adjunct to overall conditioning.

The key considerations are frequency, decibel level [see figs. 1a and 1b] and associative influences. Extremely high and low pitched sounds can be utilized to varying effect. Extremely loud noises can jar sleep patterns; in the case of solitary confinement, extremely soft noises—ex. the sound of rats—can enhance overall feelings of unease.

Associative sounds—those which are clearly recognizable to the subject, i.e., the cries of loved ones or sounds of general trauma and chaos—can all be highly effective. Be creative.

Inside the box, the world went shrieking white, as lights recessed into the ceiling suddenly glared to life, hidden speakers simultaneously blasting a recording of a fire alarm, like the world's loudest alarm clock. Wells screamed and fell off the bunk, trying to shield his ears and eyes. The ringing stopped. Wells scrambled for cover, disoriented, as Paul opened the door and stepped inside.

"Wakey, wakey," he said humorlessly, placing the tray of food on the chair. The door hissed shut behind him, closing with a heavy click.

Wells struggled to his knees, blinded by the sudden onslaught of light. His leg chain rattled against the floor. He looked up at Paul, through dark hair now matted with sweat.

It took him a moment to place the face, then Wells's eyes suddenly widened with fear and loathing.

"You," he gasped. "Why are you doing this to me?"

"Why, indeed," Paul admonished, cutting him off. He glanced at his watch. "Feeding time. You've got five minutes."

Wells squinted, saw a dry baloney sandwich, an apple, a little carton of milk. Lockup fare.

"Fuck you!" the boy spat and swept the food from the tray. The meager rations flopped onto the floor; the milk carton hit the wall and split open, bleeding white.

Paul watched impassively. "I read your psyche reports, you know," he said. "IQ's what . . . one thirty-four? You're a bright boy." His tone was perfectly calm, almost conversational; the look in his eyes was decidedly less so. He leaned in. "So who's fucked here, me or you?"

Wells glared back, eyes adjusting. "I want my lawyer," he said. "I got rights."

"Rights?" Paul sat on the arm of the chair, feigned looking around. "Sorry," he said. "No rights here. No lawyers, either. Guess it's just the two of us." He gazed down on the boy.

"The cops," Wells said defiantly, clearly nervous now. "They'll be looking for me . . ."

"Oh, they're looking," Paul replied. "You're a fugitive from justice, Will—mind if I call you Will?"

"I don't care what you call me," Wells hissed.

Paul shrugged. Whatever. "As I was saying," he continued, "you're a fugitive. You jumped bail and ran."

"I didn't run," Wells countered. He struggled to get up, fell backwards weakly. "You fucking brought me here. You did this to me . . ."

Paul brought a mocking finger to his lips. "Shhh," he whispered, then added, "our little secret. Right now, they're looking for you everywhere." Paul smiled grimly. "Everywhere but here."

He paused, let the reality of it sink in. "See, as far as the world is concerned, this place doesn't exist," he said. "And since you're here, that means *you* don't exist. You're out there somewhere." Paul gestured to the world outside the box. "You're a rumor. And what happens next is up to you."

The boy glared at him, slit-eyed and wary. "What the fuck are you talking about?"

"I'm talking about, you killed my daughter, shithead," Paul hissed. "And you have to answer for it. To me."

The boy's eyes widened; his dark hair was matted with sweat and distress. "You're crazy . . ." he said.

"Maybe so." Paul shrugged. "But then, where does that leave you?" He glanced at his watch. "Time's up," Paul said. "We'll talk more later."

Paul picked up the tray and moved toward the door. As he did, Wells suddenly lunged, clawing at Paul's leg. Paul wheeled and smacked Wells in the head with the tray. The boy collapsed, head banging against the floor. As he crumpled, Paul pulled a key attached to a thin metal chain from his pocket, inserted it into a slot in the door. The door unlocked; Paul stepped outside.

"Hey!" Wells cried out. Paul turned. "I'm hungry!" the boy said plaintively.

Paul looked at the food scattered and squashed on the floor. "So, eat," he said, then added, "pity about the milk, but there's always water, if you get thirsty enough."

Wells looked at him questioningly, then followed his gaze to the toilet. He looked back at Paul, shocked.

"Bon appetit," Paul told him.

Then closed and locked the door.

26

"Daddy . . . ?"
     The house was burning, thick clouds of smoke choking off all light, all life, all escape. The girl's voice rang out, beseeching. Paul fought his way through the blackness of the hallway, searching.

"DADDY!"

She was crying now, terrified. Paul tried to call out to her, his own voice muffled in the heavy SCBA gear. He couldn't see her, but she was close. Very close.

Fire crackled unseen before him, lost in roiling smoke. He could feel its lethal power, blistering heat baking his skin beneath the heavy canvas gear. Paul fought his way forward inch by tortured inch, checking doors. Desperately he pulled his face mask up, smoke searing his eyes. "HANG ON!" he cried. "I'M COMING!!!"

"DADDEEEEEEEE!!"

The girl was somewhere just ahead: trapped. Doomed. Paul moved faster, pressing forward. The fire roared hungrily above him. Paint bubbled on the ceiling, timbers crackling overhead. Paul reached the last door, pushed. The door would not yield; it was jammed, warped. Distorted.

Paul reared back, ploughed into it with all his might. The door cracked and gave way . . .

. . . and Paul suddenly stumbled into his daughter's bedroom, saw Kyra standing before the mirror, flames all around her. She looked at him and screamed, hands outstretched, as the mirror cracked and shattered and the flames raced up, engulfing her . . .

And Paul woke up, sweating, terrified. Alone.

His heart pounded as subconscious flames abated. He was lying in his bed in his bedroom in his home, pre-dawn light rendering shadows coolest blue. A stab of yellow light emanated from the bathroom door, which was ajar. Beyond it he heard a tiny sound of glass breaking, and Julie cursing quietly.

Paul got up on shaking legs, made his way to the door.

"Jule?" he called out. "You okay?"

He pushed open the door, found Julie seated on the fuzzy covered oak toilet seat, barefoot, in a thin cotton nightgown. The box containing her medical supplies was open on the sink; two glass ampules of insulin lay broken at her feet, liquid oozing on tile.

"I'm all right," she said quietly, grabbing another ampule, trying to load the hypo. Paul knelt and scooped up thin shards of glass, disposing of them in the trash. As he stood he saw her hands trembling. "Shit," she cursed and blinked once, twice, trying to focus. She was palpitating, looking like she was going to faint.

"Here," Paul said. He took the insulin pen from her hand, then lifted one side of her nightgown until her hip was exposed. As she leaned back he grabbed a cotton ball from the jar on the sink, doused it with isopropyl alcohol and swabbed her skin, then stuck the little 29 gauge needle in.

Julie breathed hard for a moment, then gradually brought it under control. Paul felt her forehead. "You need to eat something," he said. "What's your blood sugar?"

Julie shrugged listlessly. Wrong answer. Years of experience had taught them both that a pre-meal "take action" level should be no more than one-forty, with a hemoglobin A-IC count not above eight; hers had lately been cruising the one-seventy to one-eighty range, with an A-IC pushing double digits. Not good.

Paul reached into the medicine cabinet, withdrew her blood glucose meter: a little blue-and-white digital device that looked like a fancy stopwatch with an EZ read LCD screen, and a zippy little logo that read *Accu-check*. He checked her out, waited for the meter to register.

"One-ninety-seven," he murmured, reading the meter. "Shit." Paul felt her forehead—she wasn't feverish, which was good. The insulin would stave off immediate disaster. "Why don't you get cleaned up," he said gently. "I'll make us some breakfast."

As Paul tidied up the mess, Julie looked at him with tired eyes. "You were dreaming," she said.

"What?" Paul replied, busying himself.

"Just now," she said. "I heard you. You were mumbling something over and over . . . 'Hang on, just hang on . . . ' "

Paul shrugged it off. "Just a bad dream," he said.

Julie smiled wanly, the irony in her voice as deep as the shadows under her eyes.

"Are there any other kinds?" she asked.

Paul went downstairs, made coffee, toast, filled a pot with water and set eggs to boil.

She's got to take better care of herself, he thought as he worked. *Diabetes is nothing to screw around with.* Left unchecked, the litany of horrors was impressive: heart disease, blindness, kidney failure, and more. Beyond the daily regimen, exercise was good, but Julie's aerobics had gone out the proverbial window. Weight loss was no longer an issue; it was all she could do to keep the weight she had, and she had easily dropped five pounds from the stress. Stress was bad—and that they had in abundance.

Huevos boiling, Paul went back upstairs and started to make the bed. Julie appeared in the doorway, showered now and wrapped in a towel, looking gaunt and frail. She leaned against the frame, watching him. Paul pretended not to notice, kept working, diligently erasing all traces of sleep. Finally, she spoke, her voice curiously flat, like the verbal equivalent of a thousand yard stare.

"How do you do it?" she asked.

"Do what?"

"Remain so invulnerable," she replied. Paul paused in mid-tuck, then continued.

"I'm not . . ." he said, adding quietly, ". . . invulnerable."

"Aren't you?" she countered. "Making the bed, making breakfast, working at the station, working here, working at that damned house. Kyra's gone, and that little bastard is *out* there somewhere, and I have to keep reminding myself that one breath follows another, and you just keep working like nothing's wrong. So how do you do it, Paul? What's your secret?"

Paul bristled at the word *secret*, tried not to show it. He didn't know what to say. Saying anything felt dangerous, like unleashing something inside himself, and as much as he wanted to go over and hold her, he wanted to push her away. He kept his distance, masking wariness with weariness.

"Maybe I don't have the luxury of falling apart," he told her. "Maybe I'm afraid if I stop, *it* will."

Julie shook her head. "Typical," she murmured, then moved toward the rocker, picking up her robe and slipping it on.

" 'Typical'?" Paul said incredulously. "What's *that* supposed to mean?"

"It means sometimes I think I know you," she answered, "then sometimes I look at you and I don't know you at all. But by then, you're usually off trying to save the world."

"I'm not trying to save the world," he muttered. "I'm just trying to make some sense of it."

"But what if it doesn't make sense, Paul?" Julie replied. "What if it just . . . doesn't?"

Their eyes met again. Paul didn't have an answer for that. At least, not one he felt comfortable, or capable, of sharing. Julie looked at him—she seemed incredibly tired, incredibly fragile. He desperately wished he could open himself to her, instinctively sensed he couldn't. In their almost twenty years together, the ability to talk to each other was, in his estimation, one of their greatest gifts. Paul and Julie could always talk about anything, from metaphysics to *Mystery Science Theatre 3000*, with equal aplomb. It was the heart and soul of their intimate rhythm, and it kept them solid, kept them tight.

This, too, had been taken.

Paul said nothing, but went to her and hugged her, wrapping her slender form in his arms. She hesitated a moment, then buried her head against his chest, hands coming up to clutch at his back. There were tears in her eyes, tears in his, and though neither cried, they stood, hearts beating within inches of each other, yet light-years apart.

Paul held her as close as he possibly could.

And never felt farther away.

27

The doors to Mercy Emergency burst open.

"Got a fourteen-year-old G.S.W. to the head," Paul called out as they maneuvered the cart down crowded hallways. Strapped to the sheets was an adolescent boy in brightly colored sweats and hundred-and-fifty-dollar Nikes, blood seeping from under the bulky white pressure bandages obscuring his features. It was their fourth time in tonight, and it was only nine-thirty.

The ER team scrambled as Paul and Dondi rattled off stats. "Pulse one-sixty, b.p. one-thirty over palp, rear entry wound," Paul said. Dondi concurred, adding, "Small bore, maybe twenty-five caliber, left frontal lobe. No exit wound. The bullet's still inside."

"Bangers?" Linda Lopez, the attending physician, asked warily. She was a pretty, overworked woman in her late twenties; her brow creased as she loped alongside the cart, dark hair brushed hastily back, white lab coat already soiled from the evening's travails. It was more a tactical consideration than anxiety: it was common for gang shooters to finish what they started, even to blowing away rivals while they were still in surgery.

"Nah," Paul said. "Somebody wanted his shoes."

"Nice," Lopez mumbled, peeling back the bandage. Blood jetted from the wound, spritzing the corridor tiles. They rounded the corner into Trauma; the orderlies wheeled a fresh cart alongside and scrambled into position. Paul and Dondi stepped back—they were the grunts to Emergency, who in turn were peons to the OR surgeons and higher-priced specialists. Lopez leaned over the boy, peeled one eyelid back and shined her penlight into the glassy orb. The pupil irised down, stared blankly.

"Pupils nonfixed but nonresponsive," she said to her team, then added, "call up to OR, tell 'em to prep for neuro, see if Henderson is in. I need X-rays, CAT-scan, blood-gas and tox screens, intubate him, IV saline and Lidocaine." She paused, looked at Paul and Dondi. "Has anybody notified his family?" Heads shook all around. Lopez shrugged.

"Okay, on my count," she ordered, "one, two, three . . . lift!" In unison the Trauma team hoisted the boy up, laid him on the table. One of the orderlies pulled off the victim's blood-spattered sneakers and tossed them to the floor, then began cutting away the gore-streaked sweats.

Dondi rolled the cart out into the hall. "No offense," she called out to him. "But you guys don't have to save the whole world single-handed."

"Yeah," Dondi said, rolling his eyes. "Tell him that."

But Paul was already gone, wheeling the cart back down through the maze of pain, heading for the exit and the waiting rig. Dondi shrugged; Lopez turned back to the waiting abattoir. The door swung shut behind her.

Paul was standing outside the entrance, staring into the night, as Dondi stepped through the doors. The horizon glowed yellow, courtesy of the sprawling Exxon refinery banking the distant Hudson.

"You ready?" Paul asked.

"Yeah, sure," Dondi replied sarcastically. "I was just thinking if you have a stress-embolism, we could take a break."

"Come again?"

"It's a joke, son," Dondi grumbled. "A pathetic stab at humor?"

"Oh," Paul murmured.

Then climbed into the rig.

The drug house on Helm Street was an abandoned five-story brick structure on the dilapidated waterfront a quarter mile from the sight of William Wells's ersatz vanishing act: a defunct shoe factory turned homeless squat, long condemned but popular with transients, addicts, and street dealers.

Though periodically swept in raids, both location and consumer demand kept it viable; as tastes changed from ganja to coke to crack to meth, so, too, did the caliber of its clientele, going from mellow to twitchy to tweaked in an ever sinking cycle of despair. Finally, a handful of underground entrepreneurs decided that supply and demand need not feature costly imports, especially when five hundred dollars' worth of readily available, if highly volatile, chemicals could be cooked into five thousand dollars' worth of extremely addictive product. A cottage industry was born. It had been thriving for months.

At 11:47 that night, it blew itself straight to hell.

The initial explosion was of teeth-cracking intensity, setting off car alarms and rattling casements for six blocks. By the time Rescue One first deployed some seventeen minutes later, the fire was already licking out shattered windows on floors two, three, and four, and the building looked on the verge of an inferno. Toxic smoke billowed skyward, black and gray and ash white. Within the hour, Engine and Ladder companies from Elizabeth, Iselin, and Jersey City were called in for backup, along with every available ambulance and Rescue crew in the area. It was still not enough.

Paul and Dondi descended from the fifth floor in the basket of an Iselin aerial tower truck. Mack engines growled as the articulated boom pivoted like a one-hundred-and-fifty-foot steel arm, arcing out to clear the fire streams surging up from the attack teams below, then sweeping down to allow the men to offload their damaged human cargo. As the basket gate opened, Wallace rolled a gurney forward to meet them, looking completely freaked. Paul shot him a look.

"Get over here!" he barked.

The probie wheeled the gurney into position. Paul and Dondi reached down to the floor in tandem; a beat later they hauled up a bundled form in a bunker drag, using a blanket to avoid putting undue contact on the victim's limbs. They laid their load on the gurney as gently and quickly as possible, then wrapped the edges of the blanket over to shield the body.

"CLEAR THE WAY!" Paul called out. The three men rolled across the lot and into the street, dodging rubble, charged hoses, and other firefighters as best they could. The air was thick with the hiss and roar of water and fire; with stinking smoke, stinging spray, and cacophonous blasts of sirens, with shouting and garbled radio cross talk. With every bump and jostle, the victim moaned piteously.

They reached the Rescue One rig, which had set up on the outer periphery of the chaos. As the first unit on scene it had won the dubious honor of de facto way station for the evacuation of the injured. A cordon of police cruisers stretched past them to the end of the block, forming a convoy channel, lights strobing asymmetrically.

Andy Vasquez was on-site as Paul and Dondi approached, filthy, raggedly out of breath. He was off shift but had raced over to help.

"I caught the call on my scanner, got here as soon as I could," Andy said, then glanced around, looking for Tom and Joli. "Where're the steroid twins?"

"Still inside," Dondi said, hocking a loogie of black spit onto the sidewalk.

"How bad is it?"

"Total cluster-fuck," Dondi said, shrugging out of his breathing apparatus. "Someone was cooking crystal on the second floor, and it went boom. Blast pancaked floors three and four."

Andy looked back at the blazing building. "How many vics?"

"Not sure," Paul said. "Too many." He stripped off his own gear, gestured to the bundle. The men gathered round, each grabbing a portion of the blanket. Wallace hovered nervously. "Grab the gurney," Paul told him. "When we lift, pull it out, quick." The probie nodded and grabbed ahold. The men heaved to, opening the blanket and lifting, as Wallace hauled the gurney out and wheeled it to the side. He turned back and stopped, in shock. "Jesus," he murmured.

The thing on the blanket was once young and female, but it was almost impossible to clearly discern age, gender, or even race. Her hair and most of her clothing were seared and scorched off the blistered, cindered flesh; fingers, toes, ears, nipples, and facial features had gone molten, lumpen, like a wax mannequin pulled from an oven. Wisps of rancid smoke wafted off ruined dermis. She was burned almost beyond recognition, unconscious, oblivious. But she was still breathing.

Wallace whirled and promptly vomited. Paul ignored him, checking for vitals as Andy grabbed the medbox and Dondi went to radio the Fire Chief. "Second and third degree thermal and chemical burns," Paul said.

Wallace recovered, looked at the men. "She gonna make it?"

Paul didn't answer, scanning the scene. Other victims in varying states of destruction were bundled and huddled and waiting, a grim chorus line. "Christ," he muttered. "Where're the fucking ambos?"

Just then, a distant whoop, as the first Jersey City ambulance turned the corner at the end of the block, coming up the flashing gauntlet. In the background, another dull thump shook the building—a chemical barrel going up like a fifty-five-gallon bottle rocket. Dondi came around the corner of the rig.

"Chief wants us to stay and pee gee the vics," he said. "Let the other crews transport."

"Fuck," Paul hissed, then looked to Andy. The ambulance was threading its way toward them. "Hit 'em up," he said. "See what you can scrounge. We need more shit."

"You got it," Andy said, then took off to meet the incoming crew. Wallace looked to Dondi, confused. "What's 'pee gee'?" he asked.

Dondi looked from Paul to the kid.

"Play God," he replied.

Triage. Fourteenth-century French, original meaning, *to sort according to quality.* A fancy term for playing eenie meenie miney moe with other people's lives.

For the next forty-five minutes they worked down the line prioritizing mortality. Paul headed the triage, Wallace in tow, laboring feverishly, trying to stay focused.

High priority: breathing, stopped or labored . . . bleeding, severe or uncontrolled . . . head injuries, severe . . . cardiac arrest and stroke . . . shock, severe . . . abdominal or chest wounds, open . . .

The injured screamed or moaned or sat, rocking with shock and shivering in the cold. There were plenty to go around—a ragtag assemblage of the lost and the worthless: dealers, pipe heads, needle monkeys and quim queens, bound by bad luck and bad habits, their newfound value assigned by rude logic that dictated the worst come first.

Secondary injuries: burns . . . multiple fractures, open or closed . . . spinal injuries . . .

Ambulances came and went in a steady stream, loading as many as each could haul before howling off into the night. Paul assessed and moved, assessed and moved, tagging those they could treat, queuing those he couldn't, working his way down.

Low priority: minor fractures . . . minor cuts and bruises . . .

Until the process came perversely full circle and Paul found himself at the proverbial end of the triage line: the lowest of low priorities. It was the point rescue crews called "paramagic" because there was nothing short of miracles left to do . . .

Lowest priority: Injuries so severe that death appears certain or has already occurred . . .

And no one embodied that concept more starkly than the burned girl.

"Holy shit," Paul muttered as he knelt beside her, motioning to Dondi; Dondi hustled over as fast as his bulk and exhaustion would allow. If they had had time to think, which they hadn't, they would have thought she had already died. But the girl rasped weakly, tenuous life clinging stubbornly in the face of doom.

"She going out?" Dondi asked.

Paul shook his head. "I think she's coming to," he said.

"No way," Dondi countered.

"Way," Paul said, stripping off his coat and placing a stethoscope to her chest. The dermis had gone sticky with lymph secretions, the body desperately trying to cloak its ravaged vulnerability; scorched and sightless eyes fluttered, consciousness swimming up from oblivion. The girl began to moan.

"Shit," Paul hissed. Death was a foregone conclusion, but the mere idea of awareness returning to such pain was beyond comprehension. He saw Andy's medbox, the name VASQUEZ stenciled in black across its top. He turned to Wallace. "Check Andy's box for a stinger," he said urgently.

Wallace looked at him like Huh?, then dug into the medbox, came up empty. Paul pushed him out of the way, delved inside and withdrew a small plastic packet with a short, capped needle attached—morphine, military-issue, courtesy of Vasquez's Army Reserve contacts.

Paul uncapped the needle, found a spot of relatively uncharred thigh, stuck her up. The girl moaned again as the drug kicked in, less a cry than a final exhalation. They watched as she seemed to visibly deflate, narcotic dreams overtaking the nightmare of her final moments. Two hours before she was a street ho trading blow jobs for blow, somebody's wayward wife or mother or sister or daughter. Not anymore.

Paul covered her body with the blanket and stood wearily; Dondi patted him tiredly on the back. In the background the inferno was at last yielding to the efforts of the various crews. The roof of the building collapsed inward under the weight of tons of pressurized water, sending up a vast fireball of sparks, the flames winnowing down to smoke and hiss and char. Paul told Wallace to get a body bag off the rig; as he hustled off, Tom and Joli came around the side, damp and dirty and high on adrenaline and fatigue, in obscenely good cheer.

"Man oh man oh man what a motherfucker," Tom chortled. "D'ja see that thing go?"

Wallace came back bearing a bundle of thick black zippered plastic. Paul took it, started unfolding the bag on the ground. As he did, a stray gust of chill air blew the edge of the blanket, exposing incinerated skin. "Damn," Tom whistled low.

"Bitch got big time Kruegerized," Joli remarked caustically. "Fuckin' Nightmare on *Helm* Street."

The men snickered and groaned. Paul stood. And punched Joli square in the face.

The blow landed hard, crunching brittle bone and cartilage, knocking Joli flat on his beefy ass. Joli's nose geysered blood; he grabbed it in shock. "Jethuth Chrith!" he bellowed through mashed sinuses. "Kelly, you thyco fuck! You bwoke my nothe!"

"Shut up," Paul growled. "Just shut up."

Joli leaped to his feet; Paul stood his ground. Dondi, Tom, and Wallace instinctively placed themselves between the two, holding them back. "Knock it off!" Dondi warned, pushing Joli back.

"Me?!" Joli bitched. "It wath a fuckin' joke!" He glared at Paul, pissed and hurt; Paul glared back coldly. Dondi grabbed Joli, checked his hammered schnozz. "You'll live," he said, then turned to Tom. "Take care of him," he ordered, then said to Wallace, "Start policing up the gear. Now!"

Tom and Wallace nodded and headed off, taking the wounded Joli, who was still holding his nose. As they left, Dondi turned to Paul.

"Jesus, Paulie," he said. "What's your fucking problem?"

"Sorry," Paul muttered, feeling suddenly embarrassed, exposed.

"Yeah, well, sometimes 'sorry' doesn't cut it," Dondi replied sternly. "You were outta line."

Paul nodded; he knew. "I'm gonna have to write this up," Dondi said. "Sorry."

"Yeah." Paul sighed. He looked away; in the distance, the last of the survivors were being packed off. The auxiliary Engine and Ladder companies were packing it in, rolling hoses and stowing gear, their task, for the moment, done. The disaster was finally, if tacitly, under control.

Which was more than Paul could say for himself.

28

Paul swung a hard right, fist landing with a heavy thud. Then a left-right-left combination, followed by a flurry of jabs. Sweat flecked off his back and shoulders as his arms pistoned onto target, the low ceiling beam from which the heavy bag hung creaking with impact. He was back on Marley Street, getting himself in the mood for the next round. And he was pissed.

Truth be told, mostly at himself. He still wasn't sure why he had snapped like that—he knew as well as any of them that Joli's joke had been born not of malice but of adrenaline. Joli was an overgrown child, and lame humor was just his way of blowing off steam—soul Teflon. Like his morbid fascination with slasher movies: make-believe horrors, to keep the real ones at bay. Juvenile, but harmless.

"Stupid," Paul hissed. "Stupid, stupid, stupid . . ."

He slammed the bag again and again, punctuating words with blows. Joli could afford to be an idiot: Paul had no such luxury. That he had lost it was irrefutable, and the ride back to the station house had been marked by a tense and awkward silence. Later they'd made amends, Paul apologizing to everyone in the sincerest of terms; Joli had sniffed through taped proboscis and shrugged it off, had even joked that it might earn him some sympathy points with lithe Liza the next time they rolled into St. Anthony's. They'd shaken hands and embraced, replete with standard issue male bonding two-pat back slaps, and all had been forgiven. But Paul had seen the look in their eyes—a fleeting hint of distrust.

And that was inexcusable.

Paul stopped swinging, mopped his brow with a towel. His breathing and heart rate were up, thudding in his skull; he took a series of long, deep breaths, willed himself calm. As he did he vowed that he would not be so careless again. He could not afford to make mistakes. And whatever was going to happen next must occur quickly. The bag twisted on its chain, winding and unwinding from the violent momentum. Paul watched it until his heart rate leveled off; then he donned his shirt and combed his hair.

"That's it," he muttered. "No more fucking around."

Paul grabbed ahold of the bag, made it stop.

Then turned his attention to the box.

CHAPTER VIII: HUMILIATION

Cases may arise in which the interviewer encounters continued resistance from the subject despite best efforts and application of less invasive techniques. In such instances, strategic use of humiliation may be desired before resorting to more irrevocable physical force.

Maximum exploitation of humiliation depends upon a basic knowledge of the subject's cultural and moral biases. Techniques range from simple verbal abuse, to more elaborate psychological and physical violations. But while effectiveness can only be truly ascertained by careful study of the subject, certain techniques can be universally applied, such as stripping, forced contact with urine or feces, or various forms of disfigurement, ranging from temporary to permanent [see appendix viii]. While the mere threat of such action is often sufficient, with particularly determined or recalcitrant subjects, action may be considered a must.

A soft click as a ventilator fan kicked in. Then, lights: blinding behind recessed wire mesh. Paul entered, carrying a paper bag and his spare medbox.

Will winced and sat up on the bunk, dazed and confused. He was a shadow of his former badass self—lupine features drawn even deeper by captivity, black hair matted and disheveled. His clothing was gone, his lean form clad only in dirty underwear and a coarse but threadbare wool blanket. He had long since lost all sense of time, the solitude punctuated by random and jarring sonic assaults, clanging alarm bells, sounds of explosions, car crashes, screams, machines grinding, babies crying. All part of the calculated effort to break him down.

Will withdrew into a defensive fetal position as Paul put the box down, looked around. The rim of the toilet was crusted with filth and vomit; even with the ventilator humming, the air inside was thick with the stench of body funk and fear. Thin smears of blood greased the walls. Paul made a tsk-tsk sound.

"Stinks in here," he said, almost conversationally. Paul pulled a little remote control from his pocket, thumbed a button. The lights dimmed a notch, enough for the boy not to have to shield his eyes. Will did not look up, but his eyes warily tracked Paul's every move.

"Din-din," Paul said, tossing Will the paper bag: out fell another miserable little sandwich and a little carton of juice. The boy hesitated a moment, then hunger overtook him. Paul watched as Will wolfed down the food and gulped the juice.

Paul then produced a small paper cup of varied colored pills. "Vitamins and antibiotics," he explained. He held out the cup, rattling it. Will didn't move. "We can do this easy, or hard," Paul admonished. "Up to you."

Wells reluctantly took the cup. Paul smiled thinly as he swallowed the pills. "Very good," he said. "Now, get in the chair."

Will regarded him suspiciously. Paul explained, "Rule number one: you do what I say, when I say. It's not negotiable." He softened somewhat, adding, "Besides, I need to check you out. No good you dying from infection before we're done. Now, move."

Will glared at him for a heartbeat, then got up from his bunk, legs unsteady, and sat in the chair. As he did, Paul grabbed his arm, began securing it with the leather strap. Will freaked, tried to struggle.

"Hold still," Paul ordered, then reached for Wells's other wrist as the boy strained. It was no contest. Paul strapped his other arm down, then reached into the box. The boy's eyes widened with fear, but Paul came up with an innocuous first aid kit. He squatted on his haunches and looked at the boy's knuckles: the skin was raw and abraded.

"Beating the walls again?" he asked. Will said nothing. Paul shrugged, applying antiseptic to the scrapes.

"Not gonna do you any good," he continued. "I built this. The walls are two inches thick. The chair? Built that, too. Anchor bolts are three inches long." Paul pulled out a stethoscope, checked Wells's pulse and respiration. "You could beat on it 'til the cows come home; it ain't going anywhere. And neither are you. Not until we've had a nice, long talk."

Paul put the stethoscope away, then looked Will right in the eye, trying to remain emotionally level. "So, tell me, Will," he said, "why did you do what you did to my little girl?"

Wells looked up, met Paul's gaze. Suddenly the boy hocked deeply and spat in Paul's face. Paul turned just as the wad hit, thin spittle grazing his cheek and trailing off in a ropey string. He stood and pulled out a handkerchief, wiped it off calmly. Then he punched Will once—a short, sharp jab to the solar plexus.

He pulled the punch at the last second, the blow landing less to inflict pain than to make a point. But Wells sucked wind and wheezed, torso crumpling in on itself. Paul's jaw clenched, then he exhaled deeply, composing himself.

"Rule number two," he said flatly. "You get back what you give out. And then some."

Paul reached into his box, pulled out a blood pressure cuff, and strapped it onto the boy's bicep. As he pumped it up, he continued. "Now that was a perfect example of non-productive communication," Paul told him. "We can go round and round like that all night if you like. But remember rule number two . . ."

Wells wheezed some more, trying to shake it off; when his head cleared, he glared at Paul with a hatred cold enough to freeze marrow. Paul unwrapped the blood pressure gauge, then stood. He was frustrated, tried hard not to show it. Paul ran a hand through his hair, sighed deeply.

"Let's try this again, shall we?" he said, turning to the boy. "I have questions. You have answers. And make no mistake, before you leave here, you'll tell me."

Wells's eyes flared, then he looked away sullenly. "I ain't telling you shit," he muttered, staring at the wall.

Paul grabbed him by the chin, pulled his face around.

"Wrong answer," he said.

A bright, tinny buzz sounded, harsh and electric, as the battery-powered clippers cut an inch-wide swath of pale through black. The swath arced up and over, like a mower dividing a field, then returned to the base, widening the gap. The boy squirmed, shorn locks tumbling and curling on the floor like little question marks.

"You wouldn't believe some of the things people have said about you," Paul said as he cut another swath. "They call you a monster, a psycho, you name it." He stood behind Wells, wielding a sleek black Panasonic beard trimmer as he calmly, determinedly shaved the boy's head.

"It's like they think you're from another planet or something, like you're not even human. But I don't believe them."

Wells clenched his fists futilely, wrists and ankles still tightly bound. There was no escape. Paul grabbed the base of his neck in a viselike grip, tilting his face down, raking tiny buzzing blades across his skull.

"I mean, I know what you are," he said. "I can read all the psych evaluations and listen to all the experts from here to hell and back, and they'll all tell me what you are. But I still don't know who you are. And you don't seem inclined to enlighten us, do you?"

More hair fell away, denuded tufts wafting in the air. Will said nothing, breath hissing through his nose in rage. Paul continued.

"Guess not," he said. "But guess what? That's not acceptable. And you're a tough little fuck, so I figure all the cops and court-appointed shrinks in the world won't get it out of you, either. And even if they lock you up, you'll probably take your little secret with you, and come out one day even worse than you are now. And that's not acceptable, either."

The trimmer buzzed madly, slicing away at Will's dignity; Paul moved around to the front, heading into the home stretch. "So I'm just going to cut through all the bullshit, pardon the pun," Paul informed him, "until I can finally figure out just . . . what . . . makes . . . you . . . tick . . ." Paul punctuated the last words with final, dramatic sweeps, then stepped back.

"Ta-da," he goaded, then reached into his medbox, came up with the little metal first aid kit. He flipped it over to the unpainted bottom and held it up to Wells's face.

Will stared at the floor, where his former hair now lay in piles. Paul rattled the box, and Will glanced up, caught a glimpse of his shorn scalp, completely bald, distorted in the polished steel surface. As he did, Paul saw something so shocking it was almost miraculous: the barest hint of a tear, welling in the corner of the boy's eye. A solitary bead, clearly born of frustration and anger and boundless rage, but nonetheless visible through the layers of attitude and carefully contrived defenses. Then Will shook his newly naked head, and it was gone.

It didn't matter. Like the fact that half the regular kids and fully three-quarters of the punk bangers Paul saw these days sported similar styles. It was not a question of fashion;

it was the fact that it had been taken from him, by force, against—pardon the pun—his will. Paul had stripped him of something, and for a fleeting moment, it had penetrated, registered, broken through.

Paul had seen it in his eyes.

It was a start.

Paul stood before the furnace, an old, converted, coal-fired monstrosity dating from the early twentieth century. Like the boiler, it was archaic and inefficient, and Paul had always known it would one day have to be replaced. Now more so than ever, he thought, if only to get rid of evidence. But it still burned hot.

The little iron door was open, flames dancing yellow and orange inside, radiating heat. A small pile of clothing lay at Paul's feet: Will's jeans, T-shirt, and battered leather jacket and sneakers, along with a dustpan filled with the sweepings from the box. He had carefully cleaned up, making sure to snag every stray hair, even checking the soles of his shoes. As he fed the sweepings into the flames, the air grew acrid with the nauseating waft of cindering hair.

Paul picked up the jacket, thought about it for a moment—burning leather. Might as well send smoke signals. The shoes, too, with their leather trim and knobby rubber soles, would be way too aromatically obvious. He set them aside for a less obtrusive form of disposal, then picked up the shirt and jeans. The shirt went in first, instantly curling into a black, embered ball. As Paul went to feed the jeans in, he noted that the left leg was festooned with intricate ball-point doodles, saturating the worn and faded denim . . . curls and spirals and angles forming into an odd personal graffiti: a leering demonic face, a giant winged gryphon, and faces, dozens of faces, cartoonish and bizarre. The kinds of scribbles a kid might do in class when bored beyond belief.

Paul looked at the drawings, and in some way had to acknowledge that they weren't half bad. It would seem that Wells was not utterly without talent, to go with all that squandered IQ. He didn't recall hearing anything about the boy being an artist, or about him being left-handed, which Paul was, too.

Paul shrugged it off. He mentally weighed saving them, as if they might contain some obscure hieroglyphic code, against the fact that they, too, were evidence. A dark thought dawned on him then, perhaps clearly for the first time—*Would the boy have need of them again?* Paul thought about it for a moment.

Then consigned them to the flames, as well.

29

The problem with trying to lead a double life, Paul was beginning to realize, is that ultimately there's no such thing. In the end, there is only one life, and everything in it must somehow be made to fit. Or else.

It was late Wednesday afternoon, the day before Thanksgiving, the weather gray and brooding. Paul stood in the still-gutted kitchen of the house on Marley Street, clad in ratty work clothes: spattered painter's pants, work boots, and a ratty sweatshirt. His toolbox was open on the floor. A little electric space heater hummed beside it, pumping out fifteen hundred watts of hot air as a battered Sony boom box on the counter played the manically upbeat refrain to Oingo Boingo's "Only a Lad."

Paul swigged a beer and studied the exposed wall studs, the frayed and ancient wiring snaking through. He was feeling pretty wired himself and just as frayed, the stress of remaining outwardly calm wearing dangerously thin. His life felt like two trains coming toward each other on the same track: they could run for a while, but sooner or later they were bound to hit. Like a perverse incarnation of some deranged Gomez Adams–style collision course, it was not a matter of if, only of when.

And along the way, there were markers. Case in point: the house itself. For as much time as he spent ostensibly working on it, very little on the surface seemed to be getting done. Not good. Sooner or later, someone was going to notice, but between work and home and his secret sessions, it was hard. Very hard. He wondered how long he would be able to keep up the façade, how long it would take to finally be done with this.

Or what he would do after . . .

Paul pushed the thought away as he knelt and checked the wire. It was worn, a fire hazard if ever there was one. As he reached for it he felt a sudden stab of pain, pulled his hand back. His finger dripped blood; the metal wrapping on the main had come unbound, the edge poking upward like a razored thorn.

"Shit," Paul hissed, putting the finger to his lips, the taste of his own blood coppery on his tongue as he shook it off, then reached into the toolbox to grab a pair of heavy-duty tinsnips. He was just about to snip the offending metal when something suddenly moved off to his left, in the hallway.

"Huh?" Paul looked up. Behind him was the door leading to the basement, a shiny new Schlage locking it tight. He reached over and turned off the music, peered down the hall to the front door. It was ajar. Someone was in the house.

"Hello?" he called out. "Who's there?"

Paul shut off the music: the place went eerily quiet. He put down the tinsnips and picked up a hammer.

"Hello?"

Paul heard a shuffling sound coming from the living room. He reached the doorway, and suddenly a dark shape lunged toward him. Paul's heart skipped a beat as the hammer came up . . .

. . . and he suddenly found himself face-to-face with Spock, jumping up to throw paws onto Paul's chest, all slobbering dog tongue and surprise.

"Jesus," Paul gasped, then said sternly, "Spock, get offa me!!"

Spock jumped down, hung his head guiltily. Paul turned the corner into the living room and saw Julie, her arms folded protectively against the chill. She was dressed in jeans and boots and a black turtleneck sweater, a long wool coat and delicate scarf, her hair pulled back in a loose bun. She was both beautiful and unnerving, and her sudden presence there caught him completely off guard.

"Julie," Paul stammered, taken aback. "What're you doing here?"

"I came to see you," she replied.

Julie looked around the room in all its undone glory, then gave a little shudder. "Cold in here."

Paul nodded uncomfortably. He had not been expecting to see her. Julie picked up on it. "Is this a bad time?" she asked.

"No," Paul replied, perhaps a bit too fast. "I was just, you know, working." He indicated the hammer, as if the presence of a tool explained anything, then slipped the hammer into the leg loop of his work pants.

"Yeah," Julie murmured. He watched as she moved from living room to dining room, the dog following, sniffing her trail. Paul followed as well, trying to look casual.

As they reached the kitchen, Julie turned. "Paul," she said. "We need to talk."

"Okay," Paul said, bracing himself. Nothing good ever followed those four words. "What's up?"

Julie uncrossed her arms, hands draping her sides as though not knowing quite where to go. "First, I wanted to apologize," she began. "I know I haven't been very easy to be around lately."

"It's okay," Paul said. "Really." He meant it; he understood. But his guard was now up, and somehow he doubted it would end there.

Julie nodded. There was something else. She took a deep breath. "Anyway," she continued, "tomorrow's Thanksgiving."

Paul nodded noncommittally, wary; Julie pressed on. "Mom called and invited us down for dinner," she said, "and I was thinking—I don't have school until Monday, so maybe we could go down for the holiday, and then go to the shore, find some nice little bed-and-breakfast, get away from all this . . ." She indicated the house, but, by extension, Glendon, their jobs, memories, everything.

"So," Julie looked at him, hopeful and tentative by turns. "What do you think?"

Paul didn't know what to say. She had clearly turned some inner corner, was taking the first halting steps to emerge from her shell of grief, achingly reaching out to him. It was like a dream come true.

And there was no way in hell he could do it.

Paul thought of the secret lying just beneath their feet, felt himself suddenly one foot into some ghastly psychological punji trap, the weight of his next words being the sole difference between evasion or puncturing the thin skin of his false reality. Julie—the old Julie—knew the old Paul too well and would catch a lie in a heartbeat. So Paul did the only thing he could do and said the first and only words that came to mind.

"Gosh, Jule," he murmured uncomfortably. "It's not really such a good time."

Paul winced even as the words left his lips: a lame nonanswer if ever there was one. It was standard issue, off-the-rack bullshit. And Julie wasn't buying it.

"Why not?" she asked, genuinely puzzled. "You could get one of the guys to fill in for you."

"It's not that easy," Paul dodged, desperately doing the mental math of five days in the box. Left unattended, anything could happen. Wells could escape. He could grow ill. Or worse. In the space of a heartbeat, Paul imagined a healing holiday weekend of reconnecting with his wife and love and life, only to come back to a corpse. Or a cop. Or worse. But he kept to the lie. Hating himself for it.

"I don't know," he said. "It's just kinda short notice."

Julie was angry now. "Jesus, Paul," she complained. "How many times have you pulled double shifts for Andy or Dondi or any of the other guys?" She looked hurt, her mood crumpling like paper. Then she nodded, grimly resolute.

"I have to get out of here," she confessed. "I need to get away for a while. Why do they always have to come first?"

"It's not just that," he said, grasping. "I've got some other stuff to do."

"What, this?" she spat back. "I *hate* this place."

Julie began pacing in slow, tight circles, as if the very walls and floor disgusted her. Spock ducked out of the way, started sniffing the baseboard under the counter. "I don't know how you can even stand to be here," she said. "I wish you'd just sell it, give it away, burn it, I don't care. Just get rid of it."

"No," Paul said, adamant. Julie turned and stared at him. "Why not?"

Paul said nothing; Julie zeroed in. "You're not the only person hurting here, Paul. I lost her, too."

"I know . . ." Paul said guiltily.

"Do you?" Julie shot back. "Do you really? I was her *mother*. I carried her *inside* me." It was her turn to pull emotional rank, awful as it was, and much as she didn't want to. She leveled him with her gaze. "She's gone, Paul, and I'm never going to get over that. But it's not going to bring her back." She threw her arms wide. "None of this will."

"You think I don't *know* that??" Paul said, guilt ceding to an almost subrational resentment. "You think I can ever get away from that for one fucking second? That's *not* what this is about."

"Then what *is* it about?" Julie pleaded. "Talk to me, Paul. I know I've been pushing you away, and I'm sorry. But we've got to find a way of getting past this somehow . . ." She was on the verge of tears, her heartache so naked and plaintive that Paul thought his own would break. "We've got to do something . . . please . . ."

Julie took a tentative step toward him, imploring. She was right. Paul wanted so badly to give in, to touch her and fade into her arms, to feel something again apart from pain and grim determination. For a moment, it seemed his whole world hung in the balance of the next breath.

And then he heard the dog.

Paul glanced over, saw Spock pawing and snuffling at the basement door. The dobie whimpered determinedly, scratching at the threshold.

Paul exploded.

"Spock, NO!!" he roared. The dog skittered back as Paul lunged toward him; as he did, the hammer hanging in the leg loop swung from the forward momentum, the wooden handle smacking the poor animal square on his long snout. Spock yelped and bounded away, fleeing the kitchen, whimpering.

"PAUL!" Julie cried. "What the hell are you doing?!" She looked at him like he was a lunatic, then turned and hurried after their pet. Paul followed, found them both in the living room, Julie huddled maternally over the traumatized dog. Spock saw Paul round the corner and yelped again, curling his big body into Julie's arms.

"Is he okay?" Paul asked.

"No thanks to you," Julie said. She looked at him as if she had never seen him before and didn't like what she was seeing. Paul went defensive.

"Jesus, Jule, it was an accident," he said. "It's not like I meant to hurt him."

"Uh-huh," she said, standing. Spock hunkered behind her like a one-hundred-pound wayward tot. Paul knelt on one knee, patted it with his hand.

"C'mere boy," he said. "I'm sorry."

The dog hesitated, suspicious. Paul gestured again. "Spock . . ." The dog didn't budge. Paul's tone suddenly shifted. "Dammit, Spock, I said COME!!" The dog sat down, shifting and squirming.

"Paul—" Julie began. Paul cut her off, stood.

"SPOCK!!!" he barked, his voice going edgy and cold. The dog whimpered; a little spritz of pee pooled beneath its haunches.

"Paul!!" Julie cried.

"What?!" Paul glared at her, enraged. He caught it almost instantly. "I'm sorry," he said, backpedalling furiously.

But it was too late.

Julie went chilly and remote. She sighed and withdrew a leash from her coat pocket, clipped it to the dog's collar, then turned to face Paul. "I'm leaving to go to my parents in an hour," she said. "You're welcome to come with me"—she paused, indicating the barren space—"if you can manage to pry yourself away."

Their eyes met for a stark moment, during which his answer passed unspoken. Julie turned away, heading for the front door, the dog in tow beside her.

"Julie, please . . ." Paul started to say. But Julie kept going. He watched as she exited without another word. Out the door.

And into the coming night.

30

If the pizza at the Gaslight Tavern was the worst in the tristate area, its jukebox was arguably the best. Big and swirling, with backlit faux deco Lucite that glowed like a reactor meltdown, it was eclectically stocked with customer favorites, Mickey D. having partial hearing loss in both ears and no pressing cultural bias, with the possible exception of gangsta rap, which annoyed him not because of the negative social messages but because no one actually sang.

As a result, in any hour of random play, one was as likely to hear Frank Sinatra belting out "My Way" followed by Sid Vicious doing his own uniquely atonal interpretation of the same number, segueing into anything from Alice in Chains to ZZ Top, depending on the vagaries of fate and whoever last wielded the quarters. It was understood by the regulars that all bets were off where the Gaslight's playlist was concerned; one literally never knew what was going to come pumping out of its booming speakers next.

It was just after ten as Dondi came in. The night had turned miserable, cold and wet, rain sheeting down onto the streets like curtains falling across a stage. Inside, the crowd was sparse, in preemptive holiday prep; on the jukebox, Amanda Marshall was crooning "Last Exit to Eden," smoky voice crying out over haunting acoustic guitars and strings, against snaky bass and drums.

Paul was bellied up to the bar, nursing a bottle of Rolling Rock and a shooter of Jack Daniel's, still dressed in his work clothes. He saw Dondi and smiled.

"Hey," Paul said. "My bro . . ." He was visibly under the influence, two out of three sheets fully to the wind. Paul slapped the barstool next to him, inviting Dondi to sit, then he called out to Mickey D., "Mickey, ya fat bastid, set us up."

Mickey lumbered over and set up glasses as Dondi took a seat. Dondi glanced at Mickey as the shooter filled; Mickey shrugged and moved away, wiping down the bar. As long as Paul didn't throw up, fall over, or pick a fight, it was none of his business.

Paul raised his glass, brimming with amber liquid. "A toast," he said.

Dondi's eyebrow arched; he had rarely, if ever, seen Paul drink hard liquor. "What are we toasting?" he asked.

"Absolutely fucking nothing," Paul said. "No, wait," he amended, intoning earnestly. "To feeling no pain."

He clinked glasses with a flourish, downed the shot. Dondi watched, then downed his. Paul caught him looking, cocked his head inquisitively.

"So," he said. "What brings you out this fine holiday eve?"

"Connie's cooking the bird," Dondi explained. "Figured I'd stop in for a sec." He paused. "How you doin', man?"

It sounded like a casual question, wasn't. "Good," Paul replied, nodding exaggeratedly. "Feeling . . . no . . . pain . . ." He drew the words out, slurring them only slightly.

"I can see that," Dondi said. Paul pulled out a cigarette, patted his pocket, searching for his Zippo. Dondi spied it lying on the bar, picked it up and lit Paul's smoke. Paul inhaled deeply, listening to the music.

"Like this song?" he asked. "Reminds me of old Blind

Faith, man. Remember Blind Faith? Clapton, Stevie Winwood, before he went all soft rock and shit . . ."

"Yeah, those were the days," Dondi said, humoring him. In the background Amanda faded out; the jukebox clicked and whirred into a U2 tune, as lead singer Bono lamented sacrifices made in the name of Love. It hit some dim associative nerve, as Paul suddenly looked to Dondi.

"Tell me something," he said, quite out of the blue, "is anything justifiable if it's done in the name of love?"

"What?" Dondi said, clearly not following. "What are you talking about?"

"Like, sometimes we do stuff we're not supposed to, because it's right to do it, right?" Paul explained. "Like that girl, the other night . . . I mean, it was right to dose her, you know? She was in pain . . ."

"Yeah, I guess." Dondi nodded warily, wondering where this was going.

"But we're not allowed to," Paul continued drunkenly. "It's not legal . . ."

"So what's your point?" Dondi asked.

"My point is," Paul replied, "legal is supposed to be 'right,' and illegal's 'wrong,' right? But sometimes, legal *isn't* right, and in order to do right, you have to do a little wrong . . . right?"

Dondi risked mental whiplash listening to Paul's circular logic. He glanced over to Mickey D.; Mickey rolled his eyes.

"So," Paul concluded, "if a good person does a bad thing for a good reason, does that automatically make them bad?"

Dondi shrugged under the weight of the question, like some booby-trapped cosmic karma pop quiz. "Fuck, Paulie, how the hell should I know?"

"Exactly my point," Paul said, swilling his beer. He shook his head. "Never mind," he sighed. "I'm just talking shit."

Dondi nodded. "Lemme take you home," he said. "Julie'll worry—"

"She's gone," Paul said.

"What?" Dondi looked at him, perplexed. "What do you mean, 'gone'?"

Paul shrugged. "Left to be with her folks," he said. "Thanksgiving, ya know. Even took the dog with her." He said it as if it were supposed to be the most normal thing in the world; Dondi was visibly taken aback.

"Whoa, time out, back up," he said. "She left to go home for Thanksgiving, and you didn't go with her?"

"It's no good." Paul shook his head bitterly. "Her mom trying to make like everything's all right, her dad eyeball fucking me from across the room . . . He blames me for what happened, ya know."

"Who does?"

"Julie's dad."

"Bullshit," Dondi snorted.

"No. Truth," Paul insisted. "Hell, he never even wanted her to marry me in the first place . . . I was never good enough. Even after Kyra was born, bastard still wouldn't cut me any slack. And now . . ." The thought trailed off morosely, unfinished. Paul put fingers to temple as though trying to rub away a great pain. "Shit . . ." he hissed.

"You're just drunk," Dondi assured him. "Nobody blames you."

"Why not? I do," Paul blurted, in alcohol-fueled confession. "I mean, we fuckin' save people every day, right? So why couldn't I save her?" A tear formed in his eye; Paul wiped it away determinedly, beating back his emotions.

"C'mon, man. This ain't right." This was dangerous territory, even for the tightest of friends. Too many trip wires; too many places for the conversation to go off. But just as suddenly as it had come on, Paul shrugged it off, signaling the bartender.

"Yo, Mickey!" he called out. "Two more! Kill us again!"

Mickey glanced from Paul to Dondi; Dondi shook his head; no way. The big bartender feigned a shrug. "Sorry, Paulie," he said. "No can do."

Paul looked affronted, turned to Dondi, caught the subterfuge. "Oh, I get it," he said. "A conspiracy. Some friend you are."

"Best one you'll ever have," Dondi said. He got up off the

barstool, put a brotherly hand on Paul's shoulder. "C'mon, pardner," he told him. "Let's get you home."

Paul nodded and sniffed, fished some bills from his pocket, put them on the bar. "Yeah," he muttered. "Home."

Wherever that was.

31

Thanksgiving offered little to be thankful for, as far as Paul could see. Not that he could see very far.

He awoke groaning, stared blearily at the ceiling, trying to focus his eyes. His head whanged, as if someone had scooped out his brains and replaced them with moldy cheese. His mouth was an arid disaster zone, offset by a vague rumbling in his guts that told him suffering would be minimized provided he did not move.

Everything past the fight with Julie was a bit of a blur. He remembered going to the Gaslight Tavern, starting an endless conga line of shooters and beers, until Dondi had rescued him from his own stupidity. He vaguely remembered returning home to a dark and empty house, bereft of even Spock's canine antics to ease his entry. He didn't remember stumbling upstairs and falling into bed with his clothes on. And what dreams may have come were mercifully muted. He awoke drooling, driven from sleep not by some haunted subconscious torment but by the simple need to pee.

"Huh? . . ." Paul sat up, startled. Bad move. His blood slammed against the inside of his skull like a bad lava lamp.

His bladder sloshed like an overfilled water balloon. He thought for a fleeting moment that he might throw up.

But it still took him another ten seconds to realize exactly whose bed he was in . . .

"What!!?" Paul jumped up, squinted at the window, late morning light shining in. As he did he caught a glimpse of his reflection in the cheval mirror: still in his rumpled, grotty clothes, hair pasted down and sticking up at odd angles, eyes puffed and baggy from drink. He looked pretty much like he felt. Shitty. Hungover. Confused.

But none of that changed the fact that he was standing in Kyra's room.

Paul turned back to the bed, saw the covers rumpled and mussed. He took a deep breath, realized he could smell the faintest trace of her perfume on his clothes.

"Oh, God," he gasped, then stumbled out of the room and into the hall, lurching to the bathroom, where he retched violently. Sixty seconds later he returned, wiping his mouth on his sleeve, and stepped back in.

It was the first time since her death that anyone had ventured beyond the door. Standing wide awake in his daughter's bedroom, Paul felt out of place, alien, an intruder. Kyra's space was a portrait in teenaged transition: a perfect snapshot of contradiction and mystery, toys and cutesy kid stuff side by side with computer and stereo, books and papers and CDs, funky clothes and lacy undergarments, cosmetics and little bottles of perfume, evidence of changing tastes and hormonal tides. On her desk, a shelf holding prospective college handbooks and SAT test prep, all neatly arranged. Kyra may have inherited Julie's looks, but her knack for organizing space was pure Paul: every inch of the room was a study in meticulously controlled chaos. A place for everything, and a reason for it to be there.

Paul carefully straightened the bed, smoothing the floral comforter. Stuffed animals lay scattered on the floor, knocked off in nocturnal thrashings: a big Tasmanian devil, a floppy Cat in the Hat doll, assorted pound puppies, beanie babies, and fuzzy hand puppets. Festive relics. He placed them all back amongst the mound of pillows, tried to make it all look the way it did before. As he did he caught a faint scent of perfume, something French in a little triangular bottle.

Trésor, he remembered, having once made the earnest error of trying to get her some cheap cologne he had seen at the counter in a Paramus mall Gap, some not so long ago shopping trip. There amongst the yuppie drone gear he remembered little silver metallic cylinders with names like Earth, Air, and Dream. Paul had thought they were kind of cool; Kyra had rolled her eyes and looked at him as though he had suggested she douse herself in yak squeezings. Even at sixteen, she knew what she wanted.

Paul moved toward the door like a burglar, the morning light inappropriately cheerful. In years past, he would have been up and about by dawn, the TV pounding out cartoons and coverage of the Macy's parade, the scent of cooking food warming the air. He had taken Kyra to the parade once when she was a little girl, bundling up and braving trains and subways and the pre-dawn midtown Manhattan crush of holiday humanity, all for the chance to hoist her seven-year-old self up onto his shoulders at the corner of 46th and Broadway, to watch giant balloons and floats and marching bands. Schmaltzy and mercantile though it might be, through a child's eyes, it was magic—Kyra had giggled and squealed and kicked her heels against his chest, utterly delighted.

In later years they would have friends or family over to gather around the table and talk and drink and stuff themselves silly; Paul had even built a brick oven in the backyard, roasting the turkey in a pan over real hickory fire, which burnt the bottom black but yielded succulent meat. The Kelly house gradually became a magnet of annual good cheer, attracting holiday orphans and the familially challenged from both sides of the marital fence: parentless friends from work and school, everyone and anyone in their milieu who didn't have a home to go to or one they particularly wanted to. Kyra would play with the visiting kids as Paul and Julie played hosts extraordinaire, seeing to it that everyone's plate or glass never emptied until guests would cry for mercy or shuffle off late in the day, sated and satisfied.

But it was more than good food and drink and conversation; it was the stuff of true family, and it went beyond the bounds of mere blood. It was the ceremonial glue that bound them all together, commemorating the bounty of a year received and ushering in the hope and promise of more. And like everything else, Paul took it seriously.

And now here he was, alone.

Paul's eyes welled with tears, and for a long, pregnant moment, he sobbed a bitter, wracking sob. "I'm sorry, baby," he said to the room, to her memory. "I'm so s-sorry . . ."

The room said nothing. Paul pulled himself together, then sighed and stepped out into the hall, closing the door softly, erasing the violation. As it shut Paul caught a vague whiff of stale body funk—his own rank odor. He felt unclean, inside and out; and while he might not be able to change much of the former, the latter was easy enough.

Time to shower, he thought, *and get ready.* His head still felt like a sack full of wet rags, but unlike other feelings, it would pass. And if there was little to feel truly thankful for, there were still certain amends to make.

And certain things left undone.

It was shortly after 3:00 as Detective Buscetti sat in the happy environs of Glendon PD, his feet up on his desk, scanning the Living section of the morning paper. Inside the squad, the mood was low-key and subdued. Thanksgiving day was generally like that: burglaries up, due to the preponderance of out-of-town holiday sojourns, but violent crimes momentarily ebbed. By mid-afternoon most of the citizenry would still be working off the tryptophan buzz of too much white meat and lethargy from starch, engrossed in football games or otherwise mollified by fleeting feelings of familial bliss; later in the day, second wind would kick in, fueled by alcohol and petty resentments, and the lines would start lighting up with domestic violence calls, drunk and disorderlies, the usual smorgasbord of DUIs, o.d.'s, and disturbing the peace calls, and if history was any judge, at least one attempted or actual homicide. Thank God he wouldn't be there.

Buscetti turned the page when suddenly he heard a familiar voice call out, singsong.

"Hell-lo? Anybody home?"

Buscetti craned his neck past the filing cabinet, saw Paul standing by the empty P.A.'s desk and little wooden gate that comprised the entry area. "Paul," he said, getting up. "How ya doing, man?" He was frankly surprised.

"Hey, Stevie," Paul replied. "Long time no see." He looked tired but freshly showered and shaved, dressed down and casual. He carried a paper bag cradled loosely in one arm. "Got a minute?" he asked.

"Sure," the detective replied, waving him in. As Paul entered, Buscetti wondered what was up. In the weeks since the Wells kid's release and subsequent disappearance they had seen very little of one another, Paul off in his world of grief and Buscetti tending to avoid the Rescue One house as a mid-shift coffee pit stop. Guilt, mostly, but also a degree of frustration—for all the initial vows of swift justice, the case had gone flat ass stone cold, and nobody knew it more than Buscetti. He still kept Kyra's file on his desk, as a reminder; he instinctively covered it with the paper as Paul took a seat in the cramped and overcrowded space.

"Good to see ya, man," Buscetti began solicitously. "How's it going?"

"Eh," Paul shrugged. "Okay. Been better."

Buscetti nodded. It was an honest enough query; he had worried for Paul in the aftermath, especially when Wells's disappearing act had inevitably cast generic suspicion on Paul as a matter of course. Standard issue stuff, dutifully if expeditiously done; Paul had alibied out down to receipts from the repair shop for his truck. Buscetti had been frankly relieved; some things one just did not want to seriously consider.

"Anyway." Paul smiled. "I stopped by your house," he explained, "but Angela said you got called in."

"Yeah," Buscetti said ruefully. "Parrish called in sick, but between you and me I think he's in Atlantic City. At least it was the eight to four." Buscetti glanced at the clock on the wall. "Another forty minutes, and I'm outta here."

"Good, that's good," Paul said, then added, "Oh . . . this is for you. Happy Thanksgiving." He held out the paper bag; Buscetti accepted it, peeked inside. A bottle of Glenlivet, single malt, Buscetti's off-duty beverage of choice. The detective smiled, craggy features crinkling appreciatively.

"Wow, thanks," he said.

"By way of apology," Paul explained, adding, "I've been kind of a jerk lately."

Buscetti shook his head. "Hey, you don't have to apologize to me—"

"No, seriously," Paul insisted. "It was fucked up. I was outta line." He paused. "We appreciate all you've done for us."

Paul held out his hand; Buscetti shook it. Peace. He waited for Paul to ask him about the case, but instead, Paul just leaned over to look not at the file but at a little Polaroid of the detective's child propped up on the desk lamp. "Oh my God," he said, picking it up. "She's so big."

"Yep," Buscetti replied, chest swelling with paternal pride. "Twelve pounds, seven ounces, getting bigger every day."

"Wow." Paul squinted. "What the hell is she wearing?"

"Don't ask," Buscetti said, blushing. "Angie got it for her for Thanksgiving . . . it's called a Goo Goo Gobbler." He rolled his eyes. "Now she looks like Tor Johnson in a turkey suit."

"Nah," Paul said. "She's a doll. She's got your eyes."

"Let's hope that's all she got," Buscetti joked. "God forbid she ends up with my mug."

Paul smiled, said nothing. Buscetti scoped him, still concerned; he couldn't help but feel that all was not well in Oz. "How's by you?" he asked. "Julie okay?"

"She's okay," Paul lied. "I guess holidays are kind of a bitch."

"Yeah," Buscetti concurred.

As if by some perverse cosmic punch line, an angry male voice suddenly sounded out in the hall by the P.A.'s desk.

Buscetti and Paul both turned to see a large, surly-looking man glowering at the gate.

"Can I get some help, please?" he intoned sarcastically, hands pounding the railing impatiently. The man was big, two-fifty plus of hard fat and bad attitude, clad in a beat biker's jacket and filthy jeans, balding pate giving way to greasy ponytail. Buscetti turned to Paul.

"Wait here," he said. Paul nodded as Buscetti moved out the door. As he did, Paul's gaze flitted across the desk, the photo, the assorted and sundry papers. He picked up the newspaper, casually perused the headlines. And then saw the file laying beneath it, the name clearly marked: H4687. KELLY, KYRA.

Paul's eyes went wide. He glanced at the doorway, heard Buscetti placating rowdy citizenry.

Then carefully opened the file.

A minute later Paul emerged from the office, found Buscetti facing off with the man, trying to get a straight story without getting pissed off or pissed on. The man was obviously drunk or doped on something, his words slurred and surly. "I told you, man, I wanna report a domestic attack . . ." He looked bad, smelled worse. "Bitch fuckin' stabbed me . . ."

"Who stabbed you?" Buscetti asked, placating.

"My old lady, man! Whodahya think?" The big man looked annoyed. "Didn't like how I was carving the fuckin' turkey," he continued. "I want her locked up, man . . . fuckin' bitch . . ."

Buscetti rolled his eyes. "Whoa, back up," he said. "First things first. Now, where did this alleged incident occur?" He meant as in location, but by way of answer the big man just turned around.

"Jesus!" Buscetti gasped. The back of the complainant's jeans were flecked and spotted with fresh, wet red; a twin-pronged carving fork poked out of the broad expanse of the man's back, tines sunk deep through leather and into flesh just above the shoulder blade. The wooden handle stuck up like a little flagpole, vibrating with every movement.

Paul's eyes went wide. "Holy shit," he gulped. The drunken behemoth snorted gruffly.

"Told ya," he said.

The excitement lasted another thirty-five minutes, give or take, as first aid was administered and ambulances called. Paul left the fork in place but did what he could to stem the bleeding; as he worked he learned that the grumpy victim had indeed not only been stabbed during a festive holiday dinner by his equally alcoholic common law wife of eight years but had also ridden down to the station on his big Harley hog all by his lonesome, eschewing medical attention in favor of legal payback. He wanted her jailed, pronto. Unfortunately, Buscetti would now have to oblige him . . . and depending on how the victim's blood tox screens came back, lock him up, too. Happy Thanksgiving.

The detective sighed as the ambo crew trundled away with their gurney-load of pissed off, bleeding biker scum, leaving Paul and Buscetti staring in amazement. Buscetti glanced out the window, saw waning sunlight giving way to dusk. "Shit," he muttered. "Now I gotta go and arrest this asshole's asshole wife, then spend half the night filling out forms to keep their sorry asses in jail." His mood turned dour, morose. He sighed. "My girl's first Thanksgiving . . ."

Paul patted him on the back. He knew the feeling, in reverse. He left moments later, bidding his friend adieu, empathizing with the unfortunate turn of events. It was a sorry situation. Buscetti would be busy and distracted for hours. Paul felt the thin sheaf of papers tucked inside his coat, the ones slipped from the middle of the case file. The case file, left neatly on the detective's desk, just the way he had found it. More or less.

Yes, Paul thought. *A sorry situation, indeed.*

And about to get a great deal more so.

32

SECTION III: EXTREMITIES

When considering the impact of more overt forms
of physical coercion on the interview process,
don't overlook the importance of the extremities.
The fingers and toes are highly sensitive and
imbued with more nerve endings and pain recep-
tors per square centimeter than virtually any
other part of the body, with the exception of the
external genitalia, and can be manipulated in a
variety of ways without risk of severe injury or
death. In other words, a little goes a long way,
and a carefully orchestrated round of "this little
piggy" can have your subject talking well before the last one goes "wee wee wee" all the way
home.

*"Cause of death of this sixteen-year-old female is asphyxia
associated with craniocerebral trauma. Homicide . . ."*

Paul's recorded voice droned a verbal recitation of Kyra's autopsy report on the secreted loudspeaker. He held a photograph up to the light.

"Time to face what you've done, Will," he said sternly, his expression grim and edged. "Time to look it straight in the eye."

Wells struggled in the chair, twisting his head this way and that. He was strapped down tightly, forehead gleaming with sweat, thin rivulets trickling through the sparse crop of skull stubble. They had been at it for almost an hour now, and he just would not cooperate. Paul was growing impatient.

"Look at it, Will," he demanded, thrusting the photograph closer to the boy's face. Wells refused, looked away.

"Decedent was menstruating at TOD; vaginal examination revealed OB style sanitary napkin containing six ccs decedent's menstrual blood type A+." The voice droned on. *"Decedent was administered emergency tracheotomy en route to hospital by paramedic personnel, accounting for small puncture wound at base of throat. Decedent D.O.A. . . ."*

"D.O.A., Will," Paul repeated. "Dead on arrival. She died in that ambulance. I watched her die," he hissed. "I *had* to look at what you did. Time for you to see it now."

He jammed the photo closer. In his hand was Kyra's image, the harsh light of the morgue rendering her in flatly forensic close-up. Her delicate features were slack and lifeless, dark smudges of post-autopsy blood pooled under the eye sockets, rendering them plum-colored, bruised-looking. Will would not look at it. Paul threw the photograph down onto the bunk, thrust another one at him.

"Look at her," Paul said.

In the background, his recorded voice monotoned. *"A deep manual furrow encircles the neck. The width of the furrow varies from three inches to one inch and is horizontal in orientation with little upward orientation. The skin of the anterior neck above and below the manual furrow contains areas of petechial hemorrhage and abrasion encompassing an area measuring approximately two by one inches . . ."*

The photo corresponded, a close-up of Kyra's neck in grisly show-and-tell.

"Stop it," Will hissed, breath rasping, desperately trying not to see. Short of popping his eyes out of their sockets or pulling an impromptu Linda Blair–style one hundred and eighty degree spin, he was trapped. But still he would not face it.

"Look at her," Paul ordered, jamming the next photo toward Wells's face. It was more than mere cruelty; Paul had read something about a radical treatment being deployed on youthful offenders in Oregon, of how psychologists compelled their subjects to confront the effects of their actions. In the study, the psychologists were trained professionals, and the treatment depended on a level of trust he could hardly expect. It was not working well.

"LOOK AT HER!" Paul roared, his voice edgy with threat.

Will momentarily looked up, not at the photo but at Paul. His eyes glared fiercely, but when his gaze flitted to the image, he saw not an autopsy photo but the year-book photo: Kyra alive and smiling, her whole life in front of her.

Wells looked shocked; Paul seized on the moment. "This is Kyra, before you came along," he said. "And this is Kyra after . . ."

He flipped to another brutal morgue shot. Will looked away. Paul kept the pressure on, flipping back and forth. "Kyra before . . . and *after* . . ." He flipped shots again. "Before . . . and *after* . . ."

"Get away from me," Wells growled.

Paul moved closer. "What are you afraid of?" he said. "Of this?"

He flashed another picture: Kyra's head and torso, laid out on the slab. A sheet was demurely pulled up, but a line of rude stitches ran between her breasts and up to her collarbone, pale flesh pulled puckered and tight. It had taken him hours to be able to bear the sight of them himself; but he had done it, forcing himself to stare at the images, steeling himself for this moment. And he would not back down now.

"You did this," Paul said.

"Fuck you," Will hissed. Paul smacked him across the face, once, for emphasis. Wells recoiled, came back, hyperventilating with rage.

"She was a beautiful girl, and you killed her," Paul said, his own voice quivering with barely repressed rage. "You snuffed her life out like a candle. She was good and decent and kind, everything you're not," he told him. "How does it feel?"

No response. Paul pushed the picture closer. "How does it feel, you little shit?"

Wells craned his neck until the muscles pulled taut as piano wire, and he mumbled something unintelligible.

"What?" Paul demanded. "Speak up."

"GETTHEFUCKAWAYFROMME!!!!!" the boy suddenly exploded. He thrashed in the chair, veins in his arms and temples bulging from exertion. In an instant he seemed to dissolve into howling, inchoate panic, voice raw and ravaged. *"GETAWAAAAY!!"*

"You *KILLED* her!" Paul screamed back, his own emotional amperage going redline.

"I don't *CARE*!!" Wells cried, voice rasping.

Paul suddenly threw the photos, sending them pinwheeling into the walls, then turned and exited the box, leaving the door ajar. A waft of cool breeze wormed its way through the crack, taunting Wells with the smell of escape. Paul's recorded voice continued, unheeding.

"Post mortem lividity present in back, buttocks and lower extremities. Rectum is intact. No traces of semen/ejaculate found in vaginal area, mouth or digestive tract . . ."

Suddenly the recording stopped. From the other side of the door, a fevered rattle of metal on metal, the sound of a search in progress. A moment later the door swung back, and Paul reentered, holding his toolbox.

"Okay, tough guy," he said menacingly. "Let's see what you do care about."

*   *   *

"Did I ever tell you about the first time I made my daughter smile?" Paul said, voice level now, deadly calm as he rummaged through the toolbox placed by the side of the chair, just out of Will's visual periphery. Will looked at him suspiciously; Paul continued. "She was all of six weeks old, and I was changing her diaper. I played 'this little piggy' with her. And she smiled." He paused, caught in the grip of memory. "You don't know what it's like to see your baby smile at you for the very first time."

Paul dug deeper, came up with what looked like an industrial-grade pair of scissors: the tinsnips. He held them up so Will could see.

"So you don't care about my little girl," he said. "You don't even care about yourself . . . you just don't care about anything, right?" He dug around some more, came up with a stub of pencil.

"I gotta tell ya, Will," he said. "I just don't believe you. I think you do care. I think I can make you care."

Paul released the locking clip; the spring-mounted hinge snicked open with an audible click. He placed the pencil in the crook of the curved steel blades. "It's just a matter of what do I have to do to get you to show me."

Paul held the tinsnips up to Will's face, closed them. The pencil sheared in half and fell in the boy's lap. Paul smiled.

"Let's you and me play a game," he said.

He pressed the blades against the boy's thigh. Wells squirmed in his seat, nostrils flaring. "What do you care about, Will?" Paul asked, tracing a line in his exposed flesh. "Do you care about *this*?" He nudged the tinsnips toward his crotch. Wells stiffened and shut his eyes, still not giving in.

"Nah," Paul decided. "Too easy. Let's say we start small, and we can work our way up. Let's start"—he traced the blades away from his crotch to his knee, then down— "here!" he exclaimed.

Pointing at Will's foot.

Will thrashed as Paul knelt and raked the point of the

shears across his toes. "So tell me, Will," Paul said. "Do you *care* about your toes?"

Wells clenched his jaw tightly, resisting with all his might.

"No?" Paul asked. "How 'bout *this* one?" He pointed the tinsnips at the big toe of the boy's right foot. "*This* one?" He continued, counting down. "*This* one? It had roast beef, you know. But this one," he moved the blade, "this one of course had none."

He moved again, finally coming to the squirming baby toe. "And *this* little piggy . . ." he began, then stopped. "You remember what this one did, Will?"

Will jerked his leg, trying to free it. Paul held the tinsnips steady against the diminutive digit, let the pressure sink in. "It said something. What did this one say?"

"F-fuck . . . you . . ." Will sputtered, chest heaving.

"No, I don't think so," Paul replied. "I'm pretty sure it said something else." He opened the tinsnips, came up from underneath to slide the toe between them. "What sound did it make again?"

Will shook his head violently; Paul slid the tinsnips up until the toe was pinned in the crux of sharp steel blades. "Last chance, Will," he warned, deadly serious now. "What was the sound the littlest piggy made?"

Will tried to resist; Paul tightened his grip on the tinsnips. Pain suddenly spiked the boy's brain.

And Will began to crack.

"*W-wee . . .*" he hissed through gritted teeth.

"What was that?" Paul asked. "I can't hear you!"

"*Weee . . .*" Will gasped, louder. "*Wee . . . wee . . . wee . . .*"

"Louder!"

"*WEEWEEWEEE!*" the boy cried. "*WEEWEEWEE-WEEEE!*"

"How far did the little piggy have to go, Will?" Paul tightened the snips; a bright bead of blood smeared the blade. "Did he have to go all the way?"

"N-no . . . *Y-YESS*!!!" Wells wailed, eyes rolling in his head, openly panicking now.

"Which is it, Will?" Paul demanded. "Yes or no? Should the little piggy stay or go?"

"*No!!!*" Will sputtered, his entire body quivering. "*Don't!*"

"Don't what?" Paul said. "Don't care? You don't care about the poor little piggy??" He squeezed harder.

"*NOOOO!!!*" Will screamed.

Paul closed the blades.

The tinsnips clicked shut; Will cracked completely, screaming at the top of his lungs. Paul stood, towering over him. The boy's screams caved in on themselves, giving way to tortured mewling. "*Please . . .*" he whispered. "*Please . . .*"

"Shut up," Paul said.

Will looked at him, mind reeling, then looked down at his foot. Twin, thin lacerations flanked the pinky toe on either side, oozing red. But it was still attached.

"Guess the little piggy's not going home, after all," Paul said. He had slid the blades off as they closed, enough to break skin and draw blood, but that was the extent of the damage done. Physically speaking.

Emotionally, it was another story. Will gazed at his foot, eyes swimming in his head. Then they rolled back altogether, and he passed stone-cold out.

Paul watched dispassionately, mopped sweat from his brow with his sleeve. The box was hot, the air close and thick with adrenaline and fear. Paul reached down and untied him; Wells crumpled and sagged in the chair. Paul picked him up and laid him out on the bunk. He put two fingers to the boy's carotid artery, felt his pulse.

"You'll live," he said.

Paul glanced at his watch: 11:57. Thanksgiving was almost over. He thought he would feel worse, but somehow he didn't. He felt tired, but weirdly good. Like he had accomplished something at last. Like he had finally broken all the way through.

On the bunk, Will moaned. Music to his ears. Paul pulled the coarse blanket up to cover him, then leaned forward until his lips were near the boy's ear.

"So you do care about something, after all," he said softly. "Even if it's as small as a toe." Paul stood and smiled grimly.

Something to be thankful for.

PART FIVE

Flashover

33

I n the life of a fire, there are many subtle forces at work. The laws of thermodynamics and volatility, the tetrahedral relationship of fuel to temperature to oxygen to uninhibited chemical chain reaction—all of these and more factor in. A bit too much of one, a bit too little of the other, and nothing happens.

Combine forces just so, and a fire is born.

Once born, other subtleties come into play. Fire is alive, and like any living thing, it does not want to die. Once born, fire will burn until there is nothing left to burn, transforming everything in its path to fuel and char, for its own sake. Once born, fire fights for its life, the only way it knows how.

But beyond the technicalities of conduction and convection and heat transfer, the pyrolysis of solid or vaporization of liquid into combustible gas, fire depends on circumstance, random chance, and fate to shape its course. Combine forces just so, and it will burn until its heat reaches everything in the room, until things previously untouched by flame spontaneously ignite, each possessed of its own distinct *thermal characteristics, each driven to its own unique flash-point.*

This is the point of full involvement: the precise moment at which random factors and the laws of physics collide, when the fire's power is never more lethal or complete. It is not a matter of bad or good. It is simply the nature of fire.

But the same could also be said for hate . . .

Paul drove his truck down the main drag of Glendon Boulevard, heading home after his tour, his thoughts swirling and abstract. It was just after 8:00 on Sunday evening, the tail end of the holiday weekend. The streets were cold and glittering. On the radio, Nat King Cole crooned about having a merry little Christmas, letting hearts be light. Paul smiled grimly at the line about troubles being out of sight.

Outside the driver's window, spindly plastic Rudolfs lashed to jolly plastic Santas flashed by, all propped on the narrow median; illuminated snowflakes and twinkly lights arced overhead, spanning the street. Cheesy, cheerful icons loomed from every storefront and shop window with manic holiday abandon. Cole's sweetly husky voice filled the cab, the melody cascading and timeless.

Paul shuddered. Thanksgiving had passed, only to usher in the season he had once hated, then come to love, and now dreaded with every cell and shred of his being. Call it Christmas or Kwanzaa or Hanukkah or whatever else one's personal taste or cultural disposition so deigned; for Paul it was all a hell by any other name. A reminder of the world he no longer felt a part of because Kyra was no longer in it.

The tune swelled into the bridge. Paul felt his throat tighten.

As a child he had hated Christmas. When it had been just his mother and him they'd been too poor to ever really enjoy it; when his mom had married Ken, Paul's newly minted stepdad had quickly converted to such a ball-breaking prick that he'd made the Grinch look like Mother Teresa. Paul's memories of their first Christmas as an alleged family unit began with Paul getting his first bike—an honest-to-God Schwinn with a metallic sparkle banana seat and wheelie bars that he had lusted for with every ounce of desire an eight-year-old heart could muster—and ended with a drunken Ken deliberately backing his car over it because Paul had forgotten, in his childish excitement, to park it in its "proper" place in the garage.

By the time Paul was a teen, Ken's escalating and alcohol-fueled holiday tirades couldn't have been uglier if the bastard had butt-fucked little Cindy-Lou Who in the Whoville town square. And the entire span from Thanksgiving through New Years became a six-week-long forced march into dysfunction, compounded by the nonstop bombardment of images designed to imply that somewhere, everywhere, happy families were gathered in loving Yuletide embrace, having merry little Christmases, one and all. And Paul hated it for that.

Until he met Julie . . .

A long dead Nat King Cole song about being together through the years, if the fates allow. Paul flashed back to their first Christmas together, positively Dickensian in its poverty; their tree, a sad little Charlie Brown Christmas reject so wilted and droopy that it leaned against the wall of their apartment as if trying to catch its breath; their presents, if not Magi-grade, humble and spare. But they were young and together and deeply in love, and Paul had never felt happier or more full of promise. And each year that followed, that feeling grew, as though they had secretly declared the year zero and started anew, erasing bad memories, replacing them with the spirit of the season, the spirit of hope.

And when Kyra was born, the promise was complete.

Through the ups and downs of the next sixteen years, through good years and bad, it had held true. Their gift-giving habits had quickly proved true to form: Julie the patient stealth shopper, secreting presents in mid-July for December deployment; Paul the eleventh hour impulse buyer, madly venturing forth with mere days or hours to spare. But whether any given year found them strapped or flush, they showered their daughter with every dream they could make come true, spoiling her horribly and rendering every other holiday in the Kelly household a pale warm-up act by comparison. Their home at Christmas was like a Frank Capra fantasy made flesh.

And now?

Now it was *It's a Wonderful Life* with Jimmy Stewart jumping the bridge and slipping beneath the inky waves, no Clarence in sight; it was *Miracle on 34th Street* with Kris Kringle consigned to Bellevue and Natalie Wood on Prozac. The very thought of it made him ill.

Stranger still was the knowledge that the only miracle in his world was the one now happening in the basement on Marley Street.

The transformation had been as stark as it had been sudden. His last session with Will had left the boy shattered; for all its bitter victory, Paul had wondered what he might find upon his return. He had awakened Friday morning feeling uneasy and restless; as the day had progressed he had vowed to be prepared for whatever may come, bracing himself for the possibility of an even more violent Round Two.

But, far from the defiant creature he had come to expect, Paul had stopped back on Friday to find Will quiet, depleted, oddly compliant. The deadened black hole stare and sullen sneer had been gone; in their place, an expression that Paul could not at first fathom. And when Paul had ordered him to stand, the boy had complied instantly, mumbling something so shocking it had taken Paul a full ten seconds to fully comprehend.

"Yessir," Will had said. Paul had handed him his meager rations. Will had uttered a quiet but unmistakable thank you.

Paul could not believe his ears. Had the boy looked up, he would have seen his captor do a fleeting but literal double take. But Will had quietly accepted the food and stood, eyes down and head slightly bowed, until Paul had bade him sit. And then he'd done that, too.

Paul hadn't known what to think. Conditioned to resistance, he was unaccustomed to success. His innate reaction had been suspicion—was this a trick? But the next day, the transformation had continued. Will had been quiet and complacent, obedient and passive. His lexicon was limited . . . "please," "thank you," "yessir," "nosir" . . . but no more. He spoke only when spoken to. And Paul had responded cautiously, like an ice fisherman venturing onto an unknown floe, searching for cracks with every tentative step. But as he was leaving, Will had ventured a question: could he please be allowed to bathe?

Paul had been taken aback. Weeks of captivity had rendered the confines of the box dank and dirty; even with the fan circulating, the stench of sweat, excreta, and adrenaline permeated the boy's skin. Paul had looked away, and nodded. Maybe tomorrow.

It was less torture than test to see how the boy would react, if his newfound attitude would sunder. But Will had merely nodded, and again murmured quiet thanks.

That night, at the firehouse, it had been dead, oddly quiet for a weekend, as though all of Glendon had declared a fleeting holiday truce. The Rescue One crew had done scut work and chilled, watching videos and playing cards; Paul had kept to himself, hanging in the bay under the guise of doing maintenance, generally keeping his distance. In the ready room, the movie *Seven* played on the VCR, Brad Pitt and Morgan Freeman en route to their final, inexorable showdown with the maniacal Kevin Spacey. Pitt's voice echoed, filtering through the open door to the bay.

"I've been trying to figure something in my head," Pitt said smugly to Spacey, *"and maybe you can help me out. When a person is insane, as you clearly are, do you know that you're insane? Maybe you're just sitting around, reading* Guns & Ammo, *masturbating in your own feces . . . do you just stop and go: Wow, it's amazing how fucking crazy I really am?"*

Paul had stayed up long after Dondi and the others had retired, wrestling with the issue and his own inner conflict. In the end he'd had to admit that it only made sense to allow

Wells this one thing. Inasmuch as defiance demanded punishment, obedience by necessity required reward. Alone in the still deep of the night, Paul resolved that yes, he would.

Which brought him to this day. Paul arrived after shift with a bucket, soap, assorted toiletries, clean sweatpants, and a T-shirt. He allowed Will to bathe and dress and brush his teeth, even granting him a measure of dignity by exiting the box as he did so. When Will called out that he was done, Paul entered.

The change was subtle but startling; clad and cleaned, the boy looked slight and unimposing, baggy clothes hanging from his wiry frame, the sparse stubble crowning his head making him look forlorn, even younger than he was. The boy's sudden, spartan cleanliness only heightened Paul's awareness of the fouled condition of the box. He glanced at the grimed walls, the threadbare blanket, the stinking toilet, then told Will he would return with cleaning supplies in the morning and allow him to clean the space. Will nodded gratefully. It was weird.

For the first time since this nightmare had begun, Will's sociopathic façade had been stripped away; in its place, Paul found something oddly vulnerable, something . . . human.

It was almost like a miracle. His plan was actually working.

God damn it.

Paul gripped the steering wheel, rumbling down the home stretch. He felt torn. He should be pleased, but something gnawed at him. Like some bent form of karmic jujitsu, the sudden emergence of Will's fledgling humanity had left Paul in sudden and serious question of his own. It was one thing to imprison and subjugate the inhuman monster who had caused so much pain, quite another to do so to a human being. And something else entirely to enjoy it.

And that was the scary part, the part that both fueled and frayed him. Inasmuch as Paul had begun the journey in pain, he now felt the cold and ravenous edge of something far darker uncoiling in his gut, snaking up his spine until his nerve endings buzzed. The thing that had let him go as far as he'd needed to crack Will's sociopathic veneer suddenly told him—if he dared admit it—that the real cause of his unease was not that he had gone too far but that he had not gone far enough. It was a primal, sub-rational thing, equal parts adrenaline, rage, and simple hate.

Yes, hate, he realized, little hairs on the back of his neck prickling at the very thought of it. He hated the little fucker—part of him did, anyway. The base part, the animal part. The part that presaged all thought and reason. It had a mind all its own.

And it did not want to stop. Not at a toe or finger or hand or foot. Not if his skin were flayed with dull razor blades, an inch at a time, until he was reduced to raw wet red.

It did not want to stop at all.

No, Paul thought, then aloud he said, "No." He shuddered again, beating back the lurid impulse to vengeance or fury. He was still in control—of himself, of his feelings, of the situation.

But driving down these well-worn streets, through the festive, fictive backdrop of peace on earth and goodwill toward men, it suddenly struck him: he had known these roads most of his life. But he was in uncharted territory now.

It made it all that much harder for him to contemplate how much farther this would go.

Or to consider its inevitable end.

The telephone was ringing as he reached the back door. Paul had arrived home hoping to find the lights on and Julie already there, desperate to seek solace in her arms even as he apologized for being such a prick.

The phone rang again as he dumped his bag and scrambled to reach it in time, only to have it stop a heartbeat before he got there.

"Shit!" he muttered. "Shit! Shit!" He picked it up, heard only a dial tone. He punched *69.

"Your custom calling feature is working," a recorded voice smugly informed him. *"However, it cannot be used with the number you have dialed."*

"Shit!" Paul growled, racking the receiver. He checked the answering machine. The little red LCD registered zero. No calls. Weird. She should be back by now. The scanner atop the refrigerator sat silent.

Paul went to the fridge and grabbed a beer, visions of breakdowns and MVAs dancing in his head. He took a swig and suppressed them, thinking of more mundane explanations. A late start. Traffic. The postholiday migration back to the city.

Paul looked at his watch. They hadn't spoken all weekend, which felt strange, but perhaps it was for the best. A little space, some think time. A weekend with her folks. A good thing.

The phone rang again. Paul's heart skipped a beat, and he lurched to grab it.

"Julie?" he said, trying to sound casual, failing miserably.

"Paul," she replied, as if surprised to hear him. "You're there . . ."

"I just got in," he explained. "Where are you, hon? Is there a problem?"

"I'm here," she said.

"Where? Your folks'?"

"Yes." Tense.

"Babe, it's almost nine," he said. "Don't you have school tomorrow?"

From the other end, a pause. Hesitant. Palpable. Paul felt confused. "Julie?"

"I'm here," she said, voice small and distant.

"I'm just asking . . . I mean, traffic's probably a bitch by now."

Another pause. "Paul," she began, "I'm gonna stay here."

"Oh." Paul sighed, his hopes of restoration deflating. But it made sense; it was already late, and as much as he wanted to be with her, he didn't feature her alone on the road at midnight. "That's good," he offered gamely. "I mean, not like the world'll end if you miss a day or anything. Want me to call you in sick in the morning?"

No answer. Suddenly he felt very odd, like something was up. What was the sound of one shoe dropping?

"Jule?" he said.

From the other end, a sigh: tremulous. Pained. "What I meant is, I'm gonna stay a while," she said. The words hung ominous in fiberoptic limbo.

"What are you saying?" he asked. "I don't understand . . ."

"I need some time," she explained, sounding wooden and rehearsed, like she was reading prepared text. "I need to sort some things out . . ."

Paul winced; in its own way it was a weird turnabout to his own bullshit of the other day. She was hedging and dodging, using trite catch phrases as emotional roadblocks; it was both alarming and pissing him off.

"Things?" he said. "What things?" His own tone ratcheted up inadvertently. "Julie, what the hell's going on?"

"I don't know," she blurted, then faltered. "I just need . . . shit . . . I don't want . . ."

"Don't want what?" Paul could hear from the rhythm of her breath that she was trying not to cry.

"I just really need to be alone right now," she said finally.

Paul's heart pounded, stomach dropping like an elevator with its cables cut. "Julie, please . . ." he murmured. "Everything will be all right, I swear," he vowed desperately.

"Paul, don't . . ."

"Just come home. Get some rest, come home tomorrow if you want. But come home. Okay?"

No reply. Paul reeled, shock waves of emotional free fall rippling through him. "Julie?"

"I can't. Not right now." She sighed, added softly, "I'm sorry."

"Julie, please . . ." Paul started to say something else, but before he could find the words, he heard the sound of the receiver cradling on the other end. The line clicked and went dead. Paul stood for a heartbeat, holding the phone, in shock. Another recorded voice sounded, followed by a horrendous, shrill tone.

"If you'd like to make a call, please hang up and try again . . . [boo dah DEEEEE . . .] "If you'd like to make a call, please hang up and try again . . ."*

The tone trilled again, snapping him back. Paul hung up the phone.

And just like that, she was gone.

34

Paul stared at the telephone, swigging his beer and pacing the kitchen as if afraid that to stand in one place would be to invite the floor to drop from beneath him, swinging down like a gallows door to pitch him into a still deeper abyss. Eventually he picked it up, hit the speed dial keyed to her folks' number. It rang, unanswered, once, twice. On the third try, someone picked up.

"Yeah . . ." Ted, Julie's dad, gruff and abrupt.

"Ted, please," Paul said urgently. "I gotta talk to Julie."

"No, you don't," he countered, in full on paternal protective mode. "She doesn't want to talk to you."

"Goddammit, Ted, I'm not kidding!" Paul barked, civility faltering, then failing completely. "Quit fucking around!"

Ted flatly told him not to call, not to come there. And hung up.

"Bastard!" Paul slammed the phone down as shock gave way to stunned disbelief, to raw, boiling anger. Son of a bitch. He could only imagine how long the old fart had dreamed of saying those words, to leverage him out of Julie's life for good. Paul punched the speed dial again. The phone rang once, rang again. On the third ring an answering machine kicked in. The one he and Julie had bought for them. The one they had never used.

It beeped, recording. Paul hung up, stood in silence. His gaze tracked wildly across the room, spied Eleanor's happy little plaque hanging above the sink.

TODAY IS THE FIRST DAY OF THE REST OF YOUR LIFE.

"Son of a BITCH!" Paul roared and heaved the beer bottle at it. It twirled end over end to hit the wall, amber glass exploding in a spray of shrapnel and suds. Next came the kitchen table, upending as he grabbed the edge and flipped it, sending a bowl of fruit tumbling to smash on the tiles. Paul picked up one of the wooden kitchen chairs and swung it like a Louisville slugger, the top of the chair clipping the hanging light overhead, sending it spinning in a mad pendulum swing. The chair came down, obliterating into a crunching pile of kindling against the heavy wooden table base. Shadows lurched and loomed wildly. The whole room looked alive and demented, its placid façade rendered in lunatic shades.

"NOOOO!" he cried again, thoughts reeling. First his daughter. Then his wife. Gone. Everything he loved in the world had been taken from him, up to and including his goddamned dog.

And now there was nothing between the man and the nightmare.

Paul turned to the kitchen counter, the dishes neatly washed and racked. He swept the plates and glass from the side of the sink. They spun and flew to the floor in a flurry of glittering fragments. Paul watched them shatter, blood pounding in his veins.

And that was just the beginning.

Monday morning came like a curse.

Paul shuffled through the wreckage, shell-shocked and spent, oddly calm. The first floor looked like a bomb had gone off in it, the rage that had consumed the kitchen spreading until it had engulfed everything within reach. Dining room and living room were mauled and mangled, furniture battered and broken, bookcases thrown over to vomit their contents across the floor. A fireplace andiron poked through the blackened television tube like a stake through a vampire's heart. Only the cabinet holding the home videos had escaped unscathed; it stood like a lone sentinel, in mute testimony.

Paul found the cordless phone in the carnage, laying under a cracked family photo. He picked up the receiver and dialed. He called Julie's school, ostensibly to cover for her, in truth in a desperate bid to maintain the crumbling façade. He was politely, if awkwardly, informed that Julie had already filed for a leave of absence, right before the holidays. An indefinite leave.

"Of course she did," he said quietly. And hung up the phone.

He felt weirdly displaced, as if watching himself from afar. He had read statistics, how fifty percent of marriages suffering the death of a child ended in divorce. Cold numbers. Meaningless. He wondered, how many suicides?

Paul turned and walked upstairs to the hall bathroom, stood before the sink. He turned the water on and splashed it across his face, then stared at himself in the mirror.

"Fine," he told the reflection. "I'm fine." Paul smiled, showing teeth, lips thin and strained. "She's fine," he said, practicing, and smiled again: better this time, more lifelike, applying just the right touch of disarming sadness.

"Everything's fine," he said, smothering the feelings. He said it again, and again, until his eyes, like windows to the soul, went dark and clouded over, masking the heat inside. Until no one would ever guess what was raging there.

By Monday afternoon the destruction had been largely repaired. Paul had diligently uprighted and restored, sweeping away the fragments, masking the damage like a shattered vessel painstakingly pieced and glued back together: seemingly whole, riddled with weakness, ready to come unglued at the slightest touch.

Paul stood at the front door, donning his coat and scarf. A little mirror hung by the coathooks. Paul zipped up and glanced up to see a perfect simulation of himself staring back.

"I'm fine," he said.

Then he turned and walked out the door.

Nightfall. Our Lady of Sorrows. Another F.L.A.M.E. meeting. Paul was again in the company of lost and lamenting souls huddled in the basement rectory, seated in the outer ring of folding chairs. He listened to the litany of suffering. The holidays loomed heavy on them all; again and again he heard quiet dread expressed, the myriad ways in which every television and radio was magically transformed into an agent of emotional ambush, every trip to the market or stroll through a shopping mall turned numbly rancid and redolent with threat, every cheery song a taunting reminder, every festive card a ransom note. Each of them bore the burden of a world that stubbornly refused to cease its turning; all felt to some degree stranded, disoriented, displaced.

Afterwards the group gathered loosely, sipping coffee and chatting in soft and muted tones. Nina was there, presiding over the proceedings; when she saw Paul she smiled and asked earnestly how he was doing.

"Fine," Paul told her. "Everything's fine."

His words carried just the right mixture of sadness and resignation; when he smiled his woeful smile, her heart melted.

"It's not easy," she told him. "It never will be. But it does get better, with time." She touched his shoulder, in purely innocent empathy. In that instant a part of him rebelled; Paul felt an urge to just blurt it all out—to tell her, tell everyone, what was really going on.

Then he looked past her, and his blood froze.

Nina saw him stiffen, turned instinctively to follow his gaze. And then she froze, too. Standing by the snack table near the double doors was a woman: same slight, frail frame, same cheap Burlington overcoat, offset by a cheap and absurdly cheerful rayon scarf. Her chestnut hair had gone dull and brittle, pale skin thin and bloodless, as though stress were aging her in dog years, leeching all color from her world, rendering her mutely monochrome. But he still recognized her, and as she looked up, Paul found himself staring, in frank and naked shock, at Kathryn Wells.

The Wells woman's eyes widened as she recognized him, too. For a moment, she looked as if she might scurry off. Then she turned and looked away, trying to hide in plain sight.

"What's she doing here?" Paul asked, instinctively glancing around for her husband. But the elder Wells was nowhere in sight. Nina looked from Kathryn to Paul, visibly uncomfortable.

"I'm sorry," she explained. "Our policy is to welcome everyone who's suffering."

"Even *them*?"

"They lost someone, too," Nina countered gently. "Kathryn's been coming for some time now. I realize this might be awkward . . ."

"No," Paul said flatly, then softened. "No. It's fine." He looked at her. "Really."

Nina started to say something else, but Paul started across the room, sliding past small knots of members chatting in twos and threes, zeroing in on Kathryn Wells. He caught up to her as she hovered before a large folding conference table, pointedly busying herself with the stacks of fliers advertising support group events. She saw him in her peripheral vision and visibly flinched, but she stood her ground. Paul cleared his throat.

"Mrs. Wells?" he said levelly. "I'm Paul Kelly."

She nodded, shrinking into herself. "Yes, of course . . ." she began, then ventured, politely wary. "How are you?"

"I've been better," he replied, paused. "And you?"

Kathryn let out a little laugh, small and entirely devoid of mirth. She uncoiled a bit and shrugged. "Oh, about the same."

Their eyes met, fleeting. Kathryn looked away. "I'm sorry for . . ." she faltered—*For what? For her son's crime?*

For birthing a murderer? For ever existing at all?—then continued, ". . . I'm sorry for intruding like that. At your house, I mean. It was a stupid thing to do."

"No," Paul said. "No, actually, it was very kind. I'm sorry we . . ." His turn to hesitate. "Well, let's just say I'm sorry, too."

She looked surprised, almost shocked; certainly Paul was the last person on earth she ever expected kindness from. "You don't have to say that," she said.

"I know," Paul replied. "I guess I just wanted to tell you, if you ever needed to talk . . ." He let the thought trail off, the conversation dying. Kathryn nodded and turned to go. As she did Paul suddenly took a tentative step forward. It felt a little like searching a burning building—pushing forth through blinding smoke, feeling for heat and contact as if by Braille. He did not know what was around the next corner. But he knew the shape of a door when he felt it.

"Kathryn," he began. She turned, regarding him. "Would you like to get some coffee?"

Kathryn Wells glanced from him to the steaming pot on the table; Paul amended. "Some actual coffee, I mean. I know they mean well, but this stuff's mostly good for tanning leather."

She smiled, faintly; it wasn't much of a joke, but any port in a storm. As she did, Paul caught a glimpse of former beauty, some hint of what the years had dog-piled into submission. It struck him that she was actually very pretty, in a shy, self-deprecating way. She hesitated, then nodded. "Yes," she answered. "Yes, I would."

Paul smiled his practiced smile. He hadn't imagined this, couldn't have seen it coming in a million years.

But just like that, a plan was born.

The coffee shop was small and out of the way, the better to not be seen—not a yuppified Starbucks, but an old Italian place on a quiet side street in East Glendon. The night air was crisp and clear, chill but not too cold. Paul and Kathryn sat outside at a small marble and wrought iron café table, nursing steaming cups of cappuccino, enmeshed in private détente.

Kathryn watched as Paul lit a cigarette. He saw her looking, held the pack forward. Kathryn hesitated, looking momentarily like a schoolgirl misbehaving, then reached out to pluck one thin white cylinder with delicate fingers. He noticed her nails were bitten short.

"Thanks," she said. As she placed it to her lips Paul flipped his Zippo open, lit it. Embers glowed as Kathryn sucked deeply, exhaling a plume of frost-tinged smoke. "Jimmy doesn't like it when I smoke," she said guiltily.

Paul shrugged, like no big deal. "Jimmy doesn't need to know everything," he remarked casually. Kathryn laughed, nervous.

"Tell that to Jimmy!" she blurted ruefully, then caught herself. She took a sip of coffee; Paul watched, his expression carefully neutral. Kathryn put the cup down, changing the subject. "So . . . how is your wife?" she asked.

"She left me," Paul said. He spoke softly, but the words landed like a slap. It was intentional. Kathryn's eyes widened.

"Oh God. When?"

"Last night, or last week, depending," he replied, then shrugged. Watching her watching him.

"I'm so sorry," Kathryn said, then paused. Paul looked quietly aggrieved. It was her turn.

"My husband is a good man," she began, protectively. "He just has his own ideas of how things should be."

Paul nodded, understanding. "He's pretty strict?"

Kathryn bit her lip, gazing out into black night sky beyond streetlight glare. She nodded.

"What about with Will?" Paul asked. "Was he very strict with Will?"

Kathryn withdrew a bit, innately defensive. But Paul just waited. A solitary tear formed in the corner of one eye. She wiped it away. Paul watched, then asked softly, "Tell me about the fire . . ."

Kathryn Wells did a double take, then seemed to sag. "I don't know," she sighed. "It's like I told the police and the reporters—it was about four o'clock that afternoon. I looked out the kitchen window, and saw smoke." Her voice trembled ever so slightly. "I went outside, and Will was standing over the trash can, feeding papers into it . . ."

"What kind of papers?" Paul asked.

"Just papers." Kathryn shrugged miserably, then added softly, "Notebook papers." Paul was looking at her neutrally; he knew she wasn't telling him everything. Kathryn tried to evade his quiet, probing stare, but more tears began to well in her eyes, like a dam giving way under relentless inner pressure. Suddenly it cracked.

"It was his sketchbook," she confessed, and started to cry. Her hands fluttered in her lap like trapped birds. "All of his drawings, everything. He just burned them . . ."

Paul thought of the designs inked on faded denim, the ones he himself had fed into the flames. "What was in the book?"

"I don't know!" Kathryn wailed, and meant it this time. "It was like his private world, he wrote and drew in it all the time. He never let me see it. He never let *anyone* see it." She shuddered under the weight of her own guilt. "And then his father came home, and just gave him hell, not because he burned it, but because he set a fire."

"Had he ever done something like that before?"

"No!" Kathryn replied, adamant and defensive. "He'd been moody all week, but he wasn't like that. He was a good boy . . ."

She drew up short as her gaze met Paul's, then flitted away. "Oh, God," she murmured, almost to herself. "It's all my fault."

"What is?" Paul asked.

"Everything," she said. "All of it . . ."

Paul leaned closer, speaking so softly it was almost like a voice in her head. "Why?"

Kathryn looked at him, and the floodgates breached and spewed forth. She began to speak the terrible, unspoken truths: of her own sense of failure, the guilt, the confusion, the bottomless remorse. She spoke about Will: a quiet and sensitive child, smart but reclusive. She spoke of his relationship with his father: the elder Wells's unerring strictness, their inability to communicate, her endless struggle with her husband to just let the boy be himself. She recounted the boy's increasing rebellion, the inevitable battles, the downward cycle she was somehow not strong enough to avert. And then she spoke—in halting, urgent tones—of the nightmare since . . . it . . . had all happened; of the prying eyes of police and neighbors and media; of the horror of knowing that the child she had once carried inside her had come to be accused of something so heinous.

And Paul nodded and listened, allowing her to unload a portion of her burden, sifting every scrap for usable detail.

"Sometimes I wish it were all over," Kathryn suddenly confessed. "Everyone says he's gone, but he's not gone to *me*." Her tone turned plaintive, deeply wounded. "I keep expecting to see him, every time I turn around. I keep expecting to hear his voice, calling out from the living room, asking what's for dinner, something . . . anything." She paused, voice trembling. "Sometimes the *not knowing* hurts more than anything," she added, almost to herself. Then, in a voice barely audible, she said, "Sometimes I think knowing he were dead would be better than never knowing what happened to him at all. At least then maybe we could move on."

Kathryn stopped, suddenly exposed, ashamed of the love she felt for her own son. "Some mother," she said. "You must think I'm terrible." She lowered her head. Paul watched for a moment, then reached out across the tiny table to place a reassuring hand on her shoulder. Kathryn sobbed quietly.

"It's all right," he told her. "It's all right."

But it wasn't all right. Not even a little bit. And they both knew it. Kathryn continued to cry, the gentle strength of his touch moving her until she seemed to visibly deflate with each new breath. Paul placed an arm around her, murmuring quiet comfort. And though he said the right words, pushed all the right buttons, Paul felt none of it. She was a cipher to him, collateral damage in his twisted mission.

His mission, which had expanded until it included nothing less than the complete destruction of her world.

"It's okay," he told her. "Just let it out. Let it all out . . ."

Kathryn cried.

And then she did.

35

It was just after 10:00 P.M. on Wednesday when Paul arrived at the Waterfront, a dank little dive situated three blocks from the piers, just past a sprawling expanse of oil refinery once owned by Exxon but now under the banner of some indeterminate multinational conglomerate who performed the same job but paid a fraction of the wages. The resulting downsizing had contributed mightily to the Waterfront's glory days being firmly behind it, and by outward appearance, it would not be missed.

Faded neon advertising Stroh's and Johnny Walker Red flickered behind fly-specked windows permanently tinted by decades of diesel exhaust and grit; the dark interior smelled of stale smoke and stale beer, with the occasional faint waft of cheap perfume, even cheaper cologne, piss, and vomit. As a workingman's joint it made the Gaslight Tavern look like the Plaza; as Paul entered, the word *shithole* came clearly to mind.

He took a seat at the far end of the bar, scanning the murky interior from a vantage point that strategically covered the door. The bartender ambled over. Paul ordered a beer. The bartender came back with a longneck Bud, which Paul proceeded to nurse. He was not there to drink.

He watched the room. The ghosts of longshoremen past may have hung in the air, but the current denizens consisted of a depressive smattering of middle-aged Teamsters parked on bar stools as if they had sprouted there, and aging low-rent hookers wearing too much makeup and not enough clothes, flashing unfortunate expanses of flesh through fake fur, spandex, and fishnets. Paul watched, waiting.

The meeting with Kathryn had been purest chance, but from it was born a new sense of purpose, a necessary recalibration of direction. He had been going about this all wrong, trying to achieve results from the outside in. Kathryn, in pouring out her sorrows, had led him to realize that it was time to shift strategies and work from the inside *out*.

That required reconnaissance, investigation, research. He was not without compassion for her; in her own way, she was a victim, too. And it was not lost on him that he could have eased her pain with a word. But he needed answers, and she might have them. And the die was already cast, such as it was. She had made her choices, as had he. And now they just had to live with them.

For Paul, that meant, among other things, maintaining the illusion of normalcy as best he could. He went to work, putting in his time. There had been another fire of mysterious origin—an abandoned house near the corner of Atkins and Middleton streets that was appropriately credited to the elusive Mr. Toast—plus the usual array of civilian screwups and random disasters. The torch job had been marginally clever—a space heater left on near a gallon of paint thinner in the basement, with bundles of newspapers spread around for kindling—but otherwise it had been hot and dirty and mundanely dangerous, and Paul had humped his load like a grunt, getting the job done but no more, and nobody had died. He said nothing about Julie or the upheaval at home to Dondi or the others, and no one asked—indeed, his crewmates seemed relieved to be freed of the burden of knowing, or caring.

His sessions in the box had likewise winnowed down to

the most perfunctory of functions. The transformation seemed to be holding, which was a good sign, but rather than press for answers, Paul had left Will alone. There were other things he wanted to know first.

Which brought him to this dark and dreary place, with its gummy floors and scarred wooden stools and dead-end loser vibe. He knew from Kathryn's later outpourings that James Wells could be found here eventually: he worked swing shift at the docks, and the Waterfront was one of his regular haunts on his way home. It was just a matter of time.

Paul stared down at his glass. Poor Kathryn. A weak woman with a good heart, married too young to know who she was or what she wanted out of life, pregnant before she was twenty, middle-aged by thirty, old before her time. Hating her was pointless, like punching a sand castle; in the end she had merely taken on the form life had molded to her, and she'd crumbled at the first swell of the tide. She was the living embodiment of everything he had never wanted for Kyra, and she was legion; you couldn't throw a rock in Jersey without hitting a Kathryn Wells.

And yet, in his dreams . . .

In his dreams, Paul had seen her, fleeting images fed by a lonely woman's grief: Kathryn, young and fair, her beauty uneroded as she welcomed him into her arms, her legs parting wide to receive him . . . her legs, smooth and sleek and trembling, spread wide to issue forth a child . . . the child in her arms, its innocence as yet uncorrupted, never dreaming that he would grow to become the monster . . . the monster who would murder his child . . .

. . . and as he watched she became Julie, in the glow of her own youth, cradling the squirming bundle in her arms . . . his daughter, his love made flesh, the tiny, fragile center of his world . . .

. . . and he knew, somehow it would be different for him with a son . . . the same love, the same care, but with it, the knowledge that one day, God willing, he would grow to be a man and he would have to let him

*go . . . but a girl, a daughter . . . even as a woman, she
would still be his little girl, she would always be his
little girl . . . and he would always be there to protect
her . . .*

*. . . and Paul smelled the stench of something hid-
den yet aflame . . . as he turned, flames roared up
behind him, a wall of heat and pain that split the floor
wide, spewing up as though bellowing from the mouth
of Hell, separating him from his woman and child . . .
Paul screamed . . . the room was burning, his house
was burning . . . Paul cried out in anguish, unable to
reach them . . .*

*. . . and as he called her name, Julie looked to him,
her eyes filled with terror, hair cindering like a glowing Medusa's nest . . . the flames exploded into
inferno . . . as Julie became Kathryn . . .*

Became Kyra . . .

Paul snapped back, looked up, breath ragged, a sheen of
sweat beading his brow. The front door creaked wide.

And James Wells walked in.

Paul glanced at his watch: 11:11. He calmed his breathing as Wells lumbered to a stool in the middle of the bar,
took a seat, shoulders hunched. Paul steeled himself, called
the bartender over . . . then watched as he made his way
back to where Wells was sitting and set him up with a shot.

James Wells watched the barkeep pour, clearly wondering what was up. The bartender gestured back to Paul. He
felt a familiar rush of adrenaline, like the feeling he got
when he strapped on his gear to enter a burning building.
Except he was alone, bare-handed, and the only fire raging
was the one inside his skull.

Paul drained his glass and stood.

"It's showtime," he said.

Wells looked up as Paul ambled over, slid up beside him. It
seemed to take a moment for him to place the face; then he

harrumphed and nodded. "It's you," he said gruffly. "For a second I thought you were a faggot or sumthin'."

"Didn't stop you from taking the drink," Paul replied.

"Drink's a drink," Wells shrugged. "If you're buyin'."

"I'm buyin'." Paul took the stool beside him. He gestured to the bartender to set them up again; as he did, Paul watched Wells. He looked half-ripped before he'd even walked in the door—as he knocked back the shot Paul caught a glimpse of spider veins lining the creases of his nostrils, visible beneath the wind-burnt skin. Maybe not alcoholic, but a man who drank hard, and long. His clothes were old and faded—fleece-lined jeans jacket, work pants and flannel shirt, the creases limned with toil; his boots were scuffed and cracked; his hands, thickly callused and oil-stained. His dark hair was brush-cut and stippled gray; little tufts of wild black strands poked from the dark folds of his ears. He looked like what he was: an under-educated, blue-collar lug whose gray matter had never been seared by a serious thought, with the vibe of a faded high school linebacker for whom life past the prom had been one long downhill slide.

Wells picked up the glass, gazing into it as if it held secrets. "No offense," he said, "but what the hell're you doin' here?" He knocked back the shot and looked at Paul through hooded, bloodshot eyes. "I mean, you ain't exactly a regular."

Paul glanced past him, taking in the ambience. He shook his head. "Guess not," he replied. "Guess I just wanted to talk to you, father to father . . . man to man . . ."

"Hmmph," Wells snorted. Paul signaled the bartender to set them up again—shots and beers this time—then waited, not hostile or threatening, but merely observant. The bartender poured and retreated. After a heavy pause, Wells grumbled, grudgingly yielding.

"Look, pal," he said at last, "I'm sorry for what happened, and you seem like an okay enough guy, but whaddaya want from me? Haven't we been through enough?"

Paul said nothing. Wells slugged back the shot. "Kid's just no damn good," he mumbled bitterly. "Never was."

Paul gave a half-nod—not agreeing, merely noting. He sensed something building up inside the older man, a thunderhead of bile mounting some grim inner horizon. He quietly slid his shot across the bar until it was next to Wells's now emptied glass. Wells didn't notice, instead sighing grievously, sinking into his own thoughts.

"I don't apologize for what I am, ya know?" he said, words slurring slightly now. "All my life, I did what I had to do. Bust my balls to put food on the table, a roof over their heads, take care of fuckin' business, don't ask nothin' from nobody . . ." He picked up the shooter as if it were his own, downed it. "I tried to raise him up right, teach him how a man's gotta be. But his mother . . ." He paused, washing down bile with beer. "Always protectin' him, always whinin' about him . . ." He sighed bitterly. "Just made him weak, is all. Turned him into a snot-nosed little shit. *We* put our house up for his bail! Guess who's gonna pay for *that*!"

James Wells squatted on his stool like a brooding gargoyle. The stench of disappointment—with his son, with his wife, with himself, with his whole miserable life—radiated off of him in waves. Suddenly he turned toward Paul, off balance and belligerent. "You think I wanted any of this?" he said, voice raising. "Think I wanted cops crawlin' all over my house, fuckin' reporters shoving their cameras at us like *we're* responsible?! I didn't take any crap off my boy, and if he ever tried to give it he got the back of my hand!" Wells held up one thick-knuckled and formidable hand, waving it menacingly. "It's *not* my goddamned fault!"

Across the room, heads turned. The bartender looked at them warily. Paul put his hands up in a gesture of easy supplication, and James Wells calmed somewhat.

"Ah, fukkit," he muttered. "S'alla buncha bullshit."

He got up off his stool, lurching toward the back of the bar and the bathrooms, his gate unsteady and plodding. The other denizens went back to minding their own misery. Paul watched him go. He'd seen enough.

He reached into his pocket, pulled out a twenty, and signaled the bartender. The bartender approached. "Anything else?" he asked.

"No," Paul told him. He handed him the bill, waved it off: keep the change. As the bartender moved away, Paul reached into his jacket pocket, surreptitiously removed a vial of small blue-and-white pills. SECONAL SODIUM 50 MG. PULVUL, the label read. Paul glanced around the room casually. Then cracked one and emptied it into James Wells's beer.

Just then Wells returned, looking slightly less combative. Paul quickly pocketed the vial, acted like nothing was wrong.

"Sorry," Wells mumbled sheepishly. "Didn't mean to crawl up your ass like that. It ain't like you did anything."

Paul nodded, then stood and raised his glass in toast. Wells followed suit.

"Whadda we drink to?" he asked blearily. Paul thought about it for a second.

"To taking care of business," he replied.

It was just past midnight as Paul manned the wheel of his truck, snaking up Route 9. It was a dreary section of secondary highway that wound past industrial parks, gas stations and roadside diners, long stretches of four-lane blacktop punctuated by the periodic stoplight. By day it was a clogged artery clotted with commuters, buses, trucks and tankers, but by the witching hour, it was a ghost road. The posted limit was fifty, but the big rigs that rumbled up and down both sides of the concrete divider routinely blew by at half again as fast. Especially in the open stretches.

So much the better, Paul thought. He was moving along at the speed limit, keeping careful distance behind a piece of shit '84 Monte Carlo with mismatched doors and an undercarriage so ravaged by rust that it looked like it had been attacked by a vehicular version of the flesh-eating virus. It strayed from lane to lane as if finding them by Braille. It was an accident looking for a place to happen, and as far as Paul was concerned, it couldn't happen to a nicer guy.

You bastard, Paul thought, picturing life in happy *casa* Wells, with a man carved from stone and a woman made of sand, and a child ground inexorably in between. *You miser-*

able rat bastard. James Wells's patented no-nothing, cro-mag concepts of how to raise a real man filled Paul with incomprehensible dread and rage. *If you hadn't been such an asshole*, he wondered blackly, *would it have happened? Would any of it?* His memories of their encounter swirled and coalesced into their purest, most concentrated essence.

Would Kyra be alive today if you hadn't been such a callous, caustic, unmitigated prick?

Paul fumed, jaw tight, fingers throttling the steering wheel. The Chevy bobbed and weaved unwittingly before him. They passed a stoplight: dead ahead lay a sweeping stretch of darkened road, perhaps a mile to the next light. And they were the only vehicles in sight.

Paul reached up and flipped off his headlights. The truck went dark, little yellow running lights and dashboard glow his sole illumination. He hit the gas.

The engine revved and roared as four hundred-sixty gas-sucking cubic inches growled into action. The truck sped up, closing the distance. The speedometer climbed . . . fifty . . . fifty-five . . . sixty. Closing the distance.

Paul waited until the big Ford was right up to the Chevy's back bumper. On the cab floor, left of the brake, was a little cylindrical footswitch. Paul stomped it. Halogen hi-beam glare instantly pierced the rear windshield, flooding the interior with brilliant white light. He could see Wells's head bob and crane around in stark shadow, stunned and disoriented. The Chevy lurched in the lane.

Paul nudged the gas, massive bumper delivering a violent love tap to the back of the car, big steel and rubber bumper guards jutting up like fangs. Tires screeched as the car careened and straightened out. Paul bumped it again. Wells racked the wheel, arcing into the left-hand lane.

Paul gunned the engine and pulled up alongside, the two vehicles now locked in a lethal duet. From his high vantage point, Paul could look down and see James Wells struggling at the wheel, mouthing obscenities, but with the sedan's wide roofline Wells could not see him. The concrete abut-ment whizzed by at a blur, inches from the Chevy's driver's side.

"Son of a bitch," Paul hissed, the hum of the road beneath him echoed by the throbbing bloodlust in his veins. He racked the wheel again. The truck crossed the line, perilously close to the car, squeezing it toward the abutment. The Chevy's tires bit narrow shoulder gravel, then Wells desperately retaliated, veering back toward Paul. Paul pulled away, playing three-ton tag at sixty per.

A sign flew by, warning CAUTION: ROAD WORK. Some two hundred yards ahead, a large metal public works sign, strobing arrows flashing ➤➤ ➤➤ ➤➤ . The road narrowed to a single lane. Paul's.

One hundred yards. Wells gunned the Monte Carlo, fighting for the right-hand lane. At sixty yards Paul suddenly cut the gas and dropped back, as Wells veered in front of him . . . then gunned it again, cutting right, onto the shoulder. He punched it, left front bumper giving Wells's right rear bumper one final, fatal tap . . .

. . . and the Chevy screeched and skid, fishtailing madly and out of control, as Paul hit the brakes and slid to a rubber burning stop. He watched as the Chevy screamed sideways, gravity and sheer momentum slamming it through the road sign with a deafening crash, then smacking into the abutment with the grinding shriek of mangled metal and shattering glass, finally flipping it all the way over, roof compacting as it came to a stop, horn keening into the night.

Paul's truck waited, growling on the shoulder like a beast of prey, headlights glaring. He stared, heart pounding, adrenaline jangling his nerves. Suddenly he jumped out, jogged over to the wreckage, boots crunching on safety glass and shrapnel. As he drew near, the Chevy's horn wailed a faltering death low against the hiss and creak of mechanical carnage; the smell of gasoline hung heavy in the air.

Paul came abreast of the wreck and saw Wells, body pinned between wheel and seat, his face a mass of glass and blood. He knelt down near the crumpled driver's door, crushed like a beer can and hanging by one hinge. Wells moaned weakly, half-conscious and in shock. He was not yet dead. Paul cursed and stood, saw a sudden flash of oncoming lights: a hulking tractor trailer in the southbound lane, air brakes hissing as it geared to a stop. The driver jumped out. Paul fought back panic, calling out urgently.

"Call an ambulance!" he cried. "Now!"

The driver nodded and reached back into his cab, grabbing his CB handset. Paul knelt and reached inside the car, checking James Wells's pulse, instantly shifting from an avenging angel to one of reluctant mercy, a trained professional, saver of lives. And hating it.

St. Anthony's. Intensive Care. 2:00 A.M. The elevator doors opened. Kathryn Wells stepped out, haggard and anguished. She saw a pair of uniform cops, an Iselin ambulance crew, a whey-faced young intern whose nametag read *Wheaton*. And Paul.

Surprise offset anxiety as their eyes met, his own features sober and concerned. He took a step toward her. She asked if her husband was all right. Before Paul could answer, the intern stepped in and explained that it did not look good. He ran down a laundry list of damage . . . *critical condition* . . . *coma* . . . *concussion* . . . *subdural   hematoma* . . . *cracked sternum* . . . *punctured lung* . . . *ruptured spleen* . . . *lacerations* . . . *broken bones* . . . plus a blood alcohol level twice the legal limit, with trace amounts of sedatives.

Kathryn nodded as he spoke, taking it in as if in a blur . . . then stopped. "Excuse me," she said, "did you say *sedatives*?"

Dr. Wheaton glanced at the tox screen chart. "Sodium Seconal," he replied. "Prescription stuff. Doesn't mix well with alcohol and automobiles."

Kathryn looked confused. "I don't understand," she began. "My husband doesn't take drugs."

Behind her, the uniforms and ambo crew rolled their eyes. "Lady, wake up," one of the EMTs scoffed. "Your husband was hammered." He gestured to Paul. "You're just lucky *he* got there when he did. Saved his goddamned life."

Kathryn looked at Paul; he looked away with what appeared to be humility, in reality was thinly masked panic. His story, confabulated in the heat of the moment—*heading home, drunken lunatic came outta nowhere, slammed into the median, who knew it was Wells?*—was supported by the big rig driver, who had only seen the aftermath, and, absent any other witnesses or reason to believe otherwise, was simply accepted. Especially when the ambo crew and the cops on the scene knew Paul by name. But Paul still worried: as stories went it had the surface cohesion of a soap bubble and would not bear up to scrutiny.

But no one was scrutinizing. Kathryn Wells regarded him not with suspicion but with gratitude. His was the only sympathetic face, the only one who looked at her with anything other than what seemed like scorn. Just as they'd known Paul, they'd recognized James Wells, too. And everyone had heard of his son: the elusive and notorious William Wells, accused killer, fugitive from justice.

She asked the intern if James would be all right; Wheaton told her they'd have to wait and see, then excused himself to make his rounds. The cops and paramedics went next, their work finished for now, pausing to pat Paul on the back and praise him for a job well done.

"No problem," he told them, knowing that in fact it was. A big one.

They exited, leaving Paul and Kathryn together, and alone. Behind them, James Wells lay in the ICU ward, a mass of bandages, tubes, and IV tethers. Monitors beeped softly, clocking mortality. Paul turned away from the window, looked at Kathryn. He didn't know what to say. But before he could speak, she hugged him.

"Thank you for saving his life," she said. "For everything."

"Don't mention it," he replied. Wishing she wouldn't. Wishing none of them would.

But of course, they did.

36

Paul stood over his daughter's grave: no flowers in hand to replace the dead ones long withered in the vase, nothing but a head full of careening thoughts, and a very bad feeling he could not seem to shake. He stared down at the polished face of the stone, saw his own reflection staring back.

"Hi, kiddo," he started to say, then paused. He suddenly wondered what he was doing—not just here, talking to a slab of rock, but with everything. He felt shaky, his thoughts skittering, unable to focus long on any one thing.

He felt like he was losing his mind.

"I . . . I did something bad last night," he told her, immediately thinking, *Yeah, right, attempted murder is bad . . . and actually doing it must be downright naughty.* "Not bad," he amended. "It was wrong." It was cold outside, but he was sweating. He wiped his eyes, hand trembling. "But the thing is," he continued, "while it was happening it felt so right . . . like I should be doing it." His voice lowered. "Only now I'm not so sure."

He flashed back to the chase, the crash, the sudden reversal of rescue . . . and the screaming irony that, by the time the morning paper hit the streets, Paul Kelly was again in the news. A stringer for the Glendon *Herald* had picked up the accident on his scanner; six hours later, a page two headline splashed HERO KELLY SAVES KILLER'S DAD, the accompanying copy luridly recounting an official regurgitation of Paul's ersatz explanation, the sole mercy being he hadn't made page one.

Paul had freaked out but of course could not show it. Every aspect of his life had become a fun house hall of mirrors, every reflection warped and distorted, every image false and askew. He had to feed everyone what they expected to see. Here, alone, could he let any of it out. And even here felt dangerous.

"I'm okay," he told her. "But it was a close call. And now I wonder . . ."

He stopped—wondered what, exactly? And therein lay the heart of it. As much as he was loathe to admit it, his brush with destruction had been nothing if not miraculous. It was almost enough to make him believe in miracles.

Almost enough to make him believe in God.

And that was the shocker, a veritable knee to the cosmic nuts. Paul felt his legs wobble, then knelt on the slushy, naked earth.

"Please, God," he murmured, voice cracking. "If you exist . . . if you're really out there . . . please help me. I need to know . . . I need to know that I'm not just crazy . . . that there's still some reason why this is all happening."

He stopped, head lowered. No thunderbolts of punishment split the sky; no beams of golden sunlight pierced the granite clouds above. Nothing. Thoughts roiling, Paul reached down to scoop up a pebble from the surface of his daughter's burial dirt. And closed it in his fist.

And all of a sudden it hit him.

Maybe he wasn't crazy. Maybe it made perfect sense. Meeting Kathryn Wells in his darkest hour. Their conversation in the coffee shop. At first it had felt like luck, or fate. Now it felt like something else. At that precise moment a lifetime of agnostic defiance crumbled inside him, and it suddenly dawned on Paul that the plan, such as it was, might not be entirely his own. Going to the bar to meet James Wells? Yes, that had been his idea. But he could have killed Wells in the wreck, and he hadn't. He could have killed him in the wreckage moments later, but he hadn't. Not for want of wanting to, or trying. But something had intervened, and it felt like more than simple chance or fate. He had not been found out. His secret was still safe. The kindness he had shown Kathryn Wells was not entirely false, and it had served a purpose he could not have imagined or foreseen, and only now could begin to fully comprehend. A purpose almost divine.

It could only mean one thing.

If there was such a thing as God, He must want Paul not to kill, not to avenge . . . but to continue. This journey. This mission. Until it was finished. God had intervened, like some mystical unindicted coconspirator, and allowed him to go on.

Paul needed to believe in something. That was as good a thing as any. Kneeling at his daughter's grave, from the depths of his despair, Paul suddenly found his Higher Power. And in so doing, trusted that somehow, he and God would find a way. He felt better even thinking it.

But God, it would seem, had other plans.

Back in the bowels of Marley Street, Will was undergoing an epiphany all his own, of a much more earthly nature. He stared at the walls, his own thoughts focused down to one overwhelming impulse. And the epiphany was this:

I gotta get outta here.

Sounded simple. Not even. Playing patty-cake with Paul Kelly was an act born not of desperation but of sheer survival. Motherfucker was crazy, and watching Kelly click off his own personal countdown to meltdown was a losing proposition, no matter how many *yessirs* and *nosirs* he choked on. Will had sucked up and kissed ass about as much as he could stand, winning concessions like light and soap, and thus far had managed, if barely, to keep all his moving parts. But for how long? Will surveyed his petty privilege of the week, his big reward for cleaning his cell and generally acting like a good little boy: a roll of toilet paper.

Fucker.

Will picked up the roll and threw it at the wall; it bounced harmlessly off and flopped to the floor, coming to a stop by the leg of the chair. Will picked it up. The crinkly wrapping depicted a happily gurgling baby and promised to be squeezably soft. Will flopped back and started bouncing it off the wall in an impromptu round of two-ply handball. Thinking.

I've got to get out of here.

But how?

Escape was futile; that much was for sure. The cell was too well constructed, his movements too closely monitored. Will knew all too well that simple force would not get him out of here. Nor would attitude. And luck was fast running out. Will realized that he was going to have to *think* his way out. And his only chance lay in playing this mad game until he could somehow get Kelly to lower his guard. Then, and only then, could he hope to strike.

Yeah, right, he thought morosely. *With what?*

Will stood, injured foot throbbing. Kelly was strong, even for an old fuck. And nuts. And Will was nothing if not used up. He wracked his brain. A fringe benefit of his cleaning spree was that it had afforded him the opportunity to scour every square inch of the box in search of something, anything, that could be fashioned into a weapon. The results had not been good. The lights were recessed behind heavy wire mesh. The bunk was useless. The chair was heavy and bolted to the floor.

Bolted . . .

Will suddenly knelt, ran his hands down the stout wooden legs. Heavy hex bolts were driven through the metal brackets that anchored it to the flooring. The edges were sharply angled, difficult to grasp. Will tapped the floor, heard the deadened thud signifying a support beam under the chair's front legs. No good.

He moved back, tapping, listening. As he reached the rear legs, Will heard the slightly hollow thunk of air space beneath. Flooring, maybe a subfloor of some kind. Then, nothing.

Not nothing, he amended. *Hope* was there.

Yes.

Will scrabbled into position behind the chair, braced his feet against the wall. The pressure on his injured foot was pure agony. He held his breath, pushing with all his strength. Nothing happened. The pain was excruciating. Tears formed in his eyes. Will released and sagged, exhausted. Then took a deep breath and pushed again. Harder this time.

The chair creaked slightly. Will pushed still harder, legs trembling from exertion, sweat popping on his skin. He was just about to pass out when the chair gave. Not a lot. A little. A tiny little bit.

It was almost like a miracle.

Will unflexed, turned to check it out. The head of the hex bolt had separated from the steel bracket ever so much. He had managed to create a millimeter of play, a hard-won window of hope. Will stripped off his T-shirt, wrapped a bit of it around the bolt head, tried to work it free. No good. It was in too tight.

He needed tools.

"Dammit!" Will hissed. "God DAMMIT!"

He was panting, pissed. If he didn't get out of there, he might as well just flush himself down the toilet, because his odds of survival were shit . . .

Shit, Will thought. An idea flashed. Suddenly Will scrambled up and over to the toilet, grabbed the toilet paper and unpeeled it. The happy baby wrapping went first, smiling image going sodden as it sank. Then he unreeled the roll, yard by yard by yard, and began stuffing it into the bowl. As the toilet began to block, Will flushed it, then flushed it again. The toilet gurgled and sputtered, water swirling.

Will flushed it again for good measure, then turned his attention to one of his other hard-won luxuries: the small bar of Dial soap. Grasping it carefully, he raked it across the edge of the bunk, slicing off thick shavings. As the bowl stopped up and began to fill, Will held up the shavings to his nose, sniffing them. He grimaced for a moment. Then took a deep breath. Put them in his mouth.

And began to chew.

Paul arrived hours later to find a trail of water leaking from the box.

"What the fuck?" he gasped and hurriedly opened the lock. He threw the door open, found the toilet flooded, water swirling over the brim to pool on the floor. Will huddled on the bunk in a fetal position, looking decidedly ill.

"What happened?" Paul demanded.

"Sick . . ." Will shuddered in the grip of a horrible cramp. "I'm sorry," he added weakly. "I tried to stop it. I'm sorry . . ."

Paul bit back anger, willed himself calm. "It's okay," he said. "Can you stand?"

"Yessir." Wells nodded feebly and started to pull himself up. He doubled over again, fell back on the bunk.

"Shit!" Paul grumbled, holding a hand to the boy's forehead. No fever to speak of, but clammy. He pressed two fingers against Will's belly, probing. Will groaned.

"It's not your appendix," Paul decided. He probed a few more points, then checked Will's pulse. Normal. Paul stood and shook his head. "It's just a stomachache," he said. "You'll be all right. Can you sit up?"

Will nodded gamely. Paul helped him up, then reached into his jacket pocket and pulled out a pair of handcuffs. He clicked one around Will's right wrist, secured the other to the back of the chair. Will did not resist.

"I'll be right back," Paul told him. "Gotta get some tools." Will nodded and watched as Paul exited the box.

And, for the first time since his capture, Will smiled.

Will sat on the floor, his back to the chair, watching. Paul's bulky toolbox lay open before him. The excess water had been scooped out and disposed of, the spillage mopped up;

Paul cursed and wielded a plumber's helper, trying to unblock the stoppage.

"Damn," he muttered. "How much toilet paper did you use?"

"I felt really sick," Will explained, mock apologetically.

"Feel better now?"

"Yessir," Will said sheepishly, eyes cast downward. He glanced at the tools jumbled inside the box. "I'm really sorry . . ."

Paul regarded him skeptically, then shook his head. "All right, all right," he said, surveying the situation. The toilet was jammed tightly between the bunk and the wall; maneuvering room was at a premium. "Hand me the snake," he said, straddling the bowl. Will looked into the box uncomprehendingly. Paul looked back, annoyed. *That* one," he said. "That coily thing, there."

He pointed to a long, flexible metal tube, coiled and wrapped around itself. Will grabbed it; as he did he spied a small Craftsman open-end wrench gleaming like a promise.

"Sorry," he said and handed it off. Paul harrumphed and unwrapped the snake, one end flopping to the floor. It was six feet long, ribbed metal sleeve housing heavy steel wire, a clawlike prong on one end and a handle on the other. Paul grasped the handle, started feeding the pronged end into the bowl. Will watched, intensely alert; as he did so, he carefully plucked the wrench from the toolbox, deftly palmed it and slipped it behind his back.

"What," Paul grumbled, "you never did this before?"

"Nosir," Will replied. Paul strained as the toilet hitched and sloshed, the snake sliding into the pipes. The scrape of metal on porcelain and sloshing water was huge in the claustrophobic space. But not huge enough.

"My dad never really wanted my help," Will suddenly said. "He always said I'd fuck"—he caught himself, reiterating—"he said I'd just screw it up."

Paul paused, his back to Will, shocked. The boy had actually spoken, actually *volunteered* a piece of personal information. It was a hallmark moment, even if happening while struggling with a plugged-up commode. Paul thought of

James Wells, lying in the ICU ward. "That's too bad," he said. "Fathers should teach their sons."

"It's okay," Will said, forlorn. "I got used to it." Behind his back, he blindly fitted the wrench to the head of the bolt as Paul finished feeding the line in and grasped the handle.

"The way this works," Paul explained, "is that the sleeve inserts through the pipes till the prongs hit the blockage. Then you just turn this little crank here." Paul twisted the crank; the toilet gurgled and gulped. Will stared at him as if rapt.

"Wow," he murmured appreciatively, all the while thinking, *Fucking psycho I hate you I hate you I hate you I hate you . . .*

Paul turned back to the task. Will started turning the bolt head in sync. Threads bit wood, softly creaking as it slowly spiraled up.

"The cable turns inside the sleeve, and the prongs chew up the blockage," Paul continued.

"Uh-huh." Will adjusted the wrench, twisting the bolt head back and forth, up and down, loosening it in its socket. "I didn't know that," he said, thinking, *But I'll try to remember that when I shove it up your ass.*

The toilet was almost cleared. He was running out of time. Will desperately tried moving the bolt with his fingers. It wouldn't give. Dammit. He tried again, squeezing as hard as he could.

Suddenly the bolt gave way with a tiny squeak. He twisted it again, moved it up, then down. He could do it. It was free. Just then the toilet made a huge slurping sound as the blockage gave way. "Got it!" Paul exclaimed, reeling the snake back out.

"Yessir," Will said. "You sure did."

Paul hit the plunger; the toilet burped and chugged, water swirling freely. As it flushed, Will palmed the wrench and slipped it back into the toolbox a heartbeat before Paul turned back to him.

"There ya go," he said. "Good as new."

Will smiled wanly. Or even better.

Paul finished the job, packed up and closed the lid of the

toolbox. He uncuffed Will from the chair, then helped him up and onto the bunk. Wells winced. Paul checked his forehead for fever. "Still kinda clammy," he said. "How do you feel?"

"All right," Will said, then looked up at Paul, not sullen or resentful, but frankly questioning. "I'm never gonna get out of here, am I?"

Paul stiffened defensively; the question caught him off guard. "I guess that's up to you," he said.

"Yessir." Will looked down. "I guess it is."

Paul stood and grabbed his toolbox. As he exited he paused at the door. "Rest," he said. "You'll feel better later."

Will nodded. Sure he would.

In fact, he already did.

37

Minutes later, Paul came up the cellar stairs carrying his toolbox, found himself quite unexpectedly face-to-face with Detective Buscetti, who was standing on the back porch, staring in through the door window. He smiled, craggy features crinkling like a worn shoe, and nodded hi. Paul opened the back door. "Stevie," he said, unable to mask his surprise. "What're you doing here?"

"Just dropping by," Buscetti said, looking around casually, his features pleasant but alert. "I was in the neighborhood . . . is this a bad time?"

"No," Paul said. "No, of course not. C'mon in." He moved to let Buscetti enter. "S'good to see you, man." Paul held out his free hand.

"Good to see you, too," Buscetti replied, taking and shaking it. Paul moved away from the basement door, which closed with a click; as he did so, Buscetti noticed the shiny new dead bolt.

"So," Buscetti said. "How're things?"

"Fine . . . everything's fine," Paul replied, a little too fast, a little too forced. He gestured to the still gutted kitchen, leading Buscetti away from the basement. "You know, old house, boiler's shot, lotta work to do. You know how it is."

"Yeah." Buscetti nodded. "I know how it is."

Paul faked a smile, moved pseudo-casually into the other room, luring the detective away. Buscetti glanced again at the lock, then followed him. Paul set the toolbox down in the living room, which had improved greatly, holes patched, drywall up and neatly plastered. Open cans of paint sat on drop cloths, a tray and roller nearby. "S'cuse the mess," he said, gesturing around. "I was painting just before you came."

"Thought you were working on the boiler."

"That too," Paul said, covering, silently cursing himself. Paul picked up one of the cans, poured it into the tray. Buscetti noticed a skin on the latex, which slid into the tray and disappeared in an expanding pool of blue. Paul dipped the roller, wetting it. "So . . ." he said conversationally. "This a personal call, or business?"

"Personal," Buscetti answered.

Paul nodded. "How're Angela and Dana Jean?"

"Angela's great," Buscetti replied. "And DeeJay's the best." Buscetti paused, suddenly awkward. Paul waved it off.

"It's okay, Stevie. I'm happy for you." He paused, smiled. "DeeJay?"

Buscetti blushed. "That's what we call her now. She's a really great kid. Wouldn't believe how big she is." He reached into his back pocket and withdrew an immensely fat wallet, flipped it open to a glassine accordion sleeve stuffed with baby pictures. He held it out to Paul, who whistled appreciatively.

"Jesus, dude, how do you *sit*?"

"With great difficulty." Buscetti grinned. For a moment, it seemed almost like the old days. Paul admired the photos.

"She's beautiful," he told the detective.

Buscetti beamed with pride, stuffed the wallet back in his pants. "How 'bout you, man?" he said. "How's Julie?"

"She's good," Paul said, but his eyes said something else. Just like that, the good feeling fizzled. Paul didn't elaborate, instead dipped the roller, painted a pale blue swath across the wall. "So . . ." he said. "Any breaks in the case?"

Buscetti shrugged. "Sadly, no," he replied. "Wish there were. We're doing everything we can, but you know how it is." He paused. "I'm beginning to wonder if he might have run into foul play."

He watched Paul for a reaction; Paul didn't turn, didn't flinch, didn't break his rhythm. "Foul play?" he remarked. "How Agatha Christie of you." He turned to the detective, his face a mask of composure. "Are you serious?" Buscetti shrugged. "What kind of 'foul play'?"

"Dunno," Buscetti replied. He sighed. "It's probably nothing. People disappear all the time. He can run, but he can't hide, not forever. We'll get him eventually."

He watched Paul for a reaction, was quietly shocked to see that Paul had none. "Speaking of Wells," Buscetti segued, "I heard about your little encounter with the dad."

"Yeah," Paul ruefully concurred. "You and the rest of the world. Fucking reporters."

"Yeah. Pretty ironic stuff, though," Buscetti ventured. "I mean, what are the odds of you and Wells being on the same road at the same hour, just as he cracks up his car?"

"Such is life." Paul dipped the roller, nonchalantly kept painting. "I ever mention, this was going to be Kyra's house one day? After she finished college, I mean." He rolled another swath. "Now I guess we'll just sell it." The blue patch grew with every sweep. "She always loved this color, though. I feel like I should finish it the way she would have wanted, first." He dipped and rolled again, covering. "How's that for ironic?"

"Yeah," Buscetti sighed, choosing his next words carefully. "I guess if anything ever happened to DeeJay . . . if anyone ever *did* anything . . . I don't know *what* I'd do." He paused for effect, verbally stalking Paul. "Easy to see how something like that could drive someone to do things he otherwise would never have dreamed of."

"I guess," Paul said, noncommittal, rolling the paint just a little bit thicker. "But we can't control what happens to us. We can only control what we do about it. Right?"

"Right." Buscetti looked around the room, taking it in. "So you don't have a problem with the thing with Wells? I mean, him being the kid's dad and you saving his life and all . . ."

Paul shook his head. "It's what I do, remember?" He looked at Buscetti like he was nuts, then softened. "Was it weird? Yeah, in all honesty, it was. But it was nothing personal. Just taking care of business."

The conversation died. Paul dipped his roller, went back to work. "So, Stevie, it's good to see you and all, but I kinda got a lot of work to do. S'there anything else you wanted to talk about?"

Buscetti looked at him, sizing him up. "Nah . . ." he replied. "I better get. Like I said, I was just in the neighborhood. Wanted to see how you're doing."

"Catch ya later, then?"

Buscetti nodded. "Catch ya later."

He started to make his way out, heading back through the kitchen. Paul paused in his busywork to watch. Buscetti moved through the kitchen, heading for the back door. He stopped at the basement, gave the doorknob a little twist. It was locked.

Just then Paul stuck his head around the corner. Buscetti let go of the knob as their eyes met. "Stevie?" he said.

"Yeah?"

"Give Angela and DeeJay my love."

"Will do," he said. Paul smiled the coldest replica of a smile the detective had ever seen. Then went back to his busywork.

He wasn't the only one.

That night found Will on his hands and knees, feverishly working at the loosened bolt. He had waited patiently on his bunk for what had felt like hours, lying in perfect, still repose, until the timer Paul had installed clicked the lights off. The moment darkness descended, Will was up and off the bunk, scrambling to the leg of the chair.

He could not see his hand in front of his face, the darkness was so complete. Will felt for the bolt head, one of the four anchoring each leg to its mounting plate. He twisted it between his fingers, Paul's words echoed in his mind: *"I built this. The walls are two inches thick. The chair? Built that, too. Anchor bolts are three inches long. You could beat on it 'til the cows come home; it ain't going anywhere. And neither are you."*

"We'll see about that," Will hissed and continued working the bolt. It squeaked and rose, thread by thread, gradually rising from its mooring . . . a half inch . . . an inch . . . with each successive turn, Will's hopes grew brighter.

And then, halfway up, it stopped.

"No." Will panicked. "Oh no no no no . . ." He tried twisting it again; the bolt would go down but would not rise further. Was it bent? Stuck?

"Fuck! C'mon, you piece of shit," Will hissed, heart pounding, breath frantic. "C'mon c'mon c'mon . . ." He clawed at the bolt head until his fingertips were bloody, desperate to the point of madness. But just when he thought there was no hope, the bolt suddenly tweaked and twisted free, the threads lubricated by his blood.

"Yes!" Will fought to keep his voice down, on the off chance his captor might be outside somewhere, listening. The bolt creaked and rose . . . two inches . . . two and a half . . . three . . . then suddenly wobbled, tipping into his hands and clattering to the floor. Will felt around in the blackness until he found it, directly under the chair. He picked it up and clutched it in awe. Will's fingers traced almost lovingly down the wide, spiraled threads, three solid inches of five-eighths-inch steel, narrowing to a sharp and lethal point.

It was beautiful.

Will sat back, elated, and used the tip to tear a strip of cloth from the hem of his shirt. He wound the shred of fabric around the bolt's hexagonal head, fashioning it into a crude but serviceable weapon, then wrapped his fingers around it, made a fist. The bolt jutted between his middle and ring fingers, a deadly spike.

"The way this works," he said mockingly, "is that you insert *this* end until it hits the blockage, and then you *crank* it." Will practiced punching the air, coming up from behind his back in a murderous roundhouse thrust; he imagined it arcing up from out of nowhere, embedding in Paul Kelly's unsuspecting throat. No, his forehead. His *eye* . . .

Maybe all three, Will thought. *Why dicker when you can have it all?*

Will pulled the drawstring out from the inside of his baggy sweats, tied the bolt to one end of the cord, then tucked it back in. The bolt tapped against his leg reassuringly. Will climbed back onto his bunk, tucking his hands behind his head. His hair was starting to grow out, prickled stubble coarse against his palms. One more reason, as if he needed it.

Fuck it, he decided. *Who gives a shit anyway?* It would grow back soon enough, and that was fine by him. Provided Paul Kelly not be alive to see it.

At long last, Will had the means.

Now all he needed was the moment.

38

Stephen Buscetti was not a happy detective. The visit with Paul had bothered him severely. Indeed, it had only served to confirm the gnawing feeling that something was seriously wrong. He didn't know, and couldn't begin to say, what Paul should be feeling or how he should be acting after all he had gone through . . . but whatever it was, what he saw today wasn't it.

I practically told him the case had gone stone cold, Buscetti thought, *and he didn't even blink.* It was so out of character, even lately—*especially* lately—that it creeped him out, big-time. And that smile . . .

Buscetti frowned. As a cop, he had long ago learned that if you really wanted to know what was going on inside someone's head, you had to lock on their eyes. Faces could lie, gestures could lie, even body language could be tricked and trained to obscure the truth. It was why lie detectors were the stuff of fiction, even when real life investigators used them—pulse and respiration and even tensile response could be controlled through Zen or zoning out or simply buying deep enough into your own bullshit. But the eyes . . .

unless the perp was crazy, psycho, or sociopathic, the eyes didn't lie.

Which was perhaps why Detective Buscetti found himself pulling up to the Gaslight Tavern, off duty and after hours, nursing an acid reflux the size of the Super Bowl and a feeling of genuine dread . . . and not simply because the words *perp*, *crazy*, *psycho*, and *sociopath* were popping into his head in such close proximity to Paul's name. But also because, while Paul's mouth curled upward in the appropriate manner, his eyes glinted darkly, devoid of feeling. And if what Buscetti didn't want to think about was true, then Paul Kelly was in some very, very deep shit indeed.

They all were.

Buscetti parked and climbed out of his car. He scanned the parking lot instinctively: Paul's truck was not there, but Dondi's Trans Am was. Good. Dondi had agreed to meet him, away from the job and with little explanation, on little more than the cryptic tone of Buscetti's voice and the suggestion that they might need to have a talk about Paul. Dondi hadn't asked for any more information, and Buscetti hadn't offered, but his instincts told him that they both wanted essentially the same thing: to speak as one friend to another, on behalf of another, mutual friend.

Buscetti hoped like hell it would end there.

Dondi sat at the Rescue One crew's regular booth, pouring from a pitcher of Michelob. He filled the detective's glass first, then his own; as he set the pitcher down the two men raised their mugs in mirthless cheer. Dondi took a hefty swig and put down the mug, absently tracing a finger around the rim.

"So you first, or me?" he said. It was not a small concern: for Dondi, it felt like ratting out a friend. For Buscetti, it felt like starting an investigation.

"I'll go," the detective replied.

"No." Dondi shook his head. "Let me."

He took a deep breath, chased it with another quick swig. "First," he began, "I love Paul to death. He's like a fuckin' brother to me." Buscetti nodded; he knew. Dondi continued. "But I'm talking to Connie today—usual husband-wife shit, blah blah blah, no big deal—when she turns around and asks how Paul's taking it. I just looked at her like, taking what? And she says, 'Julie leaving him.' "

"What?" Buscetti's eyes widened.

"My feelings exactly," Dondi said. "Except I can't say what the fuck are you talking about, because she assumes I *already* know, except I *don't* know, 'cuz Paul didn't tell me. He didn't tell *any* of us."

"You talked to the other guys?"

Dondi nodded. "Not a fuckin' word."

Buscetti looked troubled. "I saw Paul this afternoon," he said after a pause, "and I asked him how Julie was doing."

"What did he say?"

"He said she was good."

Dondi snorted. "Yeah, well, unless he's got his own personal psychic friends network that would be a tough call, since she's down at her parents' place, and according to Connie, she's not talking to him."

"Since when?"

"Since before Thanksgiving," Dondi said.

"Whoa," Buscetti murmured. He flashed to Paul's Thanksgiving Day surprise visit at the station: that made twice that Paul had answered a question with an answer that technically might not be a lie but might as well be. His cop hackles started to rise. "That's over a week now."

"Ding," Dondi said. "Give that man a see-gar. You see what I mean? He's acting really fucking weird."

Buscetti looked even more troubled than he already was. "How's he on the job?"

"I dunno . . . even when he's there, it feels like he's someplace else." Dondi took another swig. "He punched Joli's lights out on a job a few weeks back. Broke his nose." Buscetti's eyebrows arched; Dondi continued. "I just figured it was, you know, on account of Kyra . . . but now I'm startin' to wonder."

Buscetti nodded. There were plenty of things that didn't mesh or track, all of which had been covered by friendship, or loyalty, or the simple cutting of slack. "He could be in denial . . ." he ventured.

"Yeah," Dondi countered, "and I could be Princess Di, except she's dead." Dondi drained his beer. "I'm telling ya, Stevie, all is not well in Oz. Pay no attention to that man behind the curtain."

Buscetti's leathery features went cloudy, as if a shadow were passing over his thoughts. Dondi picked up on it.

"What?" he said.

"I dunno. Maybe nothing." Buscetti went on. "It's the Wells thing . . . the accident . . . skid marks indicate that his wasn't the only vehicle involved." It was Dondi's turn to look shocked.

"What was the other vehicle?"

"Dunno," Buscetti replied. "Truck of some kind; we can't get a definitive read on it yet. But it had dualies on the back."

"Jesus," Dondi groaned.

Buscetti nodded grimly, adding, "And word is at the hospital Paul was real friendly with Kathryn Wells."

"What?" Dondi sputtered, aghast. "How 'friendly'?"

"Friendly enough," Buscetti said. "Definitely on speaking terms."

"Aw, man." Dondi ran a hand through his wiry hair. "This is fucked . . . this is so fucked I don't even know what to fucking tell ya." Buscetti nodded; he knew from experience that Dondi's use of the f-word was on a direct sliding scale to his anxiety. It made him a rotten liar; the stress of mendacity turned Dondi into a Tourette's syndrome poster boy. Whereas Paul . . .

Paul Kelly. Polite. Decent. An all-around great guy. It suddenly struck Buscetti like a kidney punch to the conscience that while Dondi was a lousy liar, Paul might be a very, very good one.

The two men stared at their beers. Suddenly Dondi looked up. "Where'd you say you saw him today?" he asked.

"On Marley Street," Buscetti told him. "Working on the house. Why?"

"I don't know," Dondi said as he shook his head. "I used

to work on it with him all the time. Now he wants to do it all alone. He spends all his fucking time there."

Buscetti took it in. "When you were working with Paul on the house," he asked, "did you put in new locks?"

"No," Dondi said. "But after the break-in, I told him he oughta get some. Why?"

Buscetti shrugged; he wasn't sure. "There's a double-key deadbolt on the basement door now. A Schlage. Big sucker."

Dondi looked perplexed. "I don't get it," he said. "Why the fuck would he put a double-key lock on the basement? I mean, a single key, sure, he stores his tools in the basement. But a double key? You could get trapped down there, and nobody'd even know it." He paused, flummoxed. "What the hell would he do that for?"

Buscetti shook his head. He didn't know. The men went silent. As much as the meeting was a personal comparing of notes, it was also a bit like poker: each holding something back from the other, each upping the ante with every shared fact. Buscetti didn't tell Dondi about the missing documents: the grisly photos, the autopsy report, the copy of Will's arrest file. And Dondi didn't tell Buscetti about the house's secret stash, their illicit medical inventory—the tranquilizers, antibiotics, and assorted sedatives—or that quite a few were now missing.

Cop and firefighter faced off miserably, each holding a piece of the puzzle, both afraid to put them together. But the pieces were starting to fill in anyway.

Julie entered the chapel, a small rosary clutched in her hands. A basin of holy water stood by the entrance; she touched fingers to its placid surface, genuflected humbly.

The church was old and decrepit, so quiet that the silence itself seemed a presence. Distant shore traffic hummed outside; inside, high plaster walls extended into beamed and vaulted space. The plaster was water-stained and flaking, neglected.

A row of confessionals lined the right side, all mahogany and mystery; as she watched, an old woman emerged, silver hair wrapped in a black shawl. The door creaked shut as the woman shuffled away; as she did, Julie heard the faint rustle of pigeons nesting in the eaves. Wings flapped high above. Julie looked up to see a shadow pass overhead. Then nothing.

To her left was a narrow dais, upon which were stacked rows of small votive candles. All but one were lit. Their light twinkled comfortingly, a table full of prayers. It all felt familiar, though she was sure she had never been there before.

Julie approached the dais, took a thin stick from a holder on the side. "Hail Mary, full of grace," she whispered haltingly, fingers kneading the rosary. "Blessed art thou, and blessed is the fruit of thy womb, Jesus . . ."

She touched the stick to one of the lit candles. Julie continued. "Look down upon us sinners in this, the hour of our need . . ." She held the stick to the unlit candle, touched flame to wick. The candle lit, its own small flame glowing bright. Suddenly the flame flared, hissing, then sputtered and guttered out. A thin plume of smoke wafted up as a small voice sounded behind her.

"Mommy . . . ?"

Julie turned, heart throbbing, fine hairs prickling at the base of her neck. A gurney stood in the aisle at the base of the altar, a body lying upon it, covered by a sheet. As she watched in horror, the body sat up. It was Kyra.

"Mom?" Kyra said, not to Julie but to the entire space. "Mom, are you here?"

"Baby, is that you?" Julie gasped. "Am I dreaming?"

Kyra smiled but said nothing; Julie realized that her daughter looked as she did before death. No bruises or abrasions marred her perfect flesh; her eyes were clear and filled with light. Light glowed behind her like an aura, rendering her ethereal, serene.

"Kyra! Oh my sweet baby," Julie cried, moving toward the gurney. As she spoke, Kyra turned her head, glowing eyes searching.

"Where's Daddy?" Kyra asked, her voice suddenly alarmed. "Mommy?"

"I'm here, baby." Julie stepped forward, her own eyes

glistening. "Daddy's at home . . . we both love you very much . . ."

Suddenly overhead there came a pealing of bells; great churchbells clanging in the belfry, echoing through the rafters, followed by a great flurry of fluttering wings. Kyra's features went childish, fearful. "Please, Mommy," she pleaded. "Please don't tell Daddy . . ." Silvery tears tracked down her cheeks. *"Please don't tell Daddy I'm here . . ."*

Julie reached out to touch her. "I won't," she vowed. Her hand touched Kyra's. It was cold.

Julie gasped; as she glanced back to Kyra's face she saw her daughter lying still on the gurney, eyes closed, purple bruises deep around her throat. As the bells pealed Julie stepped back, the rosary tumbling from her grasp . . .

. . . and she looked down to see the beads hit the floor, spattering like drops of blood.

Julie screamed as the blood ran, and her daughter's body lay slack and dead. She screamed again, and the bells rang, and rang, and rang . . .

. . . and then she was awake, lying in the upstairs guest room bed of her parents' modest home. The room was small and neat, done in ersatz Ethan Allen early American colonial; a small crucifix hung on the wall over the bed. Late afternoon sun filtered through chintz curtains. The telephone was ringing.

"Jesus," Julie moaned, then muttered, "fuck me." She sat up, disoriented. The phone rang again, then stopped; a heartbeat later, there came a soft knock at the door.

"Julie, honey?" It was Eleanor, sounding concerned and maternal. "Telephone for you." She opened the door, poked her head in. "I'm sorry," she said. "I didn't know you were napping."

"It's okay," Julie replied, shaking it off. She sat fully upright; she was fully dressed. "Who is it?"

"I don't know, dear—someone named Dondi?" Eleanor looked at her, decided. "I'll tell him to call back later."

"No," Julie said. "Just gimme a minute."

"It's all right, dear," Eleanor told her. "You need your rest . . ."

"Mom, don't," Julie said adamantly, then muttered, "not like I'm getting any, anyway." She reached for the phone as her mother watched; Julie gave her a look, and Eleanor ducked out, closing the door behind her.

Julie reached for the bedside table, rooted inside the drawer, came up with a pack of cigarettes. She hadn't smoked for some seventeen years, since before her pregnancy. She'd picked it back up, last week. Julie lit one, took a deep drag, smoke flooding her lungs. Then picked up the receiver.

"Dondi?"

"Hi, Julie." Dondi's voice, mock-conversational.

"Hang on." Julie placed her hand over the phone and called out, "All right, Mother!" Over the phone came her mother's voice, defensive.

"I'm not listening!"

"Good," Julie said. "So you won't mind hanging up, then!" Eleanor huffed through the receiver; Julie listened until she heard the extension click and rack. She ran one hand through her hair, bracing herself for the question she wasn't sure she wanted an answer to.

"Okay, Dondi," she said. "What's going on?"

39

fternoon. *What was the old joke?* Paul thought. *Just because you're paranoid doesn't mean they're not out to get you.* But Paul wasn't laughing.

He was being followed.

He had meant to go to Marley Street; he hadn't been there for over a day. Now he was worried. Paul wheeled his truck around a corner, glanced in the rearview mirror. The flow of traffic on Glendon Boulevard continued unabated. He continued watching as he drove up the block, seeing a city bus, a Hyundai, a Chevy Camaro, one of those updated VW beetles, improbably shiny against gray December slush, a blue Suzuki Sidekick. All proceeding on, all oblivious. He was almost to the end of the block, half convinced he was imagining things, when the Taurus turned the corner.

It was late model, mud-spattered brown, utterly unremarkable in every way but one: it belonged to Detective Stephen Buscetti. Not a Glendon PD cruiser or unmarked sedan, but his personal car.

Or was it?

Paul reached the end of the block just as the light turned

red. He sat watching as the Taurus inexplicably slowed some sixty yards behind him, hanging back. Paul could not make out the driver's face, but he was sure it was Stevie. And if that was so, it meant Buscetti was following him and had been all day. Paul had seen the Taurus a half-dozen times already while running seemingly mundane errands—the car wash to rinse away any traces of James Wells, the grocery store to buy fresh provisions for Will—with the car always in the background, like a six-cylinder Flying Dutchman, shadowing.

Paul gripped the wheel, engine rumbling, watching the cross-flow of passing traffic. In the rearview, the Taurus creeped closer, a half block behind and crawling, as if wary of closing the distance. Paul looked up: the light was still red. Behind him, the Taurus paused. The driver held something up—a map, a piece of paper—as if scoping an address. Paul couldn't see his face.

The light was still red. Paul watched as a Dodge Neon trundled by, going with the green. Behind it, a dump truck gnashed its gears, lumbering forward. Suddenly Paul gunned it, roaring forth against the light. His truck lurched into the intersection, screeching around the corner. The dump truck driver jammed his air brakes and laid on the horn, blatting out a warning as Paul countersteered wildly, barely missing a Volvo in the oncoming lane. He glanced back to see the Taurus suddenly vault forward, tires spinning on stray ice as the Volvo hit the brakes and slid into the inter-section, barely missing collision with the now stalled dumper.

Behind him the intersection was reduced to motorized bedlam: horns honking, drivers cursing, cars splayed, brake-lights flaring. Paul roared off as the Taurus reached the grid-lock, unable to pass. He glanced into the jiggling rearview, caught a glimpse of Steve Buscetti, cursing . . . or thought he did. At the next intersection Paul wrenched the wheel, executing a hard left on the yellow, heading north. The truck took the turn hard, big wheels screaming.

And then he was gone.

*   *   *

Night. The room was dark, moon high and full through dormer windows, bathing the interior an ethereal, lunar blue. In the dream, Paul moaned as Julie moved atop him, angling her hips into a long-practiced and wonderfully familiar position. They were together again, making love with ravished, animal abandon. Her breasts heaved lushly, nipples taut and full. They were together, for the first time in what felt like forever.

Paul gazed up at his wife riding him and felt time slow, go liquid, stop altogether. It felt so good. She felt so good. He dug his fingers into the deep cleft of her naked back, pulling her toward him; as the heat of impending orgasm burned in his loins Paul closed his eyes and came up, teeth grazing her neck as Julie cried out, hips furiously pumping, flesh slapping rhythmically against his straining thighs . . .

   . . . when Paul stopped, he felt the soft bed go hard and cruel beneath him. He reached out to touch cold, unyielding wood; Paul opened his eyes to see they were no longer in their bed in their bedroom in their house. The walls were windowless, close and claustrophobic, the ceiling low and oppressive; they were fucking on the dirty little bunk in the dirty little box in the basement of Marley Street.
   Julie continued in the throes of her own violent passion, oblivious. The door to the box hung ajar, slowly creaking open; as Paul watched in horror, the walls began to blister and bubble, the air filling with the bitter stench of coiling smoke.
   "We've got to get out of here," he gasped. "We've got to get out of here now." Julie stopped and looked at him, confused, as the fear in his eyes telegraphed to her own . . .
   . . . when suddenly the walls exploded in flame, fire racing under the door to blanket the interior, swirling up and across the ceiling like a living thing, merciless

*and ravenous. Paul felt the heat sear his skin as he
grabbed Julie and held her tight, her screams co-
mingling with his own as the raging inferno rose up to
consume them . . .*

. . . and Paul awoke screaming, alone in the black
recliner in the dark and ruined living room. The TV was
dead before him, a hole punched in the grayed glass tube
staring at him like a great blind eye. The house was as quiet
as a desecrated tomb; his own tortured breathing the only
sound in his ears. Paul's heart hammered madly in a chest
constricted; for a moment he thought he might pass out cold.
He put head in trembling hands; slowly, with great effort, he
brought his body to some semblance of control.

"I'm all right," he told himself desperately. "I'm going to
be fine." He said it again, for good measure.

But even he no longer believed it.

Morning. Paul rode up the sweeping drive of the cemetery, a
fresh bouquet of flowers on the seat beside him. He wanted
to see Kyra, to find some solace or peace, however fleeting,
in the field of polished granite and earth. But there was none
to be found.

As he parked he scanned the horizon, searching for signs
of surveillance. There were none, but that meant little. The
spiral was tightening. The cops were on to him: whether Stevie had made it official or not was but a matter of time.
Dondi was distant and suspicious; indeed, the whole crew
regarded him with wary concern. And there was still the little matter of his ongoing drama on Marley Street. Lies upon
lies upon lies; Paul could no longer remember where the
truth left off and the constricting circle of deceptions began.

He walked up the rows of silent stone, came to Kyra's
grave. As he knelt and placed the flowers in the little holder,
he spoke softly.

"Daddy's in trouble, sweetie," he said. "I can't really
explain right now, and I didn't want to say anything before

because I didn't want you to worry." He paused, tears welling hot against the chill air. "Whatever happens, just remember, Daddy loves you. Daddy loves you very, very much . . ."

Paul broke down then, tears flowing out to stain the mirrored surface of her memorial. It suddenly dawned on him with brute logic: Will was right. Paul could not let him go. Not now. Not ever. It had been three days since Will was last fed; whatever Paul had first intended, it had all become a terrible mistake. But he had no clue as to how to extricate himself from his own grim machinations.

Paul turned his gaze heavenward, stared up into perfectly blue sky unblemished by cloud. "What now, God?" he asked, heart wrenching. "What am I supposed to do now?"

He stood listening, heard only silence. A bird flew by, swooping and darting through the winter air, hunting something he could not see. Suddenly a voice sounded, clear and quiet—not his, but as certain as if spoken aloud. And what it said was this:

Bury the dead.

Paul turned and looked behind him. No one was there. The voice came again, like a thing apart from him, some perverse *Field of Dreams* incantation . . . except he wasn't Kevin Costner, this wasn't a movie, and he knew it was only in his head. The voice sounded again.

Time to bury the dead.

Paul looked around a second time, stood trembling. He was utterly alone on the hill. Paul stared down at his daughter's grave.

And suddenly knew what he had to do.

40

J ulie paced her parents' living room, staring at the phone as if afraid it might bite her. Her folks had departed for the mall a scant hour earlier, Eleanor entreating her to come along, as though all of her daughter's problems could be magically washed away by a good white sale. Julie had declined as politely as she could, playing the trump card of needing to rest.

And now she was alone, not resting at all but pacing their tidy Stone Harbor home like a bug on a hot plate. Spock watched her, whining worriedly; even the pooch picked up on the vibe. She wanted to pick up the phone. She needed to pick it up. But she was afraid.

The dream tormented her, sending thin chills down her spine. But worse still was the news that Dondi had brought. He hadn't said much, mostly repeated urgings that Paul was in some kind of trouble and needed her badly . . . but when she pressed him for answers, he didn't want to say. He begged her to come back, for Paul's sake. Julie had said no. She just couldn't.

But now she wasn't so sure.

"Oh, Paul," she murmured anxiously. "What are you doing?"

A damned good question. There was only one way to find out. Julie stopped and steeled herself, reaching for the receiver. But just as her fingers touched it, it rang.

Julie recoiled, instinctively pulling back. Her heartbeat raced as it rang again. She took a deep breath, picked up. "Hello?" she said.

"Julie." Paul, sounding anxious and surprised. "Hi . . ."

"Hi," she echoed. Tears immediately filled her eyes. Julie wiped them away. "Paul," she said, as firmly as she could, "I think we need to talk . . ."

"I know," he replied. That threw her. Before she could respond, Paul pressed on. "Julie, I'm so sorry," he told her. "There are so many things I need to tell you . . ."

Julie nodded to herself, tears spilling freely now. There were things she needed to tell him, too.

"But I want to tell you face-to-face," Paul continued. He paused, hesitating. "Can't we just go somewhere for a few days? Get away from everything and everyone? I just think . . ." He paused again, choosing his words carefully. "I just think it would be nice if we could figure out where we are with each other . . . and where we want to go . . ."

Julie sniffled despite herself. She said nothing.

"I love you, Julie," Paul blurted, his voice insinuating itself through the phone line and into her heart. "I just love you so much . . ."

He stopped, as if afraid he'd gone too far. But Julie sighed throatily. "I love you, too," she confessed. On the other end of the line, Paul waited. The silence stretched, fragile as a gossamer thread, as Julie thought about it for a moment, then decided.

"New Hope," she said at last.

Paul stopped, stunned. "Seriously?" he asked. "I mean, are you sure?"

"Yeah," Julie said. "Let's go."

"When?"

"Today," she told him. "Let's just go . . ."

Paul was thrilled. He told her he'd come down and get her. But Julie told him no, she'd come up. Traffic on the Garden State would be with her that way, and besides, there were some things she wanted to pack. Paul understood and offered to help; Julie said okay. They chatted a bit more, and for a few, fleeting moments, things felt almost normal between them.

Then Julie rang off, explaining that she had to go if she wanted to make it in time. She glanced at her watch: 2:45. She would meet him at home at five. Paul agreed, hung up reluctantly, with the promise of seeing her soon. He couldn't have been happier. His last words echoed in her mind.

"It's gonna be okay, Julie," he told her. "Everything's gonna be fine. I promise."

Julie nodded and said good-bye, then cradled the receiver. She wanted so badly to believe it. She felt her heart breaking open, releasing a torrent of pent-up emotion. Spock got up from his bed by the fireplace and loped over, stumpy tail wagging. He nuzzled her leg.

"No, boy," she said, scratching his head. "You stay here."

The dog hung his head dejectedly; Julie went to the kitchen counter, started writing her parents a note. With any luck, she'd be out the door before they got back; she didn't need the added resistance of justifying herself. There were too many things she and her husband needed to talk about just now.

And a few things left to confess.

Back in Glendon, Paul hung up the phone, immediately picked it back up and called the firehouse. Andy Vasquez answered.

"Rescue One," he said. "Vasquez speaking."

"Andy," Paul said. "It's Paul . . ."

"Hey, Paulie, how ya hangin'?"

"Good," Paul replied. "Listen, I'm gonna take a few personal days. Kind of a family emergency."

"Yeah?" Vasquez sounded suddenly worried. "Everything okay?"

"No, no, everything's fine," Paul insisted. "Julie and I are just gonna get away, try to work things out."

From the other end of the line, an audible sigh of relief. "Hey, that's great, buddy," Vasquez said. "We're all rootin' for ya."

Paul winced; from Andy's tone it was clear that he had heard about Julie, which meant, by extension, that everyone had. Paul felt his paranoia rise, immediately beat it back. Vasquez assured him, no problem, everyone would understand. He promised to take care of covering Paul's shifts. They wished each other well, and that was that.

Paul hung up the phone, felt a great weight shifting and lifting off his shoulders. He was giddy, unable to contain himself. *Pack,* he thought excitedly, *I gotta pack.*

He strode through the house, heading upstairs. He made his way to the bedroom, pulled their luggage from the closet, started packing. Nothing major, some casual clothes for a few laid-back days, no big deal. Paul felt like a man reprieved, the prison door thrown wide to let in the bright light of day. It dawned on him that he didn't *have* to do this anymore . . . he could just let it all go. For the first time since the beginning of the nightmare, he felt like he had a choice. He just had to let it go . . .

Let it go . . .

Paul stopped, thought of Will and the house on Marley Street. Suddenly a thought struck like a thunderbolt from a clear sky: a thought so clear it amazed him in its stark and utter simplicity.

He could just let him go . . .

. . . and suddenly what had seemed impossible revealed itself to be all too possible, all too perfect. No one as yet knew of Will's fate; to the world at large, he was still a fugitive from justice. So what would happen if Paul just threw open the door and said, *Go*? Will could run, in so doing becoming the very thing everyone already thought he was. If they caught him, they caught him—his fate would be his own. And what could he say? Imaginary interrogations danced like sugarplums in Paul's mind . . . *So he kidnapped you and put you in a box? Uh-huh, sure, kid . . . . Oh, so he shaved your head, you didn't do it to alter your appearance? Right right right right. . . . He* almost *cut your toe off, but didn't? Yup yup yup yup.* The box would be long gone. No one would ever believe him.

And if Will *wasn't* caught?

Then he would run, Paul realized. *He would run until the day he died.* In its own perverse way, it would be fitting: a life on the lam, hiding in shadows, always afraid, always hunted. It was like no life at all. In a world without true justice, perhaps that would have to do.

But what, then, of Paul's quest—his dark, twisted mission? What, then, of the *why?*

Paul sighed. Hard as it was to accept, perhaps it was not a question to which there was an answer—at least, not one such as he had envisioned. Perhaps the answer, such as it was, was not to be found in the asking but in the *living.* To honor his daughter by living his life and making that life a living testimony to all he loved in her. To let her spirit go wherever it had gone, secure in the knowledge that the people she loved were whole and well.

Something stirred within him then, and he knew: he had a choice. He was like a man standing at a crossroads. One way leading to Julie and New Hope, and the promise of life. And the other?

Paul finished packing his things, turned his attention to Julie's. He didn't know exactly what she would want or need, but it didn't matter: if she didn't care for his choices, she could buy whatever she wanted once they got there. And with any luck at all, they'd be spending most of their time wearing very little, or nothing at all.

He grabbed a few things from the closet—her favorite jeans, some sweaters, a slinky evening dress, then moved to her bureau and opened the top drawer. Inside lay a delicate tangle of bras and panties, a Victoria's Secret wonderland of lace and cotton and smooth, sheer silk. It was a total mystery to Paul, even though in all candor he had probably bought half of what resided there; but once off the rack and esconced in the drawer, it became a veritable no-man's-land. Julie even laundered them separately, as if to temporarily reside in the same hamper with Paul's duds was to violate some obscure girl-tech taboo. Soft scent wafted from the drawer; it even smelled like Julie, the faint hint of perfume flaring his nostrils and filling him with lost feelings of lust.

Paul breathed deeply, taking it in, then reached in and started pulling out dainty pieces. Easier said than done; Julie's organizational tendencies seemed to halt outright at the border of the panty drawer. Its contents were a soft and indecipherable mess, spaghetti straps and hooks and underwires clinging together in a tenaciously perplexing mass; Paul fumbled, clumsy and ham-handed, trying to liberate a bra. It came up inexplicably attached to a half dozen other garments. Not knowing what else to do, he shook it; the bra came free, but the tangled clump of panties and sundry unmentionables tumbled to the floor.

"Shit," he hissed guiltily. Paul quickly knelt, scooping up the fallen undies. As he did, something fell from their folds, landed softly on the floor. Paul looked down, saw a small bag of potpourri; he smiled and shook his head, thinking, *What is the deal with potpourri? If I gave her a bunch of dead flowers, I'd be a schmuck . . .*

Paul picked up the bag, still smiling, then looked down. Something lay under it, also having fallen—a little pink square of neatly folded paper.

He picked it up, curious. It was a smudged and blurry NCR form—a carbonless copy of a business receipt. Its presence there was odd, out of place. One corner of the fold was curled back; Paul could make out the words MEN'S CLINIC.

Huh? he thought, feeling instantly torn. A voice in his head cautioned, *Put it back, it's none of your business, what are you doing?* Paul started to place it back in the drawer.

Then unfolded and read it instead.

The header said CHELSEA WOMEN'S CLINIC, with a Manhattan street address. Paul vaguely wondered, *What the hell did Julie go to a New York clinic for?* Then his jaw dropped as his eyes scrolled down the sheet. The information was handwritten in a neat cursive script filling in the rows of tiny boxes.

Services provided: 037 . . . Status: outpatient . . . Fee: $350 . . . Method of payment: cash . . .

She paid cash? Paul wondered. It made no sense. He flipped the form over, to where the code listings were printed in pale blue.

037: Termination.

Termination? Paul freaked. It felt like his heart stopped completely, as all the blood drained from his face in one instant, came flooding back hot. *Julie had an abortion?* He couldn't believe his eyes. He flipped the receipt back over, saw the date: *September 23.* His wife had had an abortion almost four months ago and had never told him? It still made no sense. Paul's eyes scanned the form, and suddenly went wide: he lurched forward, leaning against the bureau, breath heaving violently. The paper dropped from his grasp, wafting down to land faceup in the drawer.

"No," Paul growled. "*No . . .* " Suddenly he wrenched the drawer from its slot, flung it wildly across the room. It smashed against the far wall, contents cascading down to litter the floor and bed.

"GOD DAMN IT!" Paul screamed, grabbing hold of the bureau and sending it toppling. Photos and mementos smashed into rubble in the wreckage; in one white hot instant, all thoughts of escape, of peace sundered and immolated as Paul careened out of the bedroom and down the hall, still screaming. As he did he trod across the receipt, his boot print marking the smudgy print. It had taken him a moment to read it correctly, as his eyes had seen what he wanted to see . . . or rather, had *not* seen what he could not allow himself to.

A name, written clearly, in the box marked Patient.
Kelly. Kyra Anne.

"NOOOO!" Paul howled. The receipt lay torn and crumpled, the bedroom in shambles, as he pounded down the stairs, slammed the back door behind him.

It was 3:55.

41

It was 4:10 when Paul's truck thundered up to the Rescue One parking lot and screeched to a halt. He left the engine running and jumped out, his thoughts boiled down to a blood red rage.

Paul entered the station through the rear door to the bay. The space was cavernous, empty: both rig and crew were gone, off on a run. More than coincidence. Paul had pulled the fire alarm himself, some ten blocks hence. Pulling a false alarm was a felony.

Paul didn't care. Not anymore.

She lied to me. The thoughts roiled in his brain. *They both lied.* In the blink of an eye, his past had shifted like scorched sand beneath his feet as his image of Kyra crumbled and reformed, became alien, a stranger. And Julie . . .

Why? the voice in his head wailed. *Why why why why?*

At that moment the whys which had driven him for so long melted into each other, melding into one burning, primal need to know. He felt betrayed, anguished, incensed. Enraged.

Paul crossed the concrete floor, came to the steel storage

cage. He quickly unlocked the padlock, threw open the door with an echoing clang. He opened the door of the storage cabinet, grabbed a handful of amyl nitrate poppers, stuffing his pockets. Paul slammed the doors shut and turned.

The spare defibrillator unit sat on the table, charge light glowing green. It was a small device built by a company called MedTech, about the size of a typewriter case, with recessed slots for the retractable, corded shock paddles and rows of dials and switches to control the voltage. Paul checked the meters. Good to go. He unhooked it and picked it up, then turned, only to come face-to-face with Wallace Clyburne, dressed in street clothes, a knapsack slung over one shoulder. Wallace looked surprised to see him.

"Paul. Hi," he said.

Paul eyeballed him coldly. "What are you doing here?"

"Nothing," Wallace said nervously. "I mean, I came in early, to study. I heard a noise, and . . ." He stopped, saw the defib unit in Paul's hands. "Where're ya goin'?"

"None of your fucking business," Paul told him, then pushed past, knocking the probie back into the cage. The metal clanged and rattled; Wallace watched in confusion as Paul kept right on going, across the bay and out the door. Not knowing what had happened to so piss him off.

And never imagining what he intended to do about it.

The back door of the house on Marley Street exploded inward under the force of Paul's boot. He shouldered his way through the shattered portal, shoved it closed behind him. The door was ruined. He didn't care.

The basement door loomed. Paul fished the key from his pocket, unlocked it. The door swung back. The basement steps yawned before him, dark and foreboding. His breath hissed through clenched teeth. His mind swirled, molten. It wasn't true. It couldn't be. But he had seen the proof. His daughter. His wife. His *family*.

Liars.

No more, he vowed. *No more bullshit. No more evasion. No more games.* Paul would have the truth, no matter the cost, and he would have it now. He did not know who was to blame. But he knew where to begin.

Paul began his final descent.

Will huddled in the box, shivering. His stomach gnawed and fluttered; he felt weak and shaky, anxious. There was no heat to speak of; the interior of the box was cold.

Suddenly the door to the box unlocked. Will pulled himself upright, surprised; as the door pried open he shoved the bolt into a crack under the lip of the bed, pressing its point into the wood. He tried to look innocent as Paul entered, eyes blazing, jaw set as if carved from stone.

Will stood on shaking legs, trying to make fake-nice. "What's wrong?" he asked.

Paul decked him.

The blow landed hard, caught Will completely off guard. The sheer force of it buckled his legs as the boy collapsed, head banging against the side of the chair. Will landed on the floor in a crumpled heap, his vision blurred and filled with stars.

Paul dropped the defib unit on the bunk, knelt to straddle him. "No more," he hissed, twisting to flip open the defib's lid.

Will sputtered and spat blood. "No more what? . . ." he gasped.

Paul whirled and slapped him, a backhand blow that slammed his skull onto unyielding floor. Will reeled, caught a glimpse of the bolt, hanging down under the lip of the bunk, just out of reach.

"Time to give it up, boy," Paul said, reaching down to rip open Will's shirt. Will strained to escape, but he was too depleted, Paul's weight hard upon him. His eyes swam in terror as Paul flipped the on switch, meters surging. Paul uncoiled the shock paddles and cranked the dial to one hundred joules.

As the defib hummed to life Paul took his weight off Will's chest. The pitch rose to a high keening whine as Paul quickly pulled a tube of conductive gel from his jacket pocket, uncapped it with his teeth, and greased the metal surface of the paddles. "What are you doing?" the boy asked.

The keening peaked. Paul turned and thrust the paddles to Will's chest.

The shock hit like a Mack truck, slamming through the boy's nervous system at the speed of light. Will went rigid and spasmed, veins in his temples bulging to the burst point as his teeth chattered like castanets. His bladder voided instantly, darkening the crotch of his sweats; his heels pounded a mad staccato rhythm against the floor. Paul waited for the spasm to subside, then cranked the dial to one-fifty.

"Why did you kill my daughter?" Paul demanded.

Will's eyes focused and glared, defiant. His good boy vibe evaporated along with any hope of mercy. *"F-fuck you,"* he said.

Paul shocked him again.

He waited as the tremors raged and retreated, cranked the dial up again. Two hundred.

"Why did you kill her, Will?"

"B-bastard," Will snarled, coughing up raw spittle. *"You fucking b-bastard . . ."*

Paul shocked him again. Will convulsed, passed out. Mucus streamed from his nostrils; his pulse and respiration flailed. Paul pulled a popper from his pocket, cracked it, waved it under Will's nose. The boy coughed and retched, blearily coming to. Sweat tracked the surface of his skin as Paul upped the voltage to three hundred. The defib unit whined, charge building.

"Last chance," he warned. "Why??"

The question hovered. Will sneered, tears spilling from his eyes. He mumbled something unintelligibly. Paul loomed over him.

"What?" he said. "Speak up, you little fuck! Why'd you do it??" Paul roared. "WHY???"

"BECAUSE I LOVED HER!!!" Will suddenly howled, a torrent of anguish spilling out. He glared at Paul with eyes afire. *"Because I fucking loved her!!!!"*

The boy broke down then, sobbing bitter tears that had nothing to do with the torture. Paul hesitated, stunned and suspicious. He dropped the paddles, grabbed Will by the shoulders. "What are you saying?"

Will looked up; their eyes met, held. And Paul hummed like a high-tension wire as Will finally disgorged the secret he had fought so hard to hide . . .

They were lovers. No one knew. She saw things in him that no one else could see, as he did in her—the people they were inside, the people they wanted to be. When they were together, the world disappeared, and they dreamed of a life free. But she knew that Paul would not allow it; would never allow Will to be. So they hid their love from everyone. They were a universe of two.

And then she got pregnant . . .

. . . and she was scared, so scared. Kyra feared what Paul would do: to her, to Will, to the love they shared. She was afraid of the look she imagined in his eyes. Her whole life was planned, from boyfriends to college to career to the house she'd share with the perfect Mr. Right. It was a wonderful life, with one small defect: it wasn't hers, and never had been. It was Paul's: the one he demanded of her. The only life his perfect girl could ever be allowed to have . . .

. . . and Will said let's run, go somewhere no one knew, somewhere they could be themselves. She was the only good thing he had ever known. But she wasn't strong enough. And she told him no.

Will died when he saw the pain in her eyes, died again when she tried to avoid him, for days, then weeks, a month. He begged her to see him just one more time. Finally she agreed, and they met in secret on Marley Street, as they had so many times before. Will was hurt and angry, tired of hiding. He wanted them to be together. She said she couldn't do it to her family, to her father. Will said they'd make their own family. Live their own lives.

She was crying. She said she was sorry to hurt him like this. But her answer was final. And the answer was no.

But what about the baby? he asked achingly. Kyra crumbled, an empty shell.

There is no baby, she told him. Not anymore.

Will was slaughtered, betrayed, a shell himself. The world blurred and ran red, as love became hate became endless boundless bottomless rage . . .

Kyra turned to go . . . Will said no . . . he reached for her . . . she pushed him away . . . and his hands were on her throat . . . and she fought to escape him . . . and his hands were on her throat . . . and she cried out for daddy . . .

. . . and his hands were on her throat . . .

Will stopped. Emotionally stripped. Physically ravaged. His soul, an open wound.

Paul slumped back; shell-shocked, confused. His gaze drifted away, searching the walls, the floor, the wretched confines of the prison he'd built with his own two hands. His head began to slowly shake. "The fire . . ." he croaked.

"Letters," Will croaked back. "Notes. Stuff she wrote me. Stuff I wrote her. Stuff I drew. Everything. I burned it all. I didn't want it any more. Even before I went there, I knew she'd never be able to go. She was too fucking scared."

"Of you," Paul said.

"No," Will said flatly. "Of you . . ."

Paul glared at him. "Bullshit," he growled. "That's not true."

"Yeah," the boy snorted derisively. "Like *you* would know."

Paul winced, the truth of it piercing his emotional armor. Suddenly he could see it: Will, burning his dreams, burning his history, erasing himself in a preemptive emotional kamikaze run. Paul winced again, as if recoiling from the acrid fumes.

Will felt nauseous and weak, but even in his pain he knew: this was his chance, the last one he'd ever get. As

Paul's head shook, Will's arm snaked out and under the bunk, blindly searching.

"I don't understand," Paul murmured, lost in his own mad thoughts. "You could've said something." Paul looked at the boy, the box that held them, the whole hideous nightmare incarnate. Will's eyes narrowed. "Why didn't you?"

"Because I hate you," Will hissed bitterly. His fingers found the bolt, closed on it. "I hate your fucking perfect little bullshit world." The boy laughed and coughed blood, a weak and caustic outpouring. "You think you're so fucking great, but you're so full of shit . . ."

"Shut up," Paul growled, blinking back sweat. *"Shut up . . ."*

But Will would not shut up. His words hit like bullets, punching holes in Paul's soul. "You thought you were so fucking tight," Will continued, "but you didn't even *know* her!"

Paul winced again, thoughts pounding his skull. In his mind's eye he saw Kyra, crying . . . Kyra, pulling away . . . but from whom? From Will? Or from him? Paul shook his head. "You ruined her life," he said.

"Me??!!!" Will scoffed. "What about *you*??" His words boomed out through a voice raw and ravaged, somehow larger than the body from which they issued, or the walls that constrained them. "You never even *knew* who she really was, 'cuz you were too fucking busy trying to make her into something else!"

Paul winced again, thoughts flashing to Julie's dad, scowling, imperious . . . the older man's searing, unspoken indictment: *I blame you . . .*

. . . and Will kept on, wielding the truth like a blade, sticking it in and twisting. "Don't you fucking *get* it??" he cried. "I *loved* her! She loved *me*! We could've been a *family*!! We could have been *happy*!" His voice went tight, choking on his own grief. "But we never even had a fucking *chance*!!"

"No . . ." Paul hissed, head shaking furiously.

"NO?!!" Will scoffed. *"FUCK* you, man! You're as much to blame as me!! *She killed our baby because of YOU!!"*

And that's when Paul snapped.

"NO!!!" Paul knocked Will back and grabbed the shock paddles. The defib hummed its lethal song as Paul turned back to deliver the killing jolt . . .

. . . and with his last shred of strength Will wrenched the bolt free, swung his fist out and up: a straight-armed piston thrust aimed at Paul's head. Bolt smacked bone inches from Paul's eye, raking from temple to ear. Blood gushed as Paul howled and descended, the shock paddles blasting the boy's tortured flesh. Will dropped the bolt as his nervous system fried, seizing up, violently thrashing. Then he sagged, went slack and still.

Paul hovered above him, blood coursing from the gash in his head.

Then, blackness.

42

I t was just before five when Julie pulled her car into the driveway of their house. She'd made good time, hoping somehow that it was a good omen of what was to come. But as she pulled around back she saw that Paul's truck was gone.

Julie parked and walked up the walk, fading sun throwing long shadows before her. The house was dark, bereft of life; not even Spock's goofy presence in the yard to inject an air of good feeling. Julie readied her keys to unlock the back door.

And then noticed it was ajar.

She stopped, a chill shivering through her. Julie opened the door and stepped inside. "Paul?" she called out. "Paul, are you here?"

She felt hypersensitized, her awareness taking in all detail. The kitchen looked wrong somehow, like everything had been taken apart and reassembled two inches to the left. She entered the living room, saw the blasted TV, the books hastily restacked, the sundry evidence of spent and demented rage.

"Paul," she murmured worriedly. "What have you done?"

Guilt hung heavy over her as Julie climbed the stairs, saw missing rungs on the railing, wooden stumps jutting up from where slats had been kicked out. The slats themselves lay splayed on the hall floor, forgotten.

"Paul?" she called out, louder this time, listening. Silence. She made her way down the hall, past Kyra's bedroom. Julie paused to touch the door . . .

. . . and she flashed back to Kyra, her eyes bright with tears. The wrenching confession. The shock and the shame. Julie asked who the father was, but Kyra would not give a name. . . .

. . . and Julie reached the bedroom, stared in horror at the bags half-packed and strewn on the obliterated bed . . .

. . . and she bit back her anger, as her daughter cried. Kyra needed not lectures but love, not condemnation but compassion . . .

. . . and Julie stepped into the room, heard the soft crunch of paper beneath her shoe. She looked down and saw the crumpled receipt . . .

. . . and she remembered the trip to the obscure city clinic; past narrow clots of protestors preaching love and life with eyes full of hate; how she had held Kyra's hand, promising that everything would be all right . . .

Julie picked up the paper, her hands trembling . . .

. . . and as they called her name in the waiting room, Kyra turned to hug her, her features childish and fearful. "Please don't tell Daddy . . ." she whispered. "Please don't tell Daddy I'm here . . ."

"Oh God," Julie gasped, staring at the smudged paper, his boot print clearly upon it. "Oh my God . . ."

She'd kept her promise. She'd never told him. But he had found out just the same.

Panic spiked her heart. She had tried to protect their daughter by keeping her secret but in so doing had fractured the very heart of their family. Because, truth be told, Julie had been the glue that had held them all together; as involved as Paul was, it was Julie who had been there day in and day out, making life happen while Paul was away for days on end, fighting his good fight, facing down death. It was Julie who had called the shots, Julie whom Kyra had turned to. It had been *her* responsibility . . .

. . . and it struck her then like a wrecking ball that she had failed her daughter, her husband, her family by building walls where none should have been, allowing Kyra's fear to take root and hold reign over them all. One way or another, they should have talked about it. One way or another, they could have worked it out. One way or another, but together. It was the lifeblood of family.

And Julie blamed herself for allowing it to spill.

"Oh my God," she said again. She had to find Paul. She had lost any hope of redemptive confession; she had lost the chance to explain her sin. And now Paul was out there, lost in a hell of her own creation, paved brick by brick with the best of intentions.

She had to find him. Before things went too far.

But, of course, they already had.

Paul came to, blinking back blood.

He was flat on his back, staring up at the light shining down on him like an all-seeing eye. He groaned and brought one hand to his temple. His fingertips came away sticky.

Paul winced and sat up, saw the pilfered bolt, its tip still moist with blood. *His* blood. He touched the wound again, gaze tracking to the floorplates, zeroing in on the hole.

"Son of a bitch," he growled.

Will lay sprawled in a heap before him. Paul crawled over, checked his pulse. His heartbeat was faint, thready. But it was still ticking.

Paul hauled himself up, grabbed the defibrillator. Then turned and left the box. The door creaked behind him, unlocked, ajar.

It didn't matter anymore. Nothing mattered but ending this.

Now.

* * *

"Whaddaya mean, he took it???"

Dondi arrived to find Wallace sputtering before a very agitated Andy Vasquez, who was busily chewing the probie a new one.

"Like I said, he just took it!" Wallace blurted. "I asked him where he was going, and he told me it was none of my business!!"

"Who took what?" Dondi asked.

"Paul," Wallace explained. "He took the backup defibrillator unit."

"When??"

"About an hour ago," Vasquez said. "*Plus* it looks like he raided the med cab."

Dondi turned to Wallace, furious. "And you *let* him???"

Wallace freaked. "What was I supposed to do?" he whined. "You shoulda seen him! I thought he was gonna kill me!"

"Fuck!" Dondi muttered. "Fuck fuck fuck fuck!"

On the duty desk, the telephone rang. Dondi was still shaking his head as Andy answered.

"Rescue One, Vasquez . . ." He paused, brow knitting. "Julie . . . no . . . no, he's not here . . . we thought he was with you." He looked at the other men, shrugged. "No, I don't know where he is . . . yeah, I will . . . I will . . . don't worry."

Andy hung up, looked at Dondi. He didn't need to explain. "What're we gonna do, el-tee?"

Vasquez only called people by rank when things got official. Dondi was acting captain; it was *his* responsibility. And friend or no, Paul had gone too far. Dondi sighed heavily.

"Call Steve Buscetti," he said. "Tell him we need him down here." Vasquez looked at him like, *you gotta be kidding.* Dondi shot him a no-bullshit look.

"Now," he said.

Five gallon cans of enamel paint. Another six of stain. Two liter cans of turpentine. Another three of thinner. Twelve square yards of drop cloth. Twenty of plastic. Plywood and pressboard in four-by-eight sheets. Two-by-four wall studs in soft knotted pine. Stacks of old newspapers. Combined just so: the stuff of restoration. Or destruction.

Paul worked feverishly, unscrewing the lightbulb in the overhead fixture, screwing an outlet adapter in its place. He plugged a cheap extension cord into the socket, then snaked the cord over to the workbench, where it plugged into an old box-steel heater. A cheesy brand name was emblazoned across the top.

Toastee Glo.

The irony was not lost. Paul had to thank Mr. Toast, he really did. In all honesty, the initial inspiration came from him. Credit where credit was due. The metal coils were dark and cool as Paul angled the box into position. In the adjacent work sink sat a coffee can stuffed with brushes, turpentine soaking, next to a plastic squeeze bottle of liquid soap.

Paul grabbed the bottle, squeezed its contents into the can, then stirred until the liquid turned viscous and slimy. He ripped a strip of drop cloth, two inches wide by six feet long, then dipped it in the can. As the cloth absorbed solvent, he picked up the newspapers, spread them randomly on the floor.

Paul pinched the strip, lifting one end from the can, draped it dripping across the big wooden bench. He laid the end across the face of the heater, stood back. It was perfect.

As a firefighter, he had seen countless cases of arson; he knew how to set one well enough. The light switch at the head of the stairs would act as a trigger; once lit, he would have maybe three minutes to effect his escape. Then, boom. The house was old, balloon-framed brick; twenty-foot two-by-fours ran all the way to the attic. Newer buildings used eight-footers, stacked floor to floor. The older studs cost more, old growth timber being much harder to find. But there was one other distinguishing, if unsung, feature. They were hell in a fire.

Paul cast one last glance back at the darkened basement. The box sat like a squat, silent sentinel. The door hung open, the better to welcome Will to Inferno.

Paul grabbed the defib unit and started up the basement stairs. As he reached the top, he flipped the switch.

Downstairs, the heater started to buzz as one side of the coils began to glow red. Paul listened to the familiar hum. Then he crossed the threshold from basement to kitchen. He closed the door behind him, turned.

And ran smack into Julie.

Detective Buscetti arrived at the firehouse at 4:45; by then, word of Paul's actions had spread through the crew. Everyone looked wary and worried. Buscetti approached Dondi, his expression fixed and grim; as he did, Dondi nodded to Andy. "Okay, guys, clear out, find something to do!" Andy ordered. "Move!!!" The firefighters grumbled and moved reluctantly, heading upstairs or into the bay. Andy turned back to Dondi.

"You, too," Dondi said.

"Me?"

"Yeah, you," Dondi replied, deadly serious. Andy sighed grievously and made for the bay. He paused at the door, looked at Buscetti.

"One of us, Stevie," he admonished. "He's one of us." Buscetti nodded: he knew. Vasquez withdrew, leaving them alone.

"Okay," Dondi said. "What'd you find out?"

"I put it out soft," Buscetti told him. "Radio cars'll call if anyone picks up his twenty. It's not official, yet." He emphasized the y-word, sighed. "But I don't know for how much longer."

"Tell me about it," Dondi replied. "If I write this up, it's his ass. If I don't, it's mine."

"Unless we can find him."

"Yeah," Dondi said. He looked at the cop, miserable. "Jesus, Stevie," he muttered. "What the fuck is he doing?"

Just then someone opened the front door. "Excuse me," a shy voice said. "Is Paul Kelly here?"

The two men turned and stared in shock.

It was Kathryn Wells.

* * *

Back in the box, Will came to: weak and aching, ears ring-ing. As his vision focused he realized that he was alive. He was alone in the box. And the door was unlocked.

Will sat up, stunned, half expecting assault. None came. Paul was gone. He looked down, saw drops of blood on the floor, trailing out past the door. *Maybe he's dead,* he thought. *Or dying. Or hurt. Or all of the above.* One thing was certain: he did not plan on hanging around to find out.

Will fought to stand, took a pained, halting step. Then pushed open the door of the box.

And just like that, he was free.

It was a toss-up as to who looked more shocked: Paul, at Julie's presence there, or Julie, who saw the dried blood tracking the side of his face, the portable defibrillator in his hands, the burgeoning madness in his eyes.

"Julie," he blurted. "What are you doing here?"

"Looking for you," she told him. "What are *you* doing here?"

Paul dropped the defib, pulled her toward him in a manic embrace. For a moment they stood, a swirl of emotions—love and anger, fear and longing, redemption and damna-tion—coursing between them. Julie hugged him back, touched his neck, his cheek, the gash on his head. "Baby, you're hurt," she said. "What happened?"

Paul winced and pulled away. "We've got to get out of here," he said urgently. "We've got to get out of here *now*." He took her by the arm, started pulling her toward the back door. But Julie twisted away.

"Paul!" she said. "Stop it!"

He took a step toward her, and she backed up, deeper into the kitchen. "Julie, please, I'll tell you anything you want to know, I'll tell you everything. Only later . . ."

"No." Julie stood her ground, adamant. "You tell me now."

* * *

Will limped forward, heard muffled voices upstairs: a woman and a man. His ears were still ringing from the brutal shocks. The woman's voice he could not make out, but the man's he knew all too well: Paul. Will grimaced, searching for a weapon. He saw Paul's toolbox on the workbench. Will limped over, flipped open the lid. Rooted inside. Found a hammer.

The ringing in his ears abated and was replaced by a hum. Will cocked his head, listening, then saw the space heater and the glow of heat spreading the length of the coils. As it crept toward the end Will spied the dripping cloth, the can of brushes, mounds of paper and solvents. The heat spread toward it, closing five inches . . . four . . .

"Fuck!" Will gasped, as he dropped the hammer. And lurched toward the steps . . .

Three inches . . . two . . .

"Help!!!" Will cried out, staggering up the steps. "Somebody help me!!"

Paul was still pleading as Julie heard the voice coming up from the basement. Paul heard it, too. And as she gazed back at Paul in dawning horror and disbelief, Julie saw the look in his eyes. And suddenly, she knew.

"Julie, please," he said. "I can explain . . ."

Will stumbled and clawed his way up the steps, desperate and crazed. The door was closed before him; behind and below, the glow spread the last inch . . . a half inch . . . then, *whuff.*

Ignition sparked as a small puff of flame blossomed, hungrily feeding on solvent-soaked cloth. The strip acted as a fuse, an infernal contraption, Rube Goldberg does Dante. The cloth blackened and curled as the flame picked up speed; in less than three seconds it was up to the coffee can, over the lip, and in.

KA-*BOOOSH!!* The coffee can blew up and out as a miniature fireball bloomed in the basement. Smoke billowed up, the flaming mixture of turpentine and soap spraying out and raining down like homemade napalm, spattering the papers and plastic and cloth. In seconds the fire spread, enveloping the space heater, the workbench, the neatly stacked cans of paint and thinner. The extension cord melted, sparking and arcing instantly, shorting out.

On the stairs Will coughed and clawed his way forward, momentarily shielded by the narrow walls. Downstairs, smoke filled the air as flames heated cans of highly flammable paint and thinner. Paper labels crisped and curled as the contents boiled inside. Each possessed of its own distinct thermal characteristics. Each driven to its own unique flashpoint.

And as Will put his hand to the doorknob, the first one blew.

The cellar door opened as the dull *whump* sounded. Will tumbled out, gasping; as Julie rushed toward him, fresh oxygen sucked down to feed the smoldering void. Paul raced forward, grabbed Julie, and threw her aside, then dived himself. A heartbeat later . . . *KA-BOOOM!*

The explosion was immense, rocking the row house through its foundation. The blast blanketed the basement, overpressure forcing the fire up and out, seeking escape, seeking life. It raced up the narrow hall, blasted out into the kitchen, billowing across the ceiling. Paul crawled forward as instinct and training kicked in. He squinted through the smoke, saw the back door was blocked, sealed off by flames. The blast had sent Will flying, left Julie dazed, semiconscious. Paul dragged them from the doorway, which raged like a man-made mouth of Hell, got them as far away as his strength and the seconds would allow.

And then he had to choose.

He couldn't get them both out at once. Paul dropped Will in the hall, then hauled Julie up and over his shoulder in a fireman's carry, staggering down the hallway toward the front door and escape.

Paul emerged outside coughing and carried Julie down the steps, kept going until they were safely out of range. As he knelt to lay her down on the sidewalk, Paul glanced back, saw the house on Marley Street, smoke issuing forth from its depths. Up and down the street, faces appeared: strangers peering out of windows, coming out of their homes.

Paul looked up, saw a little red box on a telephone pole. Words glinted silver across its surface. Paul knew them by heart.

PULL IN CASE OF FIRE.

Paul did.

43

Seconds later, the call came in. The alarm bell clanged hugely, echoing through the Rescue One station house. Kathryn Wells flinched and almost leapt from her skin; she had just dropped by to see how Paul was doing. Buscetti queried her urgently, to no avail. She had no idea what was going on.

Buscetti watched as Dondi and Andy hustled. The telex clattered; Dondi tore the printout free and scanned the type as Andy and the others moved. "What's the addy?" Andy called out. Dondi looked pale, his blood running cold.

"Marley Street," he said. "Five hundred block."

Buscetti and Dondi traded glances. The crew scrambled. Kathryn Wells looked at Buscetti, afraid and confused.

"What?" she said. "What's wrong?"

"Come with me," he told her.

The fire spread quickly, engulfing the structure. Paul knelt over Julie and stripped off his jacket, placing it under her head. Sirens whooped in the distance; as Paul looked up he saw Engine and Ladder companies arriving on the scene. The Rescue One rig turned the corner, air horn blatting, Detective Buscetti following in close pursuit.

Julie came to, coughing. Her eyes focused on him, filled with fear and grief. "I should have told you," she murmured. "It's all my fault . . ."

"No," Paul said, head bowed. "It's mine."

The scene whirled around them, fire crews spreading out as civilians peered from the perimeter, drawn to the spectacle. Georgie, the bellicose fire chief, bellowed in the background, throwing around his not inconsiderable weight. Buscetti's car whooped a siren song, pulling up on the sidewalk. The doors flew open; Paul saw Steve and Kathryn Wells. Buscetti pushed through the throng, Kathryn in tow. Kathryn saw Julie and stopped. Then rushed forward to help.

Behind them, another *WHUMP!* Thunderous. The house was engorged with smoke and flame. As it faded, they heard a voice calling out from inside.

"Somebody's in there!" a person cried from the crowds. Paul stared blankly, the shock of realization dawning. Necks craned and heads bobbed, morbidly alert. Dondi made his way to Paul, clad in bulky turnouts and boots, weighted with gear. Buscetti looked at Paul, eyes filled with alarm.

"Who is it?" he asked. "Paulie, *who?*"

The voice cried again, louder. Suddenly Kathryn Wells went pale as purely maternal recognition kicked in. She knew the sound, even without words, even through the chaos and noise. It was the sound of her son's cry. And it both riveted and terrified her.

"Omigod . . . my baby!" she gasped.

The others looked at her, not comprehending. Her eyes were filled with raw and primal pain. "My BABY!!" she cried out, louder this time. Julie looked at her, mother to mother, and knew. Kathryn clawed at Buscetti's sleeve. *"My son,"* she said desperately, *"my son is in there!!!"*

The weight of it hit home. Everyone looked from Kathryn to the house, to Paul, who watched as shock flickered in their eyes, brighter than any flame. One by one, realization ignited; as their stunned expressions turned to Paul, he saw the horror reflected there. And in so seeing, he glimpsed the thing he had only now come to fully grasp: his own complicity in all that had happened, not simply in the wake of his daughter's death, but all along. If they all had a sin to bear, then Paul's was pride, and hypocrisy. And if there was such a thing as God—and Paul now and finally believed there was—then there was something else, too.

There was atonement.

Somewhere inside, a massive beam fell. Flames glowed behind the windows, licking hungrily at the glass. The house was too hot for the crews to get in. Paul suddenly pushed past Dondi and Buscetti and the others, grabbed an oxygen tank and an ax off one of the rigs, started racing toward the steps.

And before they could stop him, he ran back inside.

Inside the house, the fire was alive, thick black smoke pulsing with an angry orange glow. The flames had raced from basement to attic, pooling across the cock loft, filling the narrow crawlspace, leaping from any opening. It was burning from bottom to top.

Paul came in low, fighting his way through the inferno, searching. Standing was futile; the smoke was too blinding, the heat too intense. Paul bellied down and crawled through the hell of his own making, calling out Will's name.

Something roared overhead; Paul glanced up to see a ceiling beam falling, sparks showering down as it hit inches from his face. He pushed it away with the ax head and continued.

"WILL!!" he cried. "WILL!!!!!!"

He could no longer see behind him, could barely see at all. The front door was as distant as the surface of the sun. The oxygen tank hissed; Paul sucked a great gasp, coughed and kept moving.

"WILL!!!"

Suddenly he heard him, desperately retching, dead ahead. Paul scrambled forward, found the boy huddled, blinded and choking. He quickly placed the mask over Wells's face; Will clutched and gasped greedily. Their eyes locked as Will looked up, frankly shocked to see him.

There was no time for words. No time at all. Paul grabbed Will and started dragging him back. The fire raged around them, unseen in blackness. Another great crash sounded; Paul turned just as a burning beam lurched from the void, slamming into him, knocking him sideways and down. His shoulder seared as Paul pushed Will away a heartbeat before the entire wall collapsed.

Paul hit the floor, legs pinned beneath Sheetrock and rubble. Somewhere ahead came a great liquid hiss as fire streams sprayed through shattered windows, the fire crews outside valiantly trying to beat back the flames. Paul peered through roiling smoke, caught a fleeting glimpse of the door, some ten feet away. A slim chance in hell. Then none at all.

Paul thrust the air tank into Will's arms. "GO!" he cried. "GO!!!!"

Will started to move, then stopped. "No," he gasped, then furiously tore through the pile of wreckage. He grabbed Paul's hand and started pulling him forward as Paul pushed with all his might. The rubble groaned and shifted. And suddenly he was free.

Will collapsed, gasping. Paul scuttled forward, pulled him into his arms. Searchlights swept the noxious clouds— Dondi and the Rescue crew, searching wildly. Paul called out. The men rushed forward, helping them up.

And together, they escaped, seconds before the fire consumed the room.

Outside, fire crews and police swarmed. A News 9 van arrived on-site, lights and lenses flashing and flaring. Link Lenkershem scoped himself in the van's side mirror, preening and prepping and checking his hair.

Paul and Will emerged with the others: scorched, sootsmeared, and scarred, but intact. A murmur crossed the crowds as Julie ran to embrace her husband and Kathryn did the same for her son.

Buscetti saw Will and signaled. The cops moved in. As

they took him into custody, the detective stepped up. "William Wells, you're under arrest," he said for the second time. "You have the right to remain silent. Anything you say can and will be used against you . . ."

Will looked up, hands cuffed behind him, a new kind of defiance gracing his features. All eyes were upon him— Paul's and Julie's, his mother's, the policemen's, the crowds' and cameras', the world at large. He shook his head.

"I'm done staying silent," he said. He looked at Paul, looked at them all. "I killed Kyra," he told them, then nodded to Paul. "And *he* saved my life."

Will twisted in the grip of the law until he faced Julie. "I'm so sorry," he said.

Julie met his gaze. There were tears in his eyes, tears in her own. Link Lenkershem hovered in the background, leering with joy as his cameras zoomed in, thinking, *This is great, this is so fucking great . . .*

The paramedics came forward then and hustled them back to the waiting ambulance, as the uniformed cops moved to keep the crowds at bay. Around them, hoses arced and sprayed as the engine crews battled to knock down the blaze. The structure was completely engulfed, the destruction total. The house on Marley Street would take its secrets with it.

Paul's gaze tracked from Will to Julie to Kathryn to Dondi, came to rest on Detective Buscetti. "Give us a minute, will ya, Stevie?" Paul asked. "Please . . ."

Stevie cast him a wary look, then shook his head ruefully. "Sure, Paulie," he said, but his eyes said, *We'll talk later. Count on it.* Paul nodded wearily. Buscetti turned and gently herded the others away.

As the medics tended their injuries, Paul looked to Will. The boy looked different somehow, and not merely from the deprivations of his ordeal. Something had changed in his eyes; the practiced deadness was now gone, replaced by something else—shock and pain, yes, but with it, something awake, aware. Alive.

Paul winced and watched Will watch the house burn, flames illuminating the darkened sky. And as he did, the question formed anew. "Why?" he asked. "Why did you tell them that?"

Will shrugged. "I dunno," he said softly, then added, "maybe we've both got enough blood on our hands."

Wells looked at him, and Paul nodded, humbled. And as their eyes met, something passed between them. A thousand other questions would follow, from a thousand other angles, but there were no easy answers, no simple solutions, no escaping the fact that there was a price to be paid, for all of them, a lifetime of wrongs to be righted. What was done could not be undone, and they would all have to learn to live with that, as best they could.

But as the boy faced the man, they saw each other as if truly for the first time. And in so seeing, they knew: whatever meaning was to be had was to be *made*—one day, one moment, one *choice* at a time. None of them knew what the future would bring; they could only resolve to learn from the past, and to try, as best they could. To face what they had done. To heal the damage, such as they might. And to move on. It may have seemed to some a comfortless truth. But it was the only one there was.

Paul and Will looked at loved ones and strangers alike, all backlit by the burning house, the conflagration gradually giving way under the force of the most elemental of battles. The fire would eventually falter, as fire always does; tomorrow there would be wreckage, and survivors, and an empty lot where something once had been. In the fullness of time, someone would come, as someone always does—unsinged by calamity, or bearing the scars of their own private holocaust—and would begin to build again. It was not a matter of bad or good. It was simply the nature of fire. But the same could also be said for *hope*.

It was ever thus; it ever thus would be. And as the smoke and ash settled on Marley Street, they knew: whatever else may come, something had been born there, amidst the flames.

A beginning, perhaps.

At the very least, an understanding.

No man can wear one face to himself
and another to the multitude without
finally getting bewildered as to
which one may be true.

—Nathaniel Hawthorne